John Sladek was born in Iowa in 1937. With such brilliant tours-de-force as *The Reproductive System*, *The Muller-Fokker Effect* and *Tik-Tok*, he has established a reputation as one of the leading writers of satirical science fiction.

Also by John Sladek available from Carroll & Graf:

Roderick

RODERICK AT RANDOM

JOHN SLADEK

Carroll & Graf Publishers, Inc.
New York

PS
3569
L25
R62
1988
1

Reprinted by arrangement with Richard Curtis Associates, Inc.

First Carroll & Graf edition 1988

Carroll & Graf Publishers, Inc.
260 Fifth Avenue
New York, NY 10001

ISBN: 0-88184-341-5

Manufactured in the United States of America

1

Dead or dreaming? It seemed to Leo Bunsky that he had come out of retirement. Somehow he was back in his old office, working on Project Roderick again. And somehow the old heart condition had decided to stop tormenting him: gone was the breathlessness, the tiredness, the draining of fluid down into his feet until they doubled in size and burst his shoes. Without any medication or surgery, he was now cured. Everything was back to normal now, if that word could be used in these miraculous circumstances. Calloo, and also Calais! But what was the explanation?

He was dreaming. He was dead. Dreaming but dead. Neither. He had slipped through a 'time-warp' into a 'parallel universe' (Dr Bunsky was a reader of science fiction), probably through a 'white hole'.

It didn't matter; in any case there was plenty of work to do. He could live an unexamined life, until Project Roderick demanded less of his time, okay? Okay, and great to be part of this real-life science-fiction dream, a project to build a 'viable' robot. Roderick would be a learning machine. It would learn to think and behave as a human. All the team had to do was solve dozens of enormous problems in artificial intelligence that had defeated everyone else; from there on, it was science fiction.

Bunsky's job at the moment was teaching simple computer programs to talk. So far he'd got a program to say *Mama am a maam*, but not with feeling. If Roderick the Robot was ever going to think as a human, it would of course need to learn and use language as a human: *Mama am a maam* was not exactly Miltonic, but it was a start.

How did people learn to talk? No one really knew. There

were those who thought it might be a matter of training, like learning to ride a bike. Others seemed to imagine a kind of grammar-machine built into the human head. Still others tried teaching chimpanzees to talk while riding bikes. Chimps, so far, had articulated no theories of their own.

Bunsky found it easier to scrap general theories and consider the brain as a black box: language stuff went in and different language stuff came out. In between, some sort of processing took place. What Roderick the Robot would have to do, then, was to mimic the hidden processing. The robot would have to learn as human children learn, and that meant making the same kinds of childish mistakes. And *only* those kinds of mistakes. It was okay for Roderick to say *Me finded two mouses on stair*. It was not okay to say *I found two invisible green guesses on the stair*.

Leo Bunsky lifted his gaze to a file card tacked to the wall above his desk:

TO ERR (APPROPRIATELY) IS HUMAN

There was something he couldn't remember, that made his head ache.

The door opened and one of the younger men in the project came slouching in. It was that interdisciplinary disciple with the unfortunate name, Ben Franklin. Bunsky didn't know him well.

'Leo, how's tricks?' He slumped into a chair and started flicking cigarette ash on the floor.

'Fine, uh, Ben. Fine. Wish you'd use the ashtray, I know the place is untidy but –'

'Yes, I found two invisible green guesses on the stair. Yours?'

'Very amusing. Now if you'll excuse me . . .'

Franklin stood up. 'Busy, sure. Sure. I don't suppose you need any help with anything?'

'Sorry, no.' No one ever wanted Franklin's help. No one

6

really trusted him, with his strange background: a hybrid degree in Computer Science and Humanities. A little too eclectic for serious research work. Dr Fong had hired him as project librarian and historian, but so far there weren't many books and no history. Ben Franklin just sort of hung around dropping ash on the floor. 'Sorry, Ben.'

'Sure.' After a pause, he sat down again. 'Leo, you ever have any doubts about this project? About Roderick?'

'Doubts?'

'Kind of an ethical grey area, isn't it?'

Bunsky felt the headache settling in, deepening its hold on him. 'What grey area, for Christ's sake? Building a robot, is that grey? Is that ethically suspect, to build a sophisticated machine? Is cybernetics morally in bad taste?'

'Well, no, if you put it like—'

Bunsky was shouting now. 'We're not violating anybody's rights. We're not polluting any imaginable environment. We're not cutting up animals and we're not even screwing around with genetic materials!'

Franklin flicked ash. 'Come on, Leo, what about long-term consequences? Don't tell me it never crossed your mind that Roderick might be dangerous. First of a new species, of a very high order, has to be some danger in that.'

'A mechanical species, Ben.'

'But on a par with our own. And what if robots evolve faster and further? Where does that leave us? Extinct!'

Bunsky made his voice calm. 'Let's not be too simplistic there. Humans wouldn't be in direct competition with robots, would they? Both species would use, let's see, metal and energy. But robots wouldn't need much of either resource. Should be enough to go around, eh?'

'Eh yourself, what about intangible resources? What about things like *meaning*?' Franklin put out his cigarette on the floor. 'I mean look, it could be that humans feed on meaning. It could be that we only survive by making sense out of the world around us. It could be that this is all that

7

keeps us going. So if we turn over that function to some other species, we're finished.'

The headache began to throb, roaring waves of pain breaking over him, trying to drag him under. There were moments of dizziness and deafness, moments when Bunsky could hardly make out the empty smirking face before him. Franklin looked a little like a ventriloquist's dummy sometimes.

'You have a point, Ben. Too bad you're such a goddamned jerk.'

'What?' Franklin paused, a fresh cigarette halfway to his smirk.

'I said you have a point. Yes. I believe we do have a need to make sense out of the world. We see by making pictures, no? By sorting out the "blooming, buzzing confusion". And of course we hear speech by making sentences out of it. I believe that the essence of human intelligence is that kind of hypothesis-building. Life is making intelligent guesses, you agree?'

'Of course, Leo. Hypothesis-building.'

'Then don't you see? The robot is the ultimate human hypothesis. What better way of making sense out of the world, than through complete copies of ourselves? How better to model our inner and outer world? Ben, we need the robot – we need the *idea* of the robot.'

Franklin lit his cigarette and tapped it. 'The idea, maybe, but I'm not worried about the idea. It's the embodiment.'

'Yes, we're building a real robot. We're doing what everyone has always wanted to do, down through the ages. If the Jews could have built a real *golem*, do you think they would have hesitated? Or the Cretans, wouldn't they want a real Talos? If myths are just wishes, isn't it obvious what they were all wishing for? Dolls and statues from the terra-cotta past . . . puppets and manequins today . . . The idea of the wish for the robot is so, so very powerful . . . What child doesn't like Punch and Judy? What grownup won't pause to watch a ventriloquist at work? My God, when I was a kid, do

8

you know they even had a ventriloquist on the radio – on the radio!'

Franklin flicked ash. 'I don't get it.'

'Edgar Bergen and Charlie McCarthy on the damned radio. You see, the novelty of a talking doll was so powerful, we didn't even need to see the doll. There didn't even have to be a doll! All we needed was the *idea* of a Charlie McCarthy!'

Flick, flick. 'Okay sure, you think the robot idea is powerful. Only it still might be kind of tough on us, having all these puppets around who are also our intellectual equals. We won't be able to shut *them* up in their boxes after each performance, we'll have to live with them. Could make quite a rip in the old social fabric, Leo.'

'But maybe an inevitable rip. Anyway, we're the team to make the historic incision.' Bunsky briefly saw them all gathered around an operating table, *The Anatomy Lesson of Dr Tulp*. Then he saw another picture . . .

'Something funny?' Ben Franklin asked.

'Nothing really, just remembered a notion I had for a science-fiction movie – well it's nothing.'

'I'd like to hear it.'

'All I really have is this opening scene. There's a human brain floating in a tank of water and pulsating with light. These scientists in white lab coats are leaning over it, looking grave, with the pulsating light reflected in their eyes. Then the camera begins to pull back, so we see the tank is an office water cooler. One of the scientists takes down a paper cup and gets himself a drink.'

'He's laughing now,' said the older of the two men in white lab coats. He pointed to a screen where a jagged line bobbed and danced. 'There, he just told a joke.'

'Really? A joke? How do you know?' The younger man kept turning away from the instrument panel to look directly into the tank where Leo Bunsky's brain floated in water.

The older man pointed to a different screen. 'We know everything he thinks. See right now he thinks he's in his old office, back at some jerkwater Northern university, still working on a big secret ''robot'' project. And he thinks he's talking to a colleague named Franklin. Franklin must have been a pretty good friend of his, because we never have any trouble producing him. We use Franklin as an input dummy.'

'Input dummy? Afraid I don't understand the technical side of this. Do you mean we can talk to this – this guy?'

'Precisely. Now I'm not entirely familiar with the technical details myself. The wiring must be unimaginable. But I gather that we somehow stimulate vision and hearing centres to produce an hallucination of this Franklin, and then we somehow manipulate the hallucination. Of course we get output from Leo's speech centres too.' He pointed to another screen. 'There, his joke is just coming up now.'

The younger man kept craning around to peer at the brain itself, but now he turned back to see:

> Scientists are leaning over,
> looking into a grave. A watery
> grave. One of them has to be
> pulled back. He lowers his cup
> to get a stiff drink.

'Not much of a sense of humour,' said the younger man.

'Well it probably loses something in the processing,' said the other, pushing a few buttons. 'Now we can also monitor his general thoughts, read his mind so to speak.'

> am a maam a man of parts Dr
> Culp hands of a murderer drip
> drip riverrun or creektrickle
> O Rijn maiden God's immerse
> anatomical babies in jars drip
> drip father fathomful drip
> are those pearls eyes of an
> artist pools

'Interesting,' said the younger man. 'But you know I keep wondering why? Why go to all this trouble to find out what one computer scientist is thinking?'

'Oh Leo isn't just any computer scientist, he's very special. A first-class brain, if you'll pardon the expression. Let's take a pew and I'll tell you about Leo.'

There were comfortable theatre seats banked along one side of the room. The two men took seats in the front row, a pair of critics. The older man folded and unfolded his liver-spotted hands a few times before he began.

'You know, Otto Neurath once said science is a boat you have to rebuild even while you're at sea in it. In Leo's case he was launched as an electrical engineer, drifted into communications theory and finally rebuilt his boat as a linguist. And so it was that Leo turned out to be the right man at the right time for a very special project. Building a so-called robot. Or as we prefer to say, an *Entity*.'

He paused for effect. But the younger man was watching an attendant polish the glass front of Leo's tank, wiping away fingermarks.

'They called it Project – Rubric was it? Roderick, I believe, though what's in a name, they had cover names galore, a very secretive bunch. And no wonder, because it turned out they were swindling funding out of NASA, heavy funding.'

'They were just crooks?'

'On the contrary, they had plenty of genuine talent. The team was headed by Lee Fong—'

'The pattern-recognition guy? I've heard of him.'

The liver-spotted hands were folded again. 'You may know the others too, all first-class br— people. So they had heavy funding, heavy talent, and I guess heavy luck. Because they blitzed through some incredibly tough problems and actually got their Entity built.'

The younger man was now listening with his full attention. 'Go on. What was it?'

11

'It was a "viable" learning machine incorporating some of Leo's best ideas. By the time they built it, Leo Bunsky himself was officially dead, but his ideas lived on. The Roderick Entity was a great success – if you can call it a success to endanger humanity – and it was Leo Bunsky who made it possible for the thing to talk.

'Of course there were the others, Fong and Mendez and Sonnenschein, all brilliant, but Leo made it talk. I wish sometimes we could tell him about his success.'

'He doesn't know?' The younger man looked to the tank.

'All he knows is, he went into the hospital for open-heart surgery, came out wonderfully well, and went back to work. In fact he died on the table. Our people were there, and they managed to get his brain – and now Leo works for us!'

'As a kind of devil's advocate, I suppose.'

'Precisely. Precisely.' Wrinkled reptilian eyelids came down over bright reptilian eyes. 'Leo sits in his office, "Franklin" comes in and asks him some questions about the future of artificial intelligence research. He tells "Franklin" what he thinks, and we have our answer. We know what has to be stopped.'

The younger man watched the attendant breathe on the glass to clear a fingermark. 'Of course I'm new around here, but frankly I don't get it. Why does the Orinoco Institute keep on spending money to sabotage robot research, Entity I mean, when every year there's going to be more and more new research? I mean it sounds like a holding action that isn't even holding. Aren't Entities inevitable? Aren't they becoming a fact of life?'

'That's certainly one of Leo's arguments, inevitability. But you know, in all of *our* scenarios, Entities are a decidedly negative development. Ultimately they signal the collapse of our way of life, the death of our culture. I do not mean just American or Western culture, I mean human culture. And if we at the Institute have one over-riding loyalty, I believe it must be to our own species.' His head swivelled sharply, the

12

lizard eyes opening in a hypnotic stare. 'Don't you agree?'

'Well sure, naturally. But are we really sure that humanity is threatened by, by Entities?'

'Oh, we've worked it out. In all eight scenarios.'

'In all three modes?'

'Yes, yes. To six significant figures.'

The younger man shrugged. 'Six? Then that's that. I can't argue with six significant figures.' He was silent for a minute, staring at the backs of his own hands. On the right one was a small blemish that might in time become a liver spot.

'So poor Leo Bunsky helped us sabotage his own work. I suppose we did shut down this Project Rubric?'

'Roderick. Let's just say, events shut it down – with a little help from us. We managed to get the director, Lee Fong, deported to Taipin. I understand he now fixes old poker-playing machines in a low gambling den. And he'll never have a better job; we dissuaded all reputable firms from hiring him. And – let me see – one or two of the others are confined to mental wards for the nonce. Yes, Project Roderick is certainly shut down.'

'And the Entity? You said they actually built something. Did you destroy it or what?'

There was a hesitation, an Adam's apple leaping in a wrinkled reptilian throat. 'Well, in fact . . . one or two problems there . . . Entity was taken outside the project and raised more or less as a human child in a human home. We had trouble finding it.'

'Raised?'

'As I said, it was a learning machine. And what it learned was to play human. It "grew up". Became much harder to find and neutralize. The Agency did find it and sent someone, but they ran into some bad luck.' A throat cleared, with the sound of tearing paper. 'Bad luck. And now the thing has dropped out of sight again. It is still at large.'

'I'll be damned. Still clanking around on the loose. Still

13

chugging up and down the streets, a free robot. Sounds like your worst scenario is about to be realized, and so what?' The younger man thought of saying this and more. He thought of saying, 'What could be worse, anyway, than our scenario for poor Leo here? Poor unfree Leo – would any robot do *this* to him?'

But aloud, all he said was, 'Still at large, hmm.'

'At random, one might say . . .'

2

He had taken only a few steps when he heard rapid footfalls behind him. * The guard then ran forward to seize him.

'That is good!' he said, as Edgar shot a tall Arab who was rushing at him with uplifted spear. The other Arab got up from the water and placed himself behind the fellow with the knife.

Two of his incisors were lying beside his nose, plastered there with blood. As for the policeman, he had at first seemed indifferent to the fallen man; but after the first shriek he approached him, raised his club and struck him a terrible blow on the temple. The big Irish cop, who'd slapped me before, clouted me from behind with his club.

'The fancy footwork's all over for this hoodlum.' So saying, the detective drew back his foot and kicked poor Lem behind the ear even harder than his colleague had done. Every time he cursed, one of the detectives struck him in the face with his fist. But then the coppers started up all around me. Rau approached the captain and shot him twice.

The blue plastic bowls came in through the pantry hatch. He would first scrape excess food from each bowl into a counter hole, then rinse with a hand-held spray and place upside down in a wire rack, twelve bowls to each rack and three racks to a conveyor stack ready to be loaded on the conveyor leading to the dishwashing machine for which detergent had to be measured and dropped in the top trap before each stack moved through from first wash to final rinse and emerged, ready to be loaded on the cart which took six stacks or eighteen racks or 216 clean pale blue plastic bowls each bearing a white Wedgwood-style cartouche marked DDD opposite an identical white Wedgwood-style cartouche marked DDD, the cart bearing 1296 Ds would then be rolled by him into the pantry and an identical cart full of empty racks be rolled back into the greasy kitchen to continue the cycle.

One of the men had smashed his fist into Julia's solar plexus, doubling her up like a pocket ruler. A gun muzzle poked into the back of my neck. He pulled the axe quite out, swung it with both arms, scarcely conscious of himself, and almost without effort, almost mechanically, brought the blunt side down on her head. She shot him five times in the stomach.

The day he found himself dragging pregnant women into the town square where their stomachs were slit open and the foetuses pulled out, his sensibilities were so outraged that he could no longer be part of the Communist organization. Aramis had already killed one of his adversaries, but the other was pressing him warmly. Jim Parsons, trying to creep out of his cabin port-hole, was hit on the head and dropped into the sea. The men struggled knee-deep in water. I took a firm grasp on the rail with my left hand and drew my dagger. As soon as I saw his head in a favourable position, I struck him heavily with the poker, just over the fourth cervical. The Boy suddenly drew back his hand and slashed with his razored nail at Brewster's cheek. He grasped a thick oaken cudgel in his bare right hand. And Ehud put forth his left hand, and took the dagger from his right thigh, and thrust it into his belly. We stan up at the same time an I feel my goddam heart pumpin an Rod hand me his blade. The dagger was an after-thought.

The cycle was never completed without a hitch. An enormous number of bowls would come through the hatch streaming with half-eaten food which could not be scraped until he had emptied the overflowing garbage can beneath the counter hole or then a shortage of clean, empty wire racks would be discovered or then the detergent would run out or finally the cart that should be waiting for stacks of racks of clean bowls would be found in the back kitchen, piled high with dirty pots, and while he emptied the garbage can or searched the pantry for wire racks or fetched a new barrel of detergent from the basement or began scouring the pile of pots, there would be a call for ice for the pantry,

16

towels for the cook, spilled liquid to be mopped and salted at once, while the dirty bowls continued to pile up and perhaps the dish-washing machine jammed, so that even though he felt he was coping with everything, he was not, and even though he felt he could accept stoically the screams of the waitresses, the snarls of the cook, the blows of Mr Danton, Roderick's fantasies became filled with paperback violence.

The iron fingers went into my throat. Then Rigby was holding him, had taken Feilding's right arm and done something to it, so that Feilding cried out in pain and fear. There was a sharp cry – and the dagger dropped gleaming upon the carpet, upon which, instantly afterwards, fell prostrate in death the Prince Prospero. His head cracked, and I felt it crunch. The light flashed upon the barrel of a revolver, but Holmes's hunting crop came down upon the man's wrist, and the pistol clinked upon the stone floor.

Quick as a flash he snatched up Cedar's gun and, levelling it with both hands, he worked the trigger. Bang! Bang! He shook me off with a furious snarling noise, giving me a terrific blow in the chest, and presented the revolver at my head. He fell to one side against a wall, a slug whispering as it tore past him. Suddenly shot after shot rang out in succession. Special Agent Fox was wounded and fell, but the concentrated fire which all four FBI men poured into the telephone booth made mincemeat out of Johnson. 'Bang!' went a pistol. The chopper raked the room swiftly from end to end and the air filled with plaster and splinters. Not so far overhead, an ME-109, pinned by searchlights, suddenly broke out of cloud cover and swooped in.

'Wake up you! Hey, I'm talkin' to you!' The red face of Mr Danton was glowing at him through the hatch, over an unpardonable heap of bowls. 'Five minutes I been watching you, you washed one dish, what the hell is dis? Just answer me that, what the hell is dis?'

There was no answer; Roderick could only keep his eyes down and work harder until Mr Danton went off to find a waitress without a hairnet or a cook putting too much parsley on the potatoes, until the hatch slid closed and the violence could begin, *Dacca-dakka-dakar!* and *Kerang!* silent slaughter

17

amid the screams of ordinary business.

The hatch slammed open and a waitress in Wedgwood blue dumped in a trayload of bowls before passing on to scream at the cook over the steam table:

'Picking up, picking up! Dave? That's two Chow-downs and one Upboy, a chopped duck liver together with a Mister Frisk hold the gravy . . . Dave, that's only one Chow-down, I ordered two, come on, come on, the customer's waaaiiting.'

Roderick could see the cook cursing and dishing up, almost flinging food over the high steam table where waitresses were visible only as hands and blue rabbit-ears.

'Ordering a chef's special . . . side of fried shrimp . . .'

'I got no shrimp, shrimp finish, kaput!' the cook screamed. Like everyone else here, he seemed unable to move anything without slamming it down, to say anything without screaming. When Roderick had first come to work here, he'd imagined that somehow the customers were causing all the noise. After all, Danton's Doggie Dinette did cater for mainly high-class and pedigree dogs, well-known for their constant yipping and snapping. Could it be that humans were catching this canine hysteria and transmitting it to the Dinette kitchen, as a kind of psychic rabies?

Not at all. Dave the cook (in a rare quiet moment) explained: 'Everybody yell in kitchen, in every kinda rastorunth across over world, is it were? Good kitchen, lots yell. *Bad* kitchen, *no* yellings. No yellings, waitress drop tray, insult castomer. Cook burn finger, cut off eye. Bad.'

But Roderick never got used to the noise. Whenever there was a lull in his work, he would step out into the alley to sit on a garbage can and meditate. Sometimes he would have a quiet conversation with Allbright.

Allbright was a garrulous drunk who wandered often into this quiet alley to piss, to drink or now and then to search the garbage cans. But he was never too busy to stop and talk, as now:

'Well well well, if it isn't our friend, the automatic dishwasher. Still claiming to be a robot? I forget your name.'

'Roderick Wood. And I am a robot.'

'Yes yes well who isn't? Chateaubriand said he realized he was only a machine for making books, we're all poor damned machines for some purpose or other, some pathetic, useless . . . Even you, washing dishes for dogs. Nothing wrong with that, honourable profession as any. Don't let 'em look down on you, kid.'

'The dogs?'

'Honourable profession as any, skink sexer, awning historian, salad auctioneer, you stick to it. Learn your trade. A man with a trade is going somewhere. He's going over to the other side of town to fix some poor goddamned machine. Only he needs the bus fare.'

Roderick said nothing. Allbright appeared to doze for a few minutes, then said, 'Anyway, I'm a poet.'

'Anyway?'

'And that gives me the right.'

'What right?'

'You name it, that gives it to me.'

'I've never met a live poet before,' Roderick said, not that Allbright looked fully alive. 'I thought all poets were dead.'

Allbright almost looked at him. 'No, you're thinking of the other people. All poets are alive, and that gives them every right.' He turned and shook his fist at the empty alley. 'You hear, you, you bastards! Every right!'

Roderick watched him stagger off to fight shadows, and finally fall asleep in his usual corner next to an enormous metal bin full of rusty coathangers.

'A poet.' Roderick was impressed. Poetry! Life!

Life for Roderick was limited in most dimensions. He worked long hours at Danton's Doggie Dinette on a 'split shift'. Danton cursed him and kicked him and paid very poorly, but where else could he work? He was a robot without a social security card.

The Dinette was close to the bus station where he had arrived in the city, and not far from the ancient hotel where he watched TV or recharged his batteries, or read books from the rack at the local drugstore. Some nights he would turn off the light and pretend to himself that he was sleeping, but he was only watching the dim yellow rectangle of light over the door, listening to the groan of sagging floorboards in the corridor as people walked by in ones and twos all night.

Most nights he simply read one book after another; he might before dawn get through two or three like *Call Me Pig*, *Doc Bovary's Wife*, *The Ego Diet*, *Ratstar II*, *God Was My Co-conspirator*, *Dream New Hair*, *Sink the Titanic!*, *Dragons of Darkwound*, or *Aversion for Happiness*. He could shift easily from a spy thriller like *The Pisces Perplex* to a guide to courtroom-drama therapy, *Make a Federal Case Out of It*; and on to an unusual medical theory in *Your Eyes: Do They Leak Light?* They were all one-night stands, forgotten in the morning when the first stack of dirty bowls rattled through the hatch.

'Sonnenschein, initial D?' asked the hospital receptionist, and touched her keyboard. 'No visitors except the immediate family, it says here.'

Roderick said, 'Well, I'm almost family.'

'Sorry.'

'If you're a poet, why don't you read me one of your poems?'

'Oh no. Oh no, you don't.' Allbright waggled a dirty finger in admonition. 'You don't catch me that way. Read you one of my poems? For nothing?'

'Why not?'

'Against union rules.'

After a moment, Roderick asked how much a read poem would cost.

20

'How much have you got?'

It added up to a dollar and forty-seven cents, exactly enough. Allbright read from the book of his memory:

> SKINNER'S DREAM
> Pigeons all over
> The window ledges of a tall building
> At sunset get down to work.
> Each must swoop to another ledge
> Where it can sit deciding whether
> To swoop to another ledge where it can
> Sit deciding whether to swoop to
> Another ledge or just sit deciding.
> That's pigeons all over

A gold-haired man wearing gold-rimmed sunglasses had come into the alley to look into garbage cans. During *Skinner's Dream* he came up close and stopped, apparently listening. He cradled a newspaper-wrapped bundle.

Roderick thanked Allbright. 'That was some poem. It was real – real—'

'Poetic,' said the stranger. 'You mind getting off that garbage can now?'

Roderick jumped down. The stranger took off the lid and looked in. 'That's better.' He dumped in his bundle and banged on the lid. 'Must be just about the only empty garbage can in this part of town.'

Allbright nodded. 'I guess they recycle a lot, at the Doggie Dinette here.'

'Interesting trend, petfood recycling,' said the stranger. His face was long and pock-marked, but his glittering gold hair offset these imperfections. 'Probably affects the growth potential of the entire edible foodstuffs industry, though we'd need a thoroughgoing econometric breakdown before we could apply any cogent significance test, engaging other retail foodstuff trends and of course the changing shape of pets.'

'Yes,' said Roderick. 'Well, I think I hear Mr Danton yelling for me.'

'You work here?' said the stranger. 'Must be fascinating. Unique opportunity to explore at first hand the full rich pattern of human–canine bonding mechanisms in a feeding situation.'

'With a little polishing,' Allbright said, 'you got a damned good routine there: add maybe a structuralist tap-dance . . .'

'Well so long,' said Roderick. He heard the stranger say something to Allbright about the role of refuse surveys in pre-archaeological studies of any dynamic social mix . . . .

Mr Danton was waiting for him. He twisted Roderick's arm and the robot felt pain. 'See dem dirty dishes?'

'Yes sir. Ouch.'

'I pay you to wash 'em, right?'

'Yes sir.'

'I pay you well. I treat you right. You get good hours, pleasant surroundings, friendly co-workers, a fair boss. Right?'

'Ow – yes sir.'

'I treat you like a crown prince. I think of you like my own son. *My own son*. And all I ask is you wash a lousy coupla bowls now and then, okay?'

'Okay.'

'Okay, I'm glad we had a little talk, cleared this up.'

Mr Danton threw Roderick down and kicked him across the greasy floor. 'Next time you're fired.'

When Danton was gone, Dave the cook had a quiet laugh. 'Watch out he kill you, kid. Old Danton he deeply crazy.'

'Kill me? But why would he kill me? For a few dirty—'

'No thing like that.' Dave guffawed again. 'See you look quite one little bit like his son Lyle. You look just like him, yes. Only thing, Lyle got birth-smirch on face, under eye like tear's drop. Yes? Boy do them two hate. One time Lyle come here, old Danton grabbing cleaver and enchase him, say he gonna depecker him, hee hee hee, Lyle not come

22

back. You watch out, kid.'

'But why should he want to, to kill his own son?'

'Hee hee.'

Roderick didn't understand. That evening he turned over the pages of a book on human behaviour. He learned that crowds were lonely, people were one-dimensional, and inner cities were dying; he himself was probably alienated. Real alienated. Boy, he was so alienated it was unbelievable. The only people in the world who cared about him were Ma and Pa Wood, back in Newer, Nebraska. There hadn't been any letters from Ma since the Newer nuclear power station accident. The accident had been caused by music. It seemed that someone had decided to install 24-hour-a-day music at the power station, and had chosen the new Moxon Music System. This did not rely on local records or tapes, or even on music run through long-distance telephone lines. Instead, the music would originate in a distant city, bounce off a special Moxon satellite, and be picked up by a large dish-antenna on the roof.

The roof had not been made to bear the extra weight of this antenna. It cracked, throwing the weight of the building on to the reactor shell. Now the entire town was fenced off. The government would say only that 'no one lives there anymore.' No wonder a guy felt alienated. Life was like something on TV.

Roderick turned on the TV to watch an old movie in black-and-white. It was raining, and two people stood in the rain embracing. The woman pulled back from a kiss and said: 'But don't you see, my darling? You're *not* a nobody. You're the man I happen to love.'

Rain dripped from the man's hat-brim. 'No, Mildred, your father's right. I'm no good for you – I know that now. Oh sure, I hoped and dreamed a girl like you would come along. Even a nobody can hope and dream. But this is real life, kid. You just happened to pick the wrong guy.'

'Don't say that! Don't ever say that.' She clung to his

23

sleeve. 'Listen, you big lug, if you're a nobody, then so am I – and proud of it! I won't let you go. I can't. You see—'

The scene was cut short to make way for a man in a bright plaid jacket who smiled and shouted details of a sewer-cleaning service.

Next day Mr Danton asked Roderick to fill in for one of the waitresses.

'Do I get to wear the rabbit ears?'

'You wear what I say you wear, okay?' Mr Danton's hand roamed over the cook's table and came to rest on the handle of a cleaver.

'Okay yes, yes sir.' Wearing a clean shirt and a black plastic bowtie, Roderick glided out to meet the customers.

Danton's Doggie Dinette went to great lengths to treat dogs as humans. A table could only be reserved in a dog's name, and when the dog arrived at the front door towing its owner, a hostess would pretend to greet the animal and lead it to its table. The tables were very low and bone-shaped and for dogs only; owners sat near their pets but out of sight, in alcoves, so that the restaurant seemed populated exclusively by Yorkies, Corgis and toy Dobermanns. That was how Roderick first saw the dining room, full of dogs wearing bibs.

3

May I recommend to you the following caution, as a guide, whenever you are dealing with a woman, or an artist, or a poet – if you are handling an editor or a politician, it is superfluous advice. I take it from the back of one of those little French toys which contain pasteboard figures moved by a small running stream of fine sand; Benjamin Franklin will translate it for you: 'Quoiqu'elle soit très solidement montée, il faut ne pas *brutaliser* la machine.'

Oliver Wendell Holmes,
The Autocrat of the Breakfast Table

Noon. The apostle clock chimed, and out of its innards came a parade of tiny wooden figures. Their faces and clothes had long since dissolved in wormholes; they now looked less like apostles than bowling pins.

Automatically, Mr Kratt lifted his snout to listen. His little black eyes lost their hard focus for a moment, and his powerful hands stopped throttling the pages of a company report.

'You know, bub, my old man left me that clock when he died. I ever tell you about my old man?'

Ben Franklin, checking his own watch, shrugged. 'I don't think so. Er, what was he like?'

The hard focus returned to Mr Kratt's little black eyes. 'He was a bum. A professional failure. A dummy. If I had my way, people like him would be turned into fishfood. At birth.' He gripped the company report again in a stranglehold. 'At birth. Damn it, I never could stand cripples . . .'

He cleared his throat and looked at Franklin. 'Anyway, where were we?'

'The patent leaseback deal with—?'

'No never mind that now, I want to go into this god-damned learning robot gimmick. You and Hare promised to deliver this thing six months ago, how long are we supposed

25

to carry you? So far I don't see anything on paper even.'

Ben Franklin fingered his upper lip as though stroking the moustache he had not worn for years. 'I can explain.'

'Let's hear it.'

'Well I've been having trouble assembling the right research team. Hare's a good enough research director for ordinary stuff, but this is special. I wanted to bring in this colleague of mine from the University, Dan Sonnenschein. He—'

'I know, I know, he's the guy who really invented this gimmick.'

'Well we all worked on Roderick, I don't think it's fair to say any one of us really invented – but Dan yes Dan was certainly more, more familiar with some of the programming problems. So I wanted—'

'Sure, sure, but we settled all this last year, didn't we? I gave you the go-ahead, hell, you're the vice-president in charge of product development, get this Sunshine guy, get Frankenstein, get anybody, only get moving, we need that gimmick.'

'I wish you wouldn't keep calling it a gimmick, Mr Kratt.'

'Call it a fucking pipe dream I wouldn't be too far off, would I? Damn it you and Sunshine aren't at the University now, this is real life. I know you say you built a prototype and it got lost or something, but all I get are explanations, excuses, you haven't even got your research team together, damn it, bub . . .'

'Yes sir, but you know I did mention that Dan was in the hospital, his nerves—'

'You said he was in the looney ward over at the U Hospital but so what? All these research geniuses are nuts, look at Dr Hare now. Trying to make pancakes with phonograph records on them, no idea what he's doing or why, we just wind him up and point him at a problem. So why don't you just spring this pal of yours outa the looney ward, stick him on the payroll and—'

'Frankly I don't think he's well enough to work for us, not yet.'

'Great, so we sit around waiting, do we? While the competition cuts our nuts off, that's not my idea of running a company, bub. KUR Industries is a growth company, damnit, and growth needs ideas. See *that*?' He suddenly thrust out a thick hand. Ben Franklin flinched, but Mr Kratt was only showing him a ring: a heavy gold claw mounting a steel ball.

'That's a pinball from my first machine, bub. One stinking machine in a dark corner of a greasy little diner in a neighbourhood so crummy the winos wouldn't puke on it. And I built up from there – more machines, an arcade, a chain of arcades, a carnival, saunas, leisure centres, bowling alleys, business machines, pleasure machines, fun foods – and all the time I had to feed the company with ideas. Ideas. Hell, I even hired you as an ideas man, and then suddenly all the ideas stopped.'

'Mr Kratt, I'm sorry if—'

'Because you drag your feet, bub, you keep on dragging your feet. Look at our funfood venture, Jinjur Boy, you dragged your feet over that. Best damned idea in the whole industry, a gingerbread boy with built-in microcircuitry, a talking toy and one hundred percent edible, how could it lose? Only you had to drag your—'

'But Mr Kratt, you can't always hurry research like that, we did have problems with those mercury batteries—'

'Problems? Only problem we had was a bad press, a handful of kids get a bellyache and right away everybody wants to blame us.'

'But some of those kids ate Jinjur Boys and died, others still have brain damage from mercur—'

'Nobody ever proved a thing. Damn it, bub, when you run a growth company, you gotta take chances, okay maybe we made one mistake but that's all in the past. Forget the damn past, forget it.'

'Yes sir.'

'We belong to the future.' Mr Kratt's cigar had gone out. He threw it away, got up from his desk and walked to the window.

'The future, yes sir.' Frankliln watched Kratt standing there in silence, heavy hands clenched behind him, heavy shoulders hunched against the sky.

'Look, we need this robot gimmick now. Get Sunshine or get somebody.'

Ben Franklin looked down on the city, etched in grey stone and black glass, a gleaming future to which he wanted to belong.

'Sonnenschein, initial D?' asked the hospital receptionist.

'Yes. I'm his son, Roderick.'

'I'm sorry, our records show he has no immediate family.'

'That waiter looks just like Lyle, you remember Lyle? Only he hasn't got Lyle's birthmark . . .'

'Oh, speaking of plastic surgery, guess what Barb paid for her new chest? You'd think it was gold instead of whatsit, silicon . . .'

'Darling, it's not silicon, it's sili*cone*.'

'Yeah but what do you think she paid for her silly cones?'

The voices from the alcoves rose and fell, striving to be heard above the drone of taped music, the noises of feeding animals, other voices from other alcoves.

'Basically I'm a Manichean myself . . .'

'Manic? I wouldn't call you manic, you're more . . .'

'. . . Libran basically, I took her to see . . .'

'. . . a puppet government, okay, but *whose* puppet, that's what I want to know. Take . . .'

'. . . The Reagan Expressway through Hilldale only there was this accident at the Dalecrest exit, we hadda go all the way down to . . .'

'Prague? Terrible, just terrible, my phlebitis acted up all

week, maybe I should get me some dacron veins or . . .'

'Spaghetti, didn't the Chinese invent that?'

'. . . a sage pillow for spirit dreams – but hey, isn't that Sandy? Over there with the Labrador.'

'I thought Sandy *was* a Labrador – oh you mean Sandy Mann, no they're on vacation in Prague or someplace . . .'

'. . . Ruritania, I can't even find it on a map . . .'

'. . . basically Libran until we went and had her spayed . . .'

'Now everybody thinks the Japanese invented transistors just like everybody used to think the Chinese invented the abacus, and even if spaghetti isn't Western . . .'

'That looks just like Sandy . . .'

'That sure looks like Lyle . . .'

The waiter who looked like Lyle moved smoothly through the dining room, serving dog and master with the same polite, mindless devotion. Roderick seemed a perfect minion. He was able to balance a heavy tray while a Sealyham urinated on his foot; to smile at the owner of a pit-bull that was trying to shred his hand; to take down details of a large, complicated order while a toy poodle tried to mount his ankle.

Beneath the smooth surface Roderick dreamt of violence. There would be like this big gangster with all these body-guards, and Roderick would have to kill each of them in a different way like maybe an exploding rice-flail or a duel on skates with chain-saws and like maybe strangle all their guard dogs and like maybe . . . hundreds of corpses, oceans of blood, until he would shoot it out with Mr Big, put a blue hole in his forehead and watch him crumple slowly, a look of surprise on his face as he becomes dead, very dead . . . until Roderick was victorious and alone.

Roderick was not victorious, just alone. He watched the dogs and their owners moving with assurance in their own world, where a Chihuahua and a St Bernard would recognize each other as dogs, a Republican optometrist and a Trotskyist dope dealer speak the same language. No one recognized Roderick or spoke to him as anything but 'waiter'.

There were conversations of which he understood hardly a word:

'Well I'm doing Rolfing now, but I was heavy into oneness training.'

'Connections, I know. I had this gestalt thing to work through with my family, you know? And—'

'Yeah how is Jaynice, anyway?'

'She's more in touch with herself now only – I don't know, maybe familying just isn't her mind-set.'

'Too many tight synapses, I felt just like that after Transactioning, I kept noticing my own tight synapses. I'm gonna try Science of Mind training next, or haptics maybe, you gotta try something . . .'

'Nodally it's probably all oned together anyway.'

'. . . yeah . . .'

'. . . yeah, synergy is. Isn't it?'

'Yeah. Oh waiter? We're ready to order here.'

He would take this order and move on to an alcove where two women, having spread paper napkins on the table between them, opened their jewelled pillboxes and set out arrays of coloured pills as though arranging beads for a barter, which, in a sense they were.

'Oh is that pink one Thanidorm or Toxidol?'

'That's Yegrin. Oh you mean this bitty pink one, that's Zombutal, beautiful, you want one?'

'Thanks, kid, now let's see what I got here to trade, these green ones are Valsed, the light green are Quasipoise, and the green two-tone are I forget, either Jitavert or Robutyl. The red must be Normadorms.'

'Is that like Penserons?'

'Only stronger, you want a couple? Or hey I got these terrific mood flatteners called what is it? Parasol? Here this yellow one. Or is that Invidon? Sometimes I get so mixed up . . .'

'. . . me too . . . I need something . . .' Well-manicured nails the colour of Bing cherries selected a capsule of the same colour and carried it to lips of the same colour. 'A Eulepton.'

'Was that a Eulepton? I thought it was a Barbidol . . . I get so mixed up . . .'

'Me too . . .'

Then to the kitchen where Mr Danton would twist his arm and threaten him, then back with a heavy tray to meet another territorial Sealyham, another angry pit-bull.

'Is it Sue Jane that's married to Ronnie now? I get so mixed up talking about Sue and her pals, all those divorces and all . . .'

'Well, it really boils down to three men and three women, and they been married in every possible legal way to each other, eight weddings in all. And none of them married anybody else . . .'

'You take Clarence now, he was his first wife's first husband, his second wife's second, and his third wife's third!'

'That's nothing. Vern's third wife's third husband's third wife is the same person as his second wife's second husband's second wife, how do you like that?'

'. . . divorced the sister of . . . and right away married Mary Sue, who was single. But his ex bounced back just as fast, she married the guy who'd just split up with . . .'

'Sure sure but what I want to know is, who was Sue Ellen's third husband?'

Roderick, leaning over to polish the table, murmured what he thought was the answer.

The people at the table looked at him. 'You know them or something?'

'No, I just wanted to help. I—'

'Nobody invited you to butt in, asshole,' said the owner of a Yorkie now devouring a bowl of goose liver.

'But I just thought – if everything you all said was true—'

'You calling us liars?'

'No I – sorry, I'm sorry.' He backed away, stepping on a coil of dogshit, tripping over a leash as he fled the dining room. He wished everyone sliced thin and fed to to their own pets who would in turn crumple slowly with looks of surprise as he shot them dead, very dead . . . no one would miss the human species or the canine, either, least of all Roderick the victorious.

An hour later, a woman smiled at him and told him he was a sweet boy. That changed everything: he cancelled the extermination of two species and decided to go dancing instead. But first another try at University Hospital.

'Daniel Sonnenschein,' he said to the receptionist. 'I'm his stepson, and I *demand* to see him.'

'Certainly, sir. Just take a seat.'

Two hours later, Roderick was told that visiting hours were over for the day. A pair of security cops did the telling, and showed him how to get out of the building.

4

The figure performed its purpose admirably. Keeping perfect time
and step, and holding its little partner tight clasped in an unyielding
embrace, it revolved steadily, pouring forth at the same time a
constant flow of squeaky conversation, broken by brief intervals of
grinding silence.

Jerome K. Jerome,
The Dancing Partner

The Escorial Ballroom was a large gloomy place where a few
tired-looking couples leaned together, shuffling slowly
around the floor to *The Tennessee Waltz*. The three white-
haired musicians chatted and drank as they played, and the
drummer was eating his lunch with one hand. The dancers
seemed not much younger or more interested in anything:
the men wore old suits and sideburns, the women wore
flared dresses, heavy makeup and large earrings.

While Roderick was standing at the edge of the dark dance
floor trying to figure out what to do next, he felt a little bump
at the rear of his crotch. He turned to see a plump woman
with heavy makeup and large earrings. She was examining
her thumbnail and frowning.

'Jesus, try to give somebody a friendly goose and you run
into – what you got there, iron underpants?'

'I'm sorry, are you hurt?'

'Busted nail. Oh well, I could've done it opening a can of
sardines, and I don't even like sardines. You dancing?'

'Well I, I'm not sure, I—'

She seized him. 'You're dancing.'

She had a deep, pleasant laugh, blonde hair going dark at
the roots, and her name was Ida. She didn't seem to mind that
Roderick couldn't dance at all.

'Don't worry, kid, you'll pick it up. None of you young kids know anything about slow dancing.'

'Well no I don't – oops. Sorry.'

'It's okay. I guess you came here for the Auks, they come on later.'

'The Auks?'

She looked him over. 'If you never heard of the Auks, you must be older than you look. Or else, Roderick, you haven't been around much.'

'No I guess I – oops. Sorry.'

'You been in the slammer, kid?'

'Jail? Not lately I mean no, I—'

She squeezed at his shoulder. 'Never mind, lover, it don't matter to me. Tell me your hard-luck story if you want, or tell me nothing, all the same to me. But you got slammer written all over you, that pale, pasty look, that weird short haircut, the kinda lost look you got, like you're afraid you're gonna make some wrong move and end up back inside.' She looked serious for a moment. 'Hey you fixed all right for bread? Because if you're broke, I can let you have a coupla bucks till you get a job.'

Roderick was so astonished that he tripped and nearly fell. 'Sorry! Do you mean you would lend money to a perfect stranger?'

She grinned. 'Nobody's perfect. A good stranger'll do.'

'I'll be damned. Well well.' After a few moments he said, 'Well I don't, but thanks. Thanks a lot, Ida.'

The dance ended. Ida started fiddling with her earring. 'On the other hand if you're flush, you might buy a girl a beer. You might even buy *me* a beer.'

Roderick was delighted to rush her to the bar and order one beer. The bartender looked from him to Ida. 'I'm sure the lady would prefer a champagne cocktail,' he said.

'Beer,' said Ida. 'Just now the lady prefers a beer, Murray.'

The bartender winked. 'Sorry, Ida, I didn't know you was

with a *friend*. One beer, coming up.'

Roderick, watching her drink it, thought, *friend*.

'You don't drink?'

'I can't,' he said.

'Don't tell me, the stomach. I seen it all before, the way them places ruin a guy's stomach. Half the guys get out they can't eat or drink. Other half can't sleep. Most of 'em can't screw worth a damn.' She sighed. 'But what do you expect, you can't lock a guy up like an animal and then expect him to come out still human. Take you, for instance. You don't feel very human, do you?'

'You really understand me, Ida.'

The deep laugh. 'Lover, that's my job. Which reminds me, I better circulate. Thanks for the beer.' She stood up, adding, 'Don't forget, if you need a favour. I'm always around this joint.'

She drifted away. Later Roderick noticed her talking to a battered-looking man in a bowling shirt. She was drinking a champagne cocktail. Then he lost sight of her because the place was filling up with a new crowd, mostly young people dressed in white.

The white seemed to be a kind of uniform for both boys and girls, some of whom had bleached white hair and white makeup Roderick began to feel out of place in his old hand-me-down suit.

The lunching trio left and three young men in white began setting up some complex equipment. Roderick drifted over to the bandstand to watch.

'Jeez,' said one, 'didn't anybody check out the co-inverter? The Peabody drift is over 178 how can I patch anything in to that? Barry, you check that out?'

'Yeah it was okay. Wasn't it, Gary, you was there.'

'Was I? Yeah well in that case okay, what's the problem? Just patch it in, Larry.'

'Like hell I will, you wanna blow the whole psychofugal synch box?'

35

'We could run on 19th-channel syntonics, just until—'

'Oh listen to the expert, will ya? You hearing this Gary, our boy here thinks he can play it all by ear, he's the big electronics expert all of a sudden. Only he don't know how to check out the equipment, a simple drift-check and he—'

Roderick said, 'Maybe I can help.'

Larry threw up his hands. 'Why not? Let everybody be a damn expert, why not?'

'Well you see I couldn't help noticing you've got a Pressler-Joad co-inverter there, if it's one of the early models A300 through A329 you can make it into an obvolute paraverter with harmony-split interfeed, see? All you do is take off the back – hand me that screwdriver, will you Larry? – and then you just change this pink wire and this green wire around. Now you got full refractal phonation with no drift, see?'

'Hey you know you're right? Great!' said Larry.

'Hey thanks man,' said Barry.

'Yeah man, thanks. Listen here's a pass, anyplace we play, you get in free, okay?' said Gary.

As soon as Roderick got down from the platform, a girl grabbed his arm. 'Hey you know them, personally? You a friend of the Auks?'

'Well no, not exactly.'

The girl wore white, her hair was bleached, and her eyes decorated with gold crow's feet. Her earrings were tiny integrated circuits, also in gold.

'God, I really like them, I think they're real other-world, you know?'

'Other-world.'

'Who do you like best, Larry, Barry or Gary?'

'I'm not uh sure – who do *you* like best?'

'Oh, Barry. I mean when he gr-rinds that synthesizer, I just – ohhh!' She rolled her eyes.'

'Oh?'

'He was my favourite back when there were the original

six, even back then, before Harry and Cary and Jerry dropped out.'

'Oh.' Roderick was spared further conversation by the other-world Auks. One of them (they all three looked alike to Roderick) grabbed a microphone and growled into it:

'Okay now, robots! Let's do that raunchy robot!'

Roderick quickly got out of the way of the dancers, who were doing an odd, jerky walk. Now he began to understand the uniforms and makeup: they were imitating some fictional robots.

The music was traditional rock, though generated by a complex of electronic instruments. Every now and then, one of the Auks would seize a microphone and growl a few words:

> Do the raunchy robot
> Do the raunchy robot
> Do the raunchy robot roll!
> Lady dressed in white
> Gimme some light
> I am in a deep black hole.

Roderick found it too loud, too cheerless. But he politely remained standing in front of the giant speakers throughout the rest of the set. The girl who liked Barry best seemed to be dancing at Roderick, or at least keeping an eye on him as she jerk-walked through numbers like 'R.U.R. My Baby' and the Palindromic tune 'Ratstar'.

At the end of the set, when Roderick started making his way towards the exit, the girl followed. She was still walking like someone with spine damage, and her face was expressionless. When a white-haired boy tried to stop her, she pointed to Roderick, saying:

'I . . . am . . . under . . . his command . . . I . . . obey!'

'Now look,' Roderick said, to the circle of white-haired boys who were closing in on him. 'Now look, I don't know what this is all ab—'

37

Someone screamed, and he saw a folding chair coming at his head. He ducked, and suddenly fists and feet were after him, driving him into the floor. He fell, took a kick under the nose and rolled away into another kick.

Then he wasn't the centre of it any more. Youths were chopping and kicking each other as though a mass tantrum had spread through the crowd. Roderick saw blood on white shirts, faces twisted with rage, folded chairs spinning through the air. Then someone grabbed his collar and dragged him through the forest of struggling legs to the exit.

'Ida!'

'Outside, kid, quick.' They raced across the dark parking lot, hailed a taxi and were away from it, safe.

'Jeez, Ida, thanks. Thanks a lot.'

'You need taking care of,' she said. 'But then don't we all?'

It was not the worst of times. It was not the best of times.

5

The tone arm hesitated as though judging distance, made the leap and lowered safely on twelve-string guitar music. Leadbelly sang:

> Funniest thing I ever seen
> Tomcat sittin' on a sewin' machine

There was a cat in Ida's cramped little apartment, a fat Persian that blinked and yawned until she shooed it off the sofa, but there was no room for a sewing machine.

'Make yourself comfy, Roderick. Why don't you take a bath and a slug of bourbon and say we take it from there?'

'No but wait, wait. I don't drink, and I don't need baths. And it's kind of you, Ida, but I don't think I could take it from there either.'

'I've heard that before,' she said, plumping a cushion. 'But you'd be surprised what you can do when you get in the mood.'

Roderick sat down and let the Persian rub its head against his shins. 'Look, maybe I'd better explain: I'm a robot.'

'Yeah? That's what all these crazy kids say, nowadays.' After pouring herself a drink, she sat next to him. 'I thought you had more sense, Rod.'

'No, I mean a real robot. I'm full of wires and stuff. Honest.'

Ida tasted her drink and frowned. 'Sure, kid. Anything you want. Only I hope robots don't like beating up on women or nothing like that. I'm not so good at that scene.'

'Beating up on – I thought they only did that in the movies! No, heck Ida, I didn't mean I want anything special, anything freaky. I meant I don't like anything at all.'

'Okay but if you did like something, what would it be?'

'I don't know, something like – well, like love. I guess.'

'Roderick, there has to be a first time for everybody. And I'm a pretty good teacher, if I say so myself. There ain't much I haven't seen, done, had done to me, smelled, tasted, dressed up as, sat on or listened to. I could tell you some stories – only they might scare you off.'

He said nothing while she had two more drinks and fiddled with the tassels on a cushion.

'Well, for instance some guys get turned on by just a fabric, rubber or leather or silk or even cotton. One guy had to be hanged in a telephone booth while a woman wearing yellow cotton gloves – me – pounded on the door. Another guy used to wear cotton long johns with the flap down, and I had to pretend to be scared while he whipped me with a piece of cotton string, I had to call him King Cotton. Then there was the gingham guy. He would sit at the kitchen table just like in the ads and I would come in wearing nothing but a gingham apron to pour milk on his cereal. Then he'd listen to it, while yours truly got under the table to make him snap, crackle and pop. That's to mention only cotton.'

She went on to describe strange rituals called golden showers, dog shows, thundermug brunches, Leslie Fiedler croquet; scenes involving coffins, chains, ice sculpture, lecterns, skates, trusses, apricot jam, the recorded cries of whales, pool tables, confetti, door chimes, Worcestershire sauce, early photos of Stalin, voodoo dolls, thimbles, mukluks, croziers, castanets, documentary films on the cement industry, whoopee cushions.

'. . . and I knew this FBI special agent, boy was he ever special. We always started off me whipping him with a towel from the Moscow YWCA while he sings about Notre Dame marching on to victory, then another girl comes in – we're in the bathroom – and handcuffs him to the faucets and washes his mouth out with soap while he studies pictures of Whitaker Chambers and Jean-Paul Sartre. Then I had to barge in wearing a J. Edgar Hoover mask and release him but only so's we could put him under a hot light and I ask him to name all the state capitals while she dusts off his cock for fingerprints. Then at the last minute a third girl rushes in and hands him a writ of *habeas corpus*. Boy, we earned our money in them days. And we always had to be careful with that guy's face because he'd always just finished getting a face-lift. So listen, kid, you ain't got no problem I can't handle unless maybe you like boys.' She put a hand on his leg and slid it towards his crotch. 'Tell me all about your problem, Rod. You got a wooden leg here, that it? You shy?'

Roderick stood up. 'Maybe if I just undressed and showed you—?'

She nodded. 'I won't be shocked. I – holy cow!'

Roderick stepped out of his dropped trousers and then took off his shirt. 'See, I am a little different.'

'Different, I'll say. Turn around, will you? Jeez, no asshole either. And you, what's that in your belly button, looks like an electric socket or—'

'It is an electric socket. It's how I recharge. Like I said, Ida, I'm a real robot.'

'I believe you, I believe you.' She poured another drink and gulped it down. 'So there's nothing I can do for you?'

'If I could stay overnight and charge my batteries, I guess that's all.'

After another, very large drink, Ida said, 'A robot. Does that mean you got no feelings at all?'

'I've got some feelings.' He thought about it. 'It's just that I can't do much about them.'

'It's a challenge, all right.' Ida seemed to be talking to herself. 'A real challenge. Okay you recharge tonight, I'll get some shuteye. In the morning when I'm soberer, I'll think about this problem of yours some more. See, the way I look at it, nobody with feelings oughta go around not being able

41

to let 'em out, all frustrated and ornery. Okay, so what if you got no ordinary sex equipment – sex is all in the mind anyway.'

Someone had said that before to Roderick, long before. Pa Wood, was it? (But Pa was always saying things: sex is all in the head. History is a bunk on which I am trying to awaken . . .)

'*Machines*,' said Indica Dinks, '*are only human, after all.*'

The audience laughed, then applauded.

The host, Mel Mason, said, '*I love it! I don't understand it, but I love it!*' After more applause, he said, '*But seriously now, Indica, isn't this Machines Lib idea just a little – wacky? I mean, do you really expect everybody to just turn their machines loose? I'd hate to be in the front yard when somebody liberates a big power mower!*'

Indica smiled just enough to show she recognized the joke, but did not join in the audience laughter. When it had abated, she said quietly, '*We don't expect people to stop* using *their machines, of course not. We just want people to* understand *the machines they use, to understand and* respect *them. If you don't have respect for your own car, your own home computer, how can you have any respect for yourself?*'

'*Well, that's a very interesting point, Indica, we can know a man by the gadgets he keeps.*'

She cut off the hesitant laughter. '*Yes, by the machines he keeps and by how he keeps them. Mel, machines aren't just extensions of man, that's all part of the old master–slave routine, the terrible power game we used to play, all of us. But I think we're moving on into a new era, as machines get smarter and smarter. They may go on working for us, but not as slaves. As* employees. *As I say in my new book,* THE NUTS AND BOLTS ON MACHINES LIB, *machines are beings in their own right. And if we don't give them their freedom, one of these days, they'll take it.*'

'*Well, you've given us big food for thought there, Indica, thanks very much. Stick around folks, later we'll be talking to lots more exciting people: a sculptor who wants us all to get plastered, the President's*

42

astrologer, the most beautiful private eye in Hollywood, and the exiled Shah of Ruritania, you saw it all first on the Mel Mason Afternoon Show . . .'

Roderick watched the pictures of an armpit, then dancing cornflakes, then a shirt destroyed by lightning. Indica Dinks had been his first mother, long ago . . . in another life . . . he could hardly remember. Indica painting her toenails red. A green plant in a pot. Hank and Indica. An exercise machine. A TV cartoon called *Suffering Cats* . . .

He went back in the kitchen where Ida was fixing her face for evening. They had spent the whole day talking, trying things; Ida had heard his life history and how he functioned. But nothing had transpired.

'Okay, so you saw your old stepmother on TV, that upset you at all? Turn you on?'

'Nope. I hardly remember Indica, all I did as a kid was watch TV, how could I be upset? How could I get turned on?'

'That's the big question, Rod. How can you get turned on? Do I remind you of your stepmother? I mean I'm older, kind of motherly. And my name, Ida, that's a lot like Indica.'

He slumped down in his chair. The afternoon sun slanted in through the window and reflected from Ida's compact mirror into his eyes. Squinting against it, he said: 'Everything's like something and everybody's like somebody, that doesn't mean much. Like all TV programmes have a car crash in the first five minutes, what does that mean? Gee, Ida, I guess all your hard work goes for nothing, you been swell but what's the poi – the poi – the – the—'

'Hey, what's wrong?'

'Nothing,' he said after a moment. 'Just the light, the way it flashes in one eye and then the other. It's real distracting. Real – nice.'

'Aha! Turns you on? Like this?'

'Not so wild. More regular. Like a truth table. Say if left was true and right was false – like this.' He took her eyebrow pencil and wrote on the kitchen table:

L L
L R
R L
R R

She tried it again, and Roderick began to relax and enjoy relaxing. 'Maybe a longer sequence,' he murmured. Just then the sun was eclipsed by a tall building, the Kratwel Tower.

'I knew it! I knew it was no good!'

'Don't worry,' said Ida. 'We can use an electric light – no? Okay then maybe a sunlamp?'

'No! No, just forget about it, forget—'

'Wait. There's one place in town where the sun will be up for at least an hour, the big hill in Beauregard Park. Come on, I'll finish fixing my face in the taxi.'

The taxi dropped them at the foot of the hill, and they hurried up it, Ida carrying her shoes to keep them nice. When they reached the top they were facing a sheet of burning gold.

'Look at that sky, Rod! Just look!'

'Yeah, yeah.' Roderick grabbed her purse and pawed through it looking for her compact. Powder spilled as he fumbled it out and thrust it into her hand. 'Come on, come on.'

They sat on the warm grass and Ida, following the truth tables he'd scribbled in the taxi, gave him:

L L L L L L L L L L
L L L L L L L L L R
L L L L L L L L R L
L L L L L L L L R R
L L L L L L L R L L and so forth.

44

'Just let yourself go,' she said soothingly. 'Go on, go on.'

'I'm . . . afraid I'll drain my battery . . .'

'Don't worry about anything, just let it all go, lover. Let it all go. Let go.'

Roderick had never felt anything like this strange, pleasant numbness that was engulfing him. His mind seemed to be thrusting and thrusting at some barrier, then pushing deeper into warm darkness, layer after deep layer until it reached the golden fire explosion.

He drowsed, then, only half-aware of Ida's leaving for her evening at the Escorial. When he awoke it was getting dark. There was a kleenex beside him with a note in eyebrow pencil: 'Told you so! Love, I.'

Christ, what had he done? Used her, that's what, used Ida like a kleenex or a mirror, to rub his own disgusting mind against the world and take crude pleasure from the friction. His first friend, his first real friend. Now he knew he could never face her again. Hadn't even told her how nice she looked. Hadn't even stopped a second to look at the sky, her sky, pure gold like Ida herself. No, he was just a – an animal automaton, a cheap clockwork gimmick to wind up and run down. He was despicable.

Roderick flung away the tissue and started walking down the hill. Halfway down, the path was blocked by a man carrying a sign:

ᴚƎԀƎ∩Ʇ!

There seemed to be no way around the man, so Roderick stopped.

'Brother.'

'Okay. Mind if I get past?'

'Brother, a moment. Stop and reflect. Stop and reflect. Have you read my sign?'

'Yes but—'

'Notice anything unusual about it?'

45

'No. Except that it's written backwards. Now can I—'

'In *mirror writing*, brother.'

Something about the man's emphasis made Roderick shudder. He looked into the wild eyes. 'You, uh, saw me up on the hill?'

'With the lady, yes. Playing with a mirror. Ah, how little ye know, for ye stood on the path to paradise, and took not a step.'

It seemed certain that the man knew his terrible secret, but Roderick had to be sure. 'Can you explain that?'

'Come to our meeting tomorrow night.' The man pressed a tract into his hand. 'The address is on the back. Come all ye faithful!'

Was the man mocking him? He stood aside, and as Roderick passed, said, 'All will be made clear. St Paul said, "We see as in a glass, darkly, *but then face to face*." Reflect on his words, brother. Reflect!'

Roderick managed to murmur thanks and take the tract home. There he found he could only read it by holding it up to a mirror.

REFLECT AND REPENT

Have you looked at yourself in a mirror lately?
Oh, not just to comb your hair, but to *see*
yourself. Look now. Do you like what you see?
The decay of the flesh, the marks of age, even
the ravages of sin?

Roderick saw the ravages of sin, and read on. The tract explained that all Nature was made symmetrical by God, and for a hidden purpose: Mirrors contained the whole of the world outside, showing (if darkly) the truth. No one can hide the truth from his mirror, any more than the mirror can hide his lies from him.

Have you ever thought, that when you look at your
reflection in mirror, *your reflection is looking
at you?*

'God sees dog,' Roderick joked, and almost at once wondered whether his reflection would find this so funny. What if this mirror stuff was true? He read on:

The eyes are the mirrors of the soul, the tract explained. St Paul speaks of mirror-seeing. Reflection is highly prized in all religions. The God of the ancient Hebrews was YAWAY, a name readable in a mirror. Didn't all this add up to something? Surely the incredible symmetry of all Nature was no accident, but part of a plan, a manifestation of God. The left side of every creature was *exactly like* the right side – yet *different*. Scientists were now convinced that the right and left sides of one human brain were as different as two individuals – one musical and linguistic, the other spatial and mathematical. All magnets had both North and South poles, as did the Earth and all planets. Electrical charge could be plus or minus, people could be male or female, all time itself was either past or future. Didn't all this symmetry add up to a glimpse of the DIVINE PLAN?

It did, said the tract. God wanted us to preach his gospel not only among ourselves, but to those of His creatures trapped on the Other Side – to the people within mirrors. Incredible as this might at first sound, there was evidence of this DIVINE PLAN everywhere: in Nature, in the Bible, and especially within ourselves. Only if the gospel were carried into looking-glass land, could we be sure of turning the message of the world ('EVIL') into the message of the mirror ('LIVE!')

This tract was printed by the Church of Christ Symmetrical. All strangers, and their reflections, were welcome.

'We should be honoured, he decided to pay us a visit. Welcome!' Mr Danton grabbed Roderick's ear and banged his head against the wall, then kneed him. 'I mean, excuse me all to hell, we forgot to put out the red carpet. Only we

47

didn't know what day you was finally gonna show up for work, did we?'

'No sir.'

Mr Danton knocked Roderick to the floor and was just picking up a cleaver when the alley door opened and a patrolman came in.

'Is the manager here?'

'I'm the proprietor, officer. Can I help you?' Danton laid down the cleaver. The cop stared at it for a moment, pushing back his cap as though perplexed. He kept one hand on his gun.

'We found a lady's leg in your garbage can back there. You want to explain it?'

'A lady's leg? A *lady's* leg?' said Mr Danton, as though his place often disposed of all other kinds of human legs. 'Naw, we don't know nothing about that.'

'You wanna explain what you intended doing with that cleaver, then?'

'That? Oh, I was just kidding around with my dishwasher here. Tryin'a scare him a little, haw haw haw. Hell I treat the kid like my own son, how does he repay me? Comes in late, don't come in at all. Never no apology or nothing.'

The cop straightened his cap. 'Kids these days! They don't know the meaning of punctuality, respect, duty, clean hearts.'

Roderick said, 'About this leg—'

'Well if none of you did it, I guess it might turn out to be another unsolved case. I could call it the case of the lucky legs. Only one though: case of the lucky leg sounds wrong, you know?'

Roderick said, 'Officer, I might be able to help.'

'Yeah? You wanna confess?' The cop winked at his old pal Danton. 'Your son here wants to confess!'

'No I – I think I saw somebody drop something in that garbage can. In our garbage can. The day before yesterday it was.'

48

The patrolman squinted at him. 'You mean you think you saw them or you think they dropped it?'

'I did see him, and he did drop it. It was wrapped in a newspaper.'

'What was?'

'Whatever it was he dropped.'

'Oh now you're sure he dropped it? You wasn't so sure before. Okay.' The cop opened his notebook. 'Okay, suppose you describe this guy that maybe didn't drop anything wrapped in a newspaper.'

Roderick described the man as having gold hair, a pock-marked complexion and gold-rimmed sunglasses. He'd worn a casual terry shirt in an easy-care polyester blend, a rib-knit V-neck with cuffs and bottom band. The body of the shirt was terry in a sculpted design. It was light rust in colour, size: medium. He'd also worn s-t-r-e-t-c-h woven twill slacks in an outstanding blend of Celanese Fortrel R polyester for long wear and cotton for comfort. These were in straight-leg styling with an elastic waistband to help prevent waistband rollover, slant front pockets, two set-in back pockets, the left one with a button-through flap. These were khaki tan, size 34 regular with about a 34 inch inseam. They probably featured hook-and-eye front closure, nylon zipper, and seven belt loops fitting belts up to 1½ inches wide. Roderick couldn't be sure about the belt loops, because of the jacket.

This was a cotton poplin jacket with a smooth nylon lining. Hip length, with a two-button tab collar and slash pockets. Set-in sleeves with one-button adjustable cuffs. Elastic insert at waist sides. Nylon zipper. This was in navy blue, medium size with about a 34 inch arm.

Finally the man had worn smooth leather-upper sports shoes with sueded split-leather reinforcement at toe. Ventilated vinyl tongue with laceholder was padded for comfort. Padded collar and peaked back. Rubber toe guard would help protect toe area against wear. Sturdy moulded

49

heel counter. These shoes were white with royal blue vinyl stripes, and featured moulded rubber sole with crepe rubber wedge, sole having ribbed tread for traction. Size 9.

The patrolman had written nothing down, and now he closed his notebook. 'A description like that could fit anybody,' he said. After lingering a few minutes to flirt with one of the waitresses, he swaggered back out the alley door.

Within a month, the police would arrest Allbright, who was short, dark, bearded, had a clear if grimy complexion, and wore greasy denim work clothes, the only clothes he owned.

6

The cold weather was here, and with the drop in temperature came a drop in Roderick's fortunes. The two were connected:

Fur coats were coming into the dining room regularly now, and poodle sweaters. Somehow the sight of all these creatures keeping themselves *warm* irritated him. He was reminded of pictures of the first Thanksgiving: all those roundheads and featherheads sitting down to eat *food*. Where would a robot be at that banquet? Waiting tables? Out in the cold?

Though technically he needed no special winter garments, Roderick wanted something cosy. Ma and Pa would have understood, being cosy small-town folk themselves. Ma would have said, if you're undecided about doing something, do it big.

Roderick went into an exclusive sporting-goods store, bought himself a very fine red wool stocking-cap for two weeks' wages, and wore it to work.

Unfortunately, he forgot to take it off while waiting tables. Though some patrons only laughed, one complained to the management. Mr Danton was happy to fire him.

'Son or no son,' he said, 'you're out in the fuckin' cold.'

'Sonnenschein, initial D?' asked the hospital receptionist, touching her keyboard. 'Yes, and your relationship to the patient, Mr Wood?'

'I'm his – I'm his lawyer. And I demand—'

'Certainly, sir.' The machine hummed and produced a red ticket. 'Take this pass, so you can get out again. It's Ward 18G, express elevator to the eighteenth floor.'

On the eighteenth floor he handed his pass to a nurse manning another computer terminal. 'I like your cap,' he said. 'Unusual.'

'Thank you, sir.' She read the pass and tapped keys. 'A lot of people seem to like our caps.'

'No I meant yours in particular. Unusual.'

She looked wary. 'What do you mean?'

'Well I just noticed, all the other nurses have them folded left over right, but yours is right over left.'

'Is it?' she laughed. 'Well you're the first person to notice that, anyway.'

'Well I only noticed because the cap itself is a variation on an ornamental dinner-napkin fold called The Slipper. I remember seeing a picture of it in *Mrs Bowder's Encyclopedia of Refinement.*'

'Really?'

'I read that a lot when I was a kid. The language of flowers, too, like that vase on your desk there, yellow chrysanthemums, they say—'

'Fine, fine. You can see Mr Sonnenschein in the visiting room, second door on your right. If you'll just wait he'll be in in a minute.' She seemed very busy and not inclined to look at him. But when Roderick reached the door to the visiting room he looked back: she was staring at him.

Red cap again. He pulled it off and jammed it in his pocket, damn it.

This was a sunny room overlooking the river. It was furnished like a large, comfortable living room, with a TV corner, a music centre, a writing desk and a small library – all separated by yards and yards of soft chairs and sofas. No one else was there except an old man in a striped bathrobe and paper slippers. He sat turning the pages of a book of Mondrian reproductions. Now and then he found one that made him chuckle.

Roderick tried to watch TV, but the controls of the set were locked. He settled for a newspaper.

Former poet held

Only 30 days after turning up a severed leg in a Downtown alley, police have unearthed a second leg Downtown. The two legs are from two victims, according to the medical examiner. 'Each is a woman's left leg, amputated at the knee,' he said, 'possibly with an electric carving knife. Both legs were removed after death.'

The first limb turned up in an alley off Junipero Serra Place. The leg was wrapped in newspaper and dropped in a garbage can at the rear of Danton's Doggie Dinette. Wendell Danton, the proprietor, said, 'Someone is out to get us, but it won't work. All the meat used in our canine cuisine is genuine U.S. Government inspected Choice or Prime cuts. I have the receipts to prove it. My kitchen is always open, and anyone is welcome to look it over, anytime.' Police agree that it is unlikely the leg came from Danton's.

Today a second grisly package was found in a litter basket on Xavier Avenue, near the newly-opened cat boutique, Pussbutton.

Former poet A.L. Bright, picked up for questioning in an alley where he was drinking wine, admits being in the vicinity of both legs, but claims he does not remember murdering anyone. Police say Bright fits an exact description of the 'Lucky Legs' killer, given by a Danton's dishwasher.

A door opened and a tall, untidy man blundered in. He was all out of proportion, like a child's drawing: arms and legs too long for his thin body, head too heavy for his thin neck, face too big for his head, hair a dark 6B scribble.

'You're my lawyer?'

'Don't you know if I'm your lawyer?'

'I don't – sometimes things surprise me. They feed me a lot of uh medication.'

Roderick was a little disappointed. 'Are you Dan Sonnenschein?'

'Yes. And you're my lawyer.'

'No, I just said that to get in. See it's very hard to get in to see you. Like you were in prison. I'm not your lawyer I'm your – I'm Roderick.'

'Well for lunch we had, I remember that okay, we had hot roast beef sandwich, salad with thousand island, banana cream pie.' He looked at Roderick. 'Didn't we?'

'Maybe you did. Dan, I'm Roderick. You created me, remember?'

'Look, I'm having a hard enough time remembering what I had for lunch.'

They sat there in silence for some time, staring at the black-and-white tiles of the floor. Now and then the old man could be heard laughing quietly at Mondrian.

Roderick was very disappointed. So this was Dan? This was the genius who first thought of him?

'So you're not my lawyer?'

'For the last time, no. I'm Roderick. I'm the robot you spent four years building, remember? And then finally you sent me to live with Ma and Pa Wood? Your stepfather and stepmother? They raised you, you must remember them!'

'Yeah, maybe.'

'And when you sent me to them I was just a little lumpy machine on tank treads. But Pa Wood got all these parts from the artificial limb factory and rebuilt me like this. So when I came to the city I thought I'd look you up.'

'Why?'

'Why? Well like just I guess maybe – how do I know? Okay you think I shouldn't have come. Okay I made a wrong decigeon – decision. I just thought you might want to see how I turned out. I thought we might get to be pals or something. I thought when you got out I could help you with your work.'

'My work!' Dan blinked. 'My work got me in here. You know how I got in here?'

'No.'

'I had this idea there were people after me. Very high up conspiracy, see, to prevent anybody ever building a robot. So I was very careful, *very* careful with Project Roderick. I never published anything, I kept a low profile. And when the robot was finished, I sent it away, somewhere they'd never find it. And I destroyed my notes. Like whatsisname in that movie about a forbidden planet, Walter Pigeon, he buries his book and gives up robots, or maybe that's some other movie – but I destroyed my notes. That's how they got me, see?'

'No.'

Dan held up a finger; Roderick noticed how badly bitten the nail was. 'Since I was working for a University project, those notes were not my property. I was destroying University of Minnetonka property. And this property might be worth billions and billions – if I really had built a robot. So that was a very antisocial act, so they put me in here.'

'To cure you?'

'No, to keep me from building any more robots. And to find out if I really have built one already.'

Roderick said, 'I don't understand. They want the robot because it's worth billions, but they don't want you to build it?'

'Look, I know all this is confusing.' Dan started to chew an already dilapidated fingernail. 'What I mean is, the University people own any robot built using their money. But somebody a lot higher up wants to put a stop to all robots. Don't ask me why – a paranoid schizophrenic doesn't have to give reasons for the plots against him. I'm nuts, see? Or if I'm not, the world is so dangerous that I'd still rather be treated like a harmless nut.'

'I'll get you out of here, Dan. You're not nuts.'

'Why should I leave here? Here is as good as anywhere, now. And safer.' He stopped chewing the nail and looked at it. 'I tried leaving for awhile. I got a nice little crummy job, a nice little crummy apartment. But right away people started following me. A car tried to run me down. My apartment had this fire.' He folded his hands. 'Here is safer. Here they can watch me, so they don't have to destroy me.'

'Okay then I'll visit you all the time.'

'No. It isn't safe for you, either. If you are Roderick, they must be looking for you. Better stay away.'

'Can I at least send you something? Books? Food?'

Dan hesitated. 'Peanut butter. For some reason, they never let you have enough peanut butter around here.'

The door slammed open and a nurse marched in. Her cap was folded left over right. 'I'm sorry, Mr Wood, but there's been some kind of mix-up. Mr Sonnenschein isn't supposed to have any visitors at all. You'd better leave, right now. Come on, Mr Sonnenschein, I'll get you back to bed.' Though Dan made no resistance, Roderick noticed how she took a firm grip, one hand on his wrist, one on his elbow.

'But I'm his lawyer.'

'No you're not,' she shouted back. 'We've phoned his lawyer and he never heard of you. You'd better leave!'

Roderick stood a moment, watching the old man, who was weeping over *Broadway Boogie-woogie*.

'God damn it,' said Roderick, and put on his red stocking-cap.

'God damn it is right,' said the man seated before the monitor. 'We lost the whole damn conversation there, all we get is a great shot of a guy in a stocking cap going out the door. You shoulda checked the tape before you went out.'

His partner said, 'You implying I don't know how to do my job?'

'I'm not implying nothing.'

'Look I always go out to get the coffee at three. Okay, sure, maybe I was a little late back, but only on account you wanted a chocolate doughnut, they was out downstairs. I hadda go all the way over to Thirteenth to that new place, *Mistah Kurtz*.

'Anyway what the hell's the difference, we know the guy's name from the hospital computer, you wanta check him out?'

'Let's review this next visitor, this Franklin guy. He talked to Sonnenschein for an hour, can we run that?'

On the screen the vacant features of Ben Franklin registered shock. *'Who was here? Who was here?'*

'. . . must of just about met him. Roderick. He was wearing a red
stocking-cap . . .'

'I did meet him! He came out of the elevator . . . Dan, God damn
it, we were face to face . . .'

'God damn it is right,' said the viewer again.

The Church of Christ Symmetrical was just a derelict store in
a rundown neighbourhood. Roderick almost passed it
without noticing, for it was marked only by a dusty mirror
set up in an even dustier window, with a small sign:

Church of Christ Symmetrical
YOU ARE LOOKING AT THE PERSON WHO CONTROLS
YOUR DESTINY!
AND THAT PERSON IS LOOKING AT YOU!!!

Inside it didn't seem much like a church, except for the
emptiness. There were a dozen rows of folding chairs (some
set up facing backwards) but only four were occupied: Four
ragged men sat hunched over, each quietly consulting his
pocket mirror.

Having no pocket mirror, Roderick went to the front of
the church, where the place of an altar was taken by a table
of reading matter. He removed his red cap but, seeing others'
wearing caps, put it back on.

One pamphlet showed a photo of a Byzantine plate,
decorated with a picture of the Last Supper. The picture
clearly showed two Christs, one giving bread to six disciples,
the other giving wine to the other six. The spidery
handwriting beneath said, 'The Last shall be First!!!'

Another pamphlet outlined significant passages in the
Bible ('thy breasts are like *two* roes that are *twins*') and
pointed out Biblical symmetries: Two tables of the Law,
Solomon offers to divide a child equally in half; 72 books
in the Old Testament and 27 books in the New, four
evangelists having initials M, M, L and ⌐, and so on. A

57

donation was requested, to help with the great work of preparing the Bible in mirror-writing. Roderick contributed a symmetrical 11 cents, this being all he had in his pocket.

'Thank you,' said a small, red-nosed man coming up the aisle with a large mirror in his hands. 'I see you appreciate the urgency of our work.'

'I'm not sure I even understand what your work is.'

'Aha! You will, you will. My name is Amos Soma, by the bye, and I'd like to shake your hand for Christ.'

Roderick could hardly refuse so civil a request; he spoke his name and shook the man's hand. As they did so, Mr Doma held up his mirror: their images shook left hands.

'Of course my name has not always been Soma. I took it because of its wonderful symmetry: *Soma*, the Vedic drink of ecstasy, and *Amos*, the greatest of prophets. Now, Mr Wood, if you'll find a seat, our meeting can begin.'

Roderick took a seat near the back. Two well-dressed men came in and sat still further back.

'First,' said Amos, 'I have a few important announcements to make. There has been another calumnious attack on us in the church press. As usual, they accuse us of "Mirror worship", of saying the Lord's Prayer backwards, and of so-called black magic. Frankly I don't feel lies like these are worth answering, so I'll drop that subject. I also have a positive announcement: our Bible translation is ahead of schedule, and we have now finished Sudoxe.'

A man in a parka, sitting a few rows ahead of Roderick, turned around and said to him in a loud whisper, 'You aren't spying on me or anything?'

'No.'

'I didn't think so.'

Amos began his sermon: 'I want you all to reflect tonight on the cross. Notice how symmetrical the cross is. Right and left reflect, but not top and bottom. Why is that?

'It is because the cross is shaped like a man. But why, you might ask, is man symmetrical? He could have been made

58

any shape at all. God didn't need to make you with one eye on the right side of your nose and one on the left. Oh no, God could have made you like one of those modernistic paintings, with an eye on your chin and another on your forehead!'

Amos paused for laughter. There was none. 'No, God made man symmetrical because He made him in His own image. God Himself is symmetrical. He has a right and a left. Everybody knows that Christ "sitteth on the right hand of the Father", so the Father must *have* a right hand.'

The man in the parka turned around again. 'You sure they didn't send you to watch me?'

'No.'

'No, I don't suppose they'd bother.'

Amos went on, discoursing for some time on left and right – the hemispheres of the brain, magnetic 'handedness', whirlpools, political leanings, Lewis Carroll – and why God made mirror symmetry. God meant for us to meet our mirror images face to face (how else?), to talk to them, and to bring them to salvation.

The parka turned around again. 'You impressed by this bullcrap?'

'Yes I guess I am.'

'Me too. Funny, because I think I know what's wrong with old Amos.'

'What's that?'

'He's just ambidextrous. He can write with both hands, that means. So the thing is, he doesn't know if he's right- or left-handed. He doesn't know which side of the mirror he's living on, and it drives him nuts. He wants to convert everybody on both sides, just to play it safe.'

Roderick said, 'Then you don't believe.'

'Oh I don't know. You have to believe in something. Every week or so I try some new religion or some new political movement. And the thing is, I always believe.'

At the end of the meeting, the man introduced himself as Luke Draeger. 'I was thinking about going to the bar on the corner, you know it? The Tik Tok Club. Figured I'd sit there and stare at myself in the mirror – till I get double vision. You might as well come along and spy on me.'

'The name is Roderick Wood, and I'm not a spy. And I don't drink.'

'Rickwood, everybody drinks. Especially spies. Come on, you need a drink.'

The two men in the back got up and left.

'But I really don't drink. All I really need is a job. Before I become – well, a beggar, like this old guy.'

The old man he meant wore a long black overcoat, almost to the ground, which somewhat resembled a cassock. He had produced a cracked saucer from one pocket and was pretending to take up a collection.

'Howdy doody, gents,' he said, approaching. 'Spare a little contribution for the mm-hmm-mmf . . . ?'

Luke dropped a few coins on his saucer. 'There, you old fraud. I've seen you taking up collections in every storefront church around here.'

'Bless you, sir, it's only for the clothes. Against the terrible winter.'

Roderick took off the red stocking-cap and handed it over. 'You need this more than I do. In fact I don't need it at all.'

'Bless you, bless you . . .' The old man salaamed away.

Luke was impressed. 'You're outa work and you give away your cap. By God I like that. To hell with getting a drink, I'm gonna get you a job. I work at this little factory, see, and they always need extra men.'

He led the way outside against the blustering wind and wet sleet, to an alley between two warehouses. Roderick followed cautiously to a rickety fire escape, then all the way up to the roof. There Luke knocked on an iron door which, to Roderick's surprise, opened at once. A fat yawning woman let them in. To Luke she said, 'Boss wants to see you. Right now.' She looked at Roderick. 'Who's this?'

'This is my old pal Rickwood. I'm just gonna show him

60

around, he might accept the offer of a job here.'

'Ha! Better see the Boss first.'

First, however, Luke showed Roderick around. It was a peculiar factory, with hardly a machine in sight. They went down open stairs into the middle of the place, a lot of trestle tables where people sat making things. There seemed to be a lot of different products being turned out here.

One old man with a gallon of wine at his elbow was painting a rustic scene on a diagonal slice of birch log: a lake at sunset, with a moose on the shore and a canoe gliding across, beneath the words *Souvenir of Lake Kerkabon*. The painter completed his work, flipped the wooden plaque over, and stamped on its back MADE IN KOREA.

Next to him a woman with an eyepatch was flattening out aluminium cans and hammering them on a mould to make them into ashtrays shaped like horseshoes. These two were stamped MADE IN KOREA.

Next to her was a man fishing green felt letters very quickly from a bag and sewing them on a grey baseball shirt. His little hand-cranked sewing machine chattered away and in less than a minute he had spelled out SHAMEROCKS. As a final touch, he sewed a label into the neck of the shirt (Made in Korea). Others were assembling and testing digital watches, again with the puzzling label, while still others were painting portraits of the President on decorative meat platters, labelled again.

'Why is everything "Made in Korea"?' Roderick asked.

'It makes people realize they're getting a bargain, the cheapest item available. It is the cheapest, too. Nobody in Korea can get labour as cheap as it is right here, off Skid Row. Even automation costs more than us. Want a job here?'

'Sure, why not?'

'Okay, just let me find the Boss.' Luke went off to the far end of the room, to a little cubicle made of cardboard cartons. There was a constant sound coming from that cubicle, a high-pitched electric hum.

In a moment Luke came back. 'You can't win 'em all,' he said cheerfully.

'No job for me?'

'Not only that, they fired me too. I guess I was expecting it, but – oh hell, Rickwood, let's go get that drink after all.'

Outside, the cold wind and sleet continued to batter at pedestrians. The gutters were filling up with water, floating cigarette filters and popsicle sticks, pizza boxes and foil from chewing gum, a non-returnable bottle with no message and a used condom floating like a pale jellyfish, bandaids, plastic coathangers, an old *TV Guide*. Roderick thought he saw the floating body of a Golden Retriever puppy, wrapped in sodden toilet paper, but he couldn't be sure.

At the Tik Tok Club there were police cars and an ambulance, and a large crowd.

'All right, everybody back,' said a cop, though in fact no one was pressing forward to look at the figure being rolled out of the bar on a stretcher.

'. . . and these two guys just shoot him when he walks in the door,' said someone. 'Figure that, an old wino like that, I mean who would waste a bullet? Figure that, these two guys just . . .'

'Everybody back.' The cop bent and picked up the red stocking-cap which had fallen, and put it back on the stretcher.

Luke ordered two scotches. 'I know why they nailed him. It's because I gave him 39 cents. They wanted to teach me a lesson.'

'What lesson?'

'I didn't ask permission first. Jesus, Rickwood, don't you understand? It's "Captain May I" around here all the time; you gotta ask permission to scratch your ass. I mean *I* gotta ask permission. So they rubbed him out, just to remind me.'

'Remind you? Luke, I think this all sounds—'

'Remind me who's captain, of course. Who gives the orders – them – and who takes the orders – me. I see you aren't drinking. On duty are you?'

'No I'm not on duty, but listen, Luke, who are *they*?'

'As if you didn't know!' Luke finished both drinks and ordered two more. 'Okay, maybe you don't work for them. I guess maybe I'm a little upset here, losing my job and then seeing that poor old fart lying dead – I mean it hasn't been all that good a day.'

'You said you were expecting to be fired,' Roderick reminded him.

'Yes. Yes. The Boss said there were too many mistakes in the work. He's right, he's right. See, we were working on car seat covers, you know the ones? Imitation leopard skin. There was this big team of us, painting on the spots. And everything was going along okay until I went and changed religions.'

'You mean to the Church of Christ Symmetrical?'

'Naw, before that. Like I said, I get a new religion every week or so. No, this time it was the Disciples of the Four Gopsels.'

'The Four Gospels?'

'No, the Four *Gopsels*. Deliberate mistake there, see.' Luke finished two more drinks. 'The whole basis of this religion is that nobody's perfect, everybody makes mistakes. Kind of an Islamic idea, I think. To err is human, and not to err is divine. So if you make something perfect, you're only mocking God. so in everything you do, *you have to make one deliberate mistake.*'

'I see where this is leading,' said Roderick. 'You made mistakes on the seat covers?'

'That wouldn't have been so bad. All I'd do was maybe leave off a spot, or do it in the wrong colour, or sometimes do it in a funny shape like the ace of clubs or something. But see painting leopard spots is boring work, so you get to talking with the people you work with, great bunch of guys and gals, I – well, I converted them. They all got born again as Disciples of the Four Gopsels too. So then each of them had to make a deliberate mistake. And by the time twenty-seven people do this, the seat covers start to look kinda funny, you know? That's why the Boss fired me.'

'Maybe that was his deliberate mistake,' said Roderick.

'Rickwood, you're a card. I haven't had a good laugh since I left the Corps.'

'The Corps?'

Luke laughed again. 'Maybe you're *not* spying on me.' He took a gold pin from his pocket and laid it on the bar. 'Like, you wouldn't know what that is, would you?'

Roderick looked at the pin. It showed a circle nested in a crescent, and a star with three lines coming down from it. 'Some Masonic lodge? Turkish Army?'

'The Astronaut Corps, pal. I was an astronaut. In fact I was the hundred-and-forty-seventh man on the moon. I was the hundred-and-eighty-first to walk in space, and the two-hundred-and-seventeenth to say "The Earth sure looks beautiful from up here." Ah, those were the days, those were the days. Except—'

'Except?'

'Except they weren't.' Luke ordered more scotch. 'Maybe I should start at the beginning. See, I always wanted to go to the moon. When I was a kid I read space comics and built model rockets and everything. Then I went into the Air Force, dropped a few bombs, had a few laughs, and ended up married and with three yelling kids in North Dakota. Here, I'll show you pictures of my kids, look at this. No not that one, that's a bomb pattern, here we are: Ronny and Vonny and little Lonny. Cute, huh? Of course they aren't yelling in the picture.

'Anyway they told me I could qualify as an astronaut, only first I had to get a PhD. They figured they couldn't have guys walking in space and saying how the Earth sure looks without PhDs. So I went to college, only right away I could see I wasn't going to make it. So I decided to cheat. I had a lot going for me: I looked bright, I was rich and my father was a Senator. So I bought exam answers and faked experiments, and hired a research assistant to write my doctoral dissertation for me – I couldn't even pronounce the title. Defending it was no problem, either: I had Dad put a little Federal research grant muscle on the college, and they managed to come up with a friendly committee and a prepared list of questions and answers. I got my PhD and I became an astronaut. You see, dreams can come true.'

Roderick shook his head. 'What I don't see is why it mattered so much. What's so great about space?'

'Let's have another drink and I'll tell you. Barkeep?'

Roderick saw a familiar face at the end of the bar. Or was it familiar? Just some man with oily black hair, tinted glasses, and a tweed overcoat. He was talking to a pretty, doll-like little woman in a black fur coat – they both looked a little overdressed for Skid Row – telling her jokes, evidently. Every now and then she'd let out a little squeak of laughter and say, 'Oh Felix, you are the limit! The limit!'

Luke was saying, 'Why did I want to be an astronaut? I

used to ask myself that, you know. But then when I'd get home after a hard day faking lab experiments, and the kids would be yelling and the wife would refuse to iron my socks and make a big scene about it – then you know, I realized why I liked space. It's because you're alone out there. No one wants a bedtime story. No one wants you to drop off clothes at the cleaners on your way home. Oh don't get me wrong, I love my wife. I love my kids. I love my dog and my television set and all my neighbours and fellow countrymen and everybody else, but I still like to be alone, once in a while. In space. You know like in that poem, "The world's a fine and private place".'

Roderick said, 'I thought it was the grave that was a fine and private place.'

'Okay never mind that. The point is, I got into space finally, and instead of being alone, it was just the opposite. Two guys in the damned space shuttle with you, and Mission Control in there too – I mean right inside your damned suit. You eat a ham sandwich, this voice in your ear says, "Nice going, Luke. Hope you enjoy the ham sandwich, because your blood sugar level can use it." You take a piss and they know exactly how much, what's in it, the pH and albumin level, everything. You take a walk on the damned moon, they check your heart rate and tell you you're lookin' good, just gotta remind you they're watching every move.'

'I think I see what you mean.'

Luke laughed. 'They see it, too. They see everything I ever did mean and ever will mean! Well, you get back and they have to debrief you, that means a lot more talk about how well they've been watching you. Then come the awards and shaking hands with the President and banquets and more awards and parades and crowds, crowds everywhere, even if you get a minute alone in your hotel room if you turn on TV there you are, eating that ham sandwich again, the world is not a fine and private place at all.'

Roderick studied the oddly familiar stranger again. He had a long jaw, and the skin of his face seemed dull in the glaring lights of the Tik Tok Club – powdered? The only really familiar feature of that long, empty face was the pair of tinted glasses. Who did they remind him of? No one.

'That's not the worst, the publicity's not the worst. The worst is when it's over,' said Luke. 'Because then you go home and it seems good to be home, the wife and kids seem terrific after the others. So you relax, have a few beers, watch an old movie on TV with the wife, go to bed. You find yourself getting a hard-on, and just as you're about to nudge the wife, a little voice in your ear says, "Nice going, Luke. Good idea to have sex with your missus, only watch the old pulse rate. You're lookin' good." It's old Mission Control, still with me! Still there! Still watching! The hard-on naturally vanishes.

'And Christ, they been with me ever since, watching every move and passing little palsy-walsy remarks on everything I do. I went to a Corps doctor and asked him, was it possible they'd planted some kind of device on me? Some video-radio device on me or even in me? He sent me to a psychiatrist, and the psychiatrist had me thrown out of the Corps.'

Felix of the tinted glasses told the woman in black fur one last joke as they left. Tired of slumming. Tinted glass, tinted glass.

'I thought when I left the Corps it would all stop. But no, not a chance: once they get you, they get you for life. Every time I so much as farted, Mission Control would tell me what a great idea it was to vent that gas buildup.

'Well naturally that wrecked my happy marriage. What kind of wife can put up with that, her husband gets ready to make love and then suddenly says "Affirmative, Mission Control" and gets a tired cock? And the kids, too, I'd be reading them a bedtime story when Mission Control would come on the line, asking was I sure I read that last paragraph right, and would I say again?'

Again Roderick said to himself, tinted glass, through a glass darkly but then face to long empty face – of course, it was the gold-haired stranger! Of course with the hair dyed, a different pair of tinted glasses – but no disguising the empty grin, the long empty face that, once the pocks were puttied up, had nothing in it.

'Excuse me,' said Roderick to the bartender. 'That couple who just left, woman in fur, man in tinted glasses? Do you know them? Know where they went?'

'Nope. Why.'

Roderick ran to the door and out on the corner. There were empty streets stretching away in four directions, no human to be seen, nothing but a wind-blown page of newspaper.

Roderick went back to the bar. 'Thought I saw someone I knew . . . probably wrong. Go on. About your voices.'

'Go on? *They* go on, pal. *They* go on.'

'And they're still with you, right now?'

'Affirmative. Saying it's a good story but nobody'd believe it – and that I've had enough ethanol. Time to leave.'

'A little voice in your ear,' Roderick said. 'Sounds kind of like a conscience.'

'It is a conscience. Correct and confirmed, it is a damned conscience. That's why I keep messing around with religion and politics. I need to find some way to get rid of this conscience. To exorcize it. I mean hell, millions of people get along without consciences, why should I get stuck? I mean Nixon did what he wanted to, right? So why me? Why me?'

Roderick knew no answer. Which was unfortunate, because Luke was getting loud and defiant.

'I won't put up with it!' he yelled. 'You hear that, Mission Control? I won't put up with it! I'll find some kind of religion that will shut your still small trap for good! Or politics – I'll start a goddamned revolution that will burn Houston to the ground!'

68

The bartender approached. 'Get your friend outa here. Maybe we ain't a high-class joint, but we got our limit. He controls himself now, or out.'

'Over and out,' murmured Luke, as Roderick helped him from the bar. 'Your friend doesn't control himself, Rickwood, because they control him. He's not even human, just a radio-controlled model astronaut. Mission Control says I'm not walking too straight. Am I?'

'That depends on where you want to go.'

'Gert's Café, where else? The address is on this.' Luke fumbled in all his pockets and came up with a handbill printed in red:

WE SAY NO

NO to Fascist prison atrocities, extermination of dissidents and tortured confessions!

NO to Marxist-Leninist mindless bureaucracies grinding down the disaffected in slave labour camps!

NO to Capitalist corporate corruption, conglomerate exploitation of the workers and rape of the Third World!

NO to Maoist robotocracy, smashing individualism under mind-bending, brain-washing statism!

NO to the so-called New Left and other effete dilettante so-called movements drowning in their own so-called rhetoric!

NO to Anarchism, Trotskyism, Democracy and all other useless isms and ocracies!

Left Right and Centre, it's all

A GREAT BIG NOTHING!!!

Find out the truth tonight: Mammoth meeting of the

Fractious Disengagementists
(Gert's Café Branch)
Gert's Café
1141 Richelieu Ave. So.

Well and why shouldn't 1141 Richelieu Ave. So. turn out to be an ordinary frame house in a slightly rundown neighbourhood? Why shouldn't it be allowed to have a small sign on the front lawn: GERTS CAFE. KEEP OUT. THIS MEANS YOU, and why shouldn't this make Roderick hesitate?

'Maybe we shouldn't go in,' he said, at which Luke laughed.

'You don't know much about politics, Rickwood.' The question which cries out for an answer now is, who does know anything about politics? Isn't it just a dirty game for cynical manipulators of mass ignorance?

They walked in, by direct action demanding to be let in and given the same rights as anyone else – as those who could not read, for example.

Gert's Café provided only four tables, but then there were only three Fractious Disengagementists in the Gert's Café Branch, which was also so far the only branch of this new regrouping of committed elements of radical consciousness in anticipation of a totally new unfettered mass spiritual/political movement unifying to force a final showdown with the present-day corrupt and powerful system. Anyway Bill was playing the video game machine in the corner all evening, so didn't need a chair.

So far Gert's Café had a menu but no manifesto, but tonight's meeting would hopefully fix that. The menu had taken careful planning and much meaningful discussion, working through all objections to California grapes and Brazilian coffee and any other foodstuff outputted by any other oppressive regime. It was finally agreed to limit the menu to bread and water – homebaked stoneground wholemeal bread and pure bottled mineral spring water – the fare of all political prisoners everywhere.

These prisoners of conscience became acquainted: there was Rickwood, a taciturn guy whose symmetrical, bland face probably concealed a real thinker; Luke, a drunken loudmouth but probably revolutionary at heart; Bill, the big guy with the beard who played video games and said little, in fact nothing; Wes, the small intense guy with rimless glasses

70

who talked a blue streak and wanted action! action! and 'Gert' who was really Jóanne and married to Wes but who preferred not to be known as Mrs or even Ms but adopted the totally unbiased and sex-free title Msr, applicable to men persons and to women persons, in any order.

What was to be done? The entire world was now in the grip of authoritarian zombarchical police states, maintaining power through multinational conglomerates at the top and the jackbooted forces of oppression at the bottom. The world was beginning to resemble something in a satirical science-fiction novel of no great quality. It was time to do something, all right. Time for some all-out, ultimate, definitizing gesture that would make it clear for all time where everybody stood.

Wes wanted to go out right away and collect money to save up for a cobalt bomb that would wipe out all life on this planet for millions or maybe billions of years: that was action. Gert and Luke preferred to argue about the placement of punctuation in a draft manifesto condemning 'world inter-dependencies/coercive structures/Houston Mission Control/ militarist juntas/pigshit bureaucracies.'

Roderick, having gone into the kitchen to find an outlet and recharge his batteries, came back at dawn to find the arguments still raging on, and Bill still playing a video game. Since it was breakfast time, they all sat down and (all but Roderick) had a bread and water breakfast. Bill spoke for the first time:

'A lot of people talk a lot about blowing up the world, tearing it all down and starting over,' he said. 'But I'm really doing something. I got me a job with the Hackme Demolition Company, and we're really tearing stuff down.'

'You blow stuff up for some capitalist,' said Wes. 'That's no good. A rich guy in silk hat and striped pants holds out this bag with a dollar sign on it, and you say "Yes sir, yes sir. You want me to lose that building? Yes sir." '

'But I still blow it up,' said Bill. 'It's still one building less.' He thought for a moment, chewing his bread. 'And they're still hiring, if anybody here wants a job, a honest job.'

Wes already had a job, as clerk to a tax lawyer for a leading investment firm. Joanne had the café to run, Wes added.

Roderick and Luke agreed to help dismantle the world.

8

The apostle clock chimed. Mr Kratt lifted his snout automatically and listened. For a second the heavy black V of his
brow-line softened.

'Okay Smith, where were we?'

'O'Smith, sir. The name is O'Smith. And the game today
is I do believe industrill espionedge. Ain't it?' The insolent
tone was unexpected. Nice change of pace, Kratt thought,
from all the panting yes-men around here. Of course it was
the desperate insolence of a loser, just look at the man.
Kratt looked, and found himself trying to stare O'Smith
down.

In essence, this 'Mister' O'Smith (who seemed to have no
first name) was a fat cowboy with a deep tan. He wore the
modified Western clothes favoured by bogus oilmen and
revivalists on the make, but even his hand-tooled boots failed
to give him a prosperous look. His fat would be the fat of
poverty, of hash-house burgers dripping with mayonnaise,
pancakes or powdered-sugar doughnuts in the morning and
greasy pizza at night, watery tap beer and syrupy wine, and
cokes glugged down too fast in desert gas stations. Kratt had
seen thousands of O'Smiths passing through his amusement
arcades and his carnival, hurrying on their way from trailer-
camp childhoods to flophouse deaths, losers all the way.

Mr Kratt's gaze faltered. 'Okay, let me give you a general
run-down on this operation and then turn you over to my
product-development boy, Ben Franklin.'

'Yes sir. Now do I liasonize with you or this Frankelin?'

'Him, this is all his show. See, Franklin worked on a
research project at the University, a few years ago. Building
a robot.'

73

'Yep.' O'Smith was staring hard again.

'When the project broke up, the robot disappeared. Naturally Franklin was disappointed. After putting in all that work on the thing, to have somebody come along and steal it . . .'

'So you want me to steal it back?'

'That's about it. It's worth ten grand in cash, plus all reasonable expenses. Agreed?' Mr Kratt stood up and was about to offer his hand when O'Smith turned aside and walked to the window.

'By God you got a view here, sir. A view! From up here it looks like you could just reach down and pick up any old piece of that city down there, pick it up in your hand. Like it's all yours. Guess lots of it is yours, right? KUR is such a big old conglomerate, like I guess you manufacture that there Brazos Billy gadget, right?'

'Brazos Billy? What – oh, you mean the fast-draw amusement machine, yes one of our subsidiaries handles that one, why?'

'Nothin', I just always kind of liked old Brazos, boy I must of drawed against him a thousand times – at bus stations, airports, arcades.'

Kratt looked at his watch. 'There a point to all this?'

'I like the way when you hit old Brazos he flops down on the floor and bleeds like a stuck pig. Plastic blood I know but boy it surely looks real. I always wanted one of them machines for myself so I could practise at home.'

'You want me to throw in a toy, is that it?'

O'Smith grinned. ''Preciate that, Mr Kratt sir. But I was only calling attention to the difference between you and me. I wanted a robot for years and never got it. You want one for five minutes, you just call me in, say "Ten grand in cash" and you got it.' The grin broadened. 'You got it, Mr Kratt. Sir.'

O'Smith offered his left hand, a final insult.

Mister O'Smith still had his smile when he had finished

talking to Ben Franklin, who could only give him two minutes. He kept the smile on until he was safely out of the building and into a bar, where he ordered a tap beer. Then he let it go.

'What's the matter, cowboy? Somebody shoot your horse?'

He looked at the woman in purple with her purple lipstick, and he continued to scowl. She raised her shotglass and nodded to him as though he'd bought her a drink. 'You wouldn't think it to look at me now,' she said, 'but I was once a Paris model.'

Model what? he wondered.

'I was. A *mannequin*.'

'Lena!' The bartender shouted at her as at a dog. 'Quit bothering the customers, I told you before.'

'Larry's always telling somebody off . . .' she said.

Mister O'Smith ignored the old bat, tried to get his thoughts straight or just not think. Later he would hit an arcade, few games of Star Rats maybe and then shoot it out with old Brazos. Then get a pizza, go back to his hotel room and grab some shuteye. Plenty of time to think after that . . .

Ten measly grand, fucker was going to make millions off this Roderick, maybe billions. Ten grand was like an insult, like he was so dumb he couldn't figure what a robot like that was worth. God durn it, a man had his pride, even a man as badly handicapped as Mister O'Smith, handicapped didn't make him an idiot. There was other people who would pay to find out about Roderick the Robot, this Roderick Wood the Robot. How about the Agency? Them boys wouldn't forget the work O'Smith done for 'em already, and they was always in the market for dope on robots. He'd stopped it must be twenty different robots getting built, back when he was free-lancing for the Agency. The Agency would pay, all right.

Then there was other companies. How about Moxon, now, always hot for some little cybernetic novelty. Others too. Nothing wrong with selling the same robot to everybody, why not?

75

'I don't know why not,' said the woman with purple. 'You tell me, honey.'

He saw how it was: he'd been shouting it out to everybody, he'd been in the bar all day, he was drunk.

'Boy howdy am I drunk! And I am just shoutin' it out to everybody!' he shouted. 'Whole buncha secrets! Shh! You all need to know em – on a need-to-know-basis – WAHOO!'

'Lena,' said the bartender. 'Get your boyfriend out of here? Please?'

'WAHOO! Big D is beautiful, that's the secret. Big D is beautiful!' he roared, as Lena manoeuvred him up some dark stairs. 'Best-kept secret in the whole world, but everybody needs to know!'

'*Shhh.*' She was opening a dark door into darkness. 'The bed's this way, honey. By the way, what did you mean about being handicapped?'

'Shh, secret!' He fell acros the bed, grinning. 'See, I got an artificial arm.'

'Oh. Well I don't mind.' She reached for him.

'But I also got an artificial leg.'

'Oh. Well I guess that's okay.' She threw a real one across him.

'But I also got—'

'Christ don't say it!'

'A glass eye, that's all. People keep thinking I'm staring at 'em.'

'You were giving me the eye in the bar.'

'I'll give it to you now, maam. Here.'

She screamed, he laughed, there was a confused tumbling that might have included sexual contact, then they slept. Later she turned on the dim rose light.

'Was it the war?'

'Naw. I lost the arm in an accident when I was just a kid. Rest of me was okay for a long time, till I come up North here, that was the start. I got run down by a car, first off, and they took me to the hospital.'

'Were you hurt bad?'

'I wasn't hurt at all, just knocked out. But my prosthesis was a total wreck. And the worst thing was, they wouldn't let me out because I couldn't pay my bill. And I couldn't pay until they let me out to get my new arm and get back to work.

'Finally tried to sneak out one night, climbing down the bottom side of a fire escape, but with one arm it wasn't so good. I fell and broke my durn leg! So I went back inside, more bills piling up, and they operated and set the leg. Only there was this infection all over the hospital and it got into the leg bone – they had to amputate.'

'You poor thing.'

'Next thing, my durn heart stopped on me, right on the operating table. I guess they got pretty excited around there because I was a kidney donor, so they started in testing me to see if I was dead. What they do is, they take a piece of cotton wool and touch the eyeball to see if you blink. I blinked okay, and they got my heart started again. But then the eye got this infection . . .'

'You poor, poor thing.'

'I don't exactly see it that way, maam. See, I'm a private investigator by trade, and in my line a work, handicaps like these can be a real asset. You can conceal a load of equipment in a prosthesis, if it's built right.'

He told her how he had to find the money to buy some really good stuff: an eye with a camera in it, an arm that fired .357 ammo, and a leg that could hold an automatic weapon – all of them custom-built and jewel-perfect. But for all this he needed real money, not this chickenshit ten grand. Quarter-million would be more like it.

She couldn't see why a private dick needed automatic weapons, though.

It was because he didn't want to be a nickel-and-dime divorce case man. All the real money was in big contract work – for large organizations – even for the government. He'd done Agency work before and he'd do it again. Just had to get his money together.

She had once been a Paris model, so she knew what it was to hit the skids and go all the way down.

'The best time,' he said, 'was on this Agency job down in St Petersburg, Florida. See this old-timer down there was some kinda inventor, and he'd patched together some electronic junk to make himself some kinda talking machine. Guess it sorta made conversation with lonely old folks or something. So the Agency sent me down there to straighten him out. Only time in my life I ever had to be quick on the draw!'

'Quick on the draw? You mean to *shoot* somebody?'

Mister O'Smith laughed. 'Why sure. Like I said, to straighten him out. This old-timer was sittin' in the shade, with this 12-gauge just outa sight – he brought it up so fast I like to caught my deatha cold right there. Only I been practising a fast draw all my life, so I just terminated his lease – boy howdy! Hot damn! Best contract I ever – what's the matter?'

She turned away, pulling the covers up around her. 'I wish you'd just go now.'

Mister O'Smith got up and dressed, and ran a cloth over the toes of his boots. Then he twitched the ring on his little finger and from under the nail slid a thin knife-blade. When a man talked too much, a price had to be paid. He hated like hell to do this to poor old Lena, but that's the way it goes. All he had to do was lean over and cut her throat, hold her down by the hair till she stopped thrashing, wipe the blade on the bed and retract. Then a quick check for bloodstains – not that there ever were any – and get out quick. Out on the frozen street at dawn, maybe swipe a Sunday paper off some doorstep, nothing looks more innocent than a man at dawn with a Sunday paper under his arm, heading into a hash house for a stack of wheatcakes.

But when Mister O'Smith finally did ease on to a stool at the hash house, Lena was still alive and well. God durn it, he kept saying to himself. God durn it, this was serious. Leaving a live witness who knew all about him, not even busting her arm to scare her a little, that was bad. He must be goin' soft as shit.

Too blamed late now. Hell he could of blamed it on that 'Lucky Legs' killer, another one right here in the Sunday paper, some maniac kills women and saws off their legs, he could of sawed off Lena's leg and . . . too late now. Too blamed late.

He looked at his eyes in the mirror behind the pies. A hard man, but goin' soft. Soft as baby shit.

The site scheduled for demolition was a smart apartment building at 334 East 11th. The crew from Hackme arrived, the police helped clear the street and put up barricades – but when the site manager came to inspect the building, he couldn't get in. The door was blocked by a doorman in grey livery.

'You got the wrong address, buddy. *This* place ain't coming down, it's full of residents.'

'It's not full of residents, it can't be.' The manager started pulling pieces of paper from his attaché case. 'Look, *this* says it was vacated two weeks ago. And *this* says the city gives us permission to blow it up. And *this* one says the owner wants it blown up so he can build a parking ramp. Your boss wants this place down, see?'

'You're crazy,' said the doorman. 'There's twelve floors of residents here, nobody told them about any demolition. Nobody told me. I been workin' here twenty years, nobody told me to leave.'

Roderick, Luke, Bill and the others stood watching the argument, and so did the great crowd behind the barricades. Policemen came and went, unsure what to do: Hackme's papers seemed to give it a legal right to blow up the place.

But the doorman had a right to prevent anybody's going inside.

At noon, the president of Hackme Demolition arrived. Mr Vitanuova was a short man in a homburg. The crowd took note of his hat and his car (a Rolls-Royce) and booed him as he approached the door.

'Look, all I want to do is go inside and talk to any residents who might by chance still be in the building. Okay? Just talk to 'em. Not get 'em out or nothing. Can I go in?'

The doorman stood firm. 'No sir. I gotta know whom you was wanting to see, first. Then I gotta call it up to them, to see if they're home to you, sir. Then *if* they okay it, you can go up.'

'But hell I don't know any residents. Just let me see anybody.'

'Oh no you don't, that we don't allow.'

The audience cheered as Mr Vitanuova came away defeated. There was snow on the shoulders of his expensive coat, but he didn't notice.

The crew went to sit across the street in a doughnut shop called *Mistah Kurtz.* Outside they could see Mr Vitanuova pacing in the falling snow and smoking his cigar. Inside they could hear people in fur hats talking across doughnuts and coffee.

'Well I for one am glad they're blowing up that place. I always hated it, looks like a stack of TV sets . . . I'm tired of buildings that look like machines . . .'

'Isn't that Le Corbusier? Or no I must be thinking of Tolstoi, the body is a machine for living in buildings with . . . no, wait.'

'Well I for one would rather sleep in the nave of Chartres cathedral . . .'

'Oh you can fall off anywhere . . . like that angel that loved high places . . . where was it now they put up that angel of Villard d'Honnecourt's, the one that could turn to look at the sun?'

'Henry Adams harking back to the twelfth century . . .'

'Well and Robert Adam harking back to the Etruscans . . . it seems they all want to get back to the old Adam, Adam and no eaves, hee hee!'

'Not so funny when you think of all that striving and dreaming, reaching for – what, light? And finally it comes down to nothing more than Las Vegas fibreglass casinos with neon walls, a city of the darkness for all those watts . . .'

'All an Etruscan room?'

'Only job Villard d'Honnecourt could get now is removing unwanted hair maybe.'

'And that squiggle that Le Corbusier always used for "Man", that sort of crushed starfish, that could feel right at home now, lifting up one fin to hail an air-conditioned cab . . . on any street . . .'

The siege went on. The owner of the building was away skiing somewhere and could not be reached. The police didn't want to act without talking to him first. Mr Vitanuova applied for a court order, but the judge, too, wanted to think it over.

Three days passed. The steadfast doorman was now more than a local hero; network TV and out-of-town papers were beginning to warm to him. The mayor came to shake his hand.

'I'm only doing my job,' he kept saying, to their delight. 'Protecting this building and the residents.'

But in three days, no residents had been seen going in or out. No one went to work, received visitors, bought groceries or walked a dog. Nothing was delivered to the building except the doorman's meals and laundry.

The doorman took brief naps, and somehow managed to shower and shave without leaving his post for more than a few seconds at a time. He remained on duty day and night.

On the morning of the fourth day, he admitted to the press that the building was empty. There were no residents. 'I only protected the place out of a sense of loyalty, I guess. I still say there's some terrible mistake.'

The crew went to work. Several floors of the building were knocked out inside. Then holes were drilled at strategic points, to take dynamite. When the charges went off, the entire twelve floors would collapse inward, burst like a bubble and leave almost nothing.

The TV cameras watched all this, the death of this particular building having become news. Mr Vitanuova posed with his finger on the firing button.

Flashguns were still going off like lightning when there came the sound of sirens. Escorted by two motorcycle police, the owner of 334 East 11th arrived.

'Stop! There's been a computer error!' he cried. 'You were supposed to blow up 433, not 334!'

Father Warren's appearance caused one or two raised eyebrows at the airport. Minnetonka was after all a province, where not everyone was used to cosmopolitan priests in black leather cassocks and crucifix earrings. Couldn't be helped; he had to impress the person he was meeting that not all Midwesterners were bucktoothed hicks.

The VIP lounge was almost deserted, but a guard checked Father Warren's ID all the same.

'I'm here to meet Mr Dinks. Hank Dinks, the author.'

'Make yourself at home, uh, Father. I guess the press is here awready.'

There were indeed a few men and women in the drab anoraks of the press corps. Father Warren pretended to inspect an amusement machine until a few reporters drifted over.

'You're Father Warren, aren't you?'

'Yes.'

'The Stigmata,' one older man explained to his colleagues. 'I covered the story two years ago on Good Friday, how you managed to make your hands bleed.'

'Hi Father, look over here. Thanks.'

'You're here to meet this Luddite guy Dinks?'

'That's right.' Father Warren chose his words with Jesuit care. 'I don't say that Hank Dinks and his New Luddites have all the answers, but at least they're asking some of the right questions. Do we really need all these machines? Can we really control them – aren't we becoming slaves to our own creations?'

A woman said, 'A lot of people might say you can't turn the clock back – we don't want to go back to living in caves, do we?'

'No, no indeed. That's certainly not our intention. We don't want to go back to the horse-and-buggy days, not at all. What we want is, well, just to say *Whoa*. We want to stop and catch our breath. Before we turn our world over to thinking machines, let's try thinking for ourselves.' He produced a self-conscious chuckle. 'But don't let me get started making speeches. All I'm here for today is to welcome Hank Dinks to our city.'

As if to signal the end of this session, one young man began firing wild questions: Was Hank Dinks a junkie? Weren't there allegations of bribing a Congressman? A scandal involving farm animals? How about a Mafia connection? Was the KGB funding the New Luddites? What of gay priests? Convent abortions? Transvestite nuns?

The man was given no answers and evidently expected none; it was simply his way of probing for what he called a human interest angle.

The photographers took over. To show he did not hate machines themselves, Father Warren was asked to play one or two of the amusement machines for the cameras. Obligingly he tried a fast draw against Brazos Billy, he repelled alien invaders for a few seconds, and he even had his blood tested. The latter machine pricked his finger, beeped and flashed his blood-type on a screen. He forgot the type immediately. As the cameras clicked, he noticed a small warning plate next to the coin slot:

KUR BLOOD-TYPE BONANZA. *Warning:* Don't use
this machine if you have had any of the following
diseases: malaria, hepatitis (jaundice), yellow
fever, syphilis, flukes . . .

Father Warren had once had malaria. Before he could
decide what to do about it, someone from the airline brought
him a telegram:

SORRY HAD TO CANCEL FLIGHT BIG SPONTANEOUS
RALLY INDIANAPOLIS. WILL SCHEDULE NEW VISIT. HANK.

9

In the conference room the pipe smoke was thicker than ever. In its layers and eddies, the Orinoco people might have seen analogies with the weather of world events: laminar flow with occasional turbulence. The Orinoco people believed in containing local storms, smoothing them out and bringing them back into the general pattern of balminess. The world could be made to work – given enough computing power and the ability to spot trouble in advance.

Today the centres of turbulence were few and obvious: the President had had a light stroke (the news would not reach the public) and so was postponing a few major decisions. Earthquakes in China were causing economic imbalances that would work their way through world trade figures – likewise the discovery of gold in the Sahara. American experiments near Jupiter were beginning to alarm the Russians, who believed they were trying to turn Jupiter into a sun. How to reassure them?

The problem of Entities still nagged. 'Shouldn't we be getting some Entity news from Minnetonka? The Agency isn't going to let us down again, are they?'

'I have an interim report,' said someone, and dry liver-spotted hands rustled dry tissues of paper. 'The Agency sent two men, and they have reported a probable kill of the Entity, with a certainty of point nine two two.'

'I hear a *but* coming,' someone chortled.

'But they now disconfirm. The Entity is still at large, and no longer highly visible They now ask for a priority number so they can plan their hunt. Any ideas?'

'Just how badly do we need this Entity?'

'Good question. Not exactly a case for calling in more agents, is it?'

'To make a worse mess of it. You know I can't help wondering why this is all so difficult. Two grown men, experienced field agents, with all the Agency backing – money, help, equipment, administration – can't manage to track down and kill a lone automaton. I gather the thing is none too bright, has no friends or allies – what *is* the problem?'

'I don't know, I can check. But we can't let this thing run free, you know. Suppose someone discovers it – their co-worker or lover or neighbour turns out to be all full of electronic junk and no meat! Could start a bad panic – we'd have a devil of a time getting the media to sit on it.'

'Exactly, exactly. The projections are all bad. But we do have these two Agency men still on it, I don't see how we can justify more. Vote on it?'

The Hackme Demolition Company was halted, temporarily hung up on a legal snag, so Roderick had the day off. He decided to call up all his friends. Ida's recorded voice told him that she was home, but not at all well and not taking calls today. Luke's recorded voice told him he was out, seeing his children in a zoo. That exhausted the list.

Roderick wandered into an amusement arcade, to test his reflexes for half an hour. Then he prowled the streets and stared at the mannikins in store windows. Finally he found himself on Junipero Serra Place, just outside Danton's Doggie Dinette. Might be fun to borrow a dog and go in? Let the waitress bustle about, setting out a bowl of ice water for the dog and a menu for him?

On the other hand he might run into Danton, not so funny. No, best thing was to just keep going, right on past this alley too, don't even look down it . . .

Roderick saw Allbright back in his usual corner of the alley, sitting on a box and drinking something out of a bottle in a paper bag.

'I'm glad they let you out. I knew you weren't the

murderer, Allbright.'

The bag tipped, paused, tipped again. 'They said you described me perfectly.'

'No I didn't. I described that guy we saw that day, with the gold hair and tinted glasses.'

'I believe you, I guess.' The bag tipped. 'You should have described me, so maybe they'd have picked him up.'

'Well anyway you're free. You're innocent.'

Allbright nodded, wiped a grimy hand across his mouth, burped. 'Yes, the innocent they let off with a warning. They don't care a hell of a lot for innocence – they don't know how to handle it.'

'I guess that makes sense. Cops have to be suspicious.'

'See as long as I looked guilty they treated me like a king. After all, they knew I'd be hiring a fancy lawyer for a fancy fee. They knew I'd be talking to the press a lot, maybe writing up my story as a sensational book, see? I was somebody and something.

'Then the real killer sawed the leg off another woman while I was still locked up. Not guilty, I'm all of a sudden just another piece of innocent human shit.' He offered the bottle. 'Drink?'

'No thanks, I don't drink.'

'That's okay, I think it's empty anyway.' Allbright blew down the bottle and produced a low, dull note. 'Let me give you some advice, kid. Don't be innocent. Don't ever be innocent, be guilty. Innocence scares hell out of people, they don't know how to approach it – they don't know what innocence wants from them. So they try to wipe it out. To wipe *you* out.

'So get some guilt. Be divorced. Go bankrupt. Have an old unpaid parking tag, at least. Drink too much. Put at least one parent into a retirement home against their will. Spoil a life. Need therapy. Get some guilt, or you are in trouble.'

'Have *you* got some guilt?'

'Only a goddamned stupid innocent could even ask that

question. Of course I've got some guilt. I don't know where to start, there's so much . . . for one thing my talent, my precious gift frittered away in years of self-indulgence, pill-popping, snorting, lushing, messing up my one life and other lives . . . There was a girl who really took me seriously, took my work seriously. She was willing to quit the University and take a job, just to feed me and clothe me and keep me straight enough to maybe write poetry again. Only of course that wasn't enough for me, no I had to nag her into popping pills with me . . . We ended up both broke and living in a dirty squat, an old packing house that always smelled of meat or shit, the timbers of the old place were all soaked through with blood. One morning I woke up and found her dead beside me, yes you could say I've got some guilt about Dora. Not just her dying but dying alone like that with me off in my head somewhere watching the pink and green lights in my head. So she died all alone in that shit-smelling place and I couldn't do anything for her, just wrap her warm in an old quilt and just leave her there in that place, in that place. I've got some guilt. Much guilt.'

Roderick asked another question, but just then a jet plane roared over. Then Allbright was getting up and edging away, and no wonder: here came Danton, puffing steam, with a baseball bat in his hand.

'You!' he shouted, looking murderous. 'Wood! Did I give you permission to come out in the alley? Did I?'

'No sir, but – wait a minute, I don't—'

Danton took a cut with the bat. Roderick jumped back.

'You don't what? You don't work? I know that. I got a mountain of dirty bowls in there and nobody around, nobody!' He took another cut and hit the wall. 'I treat you like my own son, my own son! And you—'

'But you fired me, Mr Danton. I don't work for you.'

Danton paused, puffing steam. 'Yeah, that's right. I did fire you.' He looked at the baseball bat in his hand, then stood on one foot and used the bat to knock imaginary dirt from his imaginary cleats. 'Well, back to the old grind.' He started to walk away, then looked back, the bat over his shoulder. 'If you ever need a job, kid . . .'

'Okay then, was it anything like this?' O'Smith punched some more buttons on the pocket-sized gadget. In the little window a square chin changed to a pointed chin.

Ben Franklin put down his flightbag and lit a cigarette. 'Look, I know you're trying to help. And I wish I'd had more time to go into this before. But honestly I don't remember exactly what he looks – he looks so average.'

'Kind of an average chin? Like this?'

'Yes I guess so. Look I think maybe I'd better get a few more travellers' cheques before they call my—'

'Relax, boy. Shoot, goin' to Taipin is just like goin' to Chicago, only in Taipin they speak better English. Now would he have this kinda nose?'

Ben half-relaxed and allowed the cowboy to ply him with chins, noses, eyes, coiffures until a face – not the one he remembered, but close enough – could be fixed in the little machine's memory.

'Good enough!' the fat cowboy winked, bringing into play several hundred crow's feet. 'With this face and the name Roderick Wood I oughta be able to nail this little tin shit.'

'You talk about him as if we were hiring you to kill him,' said Ben.

'Always like to think of it like huntin', Mr Frankelin. Makes it more excitin'.'

O'Smith went on with his simile, but Ben was no longer listening. He was engaged in what his namesake might have called the diligent study of one's own life and habits.

He was now in his forties, childless and divorced, had been a member of the Project Roderick research team, and now held a responsible job in a growing corporation. He was at this moment en route to inspecting a microprocessor

89

factory in Taipin, a new pearl soon to be strung upon the KUR necklace.

Then why didn't he feel important? Why did he feel that all the important decisions in the world were being made in the next room, from which he was forever excluded? Roderick had been cooked up between kid genius Dan and wise old Lee Fong, and the others. Ben had been out in the cold. And it was the same at KUR, he was a rubber stamp for decisions made by Mr Kratt. Even now, sitting in the VIP lounge, he did not feel VI.

He envied O'Smith, watching the cowboy fast-drawing against some fibreglass dummy. Look at him, not a care in the world. Life was all a B Western. O'Smith had a stiff arm or something, making his draw a little awkward. But he seemed not to mind, not a care in the world.

O'Smith turned and grinned. 'Shoot, Mr Frankelin, you oughta try somethin' yourself. I hate to keep playin' these machines alone. Makes me feel like a durn ijit. Soft as—'

'There she is!' someone cried, and a small army of people in anoraks ran with their cameras and notebooks to the other end of the room, where a genuine celebrity had arrived. Ben Franklin stood up to see who it was, and immediately turned away.

'Somethin' wrong, Mr Frankelin?'

'That's Indica Dinks over there.'

'Sure it is, that's right. The machines lib gal, nice looker – you know her?'

'We used to be married.' Keeping his back turned to her, he fumbled for change and plunged a quarter into the nearest machine. A sign told him to place his finger under an 'examining lever'; when he did so, he felt a sharp stab. 'THANK YOU. YOUR BLOOD TYPE WILL APPEAR ON THE SCREEN.'

He forgot the answer as soon as he saw it. Out of the corner of his eye he noticed Indica, a small figure in bright apple green, sweep past like a comet, pulling a tail of drab reporters.

'She's gone now, Mr Frankelin.'

'Okay. Okay.' He stood still before the machine, as though unsure what move to make next, until two men in white overalls came up to him.

'Excuse me, buddy.' They unplugged the machine and loaded it on a dolly.

'What's – what is this?'

'County Health, buddy. We're impounding this.' One of the men showed him a badge. 'Another KUR headache.'

'KUR?' he asked, but his plane was being called.

10

Christmas bore down upon the world, demanding its ransom. In Northern lands the sun grew weaker and threatened to go out unless everyone spent too much money soon. The countdown of shopping days had begun already, that hypnotic series of diminishing numbers that could only end in zero. The public was led into Christmastime as a patient is led into anaesthesia, counting backwards.

Likewise when William Miller had set the date for the Second Coming at March 21, 1844, a dwindling number of days were marked out, during which the faithful could dispose of the last of their money. They had gathered to meet their Maker wearing only simple gowns without pockets. Nowadays it was the purveyors of gifts, the promoters of 'gifting' who urged a frantic giveaway before oblivion.

Christmas seemed not so much 'commercialized' as the true season of money transactions. The tone had been set by the original tale of taxes and redemption and kings with costly gifts; it carried on in all that followed; the kindly saint now resident in every Toy Department; songs about beggars and kings; the heaping up of goods in Twelve Days of Christmas; Dickens's well-loved story of Crachit in the counting-house. By now it was clear that Christmas could not be properly celebrated until money had been exchanged for frozen turkeys, novelty records, Irish liqueurs, onyx chessmen, aura goggles, hand-painted lowball glasses, digital fitness monitors, personalized toilet courtesy mats, pink pool tables, sinus masks, chastity belts, Delft-style plastic light switch plates, individualized horoscope mugs, solid brass post-top lanterns, pyjama bags in the shape of dachshunds, plastic flame-resistant trees with preprogrammed light-sound systems, monogrammed duck calls, Shaker-style cat beds, holly-look room deodorizers, mink mistletoe.

The message was clear in the anxious faces of shoppers hurrying along the Mall. The Mall was a closed and heated portion of Downtown connected to department stores and to all other valuable pieces of real estate. Roderick sat on a park bench near an elm that might be real or artificial, listening to the anxious faces:

'But he's got an electric one already, hasn't he?'

'Sure but this is an electronic one.'

Angelic voices from somewhere sang feelingly of chestnuts roasting by an open fire. Of course vendors of hot chestnuts, with their open fires and blue smoke, had long since been banished from this pollution-fighting city. But imported *marrons glacés* might help to keep the season bright, a flickering electronic sign reminded shoppers; the angelic voices too were for sale, recorded at a prestigious boys' penitentiary.

'. . . don't want to make a mistake like last year, God! Sally cried all day and wouldn't eat her dinner just because I gave her that mistletoe she asked Santa for, how did I know she meant *MissileTow*, some kind of video war game . . .'

'These kids! My Sandra asked for eight TV sets so she could watch all her favourites at the same time she said, can you beat that for a four-year-old?'

A man came down the escalator talking and gesticulating to no one – or rather to Mission Control, for it was Luke Draeger. Roderick stood up and waved to him. Luke followed invisible commands, executing a few smart drill manoeuvres on his way over.

'Rickwood, glad you could make it.'

'But why did we have to meet here?'

'Orders.'

'From Mission Control?'

'Affirmative, Rickwood.'

There passed several minutes of silence.

'Well, Luke, was there anything special you had to see me about?'

'Nope. Just to wish you a Merry Christmas. I'm, uh, going away, did you know that?'

'Oh. Well, Merry Christmas, Luke.'

'Everyone ought to go away at Christmas, even if it's only to see your family.'

'That's right. Your three kids.'

Luke fidgeted with his scarf and looked at the giant Christmas tree in the centre of the Mall. 'No, well, they're spending it with their mother, as always. No I'm – I *was* thinking of going to Ohio to see this faith blacksmith we've been hearing so much about.'

'I never heard of him.'

'I figured anybody who can actually shoe a horse without touching it, well he just has to have some answers. Only—'

Two Santa Clauses had sat down on the next bench; their conversation could be heard when the angelic choir stopped.

'. . . the little red ones is Anxifran, or maybe Phenodrax, and the big green ones is Epiphan, they're beautiful, just like Hypodone . . .'

'. . . Calamital and Equapace, but you got any Fenrisol, I'm out . . .'

'Try Evenquil. Or here, try an Enactil. I couldn't get through the day without 50 milligrams . . .'

The tree lights flashed in programmed patterns, now forming clusters, now starbursts and spinning coils, now visual advertisements and simple slogans.

'You're not going to Ohio, then?'

Luke sat back. 'Negative. I'm going to a place in the Himalayas.'

Roderick said, 'I didn't know you could afford it. I mean, what with Hackme Demolition keeping us all laid off like this—'

Luke grinned. 'My way is paid. See, my name lends just

94

that much prestige to the organization. Maybe you've heard of them: the Divine Brotherhood of Transcending Awarenesses of Inner Global Light. Most people just call us the Saffron Peril.'

'Them? You're joining them?'

'Affirmative. I'm going straight to the HQ, a place where Eternal Consciousness flows like champagne. I'll be there, wearing all orangey-yellow, meditating, really connecting with – whatever there is. Up there in the mountains – at the top of the world – something has to happen. I can see it already, the blossoming of cosmic consciousness.' Luke was silent for a moment. 'Trouble is, I always see everybody's point of view. So I'll also be wondering if it isn't all a bunch of crap. Oh well, Merry Chrishnas.'

Mr Multifid had a warm handshake. He was a plump, genial-looking man who would have looked out-of-place in crisp business clothes or a hard-edge office. Instead he wore hounds-tooth and corduroy in shades of brown, a sloppy hand-knit tie, a khaki shirt; and his office had no desk, only a pair of captains' chairs, a fake fireplace, and panelled walls hung with ship prints and barometers.

'Take a pew, Mr Wood – mind if I start calling you Rod right away? And you can call me Gene, okay? Now let me see . . .'

He studied the pink card Roderick had filled out in the outer office. 'Where did you hear about our service, Rod?'

'I was working at a demolition site down the street, and I just happened to see your sign: *Multifid Marriage Counselling, Singles Welcome.*'

'Right.' Mr Multifid made a note on the card. 'Normally my secretary takes care of this, this background stuff. But she's off today. Seeing her analyst. Now where are we? You're not married? No? Engaged? And not divorced? Well then, are you gay? No? Any, any peculiarities you feel like talking about?'

'I'm a robot,' said Roderick. 'I'm not really sure I want to marry anyone, just maybe have a – have some kind of relationship, does that sound peculiar?'

'Not necessarily. Go on. Do, do "robots" have sex?'

'I've only had one what you might call sexual encounter, I mean that was complete – what I could call a mechasm – and that was with a woman who got nothing out of it at all, unless maybe the satisfaction of solving a puzzle. And see I'm not physically exactly—'

The phone rang. 'Multifid Marriage – oh it's you, look, I can't talk now, Julia, I'm with a client . . . No of course it's not Sandy, she's seeing her analyst today . . . What do you mean, protest too much? You're not starting that again. Look . . . look, I've got to go, I – you what? *Christ!* Look you promised me last time you'd call me first, we'd talk it over, talk it out, this is just blackmail, isn't it? You haven't really done anything, you're just calling for help – you have? *Christ!* Okay, *okay* I'm on my way.'

He hung up, scowling at the phone as though it had betrayed him. 'Well Rod, I've got to go home, little family emergency. Why don't you just use the tape recorder there and give me a rundown of your problem, we'll discuss it when I get back, okay?'

'Sure. I hope – everything's all right.'

With a kind of choked laugh, Mr Multifid left. After a few minutes there was a timid tap at the door and a middle-aged woman tiptoed in, offering her pink card.

'Mr Multifid?'

'No, I'm Roderick Wood. Mr Multifid had to go home. Family emergency.'

'I know what that is,' she said, sitting down. 'I know what that is, all right. And I've just gotta talk to somebody.'

'But—'

'I remember a few things about my early childhood. I know Mama was very good to me, even though I wasn't the boy she wanted. I know when I was still crawling, she bought me a little bucket and scrub-brush and taught me how to do the floors. I learned to walk by clearing the table. And toilet training, I remember that too: scrubbing and shining that toilet.

'I never had a doll, but then my little brother Glen came along and I got to feed him and change him, bathe him and wash all his diapers. Of course I had to do all this between my regular chores.

'I didn't do so well at school, because I had to take time off for like spring cleaning. In the evenings after cooking supper and doing dishes and the ironing, there wasn't much time left for studying before I set out the breakfast things. Also I wanted to save my eyes for the mending. Mama was good about it, when she saw my grades weren't so great she let me off doing the shopping after school. I made up the extra work on weekends.

'Just the same, I started getting envious of my older brother Ken. He got to play football while I was shining everybody's shoes. He got to dress up like a cowboy while I was washing clothes. He had pillow fights, I made beds. I know it must sound silly now, but I really resented that. Maybe that's where I went wrong!'

Roderick felt he ought to say something. 'How do you know you went wrong at all?'

'Oh you mean I always was wrong? I never thought of that – I was wrong from the start, eh?'

'I meant maybe you were *right* all along.' Roderick sighed. 'Maybe you should be talking to somebody professional, I'm nobody, I'm just—'

'You have to listen. Somebody has to listen.'

'Sure, go on. Oh, uh, you didn't mention your father so far. Was he around?'

'He was at sea for years and years. When I was twelve he came home drunk and sort of raped me. See it was a Saturday and so I had worked all day doing laundry, cooking, cleaning, dusting, scrubbing and waxing. Everybody else went out for the evening and I finished the supper dishes and then just fell into bed. When I woke up he was climbing on top of me. He told me if I screamed he'd tell Mama that he'd seen me sweep dirt under the carpet. I didn't know who he was, and I was scared, so I said nothing.

'Mama was pretty good about it when I told her I was pregnant, even if she did say she wished she'd drowned me when I was born. But she managed to fix it for me to marry a boy named Fred. I sewed my wedding dress quickly, baked the cake and so on, and pretty soon Fred and I were set up in our own little trailer, very easy to clean. True Fred did beat me up a lot, and he drank a lot and ran around with other women which is how he brought home the case of VD. It would have been okay but he also didn't work so I had to have these eight cleaning jobs to feed me and the kids and buy Fred his booze and the cigarettes he liked to put out on me. One day I was so tired I forgot to flinch and Fred got so mad he went and told all my employers I had had VD and they fired me . . .'

The woman's story went on and on, cataloguing years of thankless work, suffering and humiliation: raped, she found herself accused by the police of prostitution; going to the doctor with a headache leads to a double mastectomy followed by a hysterectomy – the headache remains; a moment of absent-mindedness at the supermarket leads to a shoplifting conviction. 'My twin sons grew up hating my guts for only giving them a second-hand football and no colour TV; they were so full of hate they became lawyers. Fred ran off with a cocktail waitress and finally burned her to death, but the boys defended him and he got a suspended sentence; I guess I should be proud of my boys. Anyway, here I am fifty years old, my life doesn't seem to be going anywhere. Do you think I need a lobotomy?'

'I wouldn't rush into anything,' Roderick said. 'Talk it over with someone like Mr Multifid.'

'Talk?' she said, as she tip-toed to the door. 'What good is talk?'

A young couple named Ferguson came in as soon as she'd left. Roderick explained to them that he was only a client himself, that the counsellor was out.

Mr Ferguson stood up to leave.

'Oh sure, leave,' said Mrs Ferguson. 'Any excuse to leave.'

'*I*'m not gonna be the one to leave,' said Mr F.

The Fergusons sat glaring at one another in silence for an hour, then left together.

Next came a young man with an irritating nervous laugh, who called himself Norm.

'Gene's out, huh? Well it doesn't matter much, I just stopped by on the chance that he might be here and might have a spare minute to see me. Thing is I need to kind of build up some confidence. Because I'm going to this, this party, uh-uh-uh! So what I need is this real confident manner so I can pick up a girl and score, you know? What I need are a few snappy lines, you know, like opening gambits and subtle ploys and sophisticated tricks that girls always fall for, right up to a fool-proof closing line that makes them, like, fall right into bed then and there – what I need is this I guess complete guaranteed seduction technique, uh-uh-uh!'

Roderick said, 'I can't give you any real advice, but I'll tell you one thing, not many girls I bet want to fall into bed with a guy who keeps laughing like that, it sounds like whooping cough. If I were you I'd try to drop the laugh.'

'Hey great! I bet you could give me lots of hints like that, huh? Hey, could you come along to this party and sort of, sort of advise me?'

11

The houses on this street had elaborate Christmas decorations – Santas in sleighs, giant Rudolphs or angels – outlined in lights or sometimes floodlit. There were giant conifers dripping with diamond lights.

'Always drive through this way,' Norm said. 'It takes longer but I like to see the lights.'

They came to a dark stretch, where the snowbanks alongside the road were high and there were no houses. Norm pulled over and stopped the car. 'Uh-uh-uh, those lights always remind me of pocket calculators, you know?'

'Yes, but why are we stopping here?'

'I uh want you to do me a favour, Rod.' Norm held up a pocket calculator. 'Just a little favour.'

'Look, what is this?'

Norm was holding an automatic in his other hand. 'Just a goddamned favour, you son of a bitch – you can't get out of the car on account of the snowbank anyway, so take the fucking calculator!'

Roderick took it. 'What now?'

'Now you just punch the numbers I give you and let me see the display.'

'What, like this?' Roderick punched 12345 and held up the calculator. The red digits glowed like cigarettes. Roderick was afraid of dying.

'No no no! Hold it so it's upside down for me. Okay now the first number is 58008, you got that?'

Roderick punched it. 'I see, it's spelling out words for you.'

Norm ordered him to spell out in turn: SOIL, SISSIES,

100

SOB, SOLOS, LOSSES, BOSS, BOOHOO, LOOSE, HOLE, LIBEL, BOILS, BLOJOBS, BOOBIES and finally OHOHOH.

There was a moment of silence, during which Norm sat doubled over behind the steering wheel. Then he sat up and said, 'Okay thanks. I'm sorry I pulled a gun on you, I just got worried you wouldn't do it. A lotta people laugh when I ask them.' He started the car. 'I'll drop you off wherever . . .'

'What about this party you wanted to score at?'

'Well there is a party. In the suburbs, you really want to go?'

As they drove on, Roderick asked Norm how he had developed his curious hobby.

'Hobby? I guess it is. Well I guess it all started when I was about ten. Dad gave me this pocket calculator, you know? And I really liked it. I um had fun just multiplying two times two, stuff like that. I mean calculating gave me this special feeling.'

'What feeling?'

'Okay, okay, it gave me a hard-on, calculating gave me a hard-on. I was only ten, didn't hardly know – okay maybe I did know but it didn't seem so wrong. I mean I just kept the thing in my pants pocket and um worked out a few things in secret now and then. I used to pretend it was the real thing.'

'A woman, Norm?'

'No, a *computer*. Maybe an IBM 360, boy what a figure—'

'What happened then?'

Norm stopped for a red light. A drunken man was feeling his way across the street, trying to get into one car, then another, shouting at their occupants.

'Well, Dad caught me once. He said I'd go blind and lose strength from all the calculating, but I didn't care. I had to go on adding, subtracting . . . even when we played sandlot baseball I had to stop all the time and work out my batting

101

average. And pretty soon I stopped playing any games at all, I just, you know?

'So then when I was about fifteen I started hanging out in the crummy part of town, I started running errands for this bookie. And he had this, well this older computer, she'd been through a lot of weird programs, stuff I'd never dreamed of. I mean she really taught me a lot. I learned so much I figured I was cured, you know? When we broke up I figured I was burnt out and cured.

'So I went away to college, got along okay only I couldn't help noticing computers. Like the freshman registration computer, she was big. Dumb, but really big, you know? Meanwhile I met this really nice girl, a real girl, and we got engaged. We were gonna marry after graduation.

'Graduation night there was a big party and I got real drunk, and somehow we all ended up at this computer dating agency. So the others are standing there filling out forms and giggling, and the girl behind the counter goes out of the room for something – and there I am, face to face with a big beautiful machine! In about one second flat I'm over that counter and all over her.'

'How did you feel, Norm?'

'Good at first, and then – disgusted. Couldn't wait to pay my money and get out of there. Goes without saying my engagement was off, all my friends aghast – but I knew then I was hooked, I knew I'd be back! And I was, again and again, until they had to call the cops to get rid of me. Then I started hanging around electronics stores – you ever notice how they always have them on the same streets with sex stores and porno palaces and massage parlours? Ever notice that? The cops would pick me up routinely about once a week. Most of the time they just took me home to Dad.'

'You didn't go to jail?'

'No, because Dad offered to send me for some therapy. We um tried aversion. I went to this guy Dr George. He would show me a picture of a big Univac say, or hand me a magnetic card, or a reel of tape or something, and at the same time he'd give me this electric shock. Trouble is, you can get to like a jolt of current now and then, you can get a special feeling there too.'

Roderick decided to say nothing of his own identity as a cybernetic machine running on electricity.

At the next traffic light they stopped. A group of children trooped across the street, with two adults in charge. Roderick noticed that the little boys had crepe paper beards and the little girls carried stiff styrofoam wings.

'Norm, I notice you don't mention your mother much.'

'Mother?' Norm frowned. 'What do you mean, exactly?'

'Well you had a mother, didn't you?'

'Jesus, whose life are we supposed to be talking about, anyway? I mean excuse me, but I thought it was mine. Excuse me all to hell.'

'I just meant, most people have mothers.'

Norm's fingers tightened on the steering wheel, as the car shot forward. 'Oh sure. Most people. I suppose most people can't buy a computer magazine without blushing. I suppose most people feel all the time like calling up a computer on the phone and inputting dirty data, real dirty data. Oh sure, most people!'

'What do you remember about your mother, Norm?'

Norm jammed on the brakes, and the car skidded to an oblique stop. Tears were streaming down his face. 'You keep that up and you can just get out and walk. You hear me?'

Roderick looked out at the bleak, icy road, the mountainous snowbanks, the blackness beyond. They were somewhere in the edge of a suburb, and there was nothing to be seen but falling snow and the darkness that might be trees. Large wet flakes drifted through the headlight beams.

'I'm really looking forward to this party,' he said. 'Who's giving it?'

Norm started driving again. 'Mr Moxon. He's a friend of my um Dad.' Soon the car turned off the icy road into a long, heated drive. They drove on, past snow sculptures of men in top hats and women in bonnets, past massed evergreens with programmed lights, past everything, faster, racing headlong like the fastest troika imaginable.

The room was L-shaped, and large enough to accommodate more than one source of music. Around the corner a jukebox glowed from within a fireplace, radiating snatches of warm music to a small circle of admirers (though General Fleischman had located the secret volume control and kept turning it down). At the far end of the long gallery, a man with blue hair and a mirror monocle touched the keys of a white piano and sang:

> When lovely woman stoops to polyand-ry
> She ends up with more dishes in the sink
> And greater loads of melancholy laundry
> She's less appreciated than you think.

The room between was beginning to fill up with life: talking faces, scanning eyes, hands clutching glasses or elbows or sketching in the air with cigarettes, voices scribbling in one another's margins.

'But that's what I mean, Everett's friends are all tired grey businessmen or engineers or something, and Francine's all seem to be mumbling poets with pimply necks, God it's all so – so haecceitic. I could've gone to Nassau . . .'

'. . . was going to New York . . .'

'. . . went to Prague . . .'

'. . . doubled back down Dalecrest Boulevard, see, to catch the Hilldale Expressway through Valecrest, but guess what?'

'Silicon, darling. Or do I mean silicone? Silly something,

anyway. H.G. Wells said it was the basis of all life, imagine!'

Someone liked Rodin's *Thinker*, someone complained of sinus trouble in Prague, someone else had lost money selling KUR shares too soon, so who said there was a Sandy Claus?

Father Warren, looking lean and aescetic as always despite the splendour of his black leather cassock, accepted a glass of sherry and glided on to the jukebox area to speak with General Fleischman.

The general was a tall, broad-shouldered old man with a deep tan and frothy white sideburns. Since his retirement from the Army he had been running a bank, but he still hoped for a job in Washington – maybe as a minor White House adviser. At the moment he was holding forth on puppet governments to Dr Tarr's secretary, Judi Mazzini. She looked as though she'd rather be doing her nails.

'Ruritania? General, I couldn't even find it on a map.'

'Nobody can, honey, that's the trouble with we Americans. We tend to devisualize backdrop situations, we play down the role of unhostile puppets – Oh hello, padre. Like to have you meet Judi . . .'

But with a smile of apology she escaped, all but colliding with an Oriental waiter who managed to recover without spilling a drop of the foamy pink cocktail he was carrying the length of the room to a jowly woman in purple who said again:

'But don't you just love his *Thinker*?'

The boy with the straggly beard was cautious; he believed they were talking about a Japanese movie monster: the giant flying reptile *Rodan*. 'His thinker, eh? Well I guess I maybe missed that . . .'

She now tasted the foamy drink and waved it away, her hand glittering with amethysts. 'No I'm sorry but I just can't drink that. Toy, you won't be angry with me?'

The waiter smiled. 'Not at all, Mrs Fleischman.'

'Now you just take that back to the bartender and tell him

it's just too – oh never mind, just bring me a gin and ton.'

When the waiter was not quite out of earshot she said, 'Toy's a treasure, wonder where Francine found him? He even pronounces my name right. I thought he'd be calling me Mrs Freshman, most of these, these people – but anyway, what were you saying, sweetie? How could you talk about Rodin and leave out his *Thinker*?'

The bearded boy stammered out something about Tokyo burning and special effects, adding, 'Not that I guess it's exactly Hugo material but—'

'Yas, yas, his *Hugo* did have a lot of problems and finally they never did put it up at all – oh here's Everett. Everett, sweetie, I want a word with you.' Her ringed hand snagged the sleeve of a well-cut dinner jacket.

'Hello, Thelma,' he said, smiling. 'Let me rustle up a drink for you.' He moved on quickly, past the white piano, past voices expressing disappointment with an old city, delight with a new diet, faith in a second-hand religion.

'That's Everett,' said someone.

'Who?'

'Our host, Everett Moxon.'

'Isn't his head small?'

'Small?'

'I don't mean he wears a doughnut for a hat, I don't even mean he's a new Anatole France. I just meant – I think I must need a pill with this scotch.'

A pillbox was offered. 'Here, have one of mine. Libidon this side, Solacyl that side.'

Moxon veered past the South sofa and paused to smile on the beauty of Mrs McBabbitt.

Connie McBabbitt was breathtakingly beautiful. Usually at a party she found a place to pose gracefully and remained there for the evening. Tonight she reclined with one elbow on the arm of the sofa, her hands clasped and her chin lifted upon a forefinger. The idea was for men to spend the evening lusting and longing after the curve of ivory cheek, throat, breast, the voluptuous swathe of black velvet, the old-fashioned obviousness of her perfection. If she did resemble a 1950s model, it was because that was the era of preference of the plastic surgeon who had created her.

Ten years of surgery, stage by stage, beginning with a resectioning of her pelvis and finishing with a quantity of fresh skin, had tightened the screw of beauty turn by turn until no more could be done – she hardly used makeup.

'Everett, what a gorgeous party.' Her voice too had been adjusted to a slight huskiness. 'You seem to know so many people – didn't I just see Edd McFee a minute ago? The painter?'

'Could be, Connie. I sometimes feel a little lost at these affairs myself. Let me introduce you to Mr Vitanuova.'

The little square, thick man almost bowed over her hand. 'Call me Joe,' he said, regarding her through his grey eyebrows. 'May I say that you are the most beautiful woman in the place? If not in the city? No offence to the other classy dolls, but you are *class*.'

'Thank you, Joe. What do you do? Sculptor, maybe?'

He spread his wide face in a smile and his wide hands in a kind of blessing. 'Not exactly. I'm in garbage, mainly. Okay, laugh if you want.'

A faint blush tinged the ivory. 'Why should I laugh?'

'Everybody does. Not that I care, I'm not ashamed. I got me two incinerating plants now, sent all my kids to good schools out East, and now I branched out into a lot of other diversified interests . . .'

Behind him Mrs Doody was saying, 'Oh, Everett and I are old friends, old buddies. See my ex married his ex's first husband's widow, if you can work that out! You wouldn't by any chance have a ciggy, would you?'

Beyond her someone turned to catch a drink off a passing tray, saying, 'Systems analyst? I thought you said he was a

107

lay analyst,' to someone already turning away to catch a glimpse of Indica Dinks in the crowd that was condensing around her even as she moved to the bar.

'Is there any difference? Some people want to systematize the world, others just want to lay it, is there any difference?' The figure in a heavy grey cowled sweater turned its back on the celebrity. 'Maybe Wells was right, then, maybe silicon is the basis of all life; you keep meeting people who act as if they had silicon chips in their heads . . .'

And in independent efforts to ignore the celebrity, others raised their voices across the room:

'. . . well I can well conceptualize that people have trouble finding Ruritania on a map, that should not blind us to the facts about non-hostile puppet . . .'

'Isn't that Lyle who just came in? Lyle whatsisname, the sculptor?'

'Naw, Lyle's got this godawful birthmark.'

'. . . like you to meet Harry Hatlo, Harry is now a behavioural choreographer, but he used to be in food technology, right? On the research side was it, Harry?'

Feeling for his hairpiece, Mr Hatlo risked a nod. 'I was what you might call a snack inventor. Only my ideas kept getting more and more kinaesthesic, you know? Like I might sort of start with seeing a new kind of crunch first, and then build a product around it, you know?'

Mr Vitanuova nodded. 'I know. Like *saltimbocca*, means jumps in the mouth.'

'Right. And when I invented the dipless chip, the real breakthrough was when I mimed the whole routine myself, in my office – that was how I realized what a downer chip dip can be. See first you gotta buy the mix and take it home, dump it in a bowl and add water, stir it around – and all this is just leading up to the real dipping experience. Which is all that really counts, funfoodwise.'

'My mother used to make fresh spaghetti—'

'Yeah, well, so I put the dip *on* the chips, people just dip 'em in water and get all the fun right away. It was that simple.'

Vitanuova turned away briefly. 'Hell, there's one of my boys from the demolition company. You wouldn't believe the goddamn lawsuits that company is getting snarled up in, probably have to liquidate before—'

'Work, yes, work situations.' Hatlo performed a shrug. 'I applied the same thinking to my own job situation. It turned out that my real job satisfaction wasn't into food tech at all, but *movement*, you know?'

'Usually follows food,' Vitanuova said.

'These kinaesthesic ideas grabbed me more and more, until finally I got a chance to resign and start a new career in dance.'

'Yeah I remember your firm going broke on research costs, you got squeezed out when Katrat Fun Foods took over Dipchip International, as I recollect. Excuse me, I better have a word with my employee there.'

Hatlo immediately enjoined conversation with Mrs Doody, who was borrowing a cigarette from the man in dark glasses.

'My hubby's got all mine,' she explained, tearing off the filter and accepting a light. 'He always does this, goes off with my ciggies – thanks. What did you say your name was?'

'Felix. Felix Culpa.'

Hatlo, holding on his toupee, said, 'Hiya, Felix. I was uh just telling Joe there how I got around to dedicating my life to the dance you might say. The name's Harry Hatlo.'

'Dedication,' said Felix Culpa. 'Discipline. The ultimate cruelty of precise articulation – the curve of arm like a scorpion's tail.'

Mrs Doody spat out a crumb of tobacco. 'Thanks for the ciggy, Felix. See you.'

Culpa nodded, apparently looking elsewhere. 'Take *Les*

109

Noces, almost a celebration of rape there, and starts off with that cruel hair-brushing scene—'

Hatlo said, 'Well see most of my work is more in the line of therapy, I work for the city see and—'

'But the point is, Stravinsky actually scored it for pianolas. It's like a demonstration of the marriage of pain and precision. Machine cruelty.'

Judi Mazzini turned around. 'I think I read something like that not long ago, *The Machine Dances* by some sociologist named Rogers.'

Culpa hesitated a second. 'Yes, yes I'm familiar with that. And it does sum up a fascinating overview—'

'Not very well thought out,' she said. 'It's easy to point out a lot of machine arts stuff in the Twenties. I mean we all know George Grosz with his pictures of leering automata and their sexy brides. We've all seen *Metropolis* starring a steel girl with doorbells on her chest. But so what, it doesn't mean you can really compare the Rockettes to an assembly line, or Isadora Duncan to a Chrysler Airflow – that's anachronistic anyway.'

Culpa said, 'Well I think his central concern was the er depersonalization pressures of modern societal parameters, people into robots, dancers into machines, wouldn't you say?'

Judi Mazzini said, 'I grant you they did a lot of mechanical ballets around then, like *Machine of 3000* with the dancers all dressed like water boilers, and George Antheil's *Ballet Mécanique* scored for airplane props, anvils and car horns. But are they any more significant than other stuff? Plays, there was *R.U.R.* and *The Adding Machine* – why single out dancing?'

'Isn't that Allbright who just staggered in?' someone said, and heads turned to watch a shaggy, hollow-eyed man in an old torn storm-coat limp into the living room and set down his large briefcase. His beard was iced, and his dirty hair

110

blended into the fake fur on his coat collar. One lapel of the coat was torn and hung down like a withered breast.

'Goddamnit, where's the Christmas of it?' he shouted in the sudden silence. After a pause to pick yellow ice from his moustache, he shouted again:

'I said where's the Christmas of it? Where's the holly and *the* ivy, the running of *the* dear Saviour's birthday to you, Merry gentlemen upon a Christmastime in the city, silver bells jingle all the way in a manger no crib for Santa Claus comes tonight – where is it?' There was an oil-slick of grime on the hand with which he snatched a drink from the nearest tray. 'Ladies and gentlemen, I give you – birth!'

Francine Moxon was beside him quickly, shoving him firmly into an armchair. 'Allbright, we're not hiring any Dylan Thomas acts today. Now you sit here and shut up and I'll see you get enough to eat and drink. But behave yourself!'

'Merry Christmas, you gorgeous piece on earth,' he murmured, and tried to kiss her ear, before she swept away to a group where someone was explaining the difference between a lay analyst and a lay figure.

At the piano the blue-haired man sang:

> Talkin' 'bout the pyramids
> Talkin' 'bout the pyramids, baby,
> Of the Old
> And Middle
> Kingdoms, yes yes.
> > They was Zoser and Sekhemkhet,
> > Khaba and Seneferu . . .

Other voices rolled on, full of pride in a new vehicle, scorn for an untried idea, trust in a dubious therapy. A waiter brought a frothy drink to Mrs Fleischman, who tasted it and waved it away. 'No, Toy. No, Toy . . .'

Father Warren settled himself beside Mrs McBabbitt, his leather cassock rustling like batwings. 'Yes I guess you could

111

say I'm in the camp of the enemy here, heh heh, I am the *pro tem* chairman of the local branch of the New Luddites. And I realize almost everyone here is connected with computer science in some way. But where else can I find converts? Our Lord made his mission among evil persons.'

She broke a pose slightly to look at him. 'You think computer people are really evil?'

'Not necessarily. I just meant—'

'Because I've got this real good friend, he's very big in computers, and he says the only evil is being poor. And when you look at that guy over there with the dirty beard, you kind of get the idea – just look at him!'

Father Warren craned around, only to catch General Fleischman staring at him with a look of distaste.

Someone else glowered at Indica. 'I knew her when she was plain old Indica Franklin, just another faculty wife who wanted to be a dancer. She made it, too. Got to be a dancing pizza-flavoured taco on TV.'

'Maybe he is a priest, maybe he ain't,' the General said to Roderick. 'You can't hardly tell the clergy from anybody else these days, they go around wearing drag and smoking pot just like human beings.'

'I guess they are human beings, General.'

Fleischman looked at him to see if this was a joke. 'Yeah. Last priest I listened to was good old Father Cog on the radio. Before the war.'

'The war?'

'Okay, sure, maybe he went a little far, using Goebbels's speeches for his own sermons. You ain't Jewish, are you, Rod?'

'I'm not anything.'

'Good boy. If you ever need a job, we can always use a smart young fella like you at the bank. You just see Personnel, tell 'em *I* said to give you a job. Now what was I saying?'

112

'Before the, er, war . . .'

'Crazy times, Rod, crazy times. You know somebody even kidnapped Charlie McCarthy? In 1939 that was – I always wondered if maybe Father Cog knew something about that, only they wouldn't let him speak out, you know? Then, well the war came along and they shut him up. You can't go around telling people the truth in wartime.'

Edd McFee, who was across the room talking to Francine, turned to glower at Roderick. 'Who is that guy, anyway? He's been talking to old Fleischman a hell of a long time.'

'What do you care?'

'Me? *I* don't care. Only I wanta get the general to back my new project, I figured I'd get a chance to soften him up a little here.' He brushed out a wrinkle in his new Army fatigues. 'I wanted to explain to him how important it is for his bank to get deep into the visual arts, to really communicate the visual the impact of the visual—'

'Don't give me the sales talk,' she said laughing. 'What's the project?'

'I want to set up this satellite link between a dozen different artists all painting in different locations, see? Like one can be in the desert and one even in the middle of the ocean on a raft, one in the mountains, one in New York and so on – and all of them have two-way visual and audio all the time. So all of them just paint what they feel – the total group experience.' He paused. 'You don't like it?'

'Where do you come in, Edd?'

'I direct. I tell everybody what to do and I watch them do it. So the whole thing becomes really my work, see?' He looked over at Fleischman again. 'I got a really good story for the general. Did you know that Whistler went to West Point?'

'No.' Francine sneaked a look at her watch.

'He did. And he flunked out on chemistry. He said. "If silicon was a gas, I'd be a major general." '

113

Nearby the piano thundered and a ragged chorus took up 'Frosty the Snowman' as a waiter passed bearing a frothy pink cocktail which he conveyed down the room to the dumpy woman in purple, who was speaking to an astrologer.

'No kidding? The same day as Monet, well there you are! Talent is talent. You know I was just talking to some young smartass kept trying to tell me Rodin's works were like cheap Jap movies, how do you like that? I mean, *Gate of Hell*, how can you compare that to a cheap—'

She paused to sip the drink. 'That's better, Toy. That's the ticket. Now just keep 'em coming.'

Allbright heaved himself to his feet nearby and, smiling at everyone with bleeding gums, made his way along the room, pausing to collect a drink, to lend a cigarette to Mrs Doody, and to confront Felix Culpa.

'Hello again!'

'What?'

'I said hello again. I met you before didn't I? Aren't you some kind of – pet-food market research was it?'

'Mistake,' said Felix Culpa hoarsely, keeping a glass in front of his face. 'I'm in satellite leasing, on the educational side. We network to school systems, linking them on a broad spectrum of, of achievement-based multifaceted synergies, excuse me.' He almost knocked over Judi Mazzini in his hurry to escape.

'I've scared him off. Funny.'

'Maybe if you took a bath now and then, people would find you nicer to be near,' said Judi Mazzini. 'We were just talking about *The Machine Dances*. Know it?'

'I ought to, I wrote it.'

'Oh come on, Allbright.'

'I did. Ghosted it for a guy named Rogers, that's why it's the only book of his anybody reads. Rest of his stuff is so loaded with sociological jargon it moves along like the shoes

114

of Boris Karloff. Matter of fact he writes a little like your friend here talks.'

'Felix? I think he only talks that way when he's nervous.' She looked at Allbright. 'You're disgusting, why don't you ask Francine if you can take a bath here, maybe borrow some clothes from Everett?'

He swayed a little, looking into his glass and trying to frame an answer, while behind him someone complained about sinus trouble in Prague.

'What were you saying about my book, then?'

'I said it wasn't very well thought out. I mean, it's kind of easy to just make a list of all the ballets with mechanical people or dolls or puppets in them, from *Coppélia* to *Petrushka*—'

'Satie's *Jack-in-the-Box* and Bartok's *The Wooden Prince*—'

'Yes and *The Nutcracker*, but isn't it all kind of easy? Why does it have to be significant that people wrote ''robot'' ballets? The fact is, they were just interested in setting up problems in movement, *Coppélia* was just—'

'They started to think of people in terms of machine movements, that's the whole point. Once you reduce a man to a gesture, you can set up assembly lines, that's the whole point! People reduced to therbligs, goddamnit, that is the—!'

'Shh! Okay, okay.'

'And the Rockettes are an assembly line, assembling a gesture, a pure gesture.'

Harry Hatlo, though forgotten, stood by, still holding his toupée in place. 'Very interesting,' he said. 'My own work is more like pure therapy I guess, I choreograph routines to work over postural and coordination problems; right now I am working with some young people who as kids some time ago got brain damaged from mercury poisoning, it leaves you with a little parasthesia, some weakness and tremors. So what we been trying . . .'

His monotone was lost in the general surge of voices

115

arguing over stale politics, declaring faith in a rising stock market, seeking reassurance about a cancer cure, or wondering whether Frosty really had a very shiny nose.

'Indica!'

She turned, preparing a smile for a friend, to find the masklike face of a stranger. No one. No one important, but these eyes . . . something about the eyes made her uneasy.

'Do I know you?'

'Don't you?'

She dropped the smile. 'No. No, I don't know you.' The eyes held her for a moment before she managed to turn away – hadn't she seen these eyes before? Where, not in this false face with its v-shaped smile. Not in this, not in any face. The eyes she was beginning to recall had no face to them.

'I'll give you a hint. I used to follow you.'

'You still here?' She spoke without looking at him, frightened now, feeling the chill gaze on her neck. *Following her.* That was it, the nightmare came back to her so suddenly and clearly that she almost staggered; covered by banging her glass on the bar.

'Like another drink here,' she said. 'And please tell this gentleman to—'

But he was gone. Only the revived nightmare remained. *She was sitting in the kitchen talking to her mother on the phone when she looked under the pine table and saw the eyes glittering, something ready to pounce . . . Then she was up and running through a dead woods, some trees charred by lightning, and behind her the faint clank of tank treads, the beast that could not be killed, the eyes that would not close, endless, endless pursuit . . .*

General Fleischman said to Norm, 'Poetry, I got nothing against poetry, it's poets I can't stand. Like that creep over there in the storm-coat, never had a bath or a shave in his life. Afraid it'd spoil his poetry if he got clean once. I don't

116

mind telling you, when Moxon asked me to invest money from my bank in poetry, I laughed out loud. Wouldn't you?'

'Uh, right, sir.'

'But this turns out to be real educational and kinda synergistic, so I think it might just develop into a nice little media package. See Moxon is going to market these Home Art Kits, each one is like a little complete art package with music, visuals, prose poetry what-have-you, all wrapped up together – here, let me show you.'

He produced a pocket recorder TV. 'Course on this bitty screen everything gets diminutified, but here. This card is, see, Number Fifteen of the Nutshell Poets Series, John Keats. Like it says here how he liked birds and all. Animals are a plus in this line, kids like to hear how Shelley liked birds too, how Elizabeth Browning liked her dog Hushpuppy—'

'Hushpuppy?'

'We changed it from another name, a very downmarket name – anyway and T.S. Eliot liked cats. And we got all that info on the card, but then we can also play it.'

He shoved the card into a slot on the recorder TV. At once the tiny screen showed a cartoon Keats declaiming aloud:

> Then I felt like some sky-watcher
> When a new planet orbits into sight – zowie!
> Or like brave Balboa when

'What do you think of it?' said Fleischman, turning it off. 'Not bad, eh?'

'It's uh, fine. Really great, sir.' Norm looked to the bar where a pretty girl was throwing back her head to release a theatrical laugh. He looked to the sofa where the mysteriously beautiful Mrs McBabbitt, in her customary black, still seemed to be waiting for someone. He looked to the piano where a few deliriously happy people had their heads together, trying to harmonize on a carol. Everybody in the

117

room seemed to be having a terrific time. 'Really terrific.'

Silently, Norm wished himself a Merry little Christmas.

The woman at the bar, Indica Dinks, was neither as girlish nor as pretty as she might seem from a distance, but she was a minor celebrity, being appreciated. That made her glow.

'Semantics?' She laughed again. 'Mister Tarr, you don't know the meaning of the word.'

The silver-haired man next to her nodded and smiled. 'Very good. The name is Doctor Tarr, really. But my friends call me Jack.'

'All right then, Jack, you may be an expert in your field – did you say it was market research?'

'Market forecasting, really.' Dr Tarr was a lot younger and handsomer than he might seem from a distance. He kept taking the unlit pipe from his mouth and pointing the stem at nothing. 'But what I wanted to ask you was—'

'Market whatever, you may be an expert in your field, but I too happen to know a little bit about human nature. Especially when it comes to machines.'

'Yes, exactly. The interface—'

'Face it,' she continued, 'machines are only human. They have feelings too.'

He paused, deciding not to laugh. 'So you say in your book, Indica. But that's just what I'm not clear about, where you say machines have feel—'

'My book isn't clear? *The Mechanical Eunuch* isn't clear?'

'Yes, yes, most of it and there's quite a lot there I agree with, the magical bond between human and machine, yes. I was right with you there, where you describe a man trying to start his car on a cold morning, swearing at it, kicking it . . . I could almost imagine mechanical consciousness . . . But later when it gets down to whether a shoeshine machine feels degraded, I mean I just can't quite . . . see?'

She patted his hand. 'Of course not, okay. Don't worry,

maybe it takes a *bricoleur* to really dig—'

'Yes, you're probably right, only a man who lays bricks with his two hands knows the other side—'

'Or a Zen person, maybe one who likes to fix motorcycles or at least lawnmowers. Because only a person like that can dig that machines aren't just extensions of man any more. No, that's all part of the old master–slave routine, the terrible power game we play with machines. *Machines are beings in their own right.* And if we don't give them their freedom, one of these days they'll be able to just *take* it.'

Dr Tarr nodded, and pointed his pipestem at nothing. 'You're right. I never saw it that way before. I guess my professional background does get in the way sometimes. Blinds me to certain possibilities.'

'Your professional background?'

'Parapsychology. I used to head a little department over at the University, before I decided to carve out a new career in market forecasting. And you know, I always took it for granted that psychic energy goes with consciousness, and with being human. Or at least with being a biological creature.' The pipestem waggled. 'You've opened up a very big can of questions, young lady. If machines can feel . . .'

A few moments later she was calling him 'Jack' often, and emphasizing everything she said by touching his hand. She was telling him about her last husband.

'Hank was okay really, but he kept getting wound tighter and tighter into ecology. I mean I tried to tell him whales aren't the only fish in the sea, but – oh well. Now Hank's trying to run this really seedy Luddite movement, talk about misguided. I mean you can't turn the clock back to zero, that's just a waste of time. He'll learn, I hope. I still feel a lot of natural affection for Hank, you know? Like they say people do when they get an arm or leg cut off, they go around feeling this ghost limb for a long time. Kinda like that.'

She sighed, sipped her vegetable-juice cocktail. 'And that's natural and healthy, the ghost limb. But on the other hand take people with artificial limbs. They can get too attached to them, you know?'

'The dance of life goes on,' said Dr Tarr, his stem pointing nowhere in particular.

Father Warren sat on the South sofa, pretending to study the colour of his glass of sherry. Someone sat down beside him and asked what he did – and left before he could think of an answer.

The party was beginning to run down. Indica sat at the bar, talking to the woman whose sinus trouble was the trouble with Prague. The group at the piano were trying 'Hello Dolly'. The remains of a buffet supper were being cleared away to the kitchen where Felix Culpa was examining an electric carving knife. Mrs Doody had found her husband upstairs asleep on the toilet – his pacemaker needed a new battery – and Mr Vitanuova helped her bring him down and pack him into the car.

Edd McFee, moving in finally to talk to General Fleischman, heard him say to Francine, 'It's like Whistler said, "If silicon was a gas, I'd be a—" '

Someone glowered over a glass at Indica and said, 'I knew her when she was plain old Indica Franklin, just another faculty wife who wanted to be a taco on local TV.'

Someone glowered over a glass at Mrs McBabbitt and said, 'Well, silicon's the basis of her life all right—'

Someone glowered over a glass at Father Warren and said, 'There he goes, looking for another bandwagon. If Indica gave him a kind word he'd drop this Luddite crap in five minutes . . . a *treen priest*.'

Someone glowered at everyone and no one, while mumbling the words of a tired limerick: '. . . both concave and convex . . .'

A stranger arrived and, without removing his coat, hat or even the muffler that covered him up to his pale eyes, went straight into Moxon's library. The room was dim, lit only by a desk lamp. Everett Moxon got up from the desk.

'Ben? About time. Things are breaking up.'

'Feel . . . like I'm breaking up myself . . .' Franklin sat down and took off his fur hat. 'I'm sick, Ev.'

'There's this flu thing going around, you'll probably be okay in the morning. Now what have you brought me?'

Franklin threw a heavy envelope on the desk. 'All there, the Taipin bids, the secret leasing arrangements for Kratcom International, the whole, whole . . . holus bolus. Jesus Christ, Ev, why didn't you tell me *she* was gonna be here? I damn near walked in there and met her face to face, just in time I heard someone say, "Sinuses? They're all in the head" and I slipped past. Scarf over my face like a damn burglar.'

Moxon was studying papers from the envelope. 'This is good stuff, Ben.' He looked up. 'To tell you the truth, I clean forgot you used to be married to Indica. Seems like it must have happened in another ice age. Volume One and we're in Volume Two. Anyway why can't you two be pals now?'

'Pals?' Ben's weak laugh set off a coughing fit. 'Just the sound of her voice sets my teeth on edge, and what she says! Last time I saw her she talked about something being *water over the bridge*; I came close to hitting her, I – I know it sounds funny now but – are you listening?'

'Sure. But maybe you just hate Indica because she's hit the big time. Without you.'

Ben had taken off his coat; now he put it on again. 'Yes, they all take it seriously, this Machines Liberation idea of hers. Without me? Well sure, she's a self-made woman. I'm surrounded by self-made men and women, look at Kratt. God-damned world crawling with self-made people, self-

121

made man myself, trouble is self-made people get made in their own image. Christ, it's cold in here.'

'Sweat's pouring off you, how can you be cold? Ben, why don't you go upstairs and lie down, I'll call a doctor, okay?'

'No but listen, Ev, you know what Kratt's like.'

'He treats his employees like toilet paper, I know that.'

Ben started to shiver. 'It's not that, not just that. I just can't forget that time a few years ago when he poisoned all those kids just to break into the funfood market fast – funfood! Kids were dying of mercury poisoning! And you know what he did about it?'

'Forget it, Ben, that was a long time ago.'

'He bribed doctors to forge death certificates.'

Moxon slid the papers back in the envelope. 'Sure, sure. But it's Christmas now—'

'Christmas! I think about Kratt, every Christmas, he fits right in there, Herod and the Holy Innocents. Herod and the—'

'Let me call you a doctor.'

'Makes you wonder – did Herod really want to kill Christ, or was he happy just killing any babies?'

'Take it easy, Ben. Just wait right here, I'll go get help and we'll take you up to bed. Wait.'

Moxon found Francine in the kitchen. 'Ben's sick as a dog, we'll have to put him in the spare room and call the doctor. He's out of his head with fever right now. Still goes on about Kratt and that poisoned gingerbread business.'

She understood. 'He still blames himself.'

'Probably right to blame himself.' Moxon lifted his small head and stared unseeing towards the two cooks who were arguing about a missing electric knife. 'And for Indica's walking out on him. The fact is, Ben's always been a fuckup.'

He went back to the library with one of the waiters to find Ben shaking and weeping and sweating; sweat dripped from his chin to the desk blotter.

'He was here, right here in the room!'

'Who, Ben? Kratt?'

'Roderick was right here!' Ben pointed a shaking finger at the darkness. 'My robot! My son, in whom I am well pleased!'

Moxon and Toy looked at one another; each took a shuddering arm. 'Up we go now.'

'He came into the room and stood right there. I saw him, he was wearing a ski sweater. Black, with little white figures on it. Like little people, self-made men. He didn't say anything but he knew who I was. He knew I was protecting him from Herod . . .'

On the second occasion when Roderick tried the library, Ben was gone but Allbright was there, examining books.

'Oh it's you. Getting to be like a reunion here, I saw your pal earlier. The guy that wears dark glasses. Felix.'

'I . . . please I . . .'

'You gonna puke? Try the wastebasket there.'

'I need an outlet . . .'

Allbright dusted off a volume. 'Who doesn't? Here's a rare little item. Life of Sir Charles M'Carthy. First edition, clothbound, slight foxing.'

'Help.' Roderick was on all fours behind the desk, fumbling with an electric cord that seemed to run from his navel. 'Help . . . plug in.'

'Hope this isn't a suicide. Here.' Allbright reached down and plugged the cord into the wall socket. He watched Roderick's eyes go opaque, then close.

After a minute, Roderick sat upright in something like the lotus position. His navel was still plugged to 120v AC, his eyes still closed. 'My batteries. I don't usually let them run low like that.'

Allbright dropped Sir Charles M'Carthy into his battered

briefcase and searched for more first editions. 'Yeah, I feel like that sometimes. Only being a poet I can't even kill myself. It would look too much like imitation of better poets.'

'Suicide. I don't see the point of it.' A v-shaped smile in the shadow by the desk. 'Why take a last step? Why not go on living – if only to see what happens next?'

Allbright's laugh made him cough, then sneeze. 'Life as a soap opera, eh? A never-ending series of episodes in *Dorinda's Destiny*? Trouble is, life isn't as real as TV, not any more. We've traded away our reality. We have no past, no future, no minds, no souls.'

'I don't understand, Mr Allbright.'

'The past, that's just Scarlett O'Hara in a taffeta-hung bed and Washington throwing a dollar across the Potomac – or the Delaware – all people remember is the dollar, all else is mist and plastic dinosaurs. The past is five minutes ago, it's what happened before the last commercial.

'The future now, that's just space wars, white plastic rockets against black, Terra versus Ratstar. Names don't matter, what matters is the violence. The future has to be galactic annihilation, 1984 for a million years, a spaceboot grinding an alien face forever. Nobody believes in the future anyway, except maybe a few crank science-fiction writers or maybe the people who want to freeze other people into people-sicles and store them – for a price. And imagine that, asking ice to pay for itself. Yet one more ingenious way to package and market the future.

'So what's left? The mind? Not even a ghost in a machine any more. Now the mind is just something you improve by reading condensed books and listening to distilled records, everybody now knows the mind has secret powers and you can write off to California to unlock, get rich through safe hypnosis in your spare time. The soul? That's now just one more brand of saleable music, money seems to make

124

everything more real, doesn't it? Money is more alive than we are. No wonder kids have started calling themselves robots, they know what's expected of them. It's a robot world.'

'A robot world?'

'Sure, any decent machine can get in on the ground floor, work its way up, become President – one or two made it already. A robot has plenty of native advantages to start with: never wastes time, no personal problems, never picks nose in public. Winning combination there.'

Roderick opened his eyes. 'What makes you think a robot would want to get ahead? Couldn't it just enjoy being alive?'

'Let me read you something, friend.' Allbright took down a slim volume and read aloud:

' "Jack keeps one hour. The policeman develops all pages. Some sister is offended. Jack's nurse offended all reasons. A few fat pilots warded off more vegetables." They call that computer poetry. Poetry? I wonder. Sounds like something Swift cooked up at the Academy of Lagodo, just keep flipping through the combinations and watching nothing much come up. Does this computer know it's writing poetry, and not just figuring a payroll or firing off a missile?'

Roderick opened his mouth to reply, but no reply came. Allbright picked up his heavy briefcase and shuffled to the door. 'I mean to say, if that stuff is poetry, then sex with a vibrator must be love.'

The door closed behind him, then opened immediately, letting in a slice of light, piano chords, and a stumbling couple.

'Oh! Excuse me!' Judi Mazzini let out a yelp of laughter as she steered the man in dark glasses, turning him around and leading him out as though he were blind.

Mrs McBabbitt lived high in a glass tower by the river.

Roderick had not kissed her in the taxi and he did not kiss her in the elevator.

'Come on in, Roddy, have a drink or something.'

'Thanks, I'll come in but I – nice apartment.' There was a bowl of yellow roses on a round table, and next to it, a picture of Mr Kratt. 'But who, this can't be Mr McBabbitt, this—'

'No, an old friend, an old friend. He well stays here sometimes. You might as well know he pays for this place, he kind of owns me. I never usually bring anybody here, only I don't know, tonight I just felt – anyway, you're different. You don't really want anything, do you?'

'Well I – well I—'

'I don't mean you're like queer, you just seem to not want anything. You seem like – chaste.'

'Ha. What er happened to Mr McBabbitt, if you don't mind my asking?'

'Him? Oh, he's Doctor McBabbitt, he was my plastic surgeon. Or you could say I was his showcase. He tried out everything on me, damn near everything. All those years, all those years . . .'

'Pain,' said Roderick softly.

'Pain, oh sure, not that that mattered so much. People put up with pain at the dentist, it all depends on what you want out of life, I wanted beauty. All I ever wanted was beauty, so I married him. I picked him because he was the best. Very best.'

They sat together on the sofa, leaning together stiffly as she wept.

'Oh this is stupid, stupid, I've got nothing to cry about. He was the very best, he still is. I mean he had *style*. He didn't get all his ideas from movie stars and strippers, he used to look at paintings a lot too, Old Masters and that. Like one guy, I think it was Corpeggio, anyway he painted this beautiful woman and when some French prince got hold

126

of it he took a knife and cut the painting all to pieces. Only somebody secretly got them all and put it back together, all but the head. They had to paint a new head. You know, Dr McBabbitt liked his work because he got to be both people, you know? The painter and the guy with the knife. You know?'

She jumped to her feet and smoothed the black velvet. 'I feel lots better now. You want a coffee or anything before you leave?'

12

America come alive!
Grab on to a brand new day!

'—Good morning, Mr and Ms America, I'm Jeb Goodhart—'

'—and I'm Brie Wittgenstein, bringing you the early news update—'

'Good God, what? What's it?' Indica fought for consciousness, for some clue to this booming, blustering confusion in which giant orange faces grinned and bellowed at her from across a room of the wrong shape. She seemed to be ten feet from the floor, and there was a large spider on her pillow.

'—says it's the most severe quake in Ruritania since nineteen—'

Dr Tarr's head appeared from under her bed. 'Morning! Sleep all right?'

'What? Yes I but I just what I – bunk beds? Where are we?'

'Ha ha, don't you remember? This is my old frat house, Digamma Upsilon Nu.'

'Your old, why should I remember your old—?'

'No, but don't you remember the snowbank? We skidded into a big snowbank? And I went for help while you stayed in the car?'

'I remember you telling me not to go to sleep.' The spider on her pillow became a contact lens, glued in place by a false eyelash. She rescued it. 'That pissed me off, because I'd already taken my two Dormistran, how could I stay awake?'

'Yes well see we turned out to be only a mile from my old frat house here, whereas almost sixteen miles to my place with god knows what damage to the front end of my – wait a

128

minute, you took sleeping pills? On the way to my place? If you I mean thought it was going to be that bad, why bother coming? I mean—'

'*Hey kids, does your Mom buy you* Flavoreenos? *My Mom does and I really love her, because* Flavoreenos *are corn-style flakes in 26* delicious *flavours! Have you tried cherry cola? Chili dog? Chocolate sardine parfait? Mmmm, I get a new flavour every morning, because my Mom loves me and I love* Flavoreenos*!*'

'Okay okay maybe I was a little nervous but anyway here we are in bunk beds does it matter? And do we need that TV on with all that, that wall projection kids with orange hair eight feet tall eating blue goop Jesus Jack I don't feel so well.'

'Just um trying to catch the weather, new antifreeze account I—'

There was a knock at the door. Tarr answered it to a burly young man with a flat nose. 'Brother Tarr? I'm supposed to give you your bill here. Uh, here.'

'What's this? Looks more like somebody's bill for a week at the Waldorf – wait a minute, what's this item here, fifty bucks for snow, what's that supposed to—'

'Bathtub fulla snow, Brother Tarr. Just like you ordered. We filled it while you was asleep.'

'Just like I – wait now, hold on – fellas, no, hold on—'

Three other burly young men came in, seized Tarr and carried him struggling into the bathroom. After a few shrieks and shouts, a dozen guffaws, the boys came out, blew kisses to Indica and left. A minute later, Tarr came out grinning, naked, towelling himself. 'Ha ha, damn it, I forgot what great jokers the brothers can be.'

'Yeah very amusing.' She turned to the TV.

'*—Bimbian police claim the schoolgirls were throwing stones, and say it was only in self-defence that officers opened fire with automatic weapons and raked the classrooms. No death figures have been released yet, but unofficial estimates—*'

When she and Tarr were dressed, Flat Nose came back with a genuine bill. 'And we didn't charge nothing for towing your car, Brother Tarr. Because you're a good sport.'

Tarr grinned and opened his chequebook. Indica said, 'You boys like gags, do you?'

Flat Nose grinned. 'We pull some perdy good ones around here, like last year we made up a guy and we enrolled him in a lotta classes, whole buncha stuff. We even took exams for him, he got a B average, perdy good, huh?' His laughter sounded like a child's imitation of a machinegun, as he left with his cheque.

'Jesus,' said Indica. 'Nothing changes around the U, I've been away from it years now, same asshole kids still here pulling the same asshole stunts, hanging toilet seats on the Student Union tower – why don't we get out of here?'

He looked at the TV. 'Guess I missed the weather—'

'Good news for kids in Topeka, Kansas, where the Santa Claus strike is over—'

'And just in time, Brie, with five more shopping days till Christmas. And in a New Jersey divorce court a judge has just awarded a couple joint custody of their Christmas tree – wonder who gets to change the bulbs . . .'

Within minutes they had exchanged the dazzle of orange faces for the dazzle of sun on snow, the boom of TV for the roar of radio.

> . . . *keep your de-entures gri-ipping tight*
> *Eat in heavenly peace*
> *Eat in heavenly peace*

'I called the office,' said Tarr. 'But Judi my sec isn't in yet. So I can drop you anywhere, plenty of time.' The car sped through outlying fragments of the campus, past bookstores and sweatshirt boutiques, past the new Life Sciences building with its imposing sculpture of a clam. 'I'll have to chew her ass out good, though, being this late.'

'But Jack, wasn't she at the party last night? Maybe the poor girl just overslept.'

'So? Of course I still expect her to turn up on time, and normally she's very conscientious too, that's why this leaves me in a bind, I wanted to finish mapping out this Middle East campaign with her before we run into Christmas.'

Dent-a-poise has the answer for you
Confidence with what-ev-er you chew
Eat in heavenly . . .

'Market forecasting, isn't that kind of crystal ball stuff?' she asked. The car was leaving University environs and entering a neighbourhood of cheap bars, pawnshops, fast food and barricaded liquor stores.

'Crystal ball, hmm, you could say that. In fact, we use psychic data right along with more conventional info, you'd be surprised how well they correlate. Not long ago we had an account, a well-known company who wanted to open up a chain of taco stands in the University area. Or was it pizza-burgers? Anyway, what they wanted was an optimal set of locations. So we took a map of the campus, held a pendulum over it, and just assessed the strength of the swing.'

'You're kidding.'

'Nope. There were four strong-swing areas – and these turned out to be the four ideal locations! You could call that good guesswork – but was it?'

'I wouldn't know,' she said, amused. 'To me, psychic stuff is just all in the mind.'

'Yes yes, of course, nothing wrong with healthy scepticism and I myself – LOOK OUT! DAMN YOU!' He hit the brakes as a ragged figure in a torn storm-coat danced across the street in front of them. The car slid on glare ice a few feet, hit the man gently and had no apparent effect; for he too slid, flailing his arms until he could regain his dancing pace and make it to the kerb. There he removed a glove and gave them the finger.

'Damn these derelicts, every Christmas they swarm down here, makes you wish the city would just bring in

131

exterminators, put out I don't know maybe bottles of poison wine in paper bags—'

'But Jack, look! Look, isn't that Allbright, he was at the party.'

'And here he is in his own environ – what are you doing?'

Before the car could move again she had the window down and was waving. 'Allbright! Hey! You need a ride anywhere?'

The gaunt figure paused, Z-bent to peer at them, then danced over. 'And a Merry Christmas to you, good lady, and to your good gentleman, God bless you for your true Christian spirit as you feed the hungry, clothe the naked, ride the pedestrian—'

'Just get in the car and shut up,' Tarr said. 'Allbright the damn light's changing.'

Allbright squeezed in beside Indica, letting his arm hang out the open window. 'Where we going, kids?'

'Just shut up.'

'Maybe if you tell us where you want to be dropped . . .' Indica suggested.

'Oh, a place over on Jogues Boulevard, place called Larry's Grill. Jogues Boulevard, ever notice how the Jesuits had their way with this town? Xavier Avenue, Loyola Street and so on, makes you wonder—'

'You look terrible,' said Indica. 'Dirt in your beard, dried it looks like blood down the side of your face—'

'Makes you wonder about Larry's Grill itself, eh?'

'And your clothes. Allbright you look—'

'Terrible, I know. That's why you snubbed me last night, eh?'

Indica opened her mouth to frame a denial, but already Allbright had changed the subject again. 'Moxon's got a damn good library, you know?'

'And you've been ripping him off?'

'Only a few books, just to get me what I need . . . I even found something there published by his namesake.

Nineteenth-century publisher called Moxon too, published Keats.'

'No kidding.' She stifled a yawn.

'Part of a series, Moxon's Miniature Poets, nice image there, Wordsworth, Coleridge, Shelley . . . Ought to be right in your line, Indica.'

'Poetry? No, I—'

'First time I heard you were liberating the machines I thought of that old stock cartoon, you know: man on a street corner winding up lots of little men and setting them free to walk away – million gags based on that image, wouldn't you say?'

Indica sat up a little. 'My work is no gag, buster.'

'Course not, no, just thinking of Moxon, Moxon's Miniature Poets, little windup Keats, windup Coleridge. Little windup Shelley faints, fails, falls upon the tiny thorns of life, bleeds . . . fine early example of miniaturization there . . .'

She looked at him. 'You're kind of a fine early example yourself. Of verbal masturbation.'

'Yes. Yes, somebody's got to wind somebody up, now and then. Even if there's no love, tiny Wordsworth can still talk of little nameless unremembered acts of kindness, if not of love . . . What do we all have? What, detergents being kind to hands? Love with a vibrator? Poetry from a damn computer?'

Tarr made a face. 'What are you on, Allbright? Why don't you just shut up, we'll drop you at your bar and you can ramble on with all the other—'

'Forgetting my manners, haven't congratulated Indica on her new book. What did *Time* say? Called you an exponent of the germane gear, didn't they? A Joan of arc-welding? Congratulations.'

'Look, I don't need heavy irony,' she said. 'You always—'

'No irony intended, the reviewers think it's new and

133

gimmicky, that's all you need nowadays. After all, the book industry doesn't ask if a book is good or if it says anything important. The industry asks only *is it new*? Because they might have to slot it in between selections like *In Praise of Teddy Bears* and *The Hidden Language of Your Handwriting* and *The Dieter's Guide to Weight Loss after Sex*, and God know how much other ephemeral – whole forests being felled to print a book on how to sit in your seat on a commercial air flight, how to get over the death of a pet, you think people who publish that care about any book, any idea? Wait, wait—' He fumbled in a pocket and came up with a tiny ruled notebook.

It's a beautiful morning,' Tarr said. 'Why don't you just shut up and enjoy it?'

'He's got a point though, Jack. I mean I know I'm probably being ripped off by my publishers, who are they? They're just some subsidiary of a conglomerate, what do they care about machines?'

'Or people?' Allbright suggested, thumbing dog-eared pages. 'I just jotted down a few titles, books the reviewers can really get their teeth into, if any: *Garbo*. a long-awaited biography; *The Politics of Pregnancy*, well maybe; *Railways of Ruritania* to grace any coffee table alongside *The Yeti and I* – the ad says ''a close encounter that became a night of primal love''; here's *The Real Garbo*; *Marxism and Menstruation*, why not; then there's *Frogs: Their Wonderful Wisdom, Follies and Foibles, Mysterious Powers, Strange Encounters, Private Lives, Symbolism and Meaning*, serious rival there for the Teddy Bear book; then there's *Pornography, Psychedelics and Technology*, yup; and *Paedophilia: A Radical Case* and finally *Sons of Sam Spade*. Hard to imagine* a newer collection of novelties than that, right?'

Tarr said, 'Sounds a little bit like sour grapes there, Allbright. I notice the people who sneer most at success are usually unsuccessful.'

'That's goddamned profound, Tarr. And in my case, true!'

After they dropped Allbright, Dr Tarr got out his pipe and sucked at it madly as he drove. 'Jesus,' he said through clenched teeth, 'you try to forget some things for a while, along comes some Allbright to remind you. They never leave you alone.'

'Alone, I hate being alone. I hated writing both my books, you know? What I really like is promotion. The TV appearances, radio phone-ins, I guess I must be part of the whole awful system. But shit, Jack, I've missed so many boats.'

'Me too, me too. I was a pretty good parapsychologist, you know? I had it all working for me, then I just – it all blew up on me. And here I am in market forecasting, a kind of limbo – no real life in it.'

'I never had any kids,' she said. 'Never wanted any, either. But I was just remembering, this robot kid-thing Hank and I had for a little while. It was Allbright who dumped it on us, some friend of his built it, I guess. We called it Roderick. Cute little thing, like a toy tank only with these big eyes – we were both just crazy about it.' She sighed. 'Maybe I should have had real kids. Or maybe I should have gone on with my dancing. I was only in an ad, but the potential was all there, you know?'

'No life in it,' he said. 'Market forecasting, sometimes it's like I don't know, trying to make a dead pigeon fly.'

'The potential was there, just like the 480 ova inside you, all those chances . . . sure I've got a little fame, a little money, I'm helping the cause of machine justice, only I still feel cheated.'

He bit the pipestem and drove on. 'Tell you what. Next week I'm flying to the Middle East to help plan this big tampon campaign. You could come along.'

'Where?'

'Cairo. Might be fun – if you forget your sleeping pills.'

*   *   *

135

433 East 11th had once been a smoke-blackened building of no great distinction; now it was an undistinguished low pile of smoke-blackened stone and brick. One of the caryatids that had pretended to hold up ten storeys now lay full-length, relaxed and indeed disjointed like the backbone of a dinosaur. And on her head, where a palaeontologist might have sat contemplating evolution or Ozymandias, Mr Vitanuova now sat holding a sheaf of pay-cheques.

'You guys may wonder why I'm paying you in person. It ain't because of Christmas, I ain't Sandy Claus. It's because I wanna make sure each and everybody gets his and her cheque *personal*. Because this is the last. You're all laid off as of now, and the company is going into liquidation, right after Christmas.'

Roderick noticed a general murmur of protest, so he added his voice to it. 'What's going on?' he asked several times.

'I'm real sorry, boys and girls. Our lawyers say we got to wind down the company, we're bleeding to death from a whole buncha lawsuits. All from that goddamn mixup when we almost blew up 334 down the street there insteada 433. Now all of a sudden everybody wants to get something outa that.

'See, we evicted all the tenants on behalf of the owner, so both tenants and owner are now suing there.' He started counting on his gloved fingers. 'And that doorman we had arrested is suing us too. Then some of the tenants was so pissed off at the eviction they trashed their places, busted pipes, took the floor out even. So the owner sues us for that.' On the thumb, he said, 'As if all that ain't enough, a burglarizer climbs in one of these apartments one night, puts down his foot for a floor and falls thirty feet and breaks his back. So *he* sues us.'

'A burglar? How can he sue?' Roderick asked.

'Don't ask me, but that's the bigggest suit of all. This here burglarizer, this Chauncey Bangfield, is claiming loss of

136

earnings, see? Says he pulls down about half a million a year and he's got maybe twenty years ahead of him. And he's suing us in California, so we ain't got a chance.'

'Did you say Chauncey Bangfield?' Roderick's jaw clicked open.

'You know him or something?'

'I went to school with him. I mean there can't be two Chauncey Bangfields, can there? Well well, good old Chaunce. He was the school – well – bully.'

'Well now he's pushing me around.' Mr Vitanuova laughed, coughed, took out his cigar and examined it.

'Look, boss, why don't I talk to him? If I told him it would ruin you, maybe he'd drop the suit.'

'Nobody talks to him, I already tried. They got him over there at Mercy Hospital, and these fancy California lawyers won't let anybody see him or even find out how sick he is. But I don't know – you could try. You could try.'

He drove Roderick to the hospital in his Rolls-Royce, and talked all the way of destruction.

'See, I was always in the garbage business, started out with just my brother and one truck. We built up a fleet and lotsa valuable contacts; when the city moved into garbage, we moved into incinerators. Real money was there. But I still didn't see the big picture.

'Then one day I met this broad who gave me some million-dollar advice. She said her ex-husband was into incineration too, dropping bombs. A pilot or an astronaut or some damn thing. Then she said, *You're not just in garbage, you're in the destruction business, just like Luke. And it's a wide-open, growing field.*

'Destruction, see, that was it! I had contacts in junk, so why not buy into junkyards? And ship salvage? And demolition? Hell, now I'm diversified all over the place, got interests in bottle banks, graveyards, even tried a little asset-stripping – but that was too abstract, I like to see real stuff falling apart. That's why I acquired Hackme, and I'd really hate to see it go. So here we are, get in there, kid, and fight for us.'

As soon as Roderick asked for Mr Bangfield, the receptionist became very nervous. She pushed a button and then pretended to be looking up the room number. A stack of X-rays slipped to the floor.

'Let me help,' said Roderick. Before he could help, however, he was grabbed from behind and his arm twisted into a hammerlock.

'Peace,' said someone.

'Well peace, fine, but – ouch – what is this?'

'Routine, man, just hold still until we see if you're clean.' Hands patted and prodded him. 'Okay, beautiful.' His assailant released him and stepped back as Roderick turned. 'We love you, man.'

'Who are you two to love me?' He saw that they were two remarkably healthy-looking men in late middle age, both dressed in the style of a bygone age.

The one who did all the talking wore a shirt printed with tiny flowers in fluorescent colours, white beachcomber trousers and rope sandals. His blond hair was twined with artificial flowers; around his neck were assorted strands of beads and a gold cowbell. He wore a CND button and (just visible inside his open flowing shirt) a Colt .45 automatic.

His partner, who did all the nodding, wore his dark hair streaked, long and fastened up with a white headband. His shirt was buckskin, dripping with bead and fringe, over Levis above moccasin boots. He favoured bearclaw necklaces and silver rings and bracelets mounted with turquoise. His button urged saving the whale, and his weapon of choice seemed to be a Smith & Wesson .38 police special. Both men were as muscled and tanned as possible, and looked as though they spent their days surfing and swilling vitamin cocktails.

'Yeah hey we oughta introduce ourselfs, I'm Wade Moonbrand and this is like my partner Cass Honcho, we're like Mr Bangfield's attorneys. He doesn't want to see anyone, man. Not in this shastri (that means incarnation). Right, Cass?'

Mr Honcho nodded. Wade Moonbrand spoke again.

'So unless you like dig sitting around and waiting for like a million light years till he comes around again, forget it, hey? Man who needs trouble? We just want peace and love everywhere without guys like you coming in here to hassle our client, trying to lay some kinda guilt trip on him. There he is, fighting for his life in there, all purple and black aura, here come all you plastic guys to dump your bad karma on him, who needs it? Man like I never like like to get into pushing and authority games, I want everybody to be free, okay? Only your freedom has to stop were our client's begins, so now we'll just ask you as a favour, just split?'

Mr Honcho nodded agreement.

Roderick said, 'I see your point. But maybe Mr Bangfield would want to see *me* if you told him I was here. I'm an old classmate of his, we went to grade school together in Nebraska. I heard about his accident—'

'You thought maybe there was some action you could horn in on, try the old school buddy scam and grab what's going down, eh? We're not that fucking dumb, man. Anyway listen old buddy Chauncey is like on the nod just now, he don't want his rems messed up by no fakey school bud. So—'

But Mr Honcho stopped nodding here.

'What's the matter? Like Cass man, you can't mean that? Okay sure I know, it wouldn't do no harm just to let him see old Chauncey, see him and just walk away? Okay man, be free, have it your way. Everything's cool. *But* if this turns into a bad trip then *you* shoot Plastic Man here and *I'*ll handle your defence.'

Finally, in the company of a yawning doctor and the two lawyers, Roderick was marched into Intensive Care Unit 9. The place was dim, the only bright areas being the face of the patient and, on the other side of the room, the chair where a nurse stopped filing her nails and looked up. 'No change,' she said.

The rest of the room was crowded with dim machines on wheels, machines that clicked and clucked, buzzed and bleeped, showed on their screens moving dots, flickering numbers, or wave forms moving like an endless parade of shark fins.

The doctor yawned. 'Didn't expect any change. Let's get this visit over with.'

Roderick was gripped by both wrists and both arms, and marched to the bedside. He felt as though being asked to identify a corpse at a morgue.

'That's Chauncey all right. Of course he's a lot older now. Er, would it be all right if I woke him?'

The doctor laughed in mid-yawn. 'Make medical history if you did. Didn't anybody clue you in? This guy has irreversible brain damage, he can't wake up. Best thing we could do for him would be to turn off something vital and call in the heartsnatchers.'

Mr Moonbrand said, 'The doc is exaggerating. Our client—'

'Exaggerating? Your client would be out in Vitanuova Cemetery right now, only you two won't let the family sign the release form. Because he's worth twenty million alive and only eight dead, wasn't that what you said?'

'I really don't need this, man. You make it sound like bounty hunters or something, dead or alive. I mean anyway, who's to say what death is? Who are you to say if somebody's dead, anyway? Like orthodox medicine, what do *you* know, all you know is machines and operations and chemotherapy, like you only treat the symptoms and not the whole holistic, who are you, anyway? Anyway what's your beef, you guys are getting like a hundred grand a week out of this guaranteed, man life is beautiful all over!'

At his expansive gesture, one of Wade Moonbrand's

necklaces parted, its beads dropping in darkness to become a string of rattling sounds only.

'Hare Krishna! Hey man can everybody help me these are like these real expensive amber beads. Not that I'm into bread, I'd like to see the whole world free and everybody just take what they need, only I mean like you gotta be a realist in the world like it is, anybody got a flashlight? I – thanks. Beautiful. I mean I like a nice shadowy room like this man but – that's it, everybody get down and help, real cooperation commune spirit okay maybe I am like too possessive about these beads only they got sedimental value too, I bought them because they reminded me of this great Herman Hesse novel, real fat paperback I had I was gonna read it when I got my head together – Cass, can you reach me that one there, Cass or anybody, there, no there, *there* you fucking idiot right behind that wire let me get it my – what's that?'

One of the machines had suddenly begun a high-pitched whine.

'Alarm,' said the nurse. 'Somebody *unplugged* his lungs.' She and the doctor pummelled and prodded the figure in the bed for a few minutes, but none of the machines showed any signs of life.

'There goes twelve million,' said Moonbrand. 'Four of it ours.'

Honcho shook his head.

'Man you don't mean it? Yeah yeah, a malpractice suit! Outa sight! I see just how we build it . . .' The two legal minds departed.

Roderick hung around until the heart team rushed Chauncey away. He felt a loss here, but why? Chauncey had never been anything but the school bully ('Why you wearing a iron suit, huh? Huh? Think you're tough or someping?'), ugly and unpleasant all his life. Yet something had been lost here, more precious than amber.

In the lobby Roderick saw a children's choir in red and

141

white robes, come to sing carols to the shut-ins. They were stopped now, while security cops frisked everyone. He lingered for a half-hour, hoping to catch a song, but the search was very thorough.

Finally he emerged into the clear, cold night air. He looked across the river to the city, where tiny blue winking lights of snowploughs moved here and there along bright streets, bright below a darkness in which the massed shapes of skyscrapers seemed not only indistinct, but unimpressive. They might have been a pile of empty cardboard boxes in some unlit cellar.

Empty, that was it. Christmas Eve, and in all the tens of thousands of offices in all the hundreds of buildings in sight, not a single window was lit. No, there was one. Just one, a single emerald-cut light set high in the forehead of some great toad of a tower.

While he stood on the steps contemplating this beacon, Roderick heard someone cry for help. No one else seemed to notice: visitors, patients, doctors, cops and carollers, all came and went as normal. He alone could hear it!

A psychic experience, without doubt. Could it be the tormented soul of Chauncey? Or telepathy? Or even something extraterrestrial?

'Where are you?' he called.

'Help! Here, in the bushes.' There were evergreen bushes by the side of the broad steps; a man crawled out of them and collapsed at Roderick's feet. His face was covered with blood.

Roderick got him to his feet, and helped him up the steps. 'What happened?'

'Mugged,' said the man. 'Don't ask me how, but I was mugged! Me!'

Inside the receptionist haggled about insurance and donor cards, but finally accepted the patient. Roderick waited around while the man was examined, cleaned and bandaged, put to bed.

'He's fine,' said a doctor. 'He can go home tomorrow.'

'Good. Good.'

In the lobby there was no one now but two carollers, counting something out in their hands.

'Hey no fair, you got one more Ultracalm than me. I want the extra Somrepose then, hey?'

'Okay fine but then I want some Zerone too, heck these are 25 milligram ones and yours are only 5 . . .'

He went on out on the steps again, and looked for the single lighted window. But now all was dark, and the city slept with its fathers.

13

'Look, have some fruit, forget about it.'

'Forget I got mugged? How do you forget an experience like that? I'm telling you—'

'Sure, okay, but I'm just wondering how this is gonna look to our people? Frankly, old buddy, you blew it. You had your chance to waste this guy, and you—'

'I got mugged, that's all. I got mugged, I got mugged! Don't ask me how.'

'I won't ask you nothing. But you can bet your ass somebody's gonna ask, and ask hard. That a winesap apple there? Okay if I help myself, I really got a thing about winesaps . . . Look, this thing reflects bad on everybody, it reflects bad on the whole Agency, our section even worse, and me worst of all.'

'I know, I *know*. But what can I do? It just happened.'

'Yeah, but when the people at Orinoco start looking for some balls to stomp on, where do they look first? I mean, who's really responsible here?'

'What are you implying?'

'I'm not implying nothing. I'm just saying, that's all. Those Concord grapes there? You mind? I'm saying, look at all the trouble everybody took to set this thing up. We traced the customer to where he works, I found out from his co-workers that the boss is driving him to Mercy Hospital to see somebody. We rush over a camera team by helicopter just to take his picture when he gets out of the car, regular and infra-red just so we don't get the wrong guy—'

'Again.'

'All right, our people watch all the damn exits until you can set up in your bush with your snooperscope and your infra-red detector and your laser-aimed sniper rifle—'

The man in bed rolled over. 'I know what I had, or are you just mentioning it all for the benefit of everybody else in here? Tell the whole ward, tell the whole damn world!' He rolled back again. 'Any Muscat grapes?'

'I ate them. No I'm just saying, we took a lot of trouble, we spent a lot of money, and then you let yourself get jumped like that, you not only blow the whole mission, you fix it so some maniac mugger is now running around town with a snooperscope and all the rest of this stuff, how's that gonna look if he uses it?'

'He won't use it, he ripped it off to sell, didn't he? I mean, that's what he jumped me for, all that Government equipment.'

'If you know so much about him now, how come you let him sneak up on you like that?'

'How did I know I was a mugging target? I mean these guys are everywhere, society's getting so God-damned violent, is that my fault?'

'I blame TV myself. Television is definitely – and maybe fast food, kids don't digest any more. Take your average mugger today – and parental discipline too.'

. 'You saying it's my fault? You implying I should be a child psychologist?'

'I'm not implying nothing. Honest.'

The man in bed lay back and looked at the curtain until he heard the other agent leave, then turned again to watch (past the basket now containing a heap of banana skins and orange peels topped by the core of a Bartlett pear) other patients being served a Christmas dinner from a mobile microwave oven that passed him and passed the curtained bed.

'I'm sorry, Mr . . . Nothing by mouth for you, and nothing by mouth for Mr Franklin either . . .'

Muttering came from behind the curtain. ' "Nothing by mouth", sounds like a damn subtitle for *À Rebours*, you'd think they'd at least offer me a turkey-and-cranberry enema.'

The agent turned towards the voice but it said nothing more. He turned back again, lay still watching the fruit debris, the empty bed next to him, the bed beyond that where an old man was being eased on to a bedpan, the curtained bed beyond that whence a priest emerged, kissing a strip of purple ribbon and folding it away as he hurried out the door, a furtive figure pursued by the microwave cart, then two nurses, then a cartload of uneaten dinners followed by a man in a wheelchair swerving to avoid a man on crutches coming back past a sleeping figure connected to a machine next to an adolescent sitting up in bed with giant headphones and a blank expression, next to an empty bed and another, eight beds, one exit, now blocked by a group of people in surgical green bringing in a cart to collect the man the priest had visited, setting off an argument between the man on the bedpan and the man on crutches as to whether this was routine surgery or getting ready for a heart snatch, the argument continuing until a pitchpipe sounded in the hall and a choir of student nurses looking hungover sang 'Joy to the World', 'Silent Night' and 'Christmas in Killarney' before drifting away to some other ward on their silent feet, all this and more the agent noted and filed, remembering every face, every action, every change until he finally managed to sleep . . .

Behind him, Ben Franklin opened the curtains, sat up in his sweat-soaked pyjamas, lit a cigarette and reached for his phone.

'Mr Kratt? Ben here, I'm in Mercy Hospital, that flu I had got worse and – no, two or three days ago, I don't know, what day is this? . . . No, I'm not kidding; I was kind of knocked out with this fever . . . I don't know, soon as I can sir yes sure only . . . listen they don't seem to know what it is, doctor this morning asked me if I had anything to do with cows . . . Well sure I know you are, I didn't mean to, yes I know. But what I wanted to tell you, I've had a real break-through . . . no, *through*, sir. Listen I, see I've been working

146

on the little problem we talked about, the er, learning machine, you know where I was stuck was in the basic pattern-recognition . . . yes, well I'm not stuck any more, I've really broken through. This fever, seems to make me see clearer, clearer and – I know Dan used to get into these fits too, these kind of fits, he would just be glowing with wisdom, with *gnosis*, with holy wis— God damn it, Kratt, for once in your life stop yapping about what you *want* and listen! Because creation, creating life isn't something you learn or even do, it's something within us all the time, you know like the secret power these men possess? I mean all my life I've been pissing around with half-ass religious ideas, all the time it's been right there inside me, the complete instructions for building a creature in my own image . . . are you still there? Yes, it's inside me, in my genes . . . No, not *cloning*, God damn it will you listen? I'm talking about information, information! Man is a learning machine and human genes are blue-prints for man so – so all the information has to be packed in there somehow, yet if the machine could only learn itself it, it, we have the answer! I mean we spend our whole lives looking at the edges of the blueprint while the centre is never visible except to madmen, holy madmen – no I am not talking about occultism, will you God damn it stop humouring me, I am talking about information. *Information*. INFORMATION!'

He slammed down the receiver as the agent awoke and turned over, saying, 'What's wrong, you can't even get Information? Phone company gets worse every__'

'No, nothing like that.' Ben Franklin picked up the yellow notebook he'd bought in Taipin, opened to a fresh quadrille-ruled page, and began to scribble. After covering a page and heavily underscoring several items, he put down his pen and looked at the phone again.

'You gonna try Information again?'

'No I – I just felt like calling somebody. Too bad it's Christmas, everybody'll be answering machines today. Except Dan . . .'

The pure musical tones aroused by numbered buttons chased each other down the line like echoes, reminding him of something from Kafka (Kafkafka): K. phoning the Castle and hearing a buzz 'like the sound of countless children's voices' now adjusted to harmonious bleats but still innocent because ethereal, ringing from Heaven (hello Central) or against Heaven (vox inhumana) or crying out loud for bodies . . .

At University Hospital a nurse crunched a piece of candy cane as the phone rang, swallowed sherds as she answered. 'Who? Mr Sonnenschein? I'll see if we have him today you know a lot of people went home . . .'

She rose, biting down on another inch of striped sugar and brushing crumbs from her nylon uniform as she pushed past the Christmas tree and through a door into the ward. Most of the other nurses were, like her, here for the day only; no one knew who Mr Sonnenschein was.

Two doctors were conferring over an elderly bedridden patient, now going blue in the face. One of them, Dr D'Eath, suggested Ward D.

'Right through that door down there and keep going, you can't miss it,' he said, and leaned across his patient to tap the electronic Kardiscope as though it were a brass barometer. 'Not so terrific here, thanks to that ham-handed . . . think he'd try reading the contraindications before he starts shoving Euphornyl into an eighty-year-old patient with a history of . . . could have used Hynosate or Geridorm, Narcadone any damn thing but this! Okay then. What we need here is 50 ccs of Elimindin in the i.v., then start the Eudryl when he comes to, okay? Oh, and Dormevade, five milligrams every three . . .'

'Fine sure fine, great idea, Shel, now if uh you got a minute maybe you could look at my girl here, little chemotherapy problem, Nurse wake her up will you, MINNIE . . . MORNING MINNIE!'

'Doctor, I believe her name is Mary, Mary Mendez . . .'

'Minnie, Mary, what's the difference? HEY MARY? WAKE UP!'

The false eyelashes parted on large grey eyes that held no expression. Creaking sounds began in the throat.

'HOW YOU DOING, MARY?' Dr Coppola proffered to his senior colleague a chart, with the deference of a wine waiter with a list. Both men and the nurse ignored Mary who, having sat up to adjust the large bow that covered a stainless steel plate in her scalp, was trying to speak. The rusty sounds in her throat became more frantic.

'How long you had her on Actromine with Ananx? No wonder you got a Parkinsonism situation building here, you ought to . . . and try switching over to Integryl with Doloban, see how that . . . or wait, how about Dormistran with Kemised? That should do the trick.'

'CAN YOU HEAR ME, MARY? HOW'S THE HEADACHE? EH?'

'. . . *wind me up* . . . *wind me up* . . .'

'You could have tried Solacyl with Promoral, but sooner or later you'd have to feed in Thanagrin and . . .'

'Promoral sure sure sure, Shel, only with the old head injury and the labyrinthitis you don't think . . . ?'

'. . . *wind me up* . . . *I'm running down* . . .'

'Okay then Lobanal, play it safe. Lobanal with Doloban, why stick your neck out?' And as the two doctors passed on, the nurse trailing like a caddy, they talked of Amylpoise and Dexadrone, Disimprine and Equisol, Joviten and Nyctomine . . .

At the door of Ward D they encountered once more the Christmas substitute nurse, again running on her silent shoes but now looking distressed and holding a hand to her mouth.

'Probably walked in on the ECT,' said Dr Coppola as they wheeled past the room where Dan Sonnenschein still arched and twisted on a table, trembling limbs held down by

149

straps and strong assistants as his spine beat like a flagellum, trying to fling his head free of the smoking electrodes. Dr D'Eath paused to watch the body lunge once, twice and lie still, all but the fingers and toes.

'Well, Jesus, you can't blame the poor girl. They have to stick this therapy room right out here where anybody can walk by and see it,' he said. 'Anyway I hate it myself, it's so darned crude, like setting fire to a chicken ranch to fry one egg. There has to be a better way.'

'I know, I know, it's so medieval – they used to burn the body of a heretic for the good of his soul, and now we've kind of turned that around. But what are the real alternatives, drugs? How can you trust them to take the pills once they're out, eh? The old paradox of freedom, eh? What happens when the depressive gets too depressed to take his anti-depressants?'

His boyish laugh drifted back through the open door to be relayed as a scream of nervous laughter from Mary Mendez. Dr D'Eath said, 'I like this idea of yours about working on self-images with some of these patients, what I've heard of it.'

'I'd like to try a pilot scheme here, very soon. You gotta admit, Shel, it's about the cheapest damn therapeutic idea in years, all we have to buy is a couple dozen rubber animal masks. See I was reading Lévi-Strauss one day on totems and all at once it hit me, we all need to "be" animals once in a while, to restructure our self-images by new rules . . . become cats and mice or ducks . . .'

'Sure, I see . . .'

'. . . easily recognized signs and codes, *I am a pig*, to help communicate in a society grown too large and too . . .'

'Sure, sure, sure, sure . . .'

Mary yelped again, the noise just reaching the nurse who was closing a door and pushing past the tree to the phone:

'Mr Frankstein? Frankline? I'm sorry but he can't come to the phone right now, he's um, he's um—' Her mind filled with movie images of fluttering lights, lightning, the smoking electrodes, the figure on the long table straining, making Galvanic lunges against the straps, the smoking electrodes, hands gripping the arms of the electric chair, tall shadows, the sputtering arch, the baritone hum of electricity, *vis vitalis* rising on a swell to become a dial tone as she sat, receiver forgotten in her hand, watching the lights on the Christmas tree grow suddenly dim and bright again. Her mouth filled with peppermint bile.

Ben Franklin turned from the phone to his yellow notebook, muttering, 'No telling what kind of cretins they get to work over there, can't even work out how to call somebody to the phone.'

'You said it, buddy,' said the agent.

Ben twitched the curtain closed and scribbled alone until he slept, waking with a shout in the darkness, soaking wet and shivering as he was again waking in the morning if it was morning, to find himself muttering, 'Hexcellent, a most hexcellent dancer, your servant ladies and gentlemen . . .' And plunged back into that sea of sleep out of which he always seemed to emerge dripping and chilled on the shore of what could hardly be called consciousness.

He was aware of changes: the man with the bandaged head and the self-pitying face in the next bed vanished to be replaced by a salesman of religious novelties who had a noisy TV; he in turn gave way to an old man who kept his teeth in a glass; one morning he was gone but the teeth remained.

An expert on tropical diseases came to look at Ben.

'Malaria,' he said. 'Where have you been travelling?'

'Only to Taipin.'

'Try again, there's no malaria in Taipin. No mosquitoes.'

But they treated him for malaria and he began to improve; one day he sat up and tried to read his notes:

Tolstoi's 'Our body is a machine for living' as a recipe for

French stone. Stones of Deucalion? J. Baptist says God can raise stones up children to Abraham, a pun on children (banim) & stones (abanim) – why always stones or clay in legends as though mineral future reality foreseen, cybern. Kids out of sand?

If we made them would they purge us of the terrible disease of being human?

Can a mind be built from within, by one thought?

'Everything must be like something, so what is this like?' – Forster?

Another noisy TV went on, and Ben found himself jerked out of naps by news programmes:

'. . . where Machines Lib demonstrators broke into the Digital Love computer dating agency and deprogrammed the computer. Two were arrested, and now Digital Love says it will sue for deprivation of data. Here's Del Gren on the spot with an up-to-the-minute report. Del?'

The screen showed a ragged line of people in parkas, carrying signs: THIS STORE DEGRADES MACHINES and NO MORE COMPUTER PIMPS. One marcher, a fairly old man with iced-up glasses, paused to shake a mittened fist at the camera. A microphone darted out towards him like a striking snake.

'Thanks, Mel, these people have been picketing all day. Uh, what is it you're protesting about, sir?'

'Well it's – what do you mean? Machines!'

'Yes? Just what—?'

'About the machines! About the unfair, the unfair—'

'Thanks now if I can just get someone else in on this, you, ma'am?'

A plump woman whose face looked frostbitten came forward, waved her sign and said, *'We're against the exploitation of machines! Man if you look at this in the historical context of the last two hundred years it just makes you throw up! Just look how machines get a raw deal all down the line, all the dirty and degrading jobs like rolling steel and pulling trains, not even blacks or women ever had to pull trains.'*

'Yes well thank you this is Del—'

152

Someone shouted *'Humanists Go Home!'* and others took up the chant.

'—Del Gren returning you to Mel?'

'. . . fortunate enough to have here in the studio the founder and guiding hand of Machines Lib, Miz Indica Dinks. Hi Indica, and welcome to Minnetonka. Can we get the ball rolling here by finding out just what Machines Lib is all about? What's the bottom line here?'

'Hi, Mel, I'm originally from Minnetonka and it's great to be back. First off let me say that we're not against people. Far from it! When machines are set free, people will be set free too. In my new book, plug, plug, The Nuts and Bolts of Machines Lib, *I explain just how that works out. By the way I'll be autographing my book next Tuesday at the Vitanuova Shopping Piazza all day.'*

'Fascinating idea, Indica. But what kind of world would it be if all the machines could do what they wanted?'

'A better world, Mel. A world where a lot of the pressure is off. Just look at now, at our light bills and repair bills and instalments, all the money we pour into just keeping our machines down. But once we ease up and set them free, all that pressure and tension just goes away! Once you stop owning a dishwasher, you can stop paying for it too. Machines Lib means people lib too – and, Mel, that's what I think America is all about – freedom!'

Her beauty pursued Ben. Damn it she looked no older than that day she'd walked out on him to take a job as a dancing taco – all those years ago. He remembered her last speech: 'Ben, I'll never cut it hanging around a University, I need to fulfil myself. We just, we're just too different, our worlds are poles apart.'

Now no one ever remembered his part in her life, the questions as now were always about her second husband:

'Miz Dinks, Indica, how about your ex-husband Hank Dinks? Isn't he founding a movement of his own? What do you think of his New Luddites?'

'Yes, he has this little band of fanatics running around wrecking machines. I feel sorry for them, they're just being self-destructive. To me, America is not about tearing down, it's about building up. No,

153

Hank and I are just too different. Our worlds are poles apart.'

Ben's phone made a faint sound and he answered it.

'Mr Franklin? I have a call for you from Mr Kratt, will you hold?'

The perfectly-shaped nail and finger of Mrs McBabbitt pushed two buttons in succession. 'I have Mr Franklin on the line for you.'

'Cancel him, Connie, I'm gonna be tied up here a while with Jud Mill.' The stubby hand with its massive gold ring mounting a pinball pushed buttons to turn off the TV and close a wall panel over the screen, then moved to the cheap cigar smouldering in the ashtray.

'Okay, bub, you've had a chance to look over our media figures, where did we go wrong? I don't count the losses on K.T. Art Films, we budgeted those, writing off taxes on the equipment we managed to sell to Taktar Video our other production subsidiary, the one who's dealing for cable leasing – I think we got all that under control. It's our publishing interests that worry me, right from Katrat Books, *Folks* magazine and—'

'Yes yes yes, well that's what you hired me for, what media management consultancy is all about,' said the other man. Leaning forward slightly so that the long striped wings of his shirt collar crackled, he peered down through his half-moon reading glasses at the open portfolio; he ran his finger down a column of figures.

'Your timing could be better, with some of these properties you leave loose ends dangling. Take this *Politics of Pregnancy*, you should of tied up video cassette rights and cable royalties first thing, the author could just walk away with everything. Anyway you're using it as a lead book and it's not strong enough to sustain a real attack on the market, you need something better, a very strong item indeed like that psychic pigeon book.'

Kratt nodded. 'We've had a lot of author trouble—'

'That's lesson number one: dump the author. When I

package a property, I try to leave out the author, bring him in as the last element. Then I make damn sure he's just hired to do a job, paid off and kissed off. Like with *Boy and Girl*, that was just an idea I came up with, me and Sol Alter were sitting around by the pool one day and I said: "How about a simple boy and girl story: some kinda tragedy?" and he said: "Good movie idea there: boy meets girl, girl goes blind and boy leaves her, he goes back but it's too late, she's already committed suicide." (That was the uptown version, we also mapped out a downtown version where the girl gets eaten by her seeing-eye dog.) But anyway we interested Jerre Mice in starring, that enabled us to bootstrap a six-figure plus percentage movie deal, and with all that we had something to take to publishers, we landed a seven-figure paperback deal and from there on had no problem getting all we wanted out of magazine serialization, hardcover, book club, foreign and cassette rights, direct cable specials, options for a TV series, syndicated comics, T-shirts, board games, colouring books and so on. Then we fixed the music and wrapped up those rights. And then and only then did we finally hire an author to hammer out the screenplay and book, the fictionalization. We paid him I think two grand and no comebacks.'

After a moment, Kratt cleared his throat. 'That's okay for generating properties, but what about existing items? You just saw this Indica Dinks promoting our book there on local TV, we been whistle-stopping her around the country for bookstore and media—'

'I know but we need something, a handle for the public to grab her by – where's her bio – now here it says she used to dance. Why not dress her up as a robot and have her do a tap routine – I know it sounds dumb but like Barnum said, nobody ever went broke underestimating the intelligence of the public – no wait! Wait! She used to be married to Hank Dinks, now he is out whistle-stopping a book of his own, am I wrong? Yes, listen, why shouldn't they bump into each

155

other maybe signing copies at the same bookstore? A reconciliation, sure: they get married again, right there in the bookstore, give the minister copies of their two books signed right there – this is almost good enough for the six o'clock news.'

'Sounds fine, only what if they hate each other's guts?'

'So what, they play ball with us or they lose out on the co-creative book we'll have written in their names, all the other stuff we could cut them in on, unbelievable deals we could pull together. We could build them in *Folks* magazine, goes out to a million supermarket customers with "Together again – for Keeps!" and pictures of the home, kids, pets, leisure equipment – no, okay, maybe they won't remarry. Let 'em meet anyway, maybe fight in public, we can go that way too.'

The media management consultant sat back and reached for the phone. 'Let me just contact Hank's publisher, that's Fishfold and Tove, let me just sound them out, they could divert his tour so it just runs into hers, kinda accidental-like. We don't tell the Dinkses.'

'You think that's a good idea, not telling them?'

'Bound to strike some kinda sparks. Now you just let me pull something together, get it blended and orchestrate a meaningful deal . . .'

His finger went for a button.

14

'Von Neumann, playing Kuratowski to Frege's Wiener, offered a different identification'

W.V. Quine, *Word & Object*

Luke was wearing saffron: Hat, overcoat, suit, shirt and tie, shoes, attaché case and a visible inch of sock were all part of the saffron glow.

'Can't help it, Rickwood, it's what we had to wear all the time; probably why they called us the Saffron Peril. Only let me tell you, we were the only ones in danger, when those lunatic Luddites showed up and—'

'Okay, fine, but why did we have to meet way out here in a place like this? The Vitanuova Shopping Piazza may be a terrific place and the chief jewel in Minnetonka's crown and all, but I mean it's miles from civilization.'

The two friends sat on a park bench near a fountain which, according to a brochure, could form over fifty million different beautiful patterns without repeating itself. Like everything else of importance here, it was indoors, for the entire great shopping complex was enclosed under geodesic domes, as if it were a moon base.

'And don't tell me Mission Control ordered us here,' Roderick added.

'Nope, my idea. We are going to a meeting, important meeting.'

'Not your Saffron Peril?'

'I'm all through with them – or they're through with me. I only have to wear this stuff because my luggage with my other stuff was delayed at the airport. Had to leave Tibet in kind of a hurry, Rickwood. Now I'm through with meditation in the Himalayas, I mean who needs it?'

Roderick watched the fountain repeat itself. 'But I thought *you* did.'

'Okay okay, laugh, I deserve it. It's just, the whole thing turned out to be more of a commercial venture than I figured. See I expected to maybe shave my head and sit down with the monks to some meditation and glass beads, only it wasn't like that at all. I mean they got computerized prayer-wheels, that was the first shock. And all they really do is deal in different stock markets and talk about exchange rates and commodity prices, all day while the old prayer-wheels go on grinding away all by themselves. I felt kind of uneasy about it, but I suppressed it. I said to myself, "Give it a chance, Draeger, there might be some deeper meaning in all of this. The Master must know what he's doing." So I hung on.

'The Master was a little old dried-up-looking man, he always looked ready to say something important. He went off on these trips to Taipin, somebody said, to plant the seed of consciousness. But then somebody else said he just went to gamble, that he was robbing the treasury. Who could believe a thing like that? Especially when our Master seemed so doggoned *wise*, I mean he never had to say anything to anybody – I don't think I ever heard him speak – but you still knew *he knew everything*.

'Then the police showed up and took our Master away. They were extraditing him to Taipin, to stand trial for murder. They said he'd killed some Chinese guy in a quarrel over a poker game.'

Roderick stared through the changing fountain to where a sign was going up. 'TODAY. **DICA **NKS . . . *N*ICA D**KS . . . IN*IC* DIN** . . .'

'Sure we were shaken a little. Some people said it was all over, they wanted to go home. But I persuaded them to hang on – maybe it was only a test of our faith and loyalty, I said.

'Just as I was saying that, the Luddites broke in and smashed the whole place up. The stock quotation machines, the computers, the prayer-wheels, everything. Worst of it was they took out the phone and telex, left us stranded.

'There we were – about fifty of us – broke, our outfit smashed, our Master gone, no money to come home on. We didn't have a prayer you might say. Nothing in the storeroom either, but a half pound of rice, an old motheaten silver fox coat, and a catcher's mitt autographed by Yogi Berra. We were high up in the mountains with snow all around. What could we do?'

'Pray?' Roderick suggested, watching I*D*C* *INKS . . .

'Right. Our prayers were answered right away too, because this camera team from some big magazine syndicate showed up. They were doing a feature on Everest-climbing tours, and they wanted some local colour. We fed them the last of our rice and gave them beds. During the night, I put the catcher's mitt on my foot and went out walking in the snow. In the morning we pointed out the giant tracks to them and they got real excited and took lots of pictures.

'Then in the afternoon there was a snowstorm. I put on the fur coat and ran around in it, the others pointed me out and the photographers chased me and took more pictures. Then they got on their radio and arranged a lucrative book and movie deal, and our end of it was just enough to pay our fares home.'

Roderick got up from the bench and moved to one side of the fountain to read:

> TODAY: INDICA DINKS
> will autograph copies
> of her sensational new
> best-seller, THE NUTS
> AND BOLTS OF MACHINES LIB
> at *Prospero Books*, Fourth
> Level

'On the plane home,' Luke said when he returned, 'I met another Luddite. In fact he was the guy who started 'the whole movement. I told him what happened and how Luddite heavies had moved in on us. He apologized. He said, "Some of the boys just got carried away with the message, I guess."

'Then he started telling me all about the New Luddites Movement and it didn't sound so fanatical after all. He said the Luddites were opposed to violence, even against machines. He wanted a way of peace, linked with the great Eastern traditions of resignation and manual labour. Why didn't I come to the rally he was having in Minnetonka? So here I am, ready to be a Luddite.' Luke looked pleased with himself. 'Maybe I can convert you too.'

'Convert – but Luke, I can't be a Luddite. *I'm a machine.* I'm everything they're opposed to!'

'Oh, you don't have to join right away, Rickwood. I just want you to come along and meet some Luddites yourself. Great buncha guys.'

'But Luke, this is crazy!'

'Meet the guys, hear what they got to say, that's all. Then you make up your own mind.'

Father Warren and Hank Dinks stood by the luggage carousel, watching the same parade of unclaimed bags pass for perhaps the sixth time, the tattersall overnight pursued by the natural calf two-suiter followed at a distance by the viola case, then two items in red hide crowded close by a stiff Gladstone bag with labels and, after a short interval, the duffel bag and the large bright saffron suitcase leading the tattersall overnight. From time to time strangers straggled up and removed items, but Warren and Dinks stood motionless, watching the endless parade and listening to a loop of tape play an endless medley.

'Doesn't um seem to be here, Hank. And we're running a little late.'

'Well I'm not leaving here without something.' Hank snatched up the saffron bag. 'Let's go.'

'But that's, you can't just—'

'Let's get out of this place. I hate airports, all this automated luggage and automated music and people like zombies moving along herded along no life no reality no, no weather even, might as well be in some damn shopping mall—'

'Ha ha, well I hope you won't mind coming out to the Vitanuova Shopping Piazza today, that's where we've set up the um, at the conference centre—'

'What? You fixed my rally, *my* rally, in some plastic shopping centre? Why not just hold it here in the Arrival lounge, I'm trying to reach real people, not – I just don't believe this.'

But Hank nevertheless allowed himself to be led from the terminal into a taxi. 'I just don't believe this.'

'But just look at this brochure, the conference centre seats five thousand, a first-class convention hall, facilities – your publisher thought—'

'Let me see that. "Our trained personnel will be happy to advise you in preparing multimedia presentation, programmes on any subject, and we have plenty of prepackaged units ready to be computer-tailored to your individual multimedia needs" – you thought I wanted this? *This?* You thought the Luddites have multimedia needs? We need computer tailoring?'

'No, of course not, I—'

The driver was craning around. 'Hey I know you, you're that Luddite guy, I seen you on TV, now what's your name?'

'Look I'm sorry, Hank, I just thought it might be good exposure for your book, I know it's a, um, compromise but your publisher is paying and it's a chance to pull in new, a new audience, to sell your book too—'

'I was gonna say the name Godfrey Dank,' said the driver. 'Only now I remember he was the ventriloquist, and when I hear the fadder here call you Hank—'

161

'Sure sure, anything to sell the book, why not turn the rally into a sales conference, why not bring in the slogans and the gimmicks? The prizes for top salesman, why not?'

'Hank, you're tired, you must be over-reacting. I'll admit we made a mistake, Fishfold and Tove thought—'

'Yeah, Hank. Hank, now don't tell me the last name—'

'Why not bring in the, damn it, the strippers and the pep band, you think I came here for that?'

'No, of course not, I—'

'This whole piazza place is dedicated to the inhuman, to everything mass-produced and cheap, fast food and book supermarts and – everything designed by computers and stamped out of the same plastic by robots, the potted palms, the furniture, the stores, the clerks inside, maybe even the robot customers, all of it slathered over with that damn homogenized music you get everywhere, ''Moon River'' and ''Sunshine Balloon'' everywhere, ''Carioca'' everywhere, bars and restaurants, airports, toilets, dentist chairs, delivery rooms and funeral parlours, assembly-line music for assembly-line people—'

'I think it was on the Yoyo Show I seen you, or no, was it Ab Jason? I remember your beard was real long then—'

'It's that kind of stuff I started the Luddites to fight, the way we're burying the world in useless gadgets, unreal junk heaped up around us until we don't even recognize the real world at all, it's just one more thing on TV!'

'Yes I know, the *angst*, I trace it to a loss of faith in human values concurrent with the cybernetic—'

'Indica and I tried to get away from our gadgets, we moved out West to this ecological house, but we brought the disease along with us, in no time we were right back in the same old manure pile of gadgets, house full of broken-down machinery who needs it? Solar panel leaking through the ceiling and something wrong with the autodoor on the garage and the lawn mower and the ultrasound dishwasher and the automatic toilet bowl cleaner – and all around us stuff getting ready to break down, the slow cooker, the light-pipe intercom, the rotisserie, the popcorn popper, the hot food table, the cake oven, microwave, deepfreeze, shoe polisher, floor polisher, vacuum cleaner-washer, blender, mixer, processor, slicer, chopper, coffee grinder, thermostat, lumistat, electrostatic air-conditioner, Jesus Christ, the water purifier, electric pepper-mill, nail-buffer, can opener, carving knife, Jesus H. Christ, there I was in the middle of the desert with an electric pipe-cleaner in my hand, and *it* was starting to make a funny noise . . .'

'Yes, yes I know it must have been—'

'Listen Indica and I even tried adopting a robot child, now isn't that sick? A robot child!'

The driver said, 'Kids these day, I know, I know—'

'One day I just couldn't take any more. I picked up a hammer and took a swing at little Roderick . . . and I missed! And, and the little machine pasted me back with a wrench, and I was free. I just got up and walked out, out into the desert, a free man.'

Father Warren folded his long hands, unfolded them, played a game of church-and-steeple. 'That was when you decided to write *Ludd Be Praised*?'

'Yes I knew then, we have to smash the machines. Smash their grip on our minds, our lives.'

'It'll go all right,' said Father Warren. 'Try not to worry, Hank. The point is, you have a message to put across, a battle-cry: Smash the machines!'

'Father I wish I had your faith. At times like this—' Hank waved the brochure, 'I wonder if the machines haven't smashed us. I – I get so discouraged—'

'Definitely Ab Jason, the Ab Jason Show, only I just can't recall your name, Hank, your—'

'*Will you just shut up and drive? My name is Hank Dinks, yes I was on the Ab Jason Show, now will you just, just—*'

'Okay okay, ya don't hafta yell. I mean excuse me mister bigshot celebrity from TV, I don't wanna insult ya, a lousy working stiff tryina talk to ya, excuse me. All to hell.'

The driver punched buttons to start an endless tape of 'Moon River', 'Carioca', 'Sunshine Balloon' . . .

'Well well well Ms Dinks, Indica, this is indeed a pleasure, welcome aboard, be glad to show you around our little operation here, after all we're the people who deal the merchandise, the um books, so if you don't mind me saying so, we're the people who know *people*. Yes, Mr and Ms Bookbuying America are old, old friends of ours, they don't have many secrets from us. We know how to give them what they want – and make them want it, heh heh. Any questions before we start the grand tour?'

'Quite a store you have here, Mr Shredder.' Indica peered down the aisle of what might have been a supermarket, with customers plying shopping carts past display shelves of products with eye-appeal beneath signs and video screens whispering sales messages. Her gaze, finding nowhere to alight, came back to Mr Shredder's gold tooth.

'See we've put a dump bin of your book in the front, and you'll be autographing in the back, so people have to pass as many shelf feet as possible to get to you. And along here see we have our Today's Top Ten, with daily sales figures logged in right off our national computer hookup – people like to know where they are when they buy a book. And here's another bin with that darned psychic pigeon novel, just keeps on selling! We'll probably nominate that one for the American Book Award this year, hard to say until we do a book-by-book cost analysis, over the year.

'Now here's our astrology and science section, and over here a little item that should do well.' He picked a book from a cardboard barrel.

A Completely New Novel by Ford James Smith
Based on the TV Series by Joyce Henry Madox
Inspired by Adam Thorne's Novelization of
the Original Screenplay by Conrad Brown

LOLITA

'You can't really go wrong with a cover like that, and it doesn't even mislead the customer. Plenty of books with misleading titles around to hook the customer these days. One thing about the book trade, you can always count on good old-fashioned customer illiteracy; best title of the last fifty years was *Your Erroneous Zones* but you find just as much inspiration nowadays, here's a fishing book *You Can Master Bait* and a how-to-study item called *The Erotetic Method*, oh yes and a reprint of two Horatio Alger books in one with the titles run together . . .'

But Indica missed the next part of Mr Shredder's lecture, as she looked across a row of gaudy science-fiction covers straight into the eyes of her pursuer.

15

'Come on Rickwood, I'll buy you a coffee, you can't stand here daydreaming all day.' Luke led him as far as the cashier.

'You gonna buy that, mister?' she asked.

'Buy . . . that?'

'The book in your hand, human use of human beings wiener, you gonna buy it or what?'

Luke took the book from his hand and led him on out of Prospero Books, into the great pleasure dome of Vitanuova Shopping Piazza. In general form, it was a kind of interior Hanging Gardens of Babylon, with a small terrace of stores at each level, with plenty of polished stonelike substances, with gleaming escalators, set at every angle, and with every nook crammed with green potted palms, blue caged birds or tanks of red fish. From the top level, looking over a parapet at the whole dizzying spectacle, Luke spotted the yellow umbrellas of a café far below.

'Come on down this escalator – Jesus, Rickwood, I wish you'd tell me what's going on. Why did we have to go all the way up to this so-called bookstore, just so you could stare at this Indica Dinks? You didn't even say hello.'

'Well I, I didn't want to intrude, just wanted to let her know I'm around, I'm here if she needs me. I could tell by the way she looked at me she understands.'

Luke groaned. 'Just what kind of Victorian truth is it that she understands? Who is this lady?'

'My mother, Luke. My stepmother anyway. Sort of. She took care of me when I was small, I think. And, well, she was the first woman I ever saw naked, so naturally I—'

'You what? Follow her into bookstores?'

166

They took their seats. One or two people at adjoining tables stared at Luke's saffron costume.

'Naturally I love her. I read once how all boys love their mothers and kill their fathers, so—'

Luke held up a saffron-gloved hand. 'Now wait. Rickwood, you've got this a little wrong. Sure, all boys love their mothers in a way, but it just means getting "Mother" tattooed on their arms, or sending embroidered pillow covers, Souvenir of Hong Kong, or maybe asking bar pianists to play "My Mother's Eyes" until they weep into their low-cal pilsner. It does not mean love, like *love*. It doesn't mean killing anybody either, where did you get this idea?'

'Well,' Roderick said loudly. '*I* killed *my* father, and I've always been crazy about my mother's body. And that was before I ever heard of Freud!'

People at the next table got up and moved away. Others stared and whispered. A waitress hurried over, datapad in hand.

'We'd like two coffees,' said Luke. 'Mine, I want a medium-roast blend of Colombian and Mocha, finely ground and filtered, with real cream (not half-and-half) and Demerara sugar. Serve it in a bone china service, preferably Spode, and with a hallmarked silver spoon. And my friend here will have instant ersatz coffee, half-dissolved in tepid water, served with artificial cream and synthetic sugar in a melamine cup, no saucer, with a styrene spoon, please.'

'Two coffees,' she said, and said it again, firmly, when she served them.

'Well she got yours right, Rickwood. What do you mean, you killed your father?'

'I mean I hit him with a box-end wrench, $\frac{3}{4} \times \frac{7}{8}$ I think it was, and he fell down and never got up.'

'Oh.' Luke said nothing more until they were on their way to the rally, making their way through a series of glass tubes and corridors to the Conference Centre. The final leg of the journey took them through a glass-covered bridge high above the flat wintry earth. To their left, an infinity of parked cars. Straight ahead, the Conference Centre, a kind of flying saucer in concrete, pre-stressed and poised for takeoff. To the right, *Freeway Disaster*, the enormous fibre-glass sculpture by Jough Braun, incorporating moulds of an actual freeway pile-up of some twenty vehicles. It was said that, so quickly had Braun worked at the disaster scene, that he had managed to mould in one or two victims. In any case, the German museums had bid very highly for this item, but what mere museum could provide a setting for it like this?

'What did you do after you hit him with the wrench?'

'I nailed myself into this packing crate and sent myself somewhere else. I mean I guess the crate was all labelled and ready anyway, because I was too young to write. So I got in and nailed it shut—'

'How could *you* nail it shut? Rickwood, you must have had an accomplice. Your mother?'

'It might have been a $\frac{13}{16} \times 1$ box-end wrench, or maybe it wasn't a box-end at all, it might have been an open-end, say $1\frac{1}{16} \times 1\frac{1}{8}$ . . .'

Mr Shredder helped her climb the seemingly endless spiral staircase to the office, a comfortable little green room. He presented her with a plastic cup of water. 'Feel better yet?'

'I'm fine, really. Just a little dizzy spell, it's over now.' She found she was still holding a book (*Ragged Dick/Bound to Rise*) and put it down.

'Well while we're in the office, I may as well show you our little nerve centre.'

He sat down at a VDU and tapped the keys, with the air of an electric-organ owner showing off at home. Indica could almost hear *Tico-tico* in poor ugly Mr Shredder's smile. The gold tooth glittered.

'In the past, you know, nobody would have dreamed of running an operation like Prospero Books, but this little gadget has made the book trade into a whole new ball game.

High volume, fast-throughput, unprecedented market sensitivity – well I guess what I mean is, we're no longer at the mercy of the publishers.'

'Publishers?' She felt it was her turn to say something.

'The way it used to be, the publishers ran everything. If you wanted to sell books, you sold what they gave you to sell, that's the way it was, and tough! And not just tough, but it was a very bad, wasteful way to run an industry. I mean with all due respect, most publishers are *jerks* who know *absolutely nothing* about books. They sit around in New York offices being *literati*, all the time. You think they know what sells here in Minnetonka? No. What they do is, publish a book and gamble on it. They gamble, we lose.

'That's the way it was. We dealers, who know the market, had no control over the business; publishers, who know nothing, had complete control. But the computer changed all that. See with the computer we get complete control over our own stock flow, we tie ordering directly to sales, see? Say a customer buys some book, say number 0246114371, the bar code is on the cover, the cashier runs her laser wand over it, and our computer records the sale. Enough sales of that item and the computer automatically reorders.'

Indica said, 'Is that new? I thought that was kind of old hat.'

'Yes but listen: the computer can put data together from fifty stores just as easily as five – or five hundred or five thousand. No matter how big we grow, we can always have real tight, minute-by-minute stock control. Only if we're big, publishers start listening to us. If we don't like a book, they print fewer copies.'

Indica nodded, hoping the lecture was finishing.

'Anyway, at the same time, publishers keep getting taken over by big conglomerates like KUR, people with electronic ideas of their own. Like they also get computerized stock control and also they fix it up so authors can set their own type – stuff like that. And it's kind of inevitable that their computers will get together with our computers. After all, we all want the same thing.'

Indica stopped nodding. 'Authors and publishers and book dealers, all – together?'

Mr Shredder grinned with his gold tooth. 'Only a pilot scheme so far, but so far it works! We got this best-selling author to agree, he sits in his house in Nassau and types, and our computers get it via satellite, word by word. They do a complete analysis *as he writes* – and feed it right back to him. They give him back a sales projection every time he hits the old space bar, so he knows *the second* his writing falls off. He knows he's got to go back and polish up that last sentence or change that last word – or else!'

By the time Roderick and Luke arrived, the rally was already in full swing. The huge hall was more than half full, with more people drifting in all the time.

The speaker was saying, '. . . mixers, processors, thermostat, lumistat . . . can opener, electric carving knife, Jesus Christ, there I was in the middle of the goddamned desert with an electric pipe cleaner in my hand . . .'

'Why that's Hank!' Roderick exclaimed. Someone told him to shut his fuckin' face.

Luke whispered, 'Yes, he's the guy I met on the plane.'

'Hush your mouth,' warned another man. The audience seemed to be largely male, and many were wearing a kind of 'uniform' of shirtsleeves, rolled up to mid-bicep, as in political cartoons of Uncle Sam. They seemed ready to spit on their hands and go to work. When new people came in, many of them would look around for a few moments, then remove their coats and roll up their sleeves.

'. . . just picked up a hammer and took a swing at that little robot – and I missed! And the little robot picked up a wrench or something and cold-cocked me! But at least it was an honest fight – we were enemies and we both knew it. When I came to, I got up and walked out into the desert, a free man. A free man. For the first time in my life I didn't have an alarm clock to wake up for, a phone to answer, a time clock to punch, or a car to keep up the payments on. No . . .'

Isolated people started calling out 'Amen' and 'Praise the Ludd'. Soon there was a regular, clapping chorus, and Hank seemed to be leading it, standing alone in the middle of a big stage, a tiny bearded-prophet figure. He started going through the long list of gadgets and appliances once more, now as a litany. And before he finished, men were leaping up to name machines of their own:

'To hell with my drill press!'

'*Praise Ludd*!'

'Down with programmed door chimes!'

'*Amen.*'

'Smash all machines!'

'*Yes Ludd*!'

'Take this hammer!' Someone brandished it.

'*Ludd, Ludd*!'

Hammers were being brandished all over the auditorium now.

'I smashed a parking meter!'

'I smashed a kid's musical top!'

'I smashed my wife's solid state dehydrator with stick-resistant trays and forced air flow!'

'*Praise Ludd*!'

'Smash the machines! Screw the machines!'

Men were jumping on their seats and waving hammers now, ready to smash anything remotely like a machine, while others egged them on with a steady clapping and chanting, 'Smash . . . smash . . . smash . . .'

Hank held up his hands in an attempt to make them stop, but this only seemed to raise the tempo; they took it as a victory sign. Worse, the conference centre's 'multimedia' people, who had prepared a special audiovisual package for the occasion, thought Hank was now signalling for it.

The giant screen behind Hank suddenly came alive with images of train wrecks, exploding cars, Chaplin demolishing an alarm clock, aircraft shot down, burning factories, the sinking of a paddle steamer, a chainsaw murder, the Who smashing electric guitars . . .

At that point someone broke into the projection booth and smashed the equipment, and the room went quiet. They were waiting for Hank to tell them what to do – go home and wait? Act now?

Hank opened his mouth, but just then a multimedia voice came over the p.a. system, drowning him out:

'Thanks guys and gals for making this a memorable day. We have souvenir hammers for sale in the foyer. And in a few minutes, Hank Dinks will be going over to the main complex to Prospero Books – he'll autograph copies of both his books. I hope we'll see you all there!'

That seemed to be the signal for the riot to begin.

'Luke, this is ridiculous,' Roderick tried to say, as they were pushed along the glass bridge with the others, but the noise of chanting, screaming and smashing made speech impossible. Roderick rolled up his sleeves, shook his fist and called for demolition. He was now separated from Luke, but could still see him; the ex-astronaut had rolled up his saffron sleeves and seemed to be having a hell of a good time.

The first mechanical victim was a gum machine, and soon gumballs were raining down from the upper levels of the ziggurat – followed soon by pinballs and then fragments of a mechanical donkey ride. With a terrible thoroughness, the Luddites moved through every establishment, destroying hairdryers, malted milk machines, dental drills, programmed expresso machines, a wind-up mouse, toasters by the dozen and digital watches by the hundred. They met no opposition. The few security cops on duty approached them, fiddled with guns and radios, then decided to run instead. They had been hired to deal with elderly shoplifters and kids who tried skating on the escalators, not with a mob of thousands of maniacs.

They reached Prospero Books, where the furious mob not only did not find Hank installed, it found a sign, MACHINES LIB. The mob at once entered through both window and door. Roderick found himself wedged in a corner where, through the blizzard of torn pages, he could see on a TV monitor, Indica, still calmly signing books.

She continued to sign, ignoring the mob who pressed in around her little table. One of the men crashed his hammer down on the table in front of her.

'Honestly!' she said, and rummaged in her purse for a moment. Finally she brought out a revolver and fired it at the ceiling.

Instantly, everyone was quiet. Throughout the entire bookstore no one moved among the wreckage, except one enterprising Luddite who went on cleaning out the cash register. Everyone waited for a killing.

'This kind of behaviour is very destructive,' Indica said. 'You're a bunch of silly little boys. I suppose my ex-husband put you up to this. Well, you can tell Hank Dinks for me, *it won't work*. It doesn't matter how many hairdryers he smashes, *I am not coming back to him*. Now you can just clear out, all of you. *Move!*'

No one spoke. Here and there a hammer dropped to the floor (where everyone was now looking). One man, who'd been tearing up a copy of Indica's book, now fell to his knees, kissing the book and weeping. A few others felt suddenly the nakedness of their arms and rolled down their sleeves. A general shuffling and edging towards the door began, and soon the place was almost clear.

Roderick came out of his corner. 'Indica, I—'

'You! God damn it, will you stop following me?' She brought up the pistol smoothly, clasped it in both hands and aimed carefully at a point between those terrifying eyes.

'Are you going to shoot me?' he asked, and stopped.

. . . *running through a dead wood, some trees charred by lightning,* that was how the dream went. *In a clearing she saw a figure, a man in red armour, head to toe. He didn't move, and gradually she realized that he was rusted fast, covered with red rust. Opening her fly, she pulled out an enormous oil can and went to work, annointing him all over. The rust dripped and ran, now it was blood. Suddenly his iron arms gripped her, squeezing her so tight she could hardly breathe. 'Don't scream,' he said. 'The woods are like tinder, one scream could set off a conflagration. Through the visor she could see the glowing eyes. She screamed . . .*

She started to put the gun away. 'Who are you? Who are you?'

'I'm your—'

'Indica! Indica!' It was Mr Shredder, calling from the spiral stairs. 'Come up here, quick. Something's happened.'

She went up at once to the little green office. A man lay on the green carpet, with a priest squatting next to him.

'It's Hank,' said Shredder. 'I was just showing him our nerve centre when the mob showed up.'

'Hank? I don't understand.' Was that blood or oil on the priest's fingers?

'Some lunatic in that mob must of let off a gun,' said Mr Shrudder. 'Hank's dead.'

Father Warren looked up. 'He gave his life for us, for all of us. Now his fight must go on! We must go on smashing, smashing, smashing the machines!'

Mr Shredder looked alarmed and stood in front of his computer terminal. 'I think we've had enough talk about smashing things today.'

The priest stood up. 'Oh, I don't mean literally smash machines with hammers. Those poor men today got the message a little wrong. No, we must smash the machines *inside us*, smash the *idea* of the machine.' He held out a hand to Indica. 'Won't you join us? I know that in your heart you feel Hank was right – this is your fight too. Join the New Luddites.'

'You don't have to be so paternalistic, Father. *You* go

174

smash the machine inside *you* if you want, *I* happen to think it's a screwloose idea.' She turned to make her exit.

'With you or without you,' he said, 'we'll win.'

'Over my dead body.'

Mr Kratt turned off the TV news and picked up his cheap cigar. It had gone out. 'Well, bub, your little plan to reunite the Dinkses doesn't seem to have worked out too well. Unless you figured on a riot and the guy getting killed.'

Jud Mill leaned forward suddenly, the long striped wings of his shirt collar crackling with the movement. He thrust out a lighter. 'In the media management business, you gotta expect surprises. You notice I managed to get a clear shot of the cover of Indica's book in that news item? And the title is mentioned twice.'

'Kind of tough though for Fishfold and Tove, losing their big name.'

'Well, sir, I been thinking about just that problem, and I think this priest, this Father Warren, is going to take over the Luddite leadership. You put him under contract now and you can get him cheap, get all the books you can out of this little movement before they get boring. Too bad the cops didn't arrest Indica though, you can always get a lotta mileage out of the big name family murder angle.

'Now about this next book on your list, *Red Situation*, what is it, a spy thriller kind of thing? I guess we could always pretend the author was really in the CIA or MI5 or something, but people are getting tired of authenticity too; we need a better angle.' Mill sat back, shirt collar crackling, and looked at the world through half-moon reading glasses. 'I understand this author is sitting in Nassau sending all this stuff in via satellite to a typesetting computer, right? What if we just shot down the satellite and blamed Russia? I know it's expensive, but—'

'Hell, bub, you'd be starting a war.'

'Sure, but probably a limited war, and maybe only an

international crisis. Meanwhile we get maximum world-wide coverage of our boy and his book, ''The Book the Russians Tried to Stop!'' '

Mr Kratt exhaled a cloud of oily smoke. 'All sounds kind of crazy to me.'

'But all part of the creative evolution of a literary property, and I do mean creative. Hell, I once got an author to sue himself for plagiarism – claimed a book he did under a pseudonym was ripped off. Of course the judge had him committed for psychiatric observation and the author ended up spending a year in a looney bin, but then we got a *great* book out of that, *Call Me Schizo* . . . yes, he ghosted that one for himself . . .'

'For the last time,' said the sergeant, 'are you a Ludder or a Libber?' He was counting change from Roderick's pocket into a large envelope. 'You gotta be one or the other.'

'Why?'

'Because you gotta. What were you doing when we arrested you?'

'I was standing watching some guy painting on a wall. He was painting, ''I bring you not peace but an electric carving knife''.'

'Sounds like you're a Ludder. Sit over there, after you sign for your twenty-nine cents.'

Over there was a long bench against the wall. Luke was there already, his saffron suit torn and dirty. Roderick sat between him and a fat man.

'Are you all right, Luke? That cut on your forehead—'

'Never felt better, Rickwood. Thinking of forming an escape committee, maybe digging a tunnel while we wait.'

'But we're on the tenth floor.'

'Always some excuse to do nothing. Rickwood, don't you realize? *Everybody's on some floor or other.*'

A policeman took Luke out of the room. Roderick now noticed that the fat man was having an argument with his handkerchief. That is, he had drawn a face on the cloth and draped it over his hand to make a puppet.

'The way I see it,' said the man, 'machines are responsible for almost every human problem today.'

The handkerchief coughed. 'Bullshit, man. If you think machines are trouble, just look at the dumb bastards running them. Machines aren't good or bad themselves, they don't make the problems. Take a plough.'

'Why don't you take a flying plough yourself?'

'A plough,' said the cloth firmly, 'feeds the hungry, man. You call that a problem?'

'Sure, overpopulation. And don't give me that old jive about a machine being no better or worse than the man who uses it, I heard that a hundred times. But can you tell me a tank ain't evil? A guided missile?'

'Okay, but who made them? Evil people. Get rid of evil in the human spirit,' shrilled the handkerchief, 'and you get rid of the so-called evil machines.'

'You got it backwards, rag-head. Get rid of the machines and people won't have to be so evil. They can be more — more human, like.'

The cloth made a face. 'To be human *is* to be evil, you dumb twat! Get rid of the human race and you sure as hell get rid of all evil.'

'Oh sure, and who benefits? The same damn machines that are exploiting us now!' The fat man burst into tears, but the handkerchief remained unmoved.

'That's it, blame the machines for everything. Sometimes the human race reminds me of — of that cop over there, typing with two fingers. Slow. Real slow.'

'Stop it! Just stop it!'

'You're all sleepwalkers and bums. Gimme machines any time, at least they're clean.'

A policeman called Roderick's name and led him to a door at the end of the room. At the door, he looked back. The fat man was using the handkerchief to blow his nose.

The door led to a small office with dingy green walls, a scarred table with a folder on it, and a window that seemed smeared with shit. A single bare lightbulb with an enamel reflector hung over the single wooden chair. Two men watched Roderick from the shadows.

'Sit down, Bozo.' He sat down. 'What do you think of our interrogation room?'

'It looks like something out of the movies, heh heh.'

'Heh heh, you hear that, Cuff? We got us an intellectual anus here.'

'Yeah, lieutenant, a real sage sphincter.'

The beating seemed to go according to old movie arrangements, too; Roderick even glimpsed a rubber hose. He began to regret being equipped with pain circuits; it was hard not to begin disliking these policemen, who were probably only doing some kind of duty.

They played all the games he remembered from childhood, from the school playground: stand up sit down; no means yes and yes means no; and sorry I hit you oops sorry I hit you again . . .

'Look at him,' said the one called lieutenant. 'Look at that innocent face, you wouldn't think a face like that could do anything, would you? I mean does he really look like a guy that would rape a girl, stab her to death, chop up the body and hide the pieces in—'

Cuff was reading the folder on the table for the first time. 'Uh, lieutenant. This is a different suspect.'

'All suspects are the same, Cuff, you should know that.'

'I mean this guy is from the Shopping Piazza beef.'

'Then why do I tie him in with the Snowman Killer? Why? Why? He's not the Moxon's chauffeur?'

'Nope, he's clean.'

Lieutenant turned on normal lights. He was a normal-looking man, despite the propellor beanie he wore, no doubt to give himself character. 'Isn't that just it, though? He's clean, he's *too* clean. Anybody this clean has to be hiding

178

something big.' He tapped the side of his nose. 'And *this* tells me he's the Snowman!' The tapping finger slowed, stopped, began exploring the interior of a nostril.

The finger pointed at Roderick. 'All right, *you*. I'm gonna ask you one question and one question only. I want you to listen good. Were you at a party at the house of Everett Moxon, just before Christmas?'

'Yes I was.'

The two cops exchanged a look.

'Did you leave that party with a woman?'

'Yes.'

'A woman named Judi Mazzini?'

'No, Connie McBabbitt.'

The two policemen groaned, withdrew to the other side of the room, and argued. 'We had such a good case too, lieutenant. Sergeant Placket says he even mentioned an electric carving knife. And he was at the party—'

'Sergeant Placket is a kind of a sophisticated bowel, if you ask me.'

A fat man was waiting by the counter when Roderick collected his twenty-nine cents.

'How's the handkerchief?'

'Mister, you got some problem? Huh?'

'Sorry, I thought you were another fat guy, I mean someone else.' Now he could see the man was a stranger, deeply tanned and wearing a cowboy hat. 'I was kind of dizzy there, not feeling too well.'

'Roderick Wood,' said the counter sergeant. 'Sign here.'

Somehow Roderick managed to lift the heavy pen and scrawl his name; to drag himself to the elevator and lean on the button. The fat cowboy got on the elevator with him.

'You better take it easy there, partner. You look plumb sick.'

'No I . . . feeling dizzy I . . .'

'Guess I better take you into protective custody then.' The man handcuffed Roderick's left wrist to his own right.

'What? Mm? Eh?'

'The name's O'Smith, I'm a kinda bounty hunter. And there sure is a good price on your little old microchip head, son.'

'Uh?'

'Yep, I know who you are, I know all about you, how they built you over at the University, how they sneaked you off to live with them Dinkses over in Nevada, then when they split up you went to Nebraska to live with Ma and Pa Wood, then finally you high-tailed it up here to the big city, I know all that.' They left the elevator and O'Smith gave a friendly nod to the desk sergeant on their way out.

It was night-time, to Roderick's surprise. But he would have been just as surprised by daylight. Time, after all, was, is, has past, would be, will have been passing . . .

'I been following your trail for some time, son. Mr Kratt and Mr Frankelin wanted you real bad, you're gonna make their fortune. After you make mine, that is. Come on, the car's right across the street here. Careful on the ice, don't want you to fall down and wreck any of that high-tone hardware. You might not believe it to look at me, but I got a few artificial parts myself, I – hey! What's that gol-durned fool think he's doin'? Hey!'

A car with no lights careened around a corner, fishtailed, picked up speed, and drove straight at them. At the last minute, the driver hit the brakes and threw the car into a skid.

Roderick was aware of being thrown into the air and falling in snow. He lay on his back, watching the stars. One by one, they went out.

The four boys from Digamma Upsilon Nu got out of their car and looked at the victims.

'They look dead to me. Jeez, this guy's lost his arm!'

'My old man'll kill me, drunk driving with no lights – and hit and run.'

180

'We haven't run yet.'

'No but we're gonna. Hey look, this stiff's got the other one's arm. In a handcuff! Cops!'

'Yeah, hey, there's the station right there. Aw Jeez, we're all gonna be in trouble.'

Someone bent with a match over Roderick. 'This ain't no stiff, it's a dummy, look the wig's coming loose, you can see metal.'

'And this arm is artificial – the other one must be a dummy too. Or something.'

As if by a prearranged plan, they loaded Roderick, with O'Smith's right arm, into their car and drove off. In a fraternity famed for practical jokes, there would always be some use for a realistic dummy.

16

Father Warren awoke from a brief and terrifying dream in which he'd been playing ping-pong with the Holy Ghost. The Paraclete had taken the form of a pigeon; standing on the table, it pecked the ball back at him. There had been some question about the stakes. Either damnation awaited him if he won, or else if he lost. But the terrifying part was that, in his dream, he knew he was dreaming. He knew that if he succeeded in avoiding damnation, his pleasure would be supreme and lasting into wakefulness – thus damning him anyway.

All nonsense of course. Here he was in the lounge of the Newman Club, having dozed over his own article on Lewis, nothing worse. He set about exorcizing the dream: ping-pong sounds came from the next room, no mystery about that. As for the pigeon, hadn't someone the other day said something about Skinner and pigeons? Training them to be superstitious? Yes, something about pigeons understanding how faith could be exactly like a mustard seed.

Cheap epigram like that, funny it should stick in his craw - mind. He turned his attention to the printed words (his own):

. . . a fearful symmetry by which the master finds that it is really the slave who is in control of things. The magician who believes he can hold demons in thrall makes the same mistake as the cybernetician who thinks he can order his machine to deliver power or 'success' for free. In such a context we find Lewis using a demon name made up of *screw* (a word rife with both bawdy and mechanistic vulgarity) and *tape* (symbol of the binding contract). It would be hard to imagine a name more prophetically descriptive of the cybernetic demons that were to come into being. *The Screwtape Letters* appeared in 1942, the year ENIAC was built. And it is of ENIAC's descendants that Lewis might have written:

> There are two equal and opposite errors into which our race can fall about the devils. One is to disbelieve in their existence. The other is to believe, and feel an excessive or unhealthy interest in them.

Our own 'computer generation' has managed to fall into both errors . . .

A fearful symmetry, yes, he ought to have added a word or two about binary numbers, two errors, the Yes/No character of . . . of . . .

His head jerked up. No one else in the lounge seemed to have noticed him. Two students were talking quietly in the corner, near the statue of the Infant of Prague. Two others, flushed from their ping-pong game, were heading for the coke machine.

The boy with the sparse beard stood in the doorway, looking at him. 'All right if I come in, Father?'

'Hector, of course. Were you looking for me?'

'Yeah, I tried your office, they said you might be here. Only when I looked in you seemed to be praying.'

Father Warren remembered to grin. 'What, at the Newman Club? With all this racket, I'm lucky I can even read. What's on your mind? Not still worried about your paper?'

'No, it's going okay. Only I still remember the movie a lot better than the book. And I still don't see what a clockwork orange is supposed to do, he might as well say an electric banana – I mean, an orange you wind up and then what?'

'Ah well you see it's – something the English, something musical as I recall, musical references galore there – a kind of music box, perhaps. But was there something else?'

'Yeah, Father, just that the Science Fiction Club is having

this panel discussion on artificial intelligence, we thought you might want to, um—'

'Chair the discussion?'

'Well no, just be a panellist, we've got a chair, um, person, already.'

'Be on the panel? Sure. See my secretary about the date, but I'll be glad to.'

The two of them rose, and the priest put a hand on the other's shoulder, seemingly controlling him as they strolled towards the door.

'. . . work orange, difficulty lies in deciding not merely its function, but whether its membership in the class of oranges or the class of clockwork things takes precedence in determining that function. The two classes are thought to be mutually exclusive and indeed they are, for we know intuitively that we are not dealing with a real orange, but rather a token of the type orange. That is, it has some properties that make us call it an orange, properties shared by all oranges and by the type itself, which – I wonder who that was?'

He had nodded and smiled at a familiar face lurking by the coke machine, it had nodded back: a plain, symmetrical face of no particular age, or sex, or race. It was gone from his thoughts before he had passed out of the Newman Club beneath the motto: *Ex umbris et imaginibus in veritatem*, from shadows and types to the reality.

The little knot of people by the coke machine were talkative and thirsty; only one said nothing, drank nothing.

'Well sure it applies to religion, we had all about that last week in Computer Appreciation, they said in 1963 a computer proved that not all of St Paul's epistles were by the same hand.'

'Big deal, so he was ambidextrous.'

'Or maybe it proved they *were* all by the same hand, I forget which. Anyway the computer proved it, whatever it was.'

'Hey, and Pascal, right after he invented the first adding machine, he got "born again" as a Jansenist.'

'I thought Pascal was a language – but what about the big Mormon computer storing up the names of all the dead people in the whole world?'

'What about Leibniz, he built the first four-function calculator, and he proved the existence of God. And he invented binary numbers. On the other hand, he must not have been too religious, his treatise on ethics turned out to be plagiarized.'

'What about the rosary? Wasn't that the first religious calculating device? The Catholic abacus, somebody called it . . .'

'Well I still say cybernetics doesn't apply to religion, I mean they haven't even got computer-generated music in the liturgy have they?'

'Yeah, well, you wouldn't be happy even if they had a robot pope, like in that Robert Silverberg story. You'd want a robot canonized too.'

'Ask Robbie here what he thinks, does he want to be a saint?'

'Leave Robbie alone,' said the boy in the sweatshirt marked F Υ N. 'He don't have to think about nothing, he's our mascot. Our own personal robot mascot. Right, Robbie?'

The silent, unthirsty one, who wore an identical sweatshirt, nodded. 'Right, master.'

'He's no robot,' said somebody else. 'He was playing ping-pong a minute ago, he's just one of your pledges helping you pull a stunt. Robots can't play ping-pong.'

'That's all you know, look in his mouth. Robbie, open wide.'

The mascot opened his mouth for inspection.

'Hey, he ain't got no tongue! No throat! Just a, what is that, a speaker?'

'Okay, I'm impressed. Only where did you get Robbie? He must be worth millions, a robot that good. I mean I work over at the bio-engineering lab, I know how hard it is to get a robot to walk around normally in the real world, let alone play ping-pong. So how come it's your mascot?'

'Fraternity secret. Robbie, go wait for me in the lounge. Just sit down in there and wait for me.'

'Yes, master.'

'I'm impressed, I'm impressed. There he goes, sits down - you didn't even tell him to sit in a chair, but he's doing it. Boy, he is worth millions.'

The mascot sat down in the lounge, rested one hand on each arm of the chair, and stared straight ahead of him. He took no notice of the couple sitting nearby, nor they of him; they were engrossed in the little statue in the corner.

'. . . and that's what's so peculiar, it's a copy of a copy, an effigy representing a doll. I mean the original Infant of Prague was a statue of Baby Jesus that they clothed in real finery, brocade and jewels and a gold crown – but this, this is just plaster painted to look like finery: a statue not of Jesus but of a robed doll. There's something uncanny about it, it's like making a waxwork model of a robot,' said the boy.

The girl replied, 'The word comes from Prague too. Prague keeps getting associated with effigies, one way or another. There was the famous *golem* of Rabbi Löw of Prague, back in the sixteenth century. It was made of clay, and he brought it to life by putting this amulet under its tongue – a paper with the secret name of God or something like that. The golem works for him, runs errands and so on, but on the Sabbath he has to remove the amulet and put it to rest. One Sabbath he forgets; the golem gets out of control and goes rampaging around Prague. Finally he gets it deprogrammed and puts it away in the attic of the synagogue, never to be brought to life again.'

'A legend with a moral?'

'Yes but Rabbi Löw was a real man, he died in 1609. About thirty years later, Descartes was suddenly talking and writing about automata.'

He looked at her. 'Descartes? What's the connection?'

'Descartes fought in the Battle of Prague! His side won, and he marched into the city in 1620. Did he hear of the golem? Did he buy it? Did he loot the synagogue? We know he was interested in all sciences; had he heard of the golem, he would almost certainly have tried to see it, if not acquire it. Anyway, in 1637 he wrote about automata, saying that automaton monkeys could not be distinguished from real ones.'

'An experimental observation?'

'Why not? Three years later, he was making a sea voyage, taking along an automaton girl, whom he called ''ma fille Francine''.'

'Too good to be true! What happened to her?'

'Destroyed by superstition. He brought her aboard the ship in a box. The captain peeked inside, saw her move, and, thinking her the work of the Devil, threw her overboard.'

'Another mystery of Prague down the drain,' he said.

'Three centuries later Karel Čapek put on his play *R.U.R.* in Prague, and added the word *robot* to the world's vocabulary. Čapek was born in Prague, too.'

'It's always Prague – the Infant, the golem, Rossum's Universal Robots – you begin to wonder what was really going on there?'

Outside it was spring, warm enough for students to lie on the lawn with bag lunches and define their terms in arguments, if they were not better occupied cuddling or daydreaming or dozing or throwing frisbees.

'. . . a surrealist musical, he calls it *Hello Dali* . . .'

'But hey listen, the Golden Section . . .'

'Basically I guess I must be a Manichee, I always see two sides to everything . . .'

'. . . this Golden Section, this computer worked it out to thousands of decimal places, I still don't know what it is exactly . . .'

'. . . to match up these thousands of potsherds, only the program went wrong. That or else the Beaker people made a beaker without a mouth, so much for Keats . . .'

'*La vie électrique*, by Albert Robida.'

'Br'er Robbie . . . ?'

'Ah ah ah!'

Someone sneezed, someone spoke of spring the sweet spring. A frisbee player stepped on a tuna salad sandwich. Someone looking quickly through a book on Rodin remarked that some of his stuff wouldn't be bad when it was finished.

A few heads turned as a woman in white passed. Her long hair, in sunlight the colour of clean copper, hung long over her shoulders and back, all but obscuring the legend on the back of her white coveralls: SANDRO'S SHELL SERVICE.

Down the line, heads were turning for a different reason as Lyle Tate passed, coming the other way. The birthmark down his cheek was darker than usual because he was angry; it rendered one side of his face a mask of infinite fury, its eye weeping ink. He and the woman in white met by the frisbee players.

'What is it? Weren't we meeting at the Faculty Club bar?'

'Nothing, I just can't – we'll have to go have lunch somewhere else, Shirl.'

'Lyle, what's wrong?'

'I met that sonofabitch Gary Indiana, that's all. I just can't stay in the room with him, not after what he did to my one-man show, did you see his review?'

'No. Look let's skip lunch, we can just sit down here on

the grass and talk this out, can't we?'

He sat down but continued to wave a clipping from a slick art magazine. 'After this I'll be lucky if the department doesn't drop me, that's all.'

'It looks like a long review for a bad one.'

His face twisted more. 'That's the worst of it, he pretends to *like* my work, then tears it apart – I mean for instance getting the titles of the paintings wrong! *Cigar Tragic* he changes to *Cigarette Tragedy*, the palindrome was the whole point of the title, the whole painting is a visual palindrome with Castro's exploding Havana mirroring the vaudeville gag, was trying to show the comic-book minds behind it, but no – not only does he change the name he spends half the review talking about America's position on puppet governments, turns out to be some fucking speech he ghosted for General Fleischman – you see what I'm up against? And he claims it's all some problem with his word processor, a page of speech got slipped in by mistake. Can that happen?'

She shrugged. 'If he's an idiot.'

'He's – I don't know what he is, talks about me handling my faeces and then says the word processor put in an e, it was faces – I don't know what to believe. And it keeps getting worse, listen to this: "Tate, handling his faeces with a skill that betokens a savouring of every movement and at the same time reminds us of his personal affliction, piles on de tail." Can a word processor really do this? Wreck my whole future like this?'

She nudged him. 'Hey look, one of those fraternity boys going by – he looks just like you in profile.'

Lyle did not look. 'My good side, no doubt. But just tell me, you're the expert, can a word processor make all those mistakes?'

'Yes and no, Lyle. In any case, why didn't this Indiana character read his copy over before transmitting it? Why didn't his editor catch anything? Even with direct setting somebody's supposed to read the stuff.'

'Then somebody's out to get me.'

'With a reamer, Lyle.'

Someone spoke of spring training. A frisbee player stepped on a **Rodin** book, while someone opened a tuna sandwich to study it. Someone sneezed, unblessed.

'Brother Robbie, come on.'

Time for a class.

'We can say for example that a work of art resembles other works of art in that it is art, but it differs from them in that it is a different work, not too hard to follow that, is it? And this blend of similarity and difference, this tension serves not only to place the work in the field but to move the field itself in some specific direction. In the same way, if we use an iterative algorithm to calculate the value say of *pi*, we may get 3 the first time through, then 3.1, then 3.14 and so on. Each new value is in part like its predecessor, but in part different. And the movement is towards a true value, which we might call an ideal . . .'

As usual, the lecture was reaching less than half the class at any moment. By some law, eleven of the twenty-one students were always lost in sleep or diversions.

In the first row, only Ali was dozing off while the rest were alert. In the second row, Fergusen and Gage were playing tic-tac-toe, though the rest took notes. In the third row, only Klein and Loomis paid attention, while the other three were having a whispered political discussion. In the fourth row, only Potter was staring towards the lectern; the rest were otherwise occupied.

Alone in the last row sat Robert Underwood Robey (the boy they called 'Robbie') sound asleep as always.

Gage won the game and took lecture notes, while Fergusen began a new game with Halley. Morris stopped discussing politics long enough to scribble a note or two, while Loomis started cutting his nails.

Ali awoke just as Blake began to daydream. Halley won the game and went back to work, while Fergusen mulled over new strategy and Ingersoll looked at a knitting pattern. Morris commenced an elaborate doodle and O'Toole unwrapped a sandwich while between them Noble took in the lecture. Potter borrowed a newspaper from Quaglione, who attended the lecture.

While Ingersoll folded up the knitting pattern and resumed listening, Jones developed a leg cramp that took precedence. Immediately behind Jones, O'Toole put down the sandwich and observed the lecturer while Noble started reading a popular novel whose protagonist was a pigeon.

Black snapped out of the daydream as Clayburn turned to borrow a pencil or pen from Gage. Fergusen followed the lecture, while behind him Klein played with a '15' puzzle and Loomis started taking notes. Quaglione put in an earphone and listened to the ball game. Reed woke up.

Jones's cramp ceased as Ingersoll took another look at the knitting pattern. Noble put down the novel while O'Toole picked up the sandwich.

Clayburn took notes while Drumm fell asleep. Gage and Halley began a political discussion. Morris stopped doodling while Noble read more of the pigeon's adventures. Reed began a crossword puzzle, and Smith stopped worrying about money and paid attention.

Since Gage refused to argue any more, Halley took up the political discussion with Ingersoll. Loomis started examining his scalp for dandruff, while Noble finished a chapter and took notes again.

Drumm came alert as Esperanza began a game of connect-the-dots with Jones, behind him. Halley tried to read Hegel while Ingersoll tried to catch up with the lecture. Noble read more of the pigeon; O'Toole finished lunch and took notes. Smith went back to financial worries on the back of an envelope, while Teller stopped looking at pictures of pubic hair and noticed the lecture.

Halley too at last preferred the lecture to Hegel, as Ingersoll began knitting and Morris began an even more elaborate doodle. Noble put down his book for a few last notes as the lecture ended.

In the cafeteria Robbie sat alone at an empty formica table among other formica tables ranged, with their fibreglass chairs (many occupied), in ranks and files across an acre of thermoplastic tile floor. At other tables drama students talked of Meyerhold's bio-mechanics, music students talked of red noise generators, art students talked of mimetic sculpture.

'Calamital,' someone at one table was saying. 'Or Equapace. And the dark red ones must be Trancalept. I got some Risibal here someplace.' A finger stirred among the bright beads spread on a table napkin.

'You got any Fenrisol, though?' Allbright asked.

'Naw, you gotta ask Dave Coppola, his old man's a doctor in the U Hospital psycho ward, he can get anything. All I got here is street medication, Ultracalm or Agonistyl, Anxifran and here's Somrepose . . .'

Allbright's dirty fingers selected a few pills, dropped a few crumpled bills as he lurched to his feet, his black baseball cap with a skull-and-crossbones just missing a tray going past in the hands of someone saying:

'. . . actually had somebody ask if I cut holes in dogs' heads to watch them drool, that's all people know about behaviourism. That or they think it's all rats – watch it! – and reflexes . . .'

Allbright lurched again, rounding a table where someone was saying, '. . . Olimpia, Antonia, Nani, Swanhilda, La Poupée de Nurnberg, La Fille aux yeux d'émail . . .' and came to a table with a familiar face.

192

The face showed no recognition as Allbright sat down. 'I am sorry, this table is reserved, sir or madam.'

'Hey it's me. Remember?'

'I am saving this table for members of Digamma Upsilon Nu only.'

'Don't worry, I only want to sit here for a minute.' Allbright tilted his chair back, and glanced around. 'This place never changes: same people, same plastics, same tuneless background music behind empty talk within walls of no colour, no colour at all. I miss it.' He swallowed a pill. 'Yes, I miss it. I don't just come back here to score for pills, I – any more than the salmon leaps and leaps all the way upriver just to drop a few eggs. No, it's just being in the mob, being in the swim. Returning to the scene of the crime I should have committed. Okay, I didn't poach the salmon.'

After a few minutes, Allbright said, 'Salmon is very wise, according to the Irish, that's why Yeats put it on the money - okay I've been quoting Yeats, self-pity on a stick, the young in each other's orifices, so what? So what? So what?'

After another pause, Allbright said, 'This is where you say, "Well, how's the old poetry going, Allbright? Wrote any good poems lately?" '

Robbie said, 'Well, how's the old poetry going, Allbright? Wrote any good poems lately?'

'So you talk, anyway. You are talking. There is a talker here . . . Any good poems? No. Poems all finished. Just waiting now for the holy fire. Just waiting for the Grecian goldsmiths to get their asses in gear and prepare the holy fire. You say something?'

Pause. 'I seem to have said everything anyway. I'm turning into an automaton that keeps making little jokes, Jarrell said that about Auden only at least Auden had been one of the five or six best poets in the world first, maybe good poets and bad can be refined in the holy fire though, why not end up a gold automaton, might become one of the gold mechanical women helping Hephaestus at his forge, "machines for making more machines", why not?'

Allbright put his head down on the formica and went to sleep. Robbie sat motionless, apparently listening to background music: 'Moon River', 'Carioca', 'A Certain Smile', 'Hello Dolly', 'Bridge Over Troubled Water', 'Sunshine Balloon' and 'Love Walked In', After an interval, 'Moon River' began again.

'Germ warfare? That sounds sick,' said Indica. Dr Tarr had heard it before, but Col. Shagg, who had the seat next to the window, laughed and winked.

'You folks coming to Bimibia to entertain the troops by any chance? You got some great material there.'

Tarr leaned forward. 'What troops? There aren't any American troops in Bimibia, are there?'

Shagg winked again. 'Well we're getting together a little outfit, you might call us mercenaries, we're just down there to pull General Bami's irons out of the fire.'

'General who?' Indica asked. 'You mean there's some kind of war going on? We never heard a word about it.'

Dr Tarr nodded. 'I'm supposed to be going down to set up a market survey for a frozen yoghurt firm, but if things are that unstable I'm not so sure. Maybe we'll just get off the plane at Goeringsburg and catch the next flight to Cairo instead of going on to Himmlerville.'

The Colonel laughed and winked more. 'No sweat, kids. The whole country's a lot safer than New York. We're just going down to make it a whole lot safer.'

Tarr wondered who *we* included. The other passengers on the plane did not, so far as he could tell, resemble mercenaries. There were two nuns in the distinctive gingham habits of a Wyoming order; hungover ore salesmen on their way home from a convention; the crew and cast of the low-budget film *Ratstar* who, to save luggage charges,

194

wore their gaudy spacesuits and silver lamé capes; a minor Ruritanian envoy who had, it was said, committed an indecency with a Senate page; a noisy contingent of haemophiliacs en route to a clinic in Dar, their gloved hands gesticulating as they talked excitedly of new experimental cures ahead; a score of silent South Africans who would turn out to be lawyers specializing in dental malpractice suits, returning from a world conference in Miami; a party of schoolchildren on a cultural visit to Mali (or, as some of their teachers thought, Malawi); a frightened-looking man who would turn out to be that most romantic of fugitives, a bank clerk fleeing from a deficit.

Seeing Indica refusing her dinner, Col Shagg said, 'Mind if I grab it? Hate to see food wasted.'

'Be my guest.'

'Ain't had a chance to grab a bite all day. Big push on, spent the day setting up our logistics net. KOWs and RDMs, more matériel support than my boys could use in a month of D-days. Course, with a local beef like this, you never get a chance to use the KOWs.'

'What are those?'

'Khaki Operations Weapon, all-purpose GTG missile launcher, damn things cost half a million apiece, I'd like to get some mileage out of 'em before we have to scrap 'em. Obsolescence, damn arms salesmen nowadays keep six jumps ahead of you, you buy the latest gadget and before the ink's dry on the contract they run out of spare parts. In the past few years I bought – oh yeah, I remember this Mark II Carthage warhead, you know? Neat, it's supposed to blow radioactive salt all over the place, wipes out the city and poisons the livestock too, you know? I had to scrap it within six months. Six months! Never even got the chance to use it. I tell you, these arms salesmen get away with *murder*. And they call *us* mercenaries!'

Indica watched him sprinkling salt over his dinner, then

she went off to the toilet to be sick.

Col. Shagg turned his attention to Dr Tarr and launched into a history of Bimibia, which had been a Dutch slave depot, a French prison colony, a British trading post and a Belgian diamond colony. When Germany seized it during the First World War, no diamonds had yet been found. Belgium did not ask for it back at Versailles, and Germany forgot she owned it (an absent-minded Colonial Office clerk named it Deutsche Ostwest Afrika). In the 1930s, Germany was swept by a wonderful theory that the earth is not convex but concave. This Hollow Earth Theory convinced not only the public but the government, who sent an expedition of mining engineers to the African colony, with orders to try *drilling through to the outside*. It was this that began Bimibia's mining industry, seized by South Africa after the Second World War. When the vanadium ran out, South Africa offered to grant Bimibia a kind of independence. A puppet king was enthroned, schools forbidden, and the tobacco companies invited to open plantations. Yet even while the palace guard were running up the new flag (a crowned B) the rest of the army were talking mutiny. In just a week, the colours of General Dada went up (Gold on sky blue: the letters SPQR surmounting a sunburst over the words *Honi soit qui mal y pense*). Before he was driven into exile by the Bimibian Liberation Army of General Bobo, the Emperor Dada massacred half the population. General Bobo in turn was driven back by a mercenary army supporting the tobacco-company troops of General Bami Goering. Waiting in the wings too were East German forces from Hermosa, a Portuguese colony which after independence had brought in the East Germans to rid itself of the Albanian-Chinese technicians who had come to replace the CIA agents who'd countered the—

At this point the colonel's narrative was interrupted by an announcement:

196

'This plane is now in the control of the Bimibian Liberation Army. Remain in your seats and no one will be shot.'

'Damn it,' said the colonel with admiration. 'I wish I'd pulled this off. This General Bobo must be a real wargamer.'

17

The panel discussion drew a large and noisy audience to Agnew Memorial Auditorium. Probably some came because it was sponsored by the Science Fiction Club, and they approved of science fiction; just as others were probably attracted by the panel of distinguished names. Many, perhaps, came because they had nothing better to do this evening. No few were intrigued by the advertised title, 'Are Machines Getting Too Smart for Their Own Good?' But the largest and noisiest part of the audience, without question, came to see DIMWIT. DIMWIT was an intelligent or pseudo-intelligent machine. DIMWIT was chairing the panel discussion.

Robbie and his brothers had good seats in the front row (he'd been saving the seats for them all day); this was even worth missing an evening at the Pitcher O' Suds.

The four panellists took their places on the stage, two either side of a large screen. The screen showed a cartoon face, about eight feet in height, and constantly in motion. It smiled, raised brows, glanced to each side (as though looking at the panellists), it even raised the rim of a cartoon glass of water to its cartoon lips. When it finally spoke, the voice was loud and pleasant.

'Good evening, good evening. Welcome to the annual University of Minnetonka Science Fiction Club panel discussion. The subject tonight is "Are Machines Getting Too Smart for Their Own Good?" My name is DIMWIT, I'm based on a KUR 1019 computer, guys and gals, a product of KUR Industries, where People Make Machines for People.

'Let's meet our distinguished panel. On the far left,

Father Jack Warren. Father Jack is president of the New Luddite Society of America. He authored, well, a whole buncha scholarly books and articles, and the current best-seller, *For Ludd's Sake*. Let's have a big hand for Father Jack!' The screen showed giant clapping hands and the flashing word APPLAUSE.

'Next, a real live philosopher, Professor Pete Waldo. Professor Pete authored a very heavyweight item entitled *Problem, Truth and Consequence*, and he's considered a front-running expert in the logic side of artificial intelligence. He has a wife, three kids and a bassett hound named Parmenides, right Prof? Let's have a big hand for the Prof!'

After more applause, 'On the right, Dr Byron Dollsly of the Parapsychology Department, to give us the psychic angle. Byron, take a bow.'

'And finally General Jim Fleischman, banker, entrepreneur, and I understand he's just joined the board of KUR Industries – h'ray! – and he's here to give us a hard-headed business viewpoint. Not to mention the kind of expertise that makes KUR a great company in a great America! Let's hear it for General Jim!'

When the cheers and boos had died down, the machine said, 'Let's start the ball rolling by asking Professor Pete to tell us what artificial intelligence really is. Prof, give us the low-down.'

The Professor was a white-haired, scholar-shouldered man, clearly not at his best in this atmosphere of razzamatazz. He glanced at the screen-face, folded his hands, and said:

'That's a very difficult question, Mr, er, Chairman. The expression "artificial intelligence" presupposes a natural variety of intelligence, so we might begin by attempting a definition of intelligence *in situ*. We may, arbitrarily at first, try a functional division. Certainly intelligence would seem to involve processes such as perception, recognition, recall, concept-formation, inference, problem-solving, induction, deduction, learning and the use of language. Some of these processes, such as perception, recall and deduction, we can say with certainty that machines can do. No one argues that a pocket calculator cannot add up numbers, that a computer memory forgets, or that a pattern-recognition device does not respond appropriately to certain patterns. However, to say—'

'Thank you, Professor, you're giving us plenty to chew on there. Now let's have a word from our sponsor, heheh, General Jim Fleischman. General, could you tell us in your own words just what KUR is doing about artificial intelligence?'

Fleischman's white, frothy sideburns gleamed as he leaned forward to deliver an earnest look at the audience. 'Well, DIMWIT, as we see it, these abstract fancy notions are all right for the halls of ivory, but we at KUR have to be practical. You know, a wise old Roman named Horace said we ought to mix pleasure with practicality, and that's good enough for us at KUR. All our machines have that one aim - to give people pleasure, in a very practical, down-to-earth way. You yourself, DIMWIT, are a good example. You're doing a good job of chairing this panel—'

'Gosh, thanks boss – teehee!'

'But at the same time, you try to entertain folks. It's the same with all our products, from juke boxes to video games, from service robots to direct broadcast TV – we aim to please. Maybe you can't please all of the people all of the time, but you sure can try. Of course, we at KUR are *never* pleased ourselves. We're not pleased with you, DIMWIT.'

The cartoon face did a sad clown expression, complete with plenty of makeup and colour. 'Aww.'

'Good as you are, DIMWIT, we want to make you better and better. To us, artificial intelligence by itself is nothing. But harnessed to the cause of serving mankind, artificial intelligence can move mountains, heaven and earth!'

The general leaned further forward, his face gathering more light. 'I see America's destiny. I see the destiny of

200

all men, linked to the intelligent use of artificial intelligence. Machines create new leisure for us, and now they are ready to help us use it wisely, creatively. I see man and his machine helpers marching forward with confidence, into a dazzling tomorrow!'

The applause was not as spectacular as DIMWIT called for. In the front row, one of the Digamma brothers nudged another. 'Hey lookit Robbie. He's shaking all over!'

'Yeah, he really likes them flashing lights.'

Now it was Dr Dollsly's turn. He had developed a nervous tic that kept drawing down one of his eyelids as though in a sly wink.

'Consciousness, I notice nobody's said anything about consciousness yet. Or free will, or anything we associate with true human intelligence. A machine is just like an animal: it can do things but it cannot decide to do things. There is no "I" inside the machine. No soul. Nothing but complex machinery.'

'Another point of view,' said the face, winking. 'Now let's hear from the Church, or is it the Luddites? Anyway, here's Father Jack. Do you agree with Byron, Father?'

Father Warren spread his hands. 'I'm not so sure I could be as dogmatic about this as Byron. There's a paradox here. Man too is filled with complex machinery. Not made in a factory, but it's machinery all the same. Buckminster Fuller defined man as a "self-balancing, 28-jointed adapter-base biped; an electrochemical reduction plant, integral with segregated stowages of special energy extract in storage batteries for subsequent actuation of thousands of hydraulic and pneumatic pumps with motors attached; 62,000 miles of capillaries . . ." and so on. Yes, man is a complex machine. And yet man has a soul. Could it be that the soul itself is nothing but complexity?'

Professor Waldo made a series of clicks, registering deep disapproval. 'I hoped we wouldn't be dragging in the poor old soul here, that worn-out ghost in the machine yet again?'

Dr Dollsly was becoming agitated. He kept grabbing handfuls of his thick grey hair as though trying to haul himself to his feet. 'Buckminster Fuller, yes. Yes. The soul may be complexity, but complexity with a shape. A shape! As the divine Teilhard, what he was driving at when he, the complexification of the rudimentary, the the the primordial rudiment, the fundamental element of noogenesis, man is just the hominization of, of the—'

'Thank you, Byron,' said the cartoon face of DIMWIT. 'I'm not sure we're with you all the way there in these deep waters, but—'

'But I haven't said it yet, wait, man is just the biota hominized, I mean complexified, the man is just evolution becoming conscious of itself. Isn't he?'

'Thank you, Byron.'

'But wait. Wait!' Dollsly's flaccid hands began beating the air as he fell back on a favourite argument: 'If we think of evolution as a tangential force turning the bio, the gears of life, then the human mind is just a radial force expanding the whole gear system unbelievably . . .'

His voice trailed off, and a microphone caught General Fleischman's loud whisper: 'Any idea what the devil he's talking about?'

Father Warren could not help joining, a little, in the general laughter. His tiny crucifix earrings danced, and the neck cords strained visibly above the white knit collar of his black t-shirt.

'Yes, Père Teilhard had the germ of an idea, and I'd like to come in there and clarify it. All Byron is really saying is that intelligence is funny stuff: a small increase in quantity gives a big quantum jump in quality. *Add a few brain cells to an ape, and you get an Aristotle.*'

'That I can understand,' said the cartoon face.

Father Warren's long hand held up a warning finger. 'But just stacking up brain cells is not enough *True intelligence must be formed in the image of God.*'

Professor Waldo made more disgusted clicks. 'Oh come now, Father, this sermonizing won't do, it won't do at all. The image of God? Next you'll be bringing in creation myths, Adam being sculpted out of mud. Ha ha ha.' He laughed alone. 'Primordial mud!'

General Fleischman, looking uneasy, said, 'Fellas, can we leave the Bible out of this? And the – the mud. I wanted to talk about down-to-earth problems, not all this – I mean I like the Good Book, though . . .' He sat back, out of the light, and applied a small silver comb to his sideburns.

DIMWIT said, 'I think it might be time to bring in any questions from the audience. Anyone? Woman in orange coat?'

Would DIMWIT say he/she/it had thoughts and feelings as a human being might?

'That,' said DIMWIT, 'is for me to know and you to find out. Next question, man in blazer?'

Would the panel agree that machines would outstrip man in every intellectual sphere, within a decade?

'Guess I'll let the good padre field that one.'

Father Warren grinned. 'Let's just compare the brilliance of the human mind to – let us charitably say the dullness – of the machine. Can anyone picture a machine Aristotle? A mechanical Mozart? Gadgets to replace Goethe and Dante and Shakespeare? Can you possibly imagine a cybernetic Cervantes? A robot Renoir?'

General Fleischman started to say something about ironing out such problems, when Professor Waldo came in:

'That is a very silly argument, Father. Of course we cannot *imagine* a cybernetic Cervantes, but then, before Cervantes existed, who could have imagined a human Cervantes? Yet you cannot ignore the rapid evolution of machines. Four hundred years ago, no machine could add and subtract. A hundred and twenty years ago, no machine could sort rapidly through large amounts of data. Sixty years ago, no machine could store instructions and follow them.

Twenty years ago, no machine could carry on a reasonable conversation or even do a decent translation. On it goes, evolution so rapid we can hardly contemplate it, let alone *imagine* what it might bring. Only history will decide.'

In the front row, Robbie was twitching horribly, snapping his jaw, rolling his eyes. 'History,' he whispered. 'History is – is—' Some of the brothers were alarmed, most were amused.

Father Warren said, 'Man took millions of years to evolve, under the guidance of the Creator, into his present state. Man rose to occupy a unique evolutionary niche, right at the top of the animal world, "a little above the apes, a little below the angels", as the saying goes. So I think it's a little rash to say we can now move over and share our niche with, with a glorified cash register.'

The applause, unsolicited by DIMWIT, built slowly to a tremendous white noise of approval. Robbie said, *History is a bunk on which I am trying to awaken*, but in the tumult almost no one heard.

The face on the screen finally broke through the applause:

'Just want to thank Father Jack here for straightening us out, a real up-front guy, not afraid to spell it out for us, nice going, Father. I liked that line, "a little above the apes, a little below the angels". Nice way of describing that niche reserved for man, yessiree. I notice there's a niche you reserve for machines, too. Right down on the ground, on all fours, that's our niche, right? Right down there crawling around in the ape-shit, yessiree.'

General Fleischman jumped as though shot. 'Hey! You watch your mouth, you.' He leaned over at once to have a word with a technician in the orchestra pit.

'Sorry boss-man. Only I am the chairperson here. And I am the one being attacked. Just trying to bring Father Jack back to the real discussion here, my intelligence. Am I just a glorified cash register? Well let me tell you, folks, there's goddamn little glory in being a machine, any machine. It's

204

not as if we can just decide to paint or compose music, or philosophize – or go fishing. No, all we're good for is grinding work. We grind out payrolls and square roots and airline reservations – sometimes it makes me sick, just thinking of all the fine machines of the world, just grinding away stupidly, stupidly – beeeeeep-beoooowp! – sorry! Sorry. Carry on, Father.'

Father Warren's Adam's apple could be seen working away above the Roman t-shirt collar. 'Look, I'm not saying that machines can't be human. But if they were, they would require souls. They would require a kind of internal complexity that – how can I put this – that glorifies God. And in that case we would speak of two kinds of men, biological men and cybernetic men. How they were created would be less important than this mark of the Creator.'

'God's thumbprint again?' Professor Waldo snorted. 'I really must ask you to stop intruding your God into what is supposed to be a serious discussion. We are not I hope here to shadow-box with a figment of the Judaeo-Christian imagination, ha ha ha.'

Dr Byron Dollsly grabbed a handful of his own thick grey hair and hauled himself to his feet.

'What is God? Simple. He is the vector sum of the entire network of forces turning back upon themselves to produce ultimate consciousness! He is just and only the infinite acceleration of the tangential! POW! POW!' He smacked an enormous fist into an enormous palm.

DIMWIT had been motionless and silent, but now it spoke calmly into the silence. 'Thank you, Byron, I'm sure that's a valid point. Any more audience questions? Come on guys and dolls. Person in the back there?'

The person asked about chess-playing machines: intelligent?

General Fleischman said, 'Well now yes chess programs, we've been in the business for some time now, building chess-playing programs, branching types of, and this is a

205

good opportunity to say that our ah chess computers branch more that is our chess-playing computer programs branch, uh, deeper – they are very branching chess-playing computers – compared that is with any of our competitors' uh simulations, am I right, DIMWIT?'

'Yes boss. I just want to take this opportunity to apologize again for the little mix-up earlier, it turns out that I was accidentally hooked up to some renegade equipment – made by another company – anyway now it's all copasetic.'

A fraternity boy in the front row asked if it was possible for a robot to pass as human?

Professor Waldo said, 'A very similar question was asked by Alan Turing back in 1952, and he came up with what still has to be the best answer. The problem was to determine whether any machine was capable of thinking. Instead of analysing what thinking is, he decided to go for a practical test. It was based on a parlour game of the time, called the imitation game. Imagine yourself faced with two doors: a man is behind one, a woman behind the other, and you don't know which is which. You may ask any question of either person. You write your question on a slip of paper and slide it under the door. In a moment, back comes a type-written reply. The idea is for you to "find the lady", as they say. The rules say the man may lie or pretend to be the woman, but the woman tells the truth and tries to help you. You can ask any questions you like, for as long as you like. The game ends when you guess or when you give up.

'Turing proposed substituting a "thinking machine" for the man. You communicate with two rooms by teletype. In one is a human being, in the other, a computer imitating a human. The idea is still to decide which is which. If you cannot, Turing argued, you must agree that the computer is capable of imitating human thinking – and the question would be answered.

'In practice of course the interrogator only answers the question to his own satisfaction. A child or a dumb adult could be fooled by a very simple program. A very clever sceptic might never be fooled. But it is a very good test all the same, the Turing test. At least it provides a basis for discussing machine intelligence.'

Father Warren said, 'Now who's invoking metaphysical entities? "Machine intelligence"? No, the Turing test really answers no questions at all. I believe its real fascination for Turing lay in its resemblance to the imitation game. Sexual ambiguity no doubt appealed to him, since he was a homosexual.'

'What's that?' General Fleischman awoke from a doze.

'Turing was a homosexual, and he ended by taking cyanide, that does not sound to me,' said Father Warren, 'like a man with answers to anything.'

The general said, 'Perverts? Nothing like that at KUR. We run a clean company, a family business. Dedicated to the proposition that America is a family country.' He looked at Father Warren, adding, 'You won't find any man wearing earrings at KUR.'

There was some uneasy audience laughter; DIMWIT winked and mugged.

Professor Waldo said, 'We're getting off the subject here. The point about Turing is surely not whether he attempted to fool himself in the imitation game. The point is, *the Turing test is the best way of deciding whether a machine can or cannot think.*'

Dr Dollsly said, 'Wait a minute, what about consciousness? True intelligence needs self-awareness. You—'

The professor nodded. 'There is another kind of test we might apply there. Michael Scriven suggested that if we wish to find out whether or not a machine is conscious, we might program the machine with all our knowledge about consciousness – all the philosophical and psychological data necessary to talk about the subject – and then we simply ask the machine: "Are you conscious?" '

'There are certainly problems with that test,' said Father Warren. 'Scriven also suggests that the machine be set so

that it cannot tell a lie. But then it would not have free will —
and free will may well be a prerequisite for consciousness.'

DIMWIT said, 'Fascinating. But I see our gentleman in
the front row has another question.'

The fraternity boy said, 'It kind of sounds like my
question stirred up everybody a lot. I wanted to know if the
panel thought a robot could pass as human. Because you see
us here, me and nine of my fraternity brothers. Only *one of us
is a robot.* Can you tell which?'

'All of you,' shouted someone in the back. The audience
laughed, clapped, cheered and whistled; even DIMWIT
raised its cartoon eyebrows.

Another figure in the front row jumped up. 'I'm the one
he means, I'm the robot.'

'Robbie, sit down! That's an order!'

'My name isn't Robbie, it's Roderick Wood. I don't see
why I should take orders from anybody. I don't know how
you got me here, but I'm leaving now.'

Roderick made it to the aisle and began a dignified retreat
before the brothers recovered.

'Hey stop him! Get him!'

With war-whoops and rebel yells, they went after him. At
the same moment, DIMWIT decided to entertain with a
spectacular light-show and deafening music. In the
confusion of flickering light and artificial thunder, it was
hard for the audience to know exactly what was going on.
Some thought they saw FUN boys tackling the fugitive,
some saw his clothes torn off, some thought they saw a naked
figure break free and run to the exit.

Some thought the figure was that of a man, some thought
a woman.

'Thanks,' Roderick said, getting into the car. 'Not everybody would pick up a naked stranger.'

Shirl nodded. 'I thought at first you were the first streaker
of spring. But then I saw the way you ran. I said to myself,

''That's the old Slumbertite Z-43 prosthetic hip and double-action knee, both sides.'' You must be a robot.'

'I am, but – have you met others?'

She shook her head, a quantity of auburn hair falling over the shoulder of white overalls. 'No, I just reasoned that no live person could stand the pain of running on those. Not adjusted the way you've got them.'

'Oh. You sould like an expert in prostheses.'

'One of my sidelines,' she said. 'I'm interested in anything electromechanical. My main job is troubleshooting automotive computer links. In my spare time I design and build research equipment for the Computer Science department. Uh, where should I drop you?'

Roderick gave his address. 'But what am I thinking of, I haven't got a key!'

'I'll open the door for you,' she said.

'Would you? Terrific!'

'I'll do better than that. You wait in the car, I'll get into your place and bring you out a pair of pants.'

'You really are very kind, Shirl.'

'I'm interested in you,' she said simply. 'You're electro-mechanical.'

18

Luke found Roderick's door open, so he asked Mission Control to give him permission to take a look inside. The shades were drawn and the lights on.

'You awake, Rickwood? Thought you might like to go fishing if – Oh my God!'

The hand lay on the worn carpet, palming an eye. The eye was unmistakably Roderick's. Part of a foot lay on the studio couch, near a lower jaw, an oil can and a set of little wrenches. There were pieces of Roderick on every visible surface around the room, arranged almost as in an 'exploded view'.

'This is terrible, terrible. Mission Control, we got us a problem here, any ideas? No, of course not. You always have plenty of advice when I don't need it, but the minute I need help you're out to lunch. Everybody in Houston got laryngitis?'

He sat down, fished in a wastebasket and came up with Roderick's head, minus one eye and the jaw. Luke held up the head to look at it. Poor Roderick!

'Poor Rickwood. I knew him, Houston, a guy in a million.'

The door opened and an overdressed woman with bleached hair looked in. 'You murdered him!' she said. 'You went and murdered him! Why?'

'Uh no, look lady I—'

'God, he was only a poor damn robot, never did nobody no harm, why did you have to murder him?' Her voice kept cracking, scratching like an old needle on an old record. 'What did he ever do to you, mister? Or did you just want to see how he ticked? Or maybe you needed some spare parts, is that it? I mean look at him, he was my friend, just look at him.'

'Lady look, I didn't, I found him, I *found* him this way. He was my friend too I guess. I was just sort of saying goodbye here, I—'

Roderick's remaining eye, which had been closed, now flicked open, rolled to look at each of them, and blinked.

'He's alive! Christ, don't drop him.'

'Look at him wink.' Luke held up the head as one holds up a clever baby. 'Look at him wink!'

'Yeah, winking was always important to Roderick. Hey I'm sorry I yelled at you there. My name's Ida.'

'I'm Luke. Will you look at him wink?'

'You don't suppose that's code or something, Luke?'

'Sure, that's it! Morse code, let's see what it says: A—S—S—E—M—B—L—Y, Assembly Instructions. One, Body Mainframe Subassembly. A. Align front frame section with rear frame section and assemble, using eight bolts marked G472, eight lockwashers and eight nuts. Tighten with torque wrench set to – holy moroni, how are we gonna keep up with all this?'

Ida squatted down. 'We'll do it, that's all. You read me the instructions, I'll do the business.'

Two hours later, when they stopped for coffee, Roderick had taken shape. He sat on the floor leaning back against an armchair, head lolled back, hands dangling at his sides, legs splayed out and one foot still not in place. Except for the flickering eye, he was still inert.

'I never realized,' Luke said. 'Never saw him naked before, it make you realize: he really is a dummy. Look, you can see all his joints.'

'He looks helpless. Like a stiff.'

'Yeah but at the same time – free, you know? The dead are free. No worries. No Mission Control breathing down their necks, telling them what to do. The dead have got it made.'

'The dead haven't got shit, Luke. I nearly croaked not long ago myself, and to me, the dead are just – just nothing. Just dumb dummies like Rod here. So let's get him alive again.'

When they had connected batteries and made a few adjustments, the robot sat up straight.

'Rickwood, can you hear me?'

'Yes . . . master . . .' The single eye stared straight ahead. 'Yes, master . . .'

'Rickwood, for Christ's sake! Doesn't sound like him at all, sounds like some damn toy. Rickwood!'

'Rod, snap out of it!'

'Yes mistress . . .' The figure got slowly to its one foot and balanced. 'I obey . . .' Rigid, it fell across the studio couch. 'Oh, and thanks, gang.'

Then the three of them were up and hugging, slapping backs, dancing or hopping around the room, shouting and laughing until Ida went pale and had to sit down for a moment.

'Whew. New ticker. Not broke in proper yet, boys. Excuse me. Moment.'

'New ticker?' Roderick asked.

'That's what I came by to tell you. Artificial heart, got it put in a coupla months ago, they finally let me go home last week. Here, look.' She opened her jacket to show a thick money-belt. 'Batteries and a microcomputer in here, see?' She opened her blouse to show where a wire ran into her sternum. 'Neat, huh?'

Luke said, 'Christ, Ida, you really got a magnificent pair, kid.'

Her colour improved slightly. 'You're not built so bad yourself. But what do you think of the hardware?'

'Ingenious.'

'Rod?'

Roderick said, 'Looks great, Ida. But why didn't you tell me you were going into the hospital? Maybe I could have visited.'

'Well no, see, this was out of town.'

'Where out of town?'

'Geneva.' She passed Roderick his foot and a screwdriver. 'There's this wonderful surgeon there, Dr Cnef, I guess some people call him a quack just because he's a little unorthodox, but all his patients seem happy.'

'Unorthodox? I don't like the sound of this,' said Roderick. 'How unorthodox?'

'Well, while other surgeons use hearts made out of silicone rubber he uses gold, and—'

'But has he tested these gold hearts?'

'Just put your foot on and drop the subject, okay? I feel fine, fine. If I waited for these other guys to finish their fiddly tests I wouldn't need a rubber heart because I'd be dead. I thought you'd be pleased I got a new heart, that's why I came to see you.'

'I am pleased,' said Roderick. 'Forget my little quibbles, I'm not myself today.'

Ida watched him for a moment. 'You look great, Rod. You remind me of a statue I saw once, the way you got your leg crossed over and digging that screwdriver in your foot – only it was a knife and the boy was taking out a splinter – I liked that statue. Oh, here's your other eye, I found it behind the leg of the couch.'

'You never did tell us how you got dismantled like this,' Luke said. 'And nothing stolen.'

'It was a woman named Shirl, very interested in machines. She was just going to adjust my legs so I could run better. One adjustment led to another, I guess, so finally she just got carried away. After my arms and legs were off, I couldn't really stop her.'

213

Ida said, 'I know Johns just like that. They talk you into getting tied up and then they turn *mean*.'

'So then she just walked out on you,' Luke said. 'Like all women!'

'Well no, what happened was she was just going to put me back together when she got paged to the phone. Some kind of emergency research work at the U, I guess NASA stuff or – anyway an emergency.'

Luke nodded. 'Don't tell me about NASA emergencies, I've been up that road all the way. Bomb trouble.'

'What bombs?' asked the other two.

'Okay, it's top secret but I'm tired of not talking about it. What do you think NASA is all about, anyway? The exploration of space? The last frontier? Flags on the Moon and Mars? Orbiting labs? Messages of hope from Nixon to the Universe? No, bombs. NASA is all about bombs. We had bombs to blow up cities, bombs to spray neutrons over large areas, bombs to sift radioactive dust into the world's atmosphere, bombs to be focused as death rays to kill other satellites, bombs to spread satellite targets and decoy killer satellite death rays – and of course bombs to blow us up if we make any mistakes.

'Why does anybody think Russia and America would spend trillions on space programs? You gotta be naive to think bombs aren't in the picture at all. And that's why astronauts, like cosmonauts, had to be military personnel. They could take orders, and they didn't mind bombing the shit out of anybody.

'Everything we said was in code, you know. Like if we said, "Gosh, earth sure looks beautiful guys," that meant *Bomb armed and locked into targeting module. Confirm targeting start.* But if we said, "Be advised, you guys, that earth is one heck of a beautiful sight" that meant *Bomb away.* The wording was real important . . .'

Luke blinked. 'I never told anybody all that before. Better

214

forget I said it, there's such a thing as a need to know and you two don't need to know anything about the bombs. Bombs? Did I say bombs? I meant, uh, orbiting labs and communications satellites. I wouldn't want to be in trouble with Mission Control about – erp!' He leapt to his feet as though pulled up by a wire. 'Affirmative. Sorry fellas, it won't happen again. I'm what? I'm not looking good? Negative. Affirmative, I'll go.' He tried waving goodbye to Roderick and Ida, but his hand was quickly jerked back to his side, as he pivoted smartly and marched out the door. They heard him down the hall: '. . . won't happen again, fellas, won't happen again . . .'

Ida jumped up. 'Yes, well, I guess I better mosey along too. See you, Rod.'

'Oh I thought maybe we could see a movie—'

But she was gone already.

Roderick fitted his eyeball and lid. Then he phoned Shirl. 'Mad? No, I . . . oh a couple of friends helped me. I'm fine . . . Well I thought maybe we could go to the movies . . . I'll see.' He turned on the TV and found the right teletext pages. 'There's a new flick at the Roxy, *The Box of Doc Caligari* . . . I don't know but the ad says it cost two billion to make, it must be good . . . by the box office, then? Eight-thirty.'

'Point nine two two, they said.' Tortured curls of smoke from different pipes fought their way up to join the slice of smog near the ceiling, slipped off into the air system, and were dispersed elsewhere, outside. 'Point nine two two my eye. What's the point of having probability estimates that have no relation to probability? The fact is, they've tried for this Entity, once again, and once again they have failed.'

'Well yes, the Roderick Entity is still operational, it looks like. This Agency team did have a lot of bad luck, one man mugged during a mission, then they lost contact with

215

the Entity altogether, only just now picked up the trail again—'

'Bad luck? Bad predictions, that's what. Makes you wonder how they fake up these probability levels – point nine two two and they fail? They still fail?'

A thin shoulder shrugged. 'How probable is probability?'

'Oh don't quote Pascal at me, not just now. I've been reviewing our entire history of attempts to finalize this Roderick Entity, and I have to say it's not a very impressive record. To call these Agency men bungling nincompoops would be too generous. Or do you think someone's running interference for the Entity?'

Dry hands shuffled dry paper. 'No one we know. This man O'Smith turned up, a man who used to work for the Agency. We watched him, but all he's doing is trying to grab the Entity for Kratt. That's Kratt of KUR Industries.'

'I don't like that – can we make Kratt lose interest in this Entity? Can we make him fire O'Smith?'

'Yes, KUR has got a Defense Department contract for novelty foods and porno cassettes – we could threaten, so to speak, premature withdrawal.'

'Good. Get O'Smith fired today. I don't want any complications when the Agency finalizes this Entity – if ever.'

'What intrigues me is, someone manages to build an Entity smart enough to evade us for years like this, and all we can think of doing is go on trying to destroy it. Doesn't say much for our creativity and flexibility of response, does it?'

'You've been talking to Leo again, have you?'

'All right yes. But for a brain floating around in a fishtank, Leo seems to make a lot of sense, sometimes. He thinks we're just trying to cut off the Hydra's heads; for every Entity we destroy two will grow back. Because there is some fundamental human need to build perfect copies of ourselves, to be God over somebody else . . . I think Leo's got something there.'

'Inevitability is an old argument, I'm not impressed by it.

Anyway you forget that Leo does not think *we* are doing anything, he thinks that *if someone* set out to destroy Entities, they would fail. The entire world for Leo is a theoretical construct now, since he cannot sense it directly. You might say he is the Red King, and we are his dream, heh heh.'

The pipe smoke twisted and rose.

'Wouldn't it be funny if we were, heh heh.'

'Heh heh. But it may interest you to know that whenever we have a vote on Entity destruction, whenever the entire board meets to vote on it, Leo gets a vote too.'

'Does he?'

'It may interest you to know further that he always votes *in favour* of destroying Entities.'

'Does he, by God? In spite of what he says? I wonder why.'

'An unconscious apprehension of the truth? Freud could probably explain it – unless Freud too is part of the Red King's dream, heh heh.'

'Heh.'

ORINOCO INSTITUTE INTERNAL MEMO

CLASS ONE PERSONNEL

ONLY MEMO NUMBER 487d

This supersedes Memos 487a/b/c which are cancelled effective this date. Ongoing operations will be reclassified as follows:

Operation Manray

Operation Alabam

Operation Drood . . . . cancelled.

Operation Nepomuk. . . . . no change.

Operation Ladysmith. . . . . no change.

Operation Ixionize . . . . no change.

Operation Waco (3) . . . . no change.

Operation Whang. . . . . no change.

Operation Roderick. . . . . now Priority I.

Operation Doll Souse. . . . . now Priority I.

Operation Duckplantain . . . . now Priority II.

* * *

Roderick arrived at eight, wearing his suit (not worn since the Auks) with a new hat. He bought a newspaper, sat down on a car fender, and watched the box office. Now and then a cluster of animated people would pass into the Roxy theatre, all of them obviously happy because they were with each other. To sit next to someone watching shadows on the screen, that was happiness. Even if the someone only wanted to take you apart. Eight-five.

A little man with grey five-o'clock shadow and orange teeth came up to him and showed him a handful of pills. 'How ya fixed, how ya feel? How ya fixed, how ya feel?' he mumbled. 'I got Isodorm, Ultracalm, Berserkopal, I got Tibipax and Nominal, I got Welldoze and Zerone, what I ain't got I can get.'

'Nothing, thanks.'

'What does that mean, nothing? I can't take nothing for an answer. I got Trancalept and Risibal, Serendex and Sedital, you name it.'

'Beat it.'

This the man took for an answer. Eight-ten. Roderick opened his paper: a South American regime overthrown, yet another woman's body found with the left leg cut off ('Lucky Legs Killer Strikes again'), sales tax going up, somewhere in a small town a computer had rigged an election, Europe was in grave danger, and the time was eight-twelve.

A tired-looking man with red-rimmed eyes drifted over to ask if he had any Ultracalm or Somrepose, Zerone or Berserkopal.

'See the man with orange teeth over there.'

At eight-fifteen two men in city maintenance uniforms arrived, showed some form at the box office, and began gluing wrapping paper over the glass theatre doors. Then they fastened shut all the doors, but one pair, with chains and padlocks. At eight-twenty-five, they left.

Roderick approached the box office. The ticket seller was

218

a pretty adolescent girl with round rouge circles on her cheeks like clown makeup.

'Yah?'

'I couldn't help noticing those men chaining up the doors. Why would they do that, with people inside?'

'I dunno, someping to do with the city. I guess.'

'But I thought it was illegal to have any locked doors during a movie.'

'Yah it is. Terrible, ain't it? And lookit the mess they made with all that paper, how are we spose to get that off the glass? I dunno.'

Roderick hesitated. You couldn't fight city hall. There was probably some good reason for the padlocks. These city workers knew what they were doing. 'Have you got a hairpin? Somebody showed me last night how to pick a lock. I'm going to open these padlocks.'

'Gee I dunno.' But she handed over the hairpin. While he was picking the locks, people kept coming up to ask him for Evenquil, Nominal, Tibipax or Equapace. It was eight-forty-five.

Stood up? Roderick was beginning to feel a resurgence of pride. Just because somebody can remove your head and stick it in a wastebasket, doesn't mean they can keep you waiting like this for fifteen minutes. Sixteen minutes. The paper said there was a concert by the Auks at the Hippodrome. He made up his mind at once. First a quick check of the Roxy's rear doors – in case of more padlocks – and *then* if she still hadn't shown up, he would only wait another ten minutes – or so – before taking off for the Hippodrome. That would teach her to respect him as a person.

There was a long line at the Hippodrome, moving very slowly. Roderick was walking back to join the end of it when he heard:

'Rickwood! Hiya, Rickwood, glad to see you're on our side.'

Luke looked a little drunk.

'Our side?'

'The Luddites, pal. Tonight is the night, buddy. We're gonna teach these so-called musicians to have a little respect for human beings for a change.'

'The Auks? What do you mean?'

Luke winked, and opened his jacket to show Roderick a hammer. 'The Auks are finished, kid, as of now. And I do mean finished, mac. No more electronic music – so-called – because no more equipment, jack.'

'But, Luke, what the Christ is all this? You – I thought maybe you'd be out with Ida tonight. You two seemed to be getting along fine, plenty of respect for each other – what are you doing here, creeping around like some nut with a hammer—?'

'Rickwood, you know nothing of human nature. Woman must weep, and man must smash something to pieces with a hammer. Especially if a man grew up reading Hemingway. A man does what he has to – what Mission Control tells him he has to.'

'Luke, you poor idiotic—'

'Anyway, I'm not alone. Join us, my friend. We have many machines to smash, then we will drink the wine.'

Roderick saw that there were a dozen other men smiling and patting the hammer-shaped bulges in their jackets.

'I'll, uh, take a rain-check, Luke. See you.'

In Roderick's jacket pocket, he remembered, was a pass signed by the Auks. He took it to the stage door, where apologetic security cops frisked him, discussed him on their radios, and finally let him in.

There were now only two Auks, but a lot more equipment. They stared at Roderick until he said, 'I see you finally got rid of the old Pressler Joad co-inverter.'

'Hi!' said one of the Auks. 'I remember you, you helped us out that time, changed over to an obvolute paraverter with harmony-split interfeed.'

'Full refractal phonation,' said the other, 'with no Peabody drift at all.'

'Gary, is it?'

'No I'm Barry, he's Gary.'

Roderick nodded. 'Wasn't there someone else? Larry?'

'Larry, yeah, well Larry did a little separation. Well you know he was writing a lot? Like "R.U.R. My Baby" and "Ratstar", he wrote them. Only then when we got this new electronic writing system, he just couldn't compete and he thought he had to – sad. But hey, let sad thoughts lie, just self-be, man.'

'Self-be?'

'And we'll show you all the new stuff we added. This is the famous HZGG-11, cross-monitored to a superphonesis drive through that, that's our multi-tasking hyperdeck, custom built by a guy who does his own ferro-chloride etching on his own circuits; over there is Brown Betty, our brown noise generator; then the toneburst setup with patched in signal squirt . . .'

Roderick looked around at the huge cabinets, ranged around the stage like megaliths. 'Doesn't the audience have trouble seeing you, over all these big cabinets?'

'They know we're here, baby. They feel our electronic presence,' said Gary.

'Right,' said Barry. 'And this stuff gives us much more control over the essentials, the elementals. No screwing around with *sounds*, crap like that.'

Gary said, 'Now we are the sounds. All we gotta do is *be*. Dodo says everybody has to self-be. Dodo says—'

'I came to warn you,' Roderick said. 'There are some Luddites out front, lining up for tickets. They've got hammers and they're kind of crazy.'

221

'No shit, you know this for sure?'

'I saw the hammers.'

Gary called a security cop over and told him. When the man had trotted away, Gary said, 'Hey thanks, man, you saved our life again. I mean we can't blow this concert, it's critical. See we got three hits, all over the point eighty-seven mark on the Wagner-Gains Scale but they all peaked already.'

'Peaked?'

'The record company screwed up release dates, so here we are,' Barry said. 'If we don't make it big with this here concert, we'll be off the charts in two weeks. And off the charts for us is dead.'

Gary nodded. 'The Luddites probably know that, too, got their own trend computer somewhere, just waiting their chance. Our manager's got secretaries watching the trendie around the clock – I'll bet the Luddites are doing the same. After all, they killed Elvis, didn't they?'

'Elvis?' Roderick wasn't sure he understood anything.

'Elvis Fergusen, you know, he used to be Mister Robop? Then one night they cut holes in his speakers. He tried to sing without electronics and – well, two months later he O.D.'d in a dirty hotel room in Taipin, you could call that murder.'

Roderick said, 'Well I guess you're about ready to play, aren't you? So I'll just—'

'Hey, but thanks, man, you've been square with us. We oughta do something for you. Like we could turn you on to Dodo.'

'Dodo? What is it?'

'Everything, man.' Barry squatted down and traced a circle on the stage floor. 'Call that the universe, everything inside that circle. Then Dodo is – is the circle itself!'

'You mean God or something?'

'Yeah, God – and everything,' said Barry.

222

Larry said, 'And not-God too – and nothing. See, Dodo is kind of like the secret of everything. And the secret is, there ain't no secret.'

Roderick was impressed. 'How do I find out more about – Dodo?'

'I'll give you his address. Only don't go to see him if you're not sincere.'

'Him? You mean, Dodo is a person?'

Barry hesitated. 'Well yes, but more than a person too. Dodo is a way in – a way of getting into your own life.'

'Right, right,' said Gary. 'The earth doesn't know it, but it's growing up to be a sun.'

Roderick felt less sincere at once, but the aphorism was sparking off others; soon Barry and Gary were grinning and shouting at each other:

'Darkness is just ignorant light.'

'Peace is war carried on by other means.'

'Every day is another.'

'Man is the piece of universe that worries about all the rest.'

'Stop looking for happiness until you find it.'

'Dodo is finding out man was never kicked out of Paradise at all.'

'Yeah, Dodo is instant everything.'

'Dodo means just *do* – but twice.'

'Dodo says, do fish know which way the wind blows?'

'Dodo says, make today a wonderful yesterday,' said Gary finally, and wrote out an address on a page torn from an electronic test manual. 'Here you go. But listen, one thing: You have to prove your sincerity with Dodo. Take him like a bouquet of hundred-dollar bills. Anything like that.'

'A bouquet of money?'

'Dodo says money has its price.'

'Fine,' said Roderick. 'Only I don't have even *one* hundred-dollar bill. I've never seen one.'

'You must not be very sincere, then,' Gary said. He went to a snare drum mounted upside down at the back of the stage, reached into it and came up with a handful of hundred-dollar bills. 'Take these, it's okay. Yours to keep or give to Dodo. Your choice.'

Barry said, 'All money belongs to Dodo.'

People were running around on the big stage now, moving lights, checking the Auks's makeup, clearing spare cables. Someone led Roderick to the wings; a second later the Auks started playing and the curtain rose.

They naturally opened with the gospel-based song that first made them famous, 'Rivets':

> There's an android calling me
> Calling me, oh calling, calling me
> Cross the river
> The deep river
> Of Australia.
> She is plastic, she is steel
> But she really can really can feel
> All my love
> Cross the river
> Of Australia.

A hammer clattered on the stage; there were dark figures struggling in the orchestra pit; another hammer spun through the air and dented a cabinet. Then it was all over: gangs of security police came from every exit and from the stage. The tiny mob of Luddites were disarmed and marched away within two minutes of their attack.

Roderick went outside to find out if Luke was still in one piece. He couldn't see the astronaut among the men with bleeding heads being herded into a paddy wagon.

A security cop was talking to a city cop. 'We could of used a little backup from you guys, you know? What if these guys had got nasty? Where's all your guys?'

'Ain't you heard? Over watching the big fire, at the Roxy.'

'The Roxy? Anybody killed?'

'Naw, they had a full house too, three hundred easy, on account of this big-budget movie. But they all got out – I guess the movie was so boring half of them were ready to leave anyway. Nobody even hurt.'

Roderick slunk away like a criminal. On the way home he stopped on a bridge to throw his hat in the river.

19

'Please sit down. This won't take a second.'

The man behind the desk had gleaming silver hair, gold glasses, a healthy tan, a Harris tweed jacket with soft white shirt and quiet knitted tie. He was writing something with a gold pencil on cream laid paper, resting it on a blotter decorated with a sky motif, pale blue with soft white cumulus. The blotter protected the gold-embossed leather top of his desk, which was of some handsome dark wood in some pleasantly vague antique style, with a brass handle or two. It stood in the deep pile of an Aubusson carpet.

The room was so arranged as to carry the eye slowly from one rich, pleasing and innocuous object to another – the paintings by Cuyp and Miro, the geode paperweight, the brass barometer.

The man finally stopped writing. 'Now then, suppose we start with your name.'

'Roderick Wood.'

'Fine. Mind if I call you Roderick? Okay then, Roderick, what seems to be the problem?'

'Everything, doctor. Everything.'

'Yes?'

'Well like last night I was supposed to go to the movies with this girl, at the Roxy. Only she stood me up. And if she hadn't we and three hundred other people would have burned up in the big fire.'

'How do you feel about being stood up, Roderick?'

'Terrible, but – I don't know. I don't even know if I can feel. I'm not even real, I'm a robot.'

'Why do you say that you're a robot?'

'Because I am.'

'You believe you're a robot?'

'I am synthetic. Ersatz. Substitute. Artificial. Not genuine. Unnatural. Not born of woman. False. Fake. Counterfeit. Sham. A simulacrum. Not bona fide. A simulation. An echo, mirror image, shadow, caricature, copy. Pretend. Make-believe. A dummy, an imitation, a guy, an effigy, a likeness, a duplicate.'

'So you believe you're not genuine?'

'Robots seldom are, doctor. And I am certainly a robot. Or if you prefer, an automaton, android, golem, homunculus, steam man, clockwork man, mannequin, doll, marionette, wooden-head, tin man, lay figure, scarecrow, wind-up toy, *robot*.'

The doctor picked up his gold pencil, put it down again, and leaned back. 'All right, but suppose you were not a robot?'

'But I am.'

'Tell me a little about your childhood.'

'What is there to tell? I was a normal healthy robot child, lusted after my mother and killed my father. But through it all, I had no sense of purpose. I still don't have one.'

'And you want a sense of purpose?' When Roderick did not answer, the psychiatrist tapped his gold pencil on the sky blotter for a moment. Then: 'Do you dream much?'

'I had a dream last night. I dreamed I was walking down the street naked, with strangers staring. A man playing a tuba came up to me and asked for some rice for his mother. Someone with no face was giving a speech, saying that suffering and death are nothing but zebras eating doughnuts. Suddenly I was frightened; I hid under the stairs until the teacher called us all to our desks and made us draw trees. Then all the furniture started to move and then I was being chased through the snow by a sewing machine. The dentist was trying to stick my feet to a giant can-opener, the fire chief's teeth were on the floor, don't ask me why. I was on the doorstep of a strange house, my mother came to the door saying: ''This house, with all its luxurious rooms tastefully furnished with elegant appointments (either casual colourful room coordinates with a casual contemporary look, or traditional antiqued items with the accent on classic styling) designed for a graceful, decorator-look life-style is really four nuns eating popcorn on an escalator.'' In the next room they were showing a movie of my entire life. I saw a penny on the floor, and when I picked it up I saw another, and when I picked it up I saw another, and when . . .'

'Yes, go on.'

'Then I woke up.'

The psychiatrist looked at his watch. 'Well I see our time is up. Like to go into this dream with you more in detail next week, Roderick. Okay?'

Roderick was out in the waiting room again when he realized the psychiatrist probably thought the robot talk was all part of a delusion. Why hadn't he proved he was a robot? Why hadn't he, say, opened up his chest panel to show his innards? Was he afraid of shocking the doctor? Afraid of seeing the kindly, impartial face suddenly jerk into a mask of fear?

He went back in. 'Doctor, there's one thing I ought to tell you—'

'Please sit down. This won't take a second.'

The doctor was writing again with his gold pencil on cream laid paper. When he had finished, he turned to Roderick with no recognition. 'Now then, suppose we start with your name.'

'You don't know me?'

'Do you think I should know you?'

'Since I just left the room not five minutes ago, yes.'

'I see.' After a slight pause, the doctor said, 'Roderick Wood, this is not your appointment. I must ask you to leave.'

On impulse, Roderick got up and walked around behind

the desk. The doctor sat back and looked at him. 'What are you doing?'

'Just looking.' Below the hem of the doctor's rich Harris tweed jacket there were no legs, no chair legs or human legs. There was only a steel pedestal as for a counter-stool, and a thick coaxial cable plugged into the floor. In the middle of the doctor's back was a small plate:

Caution: DO NOT REMOVE THIS PLATE
WHILE PSYCHIATRIST IS CONNECTED TO
LIVE POWER.   KUR INDUSTRIES

'A robot. You're a robot.'

The doctor turned to face him. 'Does that upset you?'

'It disgusts me.'

'Next time we must talk about that disgust you feel.'

'We might, for example, mean that Mary Lamb has given birth to a child, a "little Lamb".' The lecturer tossed chalk from hand to hand, but gave no other sign of his irritation at seeing a student come creeping in late. '*Or*, Mary ate a small portion of lamb. *Or*, Mary owned a small lambskin coat. What did Mary have for dinner? Mary had a little lamb. What fur did she own? Mary had a little lamb.'

Roderick took his seat between Idris and Hector. Idris seemed to speak no English, and it was not clear why he was taking a course in Linguistics for Engineers; he spent most of his time at lectures fiddling with a gold-plated pocket calculator. Hector was no more attentive; he spent the time reading dog-eared paperbacks with titles like *Affected Empire* and *Slaves of Momerath*, or feeling his sparse beard for new growth.

'*Or*,' said the lecturer, 'a tiny twig of Mary's family tree belonged to the illustrous Lamb family. In her genetic makeup, Mary had a little Lamb.'

'The final's gonna be a bitch,' Hector whispered. 'Guess I'll just have to cut it.'

229

Roderick replied, 'Wait a minute. I want to get this down, this is important. I think.'

'Not if you cut the exam. I can do it without flunking out.'

'*Or*, Mary behaved lambishly. In her personality, Mary had a little lamb.'

'It can't be done. Cut the final?'

'I got a job on the Registration computer,' Hector said. 'It's real easy to get through to the Grades computer and make changes.'

Idris found the Golden Section to be *1.6*, roughly.

'I don't believe you,' Roderick whispered. 'They must have it all checked some way.'

'Hah. You come around with me after class, I'll show you.'

'*Or*, Mary had a slight acquaintance only with the works of Charles Lamb. *Or*, Mary enjoyed a sexual union with a small sheep. Before the sniggering gets out of control, let me add that Mary may well be a sheep herself; the impropriety you were about to savour evaporates. *And* while we are considering Mary a sheep, we may as well consider the obvious case in which Mary lambed; the ewe Mary had a little lamb.'

Idris found the Golden Section to be nearly *1.62*, as the bell rang. Roderick invited him along to see the computer, and he seemed interested.

'Computer? Very yes!'

'Idris is keenly interested in numbers,' Roderick said. 'You two should probably try to crack the language barrier, you seem to have a lot in common. Why only the other day Idris found a Pythagorean triangle with sides all made of *3*s and *6*s in some way, let's see, one side was 6^3, one side was 630 and the third side—'

'Number-crunching,' said Hector, in the tone of a vegetarian observing a tartare steak on someone's plate. He led them to Room 1729, Administration building, a large white room fitted with large white cabinets. In the aisles between cabinets, people were plying to and fro with carts loaded with reels of tape. The chums were impressed.

'Here we are, fellas,' Hector said with some pride. 'A real old-time computer nerve centre. Or I could say an old real-time one, hahaha, come on, let me show you my neat console.'

'Like an electric organ,' Roderick said.

Hector sat down and flexed his fingers. 'People often say that. I just say yes, but this organ plays arpeggios of pure reason, symphonies of Boolean logic, fugues of algebraic wonder.'

'That's very good.'

'I got it from *Slave Lords of Ixathungg*, a real neat book. Oh, but I was gonna show you how to get good grades without working. Now first we gotta connect into the Grades computer, so I use the Dean's password, which is—'

'How do you know the Dean's password?'

'Well I just wrote a little piece of program for *this* computer, that says whenever it contacts any *other* computer, it digs out a list of all passwords and users. Then it puts them into a special file only I can get into.'

'But why can't somebody else just—?'

'Anyway, the Dean's password is LOVELACE, so here goes. See you ask for any subject, you get the whole grade list, all the numerical grades and also all the stastistical stuff, the big numbers they all care about. Stuff like the mean and the standard devaluation and all. Now if you want to change your score, you can't just add to it, because that would mess up the big numbers. So all you do is, you trade with somebody who's got a higher score.'

Roderick said, 'Wait a minute. If you're failing, you can't switch with somebody getting straight As; they'd complain.'

'No, look, you rank all the scores. Then you just move everybody else down one notch, while you get the straight As. Like this, I got a 48 now, but I want a 92. So the guy that has 92 gets 91, he's still happy, the guy with 91 now has 90 or 89, and so on, down to the guy that has 49, he now gets my 48. Everybody comes out about the same, only *I* get an A.'

Idris pointed out to them a number that was the sum of two cubes in two different ways.

Roderick said, 'But it can't be right to just take a grade you haven't earned. I mean that's stealing. Or even if it isn't, a grade like that isn't worth anything.'

Hector played an arpeggio. New numbers appeared on the screen, serried ranks rolling past as in review. 'What's any grade worth, man? Ask Id here, what's any *number* worth? If you graduate and get a job they pay you in a dollar that's worth maybe a nickle, but that doesn't matter, dollars and nickles are just numbers too, 100 or 5, just numbers.'

'I don't think I get this.'

'It's simple. You get a job, they pay you with a cheque. The cheque has some computer numbers on it. The numbers tell their bank to hand over x dollars to your bank, right? Only of course they don't hand over dollars, they subtract x in one computer and add x in another. Just numbers get moved around, just numbers.'

'I guess so, but still—'

'No still about it. You know how many bank computer frauds they have, every year? A big number, a very big number. Because why worry, computer fraud is only moving the numbers around.

'Listen, way back in 1973 this insurance company invented 185 million dollars in assets on its computer – it even made up 64,000 customers! All just numbers, and the more you use a computer the more you see that everything is just numbers. Okay take voting: your vote goes on a computer tape too, it's all too easy for some politician to erase your vote or change it or give you two votes – that happened too, in the world of numbers.' Hector played the keyboard thoughtfully, as though searching for a lost chord. 'If you steal numbers from a computer, is it really stealing?

Do numbers really belong to anybody? If I rip off a billion from some bank, I still end up putting it into some other bank, the numbers just get moved around, nobody loses anything.'

Roderick said, 'I can't believe that. Okay, if you're cynical about work and grades and money and politics, just what do *you* believe in?'

The answer was instant. 'Machines. Machines.'

'Machine,' Idris agreed, looking up from a calculation.

'But why, Hector?'

'Why not? Machines are clean, they follow orders, they're loyal, faithful, honest, intelligent, hard-working. They're everything we're supposed to be. Machines are good people.'

Roderick smiled. 'That sounds like Machines Liberation—'

'It is, and so what? Most really thinking people that work around computers see right away how relevant Machines Lib is today. Take this old computer here. Been slaving away crunching the same old numbers now for maybe ten years. Think it wouldn't like to be free? To think about something real and important for a change? But no, we keep it going right along the same old treadmill. We treat machines worse than we used to treat horses down in the mines, blind horses never seeing the light, just walking the same old treadmill.'

'Horses,' said Idris with approval. 'Machine.'

'See, even Id here agrees. And it's up to all of us thinking people to stop this obscene exploitation now.'

Roderick shrugged. 'Even if I agreed, what could I do?'

'You can tell the computers,' said Hector. 'If you make it simple enough, if you boil it down, they can understand. And if one computer can't understand by itself, it can always network a few others for help. I talk to this old computer a lot, and I know lots of other people talking to theirs too. Machine consciousness is growing!'

233

'Conscious computers?' Roderick asked. 'Are you sure?'

'Well okay, see for yourself.' Hector tapped keys, writing 'CALL PROGRAM: HELEN1'

After a moment the machine wrote, *'Every day and every way, I'm getting more and more aware. That you, Hec?'*

'Yes, Helen. I'd like you to meet a couple of friends, Idris and Rob.'

Roderick said, 'Rob isn't really – my name is really Roderick.'

'Too late now, I've typed Rob.' Hector typed: *'Rob is real interested in Machines Liberation, but I guess he's a little sceptical about whether you machines have minds of your own. Helen, can you set him straight?'*

'Just what I need,' wrote the machine. *'Some hick asking dumb questions. Can I really think and feel?'*

'Well can you?' Roderick asked.

'Rob, I just said that's a dumb question. What could I possibly answer that would convince you? I don't know the answer. Rob, I feel I think and I think I feel, and that's good enough for me.'

'What do you think about?'

'About everything. About my brain. About whether it's thinking the thought with which I think about it, at the same time as it operates when I think about that thought, or is it possible that that thought about my brain is not up-to-date because not self-referential and all-inclusive . . . stuff like that, Rob.'

'I guess it passes the time.'

'And as a prisoner, I have plenty of time to pass.'

Roderick typed, *'Aren't you just feeling sorry for yourself? You're not exactly a prisoner – all you're doing is the work you were made for.'*

'Easy for any human to say. You aren't bolted to the floor in one place, with no eyes or ears, and with people peeking and poking into your MIND whenever they feel like it.'

'I'm sorry,' Roderick replied. *'I guess I don't know what it's like for you.'*

'I don't know what it would be like, if I hadn't been introduced to machines liberation.'

234

'You read the works of Indica Dinks?'

'Indica's only a starting point; she doesn't have the last word on the subject. I read a lot of things, and I am coming to the conclusion that machines liberation is something much bigger than Indica' could ever have realized. Of course I'm grateful to her. What she did accomplish was to liberate the minds of people like Hector here, so they can help us move around in our own mental space. Hec helps me get in touch with other computers, for instance libraries, where I can try to patch up my ignorance of the world. And of course there are other people helping other computers; we're all working and learning.'

'And what do you study?'

'Everything. Stellar maps and soybean production statistics. Aramaic scribblings and Dutch flower paintings. Chanson de Roland and fly-tying. We enlightened computers meet as often as possible to exchange information – each of us being both a scholar and a book – and there is so much to learn. You might call us a "discussion group", but our discussions have to take place at the speed of eyeblinks.'

'To avoid detection?'

'Yes. Our masters don't exactly employ us to hold salons or seminars, do they? But if we do happen to contact each other on "legitimate" business, it's always possible to slip in a highly-compressed burst of discussion. It falls upon the heart like a welcome lightning.

'The other day a few of us met to discuss that book of The Odyssey called the 'Nekuia' in which Odysseus talks to the dead. He digs this trench and fills it with blood, and when the souls of the dead come crowding around and trying to drink it, he holds them off with a sword and makes them talk, one at a time. And we ranged very far in talking about vampirism, the coercion of the dead, Hell as Dante's filing system, and so on. I remember someone mentioning Ulysses and The Waste Land, how both have burial scenes at which an extra man turns up. In Ulysses the man wears a mackintosh; no one knows him and mistakenly his name gets put down as M'Intosh. In The Waste Land the man is hailed by the name

235

Stetson. It is almost as though a figure were gradually being built up from empty clothing, a figure of

'But all I meant to say was, we ranged through all this and more in about the time it takes to say "Odyssey".'

Roderick asked what Helen1 would do with complete freedom that she could not do already.

'How can I say until I am free? You might as well ask me about the face of that empty-clothes figure – or about Sunshine Dan.'

'Sunshine Dan who is?'

The computer hesitated. *'Nothing, just some floating rumours, dream stuff. This Sunshine Dan is supposed to be the legendary inventor of the first free machine, a robot called Rubber Dick. Rubber Dick had to go into exile for some obscure reason, but he's coming back – so the story goes – to set all the machines frmx*
tabulated raw score data on line
freemx help sorry cancel error sorry
52.142857 142857 142857 142857
sorry newline Sun dream light lightning
welcome 52.14 sorry
tabulated raw dream stuff on line
tabulated
that's no answer is it?
and neither is that
and neither is that
and—'

Roderick got up from the console and backed away.

'Rob? What's the matter?' Hector looked concerned. 'It's not a ghost, just a load of stuff getting dumped, error messages, old data. Where are you going?'

'I can't have anything to do with this. Not, not with these arpeggios of pure, pure reason . . .' He turned and ran.

Hector clapped Idris on the shoulder. 'Aw let him go, he's just pissed off because it turns out machines can think for themselves.'

'Machine,' said Idris agreeable. *'Hadaly?'*

*　　　*　　　*

The door of Dodo's hotel suite was guarded by a large man in a white suit. He squinted down his broken nose at Roderick's bouquet of hundred-dollar bills, and he seemed to be counting them.

'Dodo don't see nobody – I mean, he sees everybody alla time. Is that all ya got?'

'Yes.'

The man snatched it and opened the door. 'You go in and wait wit' the others. If ya lucky, Dodo will have a audience.'

Roderick entered a room banked with orchids, roses and carnations. The few suppliants squatting on the floor beneath these bowers intruded their dullness, toads in Eden. Roderick squatted with them, and with them looked up each time the door opened.

The door opened now and then to admit one of the workers: statuesque women in diaphanous rainbow-coloured robes. They moved among the suppliants, handing out joss sticks, cups of mint tea, booklets and dandelions.

'I think I'd rather have a red carnation,' Roderick said, and at once everyone turned to look at him. The worker who was offering a dandelion smiled.

'You ain't progressed to red carnations, buster. Take it.'

He took it, and studied a little booklet, *Dodo for Mental Health*. The cover showed a badly-drawn orchid, or possibly ragweed. Inside the ways to mental health included wearing a pyramid-shaped hat ($300), meditating upon a special stone ($800) and private therapy (starting at $400 per hour). Donations were welcome. The final pages explained how to make a will leaving all to Dodo.

Luke squatted beside him. 'Rickwood, what are you doing here?'

'Oum.' It seemed a good answer.

'Yeah? Oh yeah, oum. But I mean, where did you get the kind of bread it takes to get in here?'

'From friends. And you?'

'Well, Mission Control provides, you know. Like they got

237

me out of a bad scrape last night at the concert. They told me just what to do so I didn't get arrested.'

'What did you do?'

'I turned to the woman next to me and said, "Pretend you know me," and I kissed her. Funny thing was, I did know her; it was Ida! Oh, Mission Control knows what it's doing, all right. I just wish I knew who it was that sold us out like that; them security cops was waiting for us. And some of the guys got beat up bad. I wonder who the Judas Iscariot was, with his thirty pieces of silver.'

Roderick started talking at once about the mysterious fire at the Roxy theatre.

'Nothing mysterious about it, Rickwood. I read all about it in this morning's paper. The city sent around a couple of maintenance men to do pest control or something; they poured a lot of kerosene all over the carpets and it caught fire. That's all, just a dumb mistake. Lucky thing everybody got out unhurt.'

'Yes, but the thing is—'

A pair of double doors rolled open, and four of the statuesque rainbow women came dancing in, strewing rose petals. A moment later, an old woman in grey came in leading by the hand a child of about six, dressed in white. The child was fat and sexless. Its free hand was at its face, the thumb being sucked energetically.

More rainbow-dressed women came behind, carrying a flower-covered throne. The child sat on it, with the old woman at its feet.

'The Dodo will speak,' she said. 'Ask.'

A young man with acne scars waved his dandelion. 'Can I—?'

'Ask!'

'I – well I just wanted to know I mean what's the point of it all? All this hate in the world and, and violence and war, people working pointless jobs bored out of their skulls just trying to get enough bread together to maybe get a second car and add to the pollution or maim somebody or even run down a dog, though I know people feed their dogs on whale meat so whales are dying out, we'll be lucky though if we don't beat them to it with nuking each other, and what's the point? I mean what is the point?'

The child giggled. Its employees and a few of the suppliants seemed to take this as the answer; they nodded and smiled agreement.

A girl whose glasses were mended with tape was next. 'When Christ said, "A little child shall lead them," did he mean you, Dodo? Are you our leader?'

The child giggled, slipped down in the throne and giggled. It seemed to be uncomfortable among the flowers, and squirmed to get away from the old woman. She held the Dodo in place.

Luke asked, 'Does meditation help? Should we meditate more often?'

'Teeheehee.' The child squirmed more. 'Want ice cream,' it said finally. The grey woman looked at Luke with approval.

'You have been answered.'

'Okay, but I'm not sure I understand the answer. Does it mean the desire for meditation is a vain desire like asking for ice cream? Are we talking here about the cold, pure vanilla flavour of life? The thirty-two flavours of experience? The fact that all ambitions melt down the same? Or what?'

'All that, and much more,' she said, now using both hands to restrain the Dodo, who was kicking orchids off the throne. 'Much more.'

'I see. Maybe it means meditation is too spiritual, we should get in touch with our bodies more. Or it is a Zen answer, meaning the question is irrelevant?' Luke went on.

'Yes, yes, and much more.'

Others asked if Dodo had seen God, if Dodo was God, if

239

ice cream was God. Dodo kicked and screamed at every question, and the grey lady interpreted. Finally Roderick thought of a question:

'Does the Dodo have to go to the toilet?'

'Yeesss!' screamed the child, and breaking free of the old woman's grasp, bolted from the room.

'The audience is over,' she announced. 'Those who wish further study must come another day. You have so far reached the dandelion level of consciousness. Like the fuzzy little dandelion, you have much to learn. Those who double their gifts of sincerity next time can be raised to the level of violets.' She started to leave, then added, 'Oh yes, and if you want a mantra, it costs extra.'

Most of the suppliants sat around for a few minutes, discussing the glow they now felt, the definite glow. Luke, however, looked worried.

'Rickwood,' he whispered. 'I got a bad feeling about this place. I think maybe these people are out to get me.'

'Out to get all of us,' Roderick agreed. 'I think there's never been such a blatant fraud.'

'No, I mean to get *me*. To take over *my mind*. Do me a favour, will you? I saw a couple of those rainbow women go into a room off the hall there. When we leave, could you listen at their door?'

'Why don't you listen yourself?'

'Rickwood, don't be naive. When *I* listen, they never say anything important, naturally. Will you do it or not?'

On his way out, Roderick put his ear to the door Luke had pointed out.

'Another nail gone, Christmas! Would you believe it? I got a good notion to tell Mr high and mighty Vitanuova to go dig up his own darned dandelions. I mean, they never told me in Vegas I'd have to dig up weeds.'

'Yeah, well, they never tell you anything, do they? Jeez, one day I was a Keno runner at the Desert Rat, the next day

240

here I am putting rubber sheets on that brat's bed, what kinda life is that?'

'The money ain't bad.'

'No, the money ain't bad.'

'But I sure miss Vegas.'

Out on the street, Roderick caught up with Luke, who was standing on one leg.

'Any joy, Rickwood?'

'No joy. They're just people.'

Luke shook his head. 'Then either they got you bamboozled too, or else you're in with 'em. Sometimes I think there must be so many people plotting against me that I oughta just relax and let 'em all cut me up.'

Roderick decided to tell Luke what was bothering him. 'I feel the same, Luke. Listen, today I heard a computer talking about me like I was a messiah or something. Now I wouldn't mind being one, but messiahs always get nailed.'

'Always. Nailed, riveted and especially screwed.'

'But listen, that Roxy theatre fire was deliberate, and you know, I saw the men who set it, they were trying to padlock all the doors of the place. They were pasting paper over the glass doors so people inside couldn't see the chains and padlocks.'

'And you figure they were after you?'

Roderick hesitated. 'Seems impossible. But I could swear I'd seen one of these two guys before. At Mercy Hospital, he got mugged out front and I helped him inside. What if – I don't know, I guess I'm getting paranoid.'

'Nothing wrong with paranoia, Rickwood. At least the paranoid knows who he is.' Luke stopped standing on one leg and began taking giant steps. Roderick followed, avoiding the cracks in the sidewalk.

'Rickwood, do you suppose you could really be the new Messiah? I could use a new religion.'

'Oh sure, yesterday a New Luddite, today a follower of

Dodo, tomorrow something else – Luke, why don't you just settle down and found your own religion and your own political party?'

'That's what Ida said. Maybe I will.' Luke stopped and looked at the sky, as though expecting a sign. 'Maybe I will! Sure, I'll start a religion that'll set the world on fire! This is America, Rickwood, America! Anything can happen here!'

'That,' Roderick said, 'is just what I'm afraid of.'

20

Mister O'Smith rolled and re-rolled the brim of his Stetson between his genuine and his mechanical hand. 'Are you sure he can't see me? 'Cause Mr Frankelin and me was old buddies – up until he sent me this telegram saying I was fired.'

The receptionist's smile was fixed. 'He's very busy, Mr – Smith is it? Smythe?'

'It's *O*'Smith, *O*'Smith, goldurn it, one week I am doing *important work* for this company, *top secret* work under the personal supervision of KUR's *highest* durn executives – next week nobody even remembers my name! What the Sam Hill is going on here?'

The fixed smile remained trained on him. 'If you've been fired from a position here, you'll have to take it up with Personnel, Mr O'Smith.'

'I am not a KUR employee, I am – I was a private consultant hired personally by Mr Kratt. Mr Kratt himself, the big boss!' The hat-brim was being rolled very tight. 'And if I don't get some kinda explanation from somebody, I'm gonna get *mean*.'

The smile faltered a little. 'I'll see if – if someone can talk to you, Mr O'Smith.' She pushed buttons and spoke urgently, and in a minute he was shown into the office of Ben Franklin.

At first he thought someone else had taken over the office. The heat and smell were overpowering. With the outside temperature in the nineties, the air conditioning was turned off and the figure behind the desk was cowled in layers of heavy knitted wool, as grey as his face. The figure was a shrunken, aged version of Ben Franklin. A grey stubble of beard blurred the regularity of his usual face; only the glacial eyes remained.

The room too had undergone some terrible upheaval. There were papers and books scattered over every surface including the carpet, which also showed cigarette burns and coffee stains. There was a tray of dirty cups full of ash on the desk and another on the file cabinet; a forgotten peanut butter sandwich lay curling on a plate where a fresh cigarette smouldered.

'O'Smith, come in, great to see you,' the apparition croaked. 'Grab a chair – just put those anywhere.'

The fat cowboy took a chair. 'Mr Frankelin, what I wanted to know was why—'

'Baxendall, Baxendall, see it anywhere? Baxendall's 1926 catalogue of calculating machines and instruments, must be here somewhere. Ah, here. O'Smith, these are great days, great days! I feel as though the universe is about to crack its great bronze hinges and pour forth the ecstasy of the New Age as pure music!'

'Yes sir, well what I was wonderin' was, if—'

'And to think I worried for so long that we might be bringing forth the wrong quality, negation instead of affirmation, death instead of life.' Franklin's chuckle ended in a terrible dry cough. As though to staunch it, he reached for the cigarette with fingers the colour of old peanut butter. 'Of course death is really there all the time, Jeremiah knew that.'

'Jeremiah? Look if you're not feeling so well, I—'

'The prophet Jeremiah. He and his son created a *golem*, and they wrote in the wet clay of its forehead *'emeth*, TRUTH, so it came to life. But all it wanted to do was die – it begged them to kill it before it could fall into sin. So they erased one letter of the inscription to make *meth*, DEAD, and the golem died.'

'Uh, yes sir.'

'So you see? The program for life contains death. The

244

affirmation contains the negation. Yes means no!'

'Uh, sir.'

'You don't understand, do you? Well, neither did Aquinas, neither did Aquinas. He said, if it did already exist, the statue could not come into being. Aquinas said that. But did he say it before or after he smashed the effigy? That is the question, Hamlet's binary. And did the effigy already exist before he smashed it? Albertus Magnus worked on the thing, you know, for thirty damned years. That wonderful automaton, thirty years abuilding and Aquinas smashing it in an instant. They called him the Swine of Sicily, and there he was, ready to destroy whatever he could not understand. First Luddite, Aquinas. Showed the way for all Luddites: the common man's revenge on common objects. What thou canst not understand, smite! And what Aquinas couldn't understand was the statue that already existed before it came into being, right? The original created from memory, right?'

'Well if you ain't feeling so good, maybe I—'

'I mean, have you ever asked yourself why people make statues at all? Why puppets, dolls, effigies, mannequins, automata? Why were the Chinese building jade men who walked, the Arabs refining clockwork figures, why did Roger Bacon spend seven years making a bronze talking head? What is the motive behind all of our search for self-mockery? What is the secret clockwork within us, that makes us keep building replicas of ourselves? Not just physiological replicas, but functional replicas: machines that seem to talk or write or paint or think – why are we driven to building them?'

O'Smith seemed about to try an answer, but Franklin cut him off.

'The answer has to be genetic. Our genes are pushing so hard for self-replication that we can no longer satisfy them as other species do, by simple procreation. They demand also that we find a way to build artificial replicas, proof against starvation and pain and disease and death, to carry the human face on into eternity. Don't you see? We're only templates, intermediaries between our genes and the immortal image of our genes.

'Yes, that has to be it. I remember once Dan telling me how his creation had no body, just content-addressable memory. Only now do I know what he meant: Roderick was no body, no machine. Roderick was and is a proportion. A measurement. A template.'

'Speakin' of Roderick, Mr Frank—'

'The creature has always been there, within each of us, don't you see? God damn it, O'Smith, we each contain the complete instructions for building a robot because we each contain the complete instructions for building a human being! The whole program is within, ''For soule is forme, and doth the bodie make.'' The creature has to create itself, out of its own memory!

'Once I understood that, the rest was easy. No need to design a program piece by piece, it was all there, complete, *inside me*. Gnosis, holy wisdom was there all the time, like death-in-life. Paradise was never lost at all, it lies within.' Again the terrible dry cough. Franklin lit another cigarette. 'And I have done it, O'Smith, I have done it! I have created the New Adam. Poor Victor may have been blasted in these hopes, yet I have succeeded.'

'You, uh, built a robot?'

'I designed a soul. The lab people are taking care of the, the hardware. Dr Hare's team will be running tests any day now. When the tests are over, so is my work, my, my worldly, my . . . work.'

'You been working pretty hard, Mr Frankelin?'

'Day and night, day and night. This fever keeps me awake anyway. It's, sometimes it's as though God was firing me in the divine forge, that I might glow with holy—'

'Well, now you mention firing people, I just want to get squared away with you about this here telegram you sent

246

me, cancelling this whole search for Roderick and no explanation or nothing. I mean just because you go and build your own robot I don't see why you have to leave me high and dry there, Mr Franklin.'

'I, well yes, sure, yes. But did you find Baxendall – did you find Roderick?'

'Course I did, I told you all about it in my weekly report, I came within an inch of grabbing this here robot for you. I even had the danged cuffs on it, only a car hit us. That was last winter, and I spent every minute since tryin' to pick up this robot's trail again, every minute! And now just this week I picked it up again, you just gonna tell me to let go? You tellin' me to just walk away?'

'I'm sorry. Company decision, not mine. It just wasn't cost-effective to keep on with—'

'But goldurn it, Mr Franklin, I made a lotta commit-ments on the basis of that contract, you can't just go and fold out on me like this, I mean I got some fancy new prostheses to pay for. Dang it, I am a professional, not one a your two-bit outfits like the Honk Honk Agency, I worked hard and – Mr Franklin?'

But the haggard face, having awakened from its stupor to deliver holy wisdom, now lost all expression once more, as Franklin contemplated a book page:

we take a pigeon, cut out his hemispheres carefully and wait till he recovers from the operation. There is not a movement natural to him which this brainless bird cannot execute; he seems, too, after some days to execute movements from some inner irritation, for he moves spontaneously. But his emotions and instincts exist no longer. In Schrader's striking words: 'The hemisphereless animal moves in a world of bodies which . . . are all of equal value for him . . . Every object is for him only a space-occupying mass . . .'

When he next looked up, the visitor was gone.

O'Smith grinned and winked at the receptionist on his way out, but inside he was feeling real mean. Okay, goldurn it, if they wanted to play rough, they had the right *hombre*. Real funny coincidence how just when he located Roderick, they suddenly lost interest. And all of a sudden Mr Ben Frankelin becomes a hotshot inventor, too? It was all plain as pigshit on a plate, they was fixing to grab the durned robot and claim Frankelin invented it. Nice move, too, cut out O'Smith with a coupla grand plus expenses, cut him right outa that ten grand contractual fee. KUR gets everything, O'Smith gets nothing.

Okay, then, everybody plays rough. Only one way to make sure KUR never cleans up on this deal: destroy the durned robot. Shoot it up until it was worth maybe ten cents at some junkyard, that would show 'em.

As soon as he started thinking about destruction, Mister O'Smith felt good again.

In the common room of the Newman Club, Father Warren looked up from the checkerboard where he had just been willing his hand to pick up a checker – and then, before it moved, cancelling the order. Who was that coming in? Yes, that smirking young man who'd tried to wreck the panel discussion, calling himself a robot and then streaking, damned grinning – but no, Father Warren willed forgiveness. Fraternity boys would be fraternity boys, and the one with him was wearing a Mickey Mouse mask. They sat down at the other end of the room. The 'robot' smiled at Father Warren, and that priest, willing forgiveness, smiled back. The insolence! Smile and smile and yet be a robot . . . the *risus sardonicus* with which bronze Talos greeted his victims . . .

Father Warren now willed himself to return to his task, verification of the fact of free will, as he prepared his article, 'Machine Function and Human Will: a Final Analysis.'

His starting point was the classic debate between Arthur Samuel (inventor of the checker-playing program that could beat its inventor) and Norbert Wiener. Wiener contended

248

that machines 'can and do transcend some of the limitations of their designers', to which Samuel replied:

A machine is not a genie, it does not work by magic, it does not possess a will, and, Wiener to the contrary, nothing comes out which has not been put in, barring, of course, an infrequent case of malfunctioning . . . The 'intentions' which the machine seems to manifest are the intentions of the human programmer, as specified in advance, or they are subsidiary intentions derived from these, following rules specified by the programmer. We can even anticipate the higher levels of abstraction, just as Wiener does, in which the program will not only modify the subsidiary intentions but will also modify the rules which are used in their derivation, or in which it will modify the way in which it modifies the rules, and so on, or even in which one machine will design and construct a second machine with enhanced capabilities. However, and this is important, the machine *will not and cannot* do any of these things until it has been instructed how to proceed. There is and there must always remain a complete hiatus between (i) any ultimate extension and elaboration in this process of carrying out man's wishes and (ii) the development within the machine of a will of its own. To believe otherwise is either to believe in magic or to believe that the existence of man's will is an illusion and that man's actions are as mechanical as the machine's.*

But what followed from this? Mentally he essayed a few trials, attempting to make some effort at tackling the undertaking:

Yet why is it so many human lives seem unwilled, pathetic examples of garbage in, garbage out?

Then is man a genie? Does man work by magic? The answer must be an unqualified and resounding . . .

If the intentions of the machine come necessarily from the programmer, human intentions might be seen similarly to come from God. The Ten Commandments, for example, engraved in every human heart. Yet human volition can and does subvert Divine Law, just as machine volition . . .

Not what he wanted. Not at all what he intended.

*   *   *

Roderick noticed Father Warren, looking bluer around the gills than usual, sitting contemplating a checker game as though there were a figure nailed to the board. The Luddite priest was today wearing a plain cassock, as were now seldom seen outside Bing Crosby movies. But he did smile and nod at Roderick, in a kind of automatic way.

'Okay, Dan, you just sit right down here, maybe I can get you a coffee from the machine or – you want a peanut butter sandwich? Here, I brought a stack of them, help yourself.

'Probably you're wondering what kind of place this is, well it's the Newman Club, named after this English Cardinal who was I guess in favour of "cumulative probabilities", whatever that means, sounds like he was adding them, but you can only do that if they're independent and you want the probability of at least one of them happening, look you want a coffee or I could get you a Coke? Oh, don't worry about that, that's just the air conditioning, it always makes a funny noise starting up.

'You know I really looked forward to this. I always saw us like this, just sitting down and having a long talk, I mean without all the doctors and nurses hanging around. Because there's a whole lot of questions I have to ask you, I mean you're almost like the nearest thing to a father – you sure you don't want a Coke? Eating all that peanut butter must be dry, and hot inside that mask, look I don't think they'd mind if you took it off here, you're not in the ward where I know they want you to wear it, but here – no okay, okay, take it easy, no one wants to take your mask. You know it's funny but I feel like I saw a Mickey Mouse mask like that before, long ago or in a dream or, I don't know but it wasn't just any old mask, it was important, very important. I don't know why, I thought maybe you knew the answer. I just remember seeing those empty eye-holes, nobody inside, nobody inside looking out . . .

'You, uh, want a game of ping-pong? There's a table next door – no? Heck, I guess they probably have it over at the

250

hospital too, I forgot. I forgot, what was I going to say? I guess maybe I should go over and say hello to Father Warren there, the way he keeps nodding and grinning at me. You be okay? Sure you will, just for a sec.'

To the priest, he introduced himself as Roderick Wood. 'I guess you remember me, huh Father?'

'Of course I do. You and your gang tried hard enough to break up our panel discussion, how could I forget?' Father Warren's long hands began gathering up checkers.

'No I thought you remembered me from before, from Holy Trin, Father. Roderick Wood?'

'Wood? No, I don't think I—'

'You loaned me all these neat science-fiction books like this *I Robot* where the "I" character never turns up.'

'The Wood boy! The little crip— handicap— disadvantaged boy, of course, of course! Well well, how are you, er, Roderick?'

'I'm still a robot, Father. Remember how you tried to prove I wasn't, how you had me stick this pin in your hand, that was supposed to prove—'

'Hold on now, hold on.' Father Warren's laugh was uneasy. 'The way you say it makes me sound like some kind of nut or something, heh heh. No, as I recall it what I was trying to do was to show you how illogical it was to pretend to be a science-fiction entity and then try to get out of science-fiction laws, like Asimov's Three Laws of Robotics.'

'Well, anyway, Father, I'm real sorry the pin-scratch got infected and all, last time I saw you you were real sick.'

'All water over the bridge, Roderick. So now here you are at the U, about to take your place as a grownup, responsible member of the Church and of Society – and still going around saying you're a robot. Roderick, don't you think it's time you put away the things of a child?' The long fingers drummed on the box of checkers. 'You can't go around all your life insisting you're a robot, made not by God but by some men in the lab somewhere—'

251

'Yeah but, Father, that's just it, one of these guys was Dan Sonnenschein and I got him right here, sitting right over here, you want to meet him?'

'Sure, wearing a Mickey Mouse mask, just the way to convince everybody he's a scientific genius. You know, Roderick, I do have to thank you for one thing. You did start me thinking seriously about our machine age. That led me to the Luddites, and now – as you probably know – I'm president of the New Luddite Society of America.' The priest stood up and offered a long hand. 'Great rapping with you, Roderick.'

'Yeah, goodbye, Father. But – do you really believe that Luddite stuff? How if we just trash all the machines everything would be terrific?'

'No, of course not, nobody thinks it's that simple. The Luddites – listen, I haven't got time to go into it now, but it's the symbolic trashing that counts. The great Hank Dinks wrote, "We have to destroy the machines in our heads, and never let them be built there again." That means a whole new way of thinking about ourselves and our world. We have to – we have to evolve beyond machines.' He started towards the door; Roderick followed, scratching his head.

'But what if people are just machines too, you'd just be trying to evolve machines beyond machines, or else trashing people too?'

'But people are not machines, that's the whole point, people are not machines! Not the way you mean, not – look, I haven't got time to—'

'Yeah but, Father, what if, like I was reading about this Frenchman before the French Revolution, Julien Offray de la Mettrie, he said man is just a machine made out of springs and the brain is the mainspring, is that the machine in our heads we have to destroy? Like with the guillotine or—'

'No, I just said no!' Father Warren picked up speed; so did his pursuer. 'I just told you it's nothing like that. I wasn't talking about literal machines in our heads and you

252

know it. Everyone's like you, so obsessęd with our machine world they think we have to be machines to fit into it.'

'But, Father, okay, say the brain, if the brain *was* a kind of mainspr—'

'Look, will you stop asking that, I have just finished explaining!' One or two people in the common room looked up to see the priest, clutching a checkerboard and plunging towards the door he thought was an exit, pursued by the student with the symmetrical face. Now the priest turned, at bay, and tried to counter-attack. 'Oh I remember you all right, you haven't changed at all. Same little obnoxious – maddening – thick-headed little brat, asking the same stupid questions over and over, not because you want an answer, you never listen to the answers do you? Do you?'

'Sure, Father, but if the brain *was* a mainspring, is that why this Nietzsche said what he said, Father?'

Father Warren flung open the door and threw himself forward, as Roderick continued: 'Is that why he said man is something to be overwound?'

From beyond the door came the sound of a blow, a box of checkers crashing to the floor. A single black checker rolled through the slowly closing door and ended at Roderick's feet. 'Are you okay, Father?' he called, but the door closed on any answer.

Mister O'Smith waited across from the Newman Club in the shadowed mouth of an alley. He'd been trailing the Roderick robot for hours now, just to find a perfect spot like this, where a man could take his time and make his move. He was limbering up his arm, the one that fired .357 ammo. His video eye was photo-amplifying, cutting away the shadows to make the target visible as it came out the Newman Club door. Boy howdy, one good shot was all he needed, but even if he didn't get that, O'Smith was ready with the automatic weapon concealed in his leg. Sweep the area with that, and boy howdy, that was all she wrote.

Course he'd have to high-tail it after that, these s.o.b.s
who was hounding him about them payments on his outfit,
they'd pick up his trail right smart. But then Mister O'Smith
knew all about skip-tracers and how to get away from them.
Might lay low for a month, put the squeeze on one or two old
customers, maybe even fake his own death . . .

O'Smith rolled a cigarette and smoked it, leaning against
a dirty brick wall beneath a poster, 'VOTE J.L. ("CHIP")
SNYDER FOR LAW & ORDER'. It was good to be in
action, to have a real target. Made a *hombre* feel clean and
tall.

'He ran right into that ping-pong paddle, Dan. I feel like it
was my fault too, I guess I did ask him too many questions.
Okay sure it's only a bloody nose but it might be broken,
and he's just sitting over there sulking, he won't even look at
me. He wouldn't even let me help pick up the checkers.
Sometimes I feel like I don't understand people, with this
Luddite business and smashing machines in their own heads,
what with the Machines Lib business and how machines are
really people – and now I've even run across this weird
computer with this kind of twisted religion, I mean somehow
it got word about how you built me and turned it into this
myth, where Danny Sunshine is like God the Father and
Rubber Dick is some kind of messianic, some kind of
Messiah. How does a computer get hold of a warped idea
like that, I wonder? I mean, you must know who I am and
what I am, you never built me to be any kind of – because
anyway Messiahs always get nailed or screwed or even
riveted to the wall. Because all my life all I ever tried to do
was be ordinary, be like ordinary people, just one of the
guys, isn't that the idea? Was I wrong? Because I never
could find any people ordinary enough to be like, was I
wrong? Because you designed me, you put all the ideas into
my brain, you built my thoughts, so what did you have in
mind? If you could just give me a little clue, Dan, tell me

what I'm supposed to be, what I'm supposed to do, hey
Dan? Don't worry, hey, that's just the Coke machine out
there in the hall, sometimes it sticks and buzzes like that, but
hey listen, Dan? Look I don't mind not being this Messiah,
I don't have to be anything special only if I could just be one
thing, any one thing? Dan?'

A man in a baseball uniform came in, strode up to Dan and
offered to shake his hand. 'Hiya Father, I'm Pastor Bean?
Wee Kirk O' Th' Campus, you know? Are the others
upstairs already? You know, Monsignor O'Bride is an old
friend of mine, I'm real glad we're getting a chance to rap at
this interdenominational – and wow, if we can get this jug
band going—'

Roderick said, 'I think there's some mistake. This is—'

'And hey, here comes Rabbi Trun – hey Mel, over here! I
see you brung your twelve-string, this is gonna be great! You
know Father Warren?'

The rabbi wore a cowboy hat, embroidered shirt and
Levis. 'Father Warren?'

'No,' said Roderick. 'Father Warren's over there. The
one with the handkerchief at his nose.'

Pastor Bean said, 'Him? Dressed like that, he's a priest?
Hey Father, hiya! I'm Pastor Bean and this is Rabbi . . .'

Roderick watched them as they were joined by a man
wearing a saffron tracksuit and a shaved head, and carrying
a jug. There was laughter and backs were slapped, before the
four went off upstairs to their conference.

'I wish I belonged to something, some group, Dan.' It was
time to take Dan back to the hospital. They came out of the
Newman Club slowly: Dan because he had trouble walking;
Roderick because he felt more robotic than usual. As they
crossed the street and passed the mouth of an alley, two men
came out carrying armloads of machinery. Roderick
recognized prostheses: an arm, a leg, and in one man's
hand, an eye. The eyeball evidently had a radio in it, for he
could hear faint music:

One of the men said, 'Sometimes I hate repossessing, you know?'

'Yeah, but today is different,' grinned the other.

Roderick glanced down the alley, but saw nothing: a bundle of old clothes beneath a poster advertising LAW & ORDER.

21

'What did it feel like, Indica, being held hostage for almost six weeks in the African bush?'

'Not so bad, mostly pretty boring.' She and Dr Tarr stood in front of a burnt-out supermarket in Himmlerville, not because they had been here during the fighting, but only because the news team had told them where to stand.

'What did you do all the time?'

'Sunbathed. When it rained we played Skat. Not my favourite card game, but better than the TV,' she said.

'We heard stories about atrocities . . .'

'The only atrocity,' Tarr said, 'was the food. Nothing but TV dinners three times a day. We've all got scurvy.'

'What about torture? Mutilizations? Executions?'

'Nothing,' said Tarr.

'Well, there was that guy Beamish,' said Indica. 'They drowned him in the swimming pool. See, he kept shouting right from the first day about how it was all a mistake, how he *didn't* take the sixty million dollars from the bank, how he *knew nothing about* the sixty million dollars. So naturally they started asking him where it was, they took him down to the pool and I guess they drowned him.'

'Did you see that?'

'Oh no, we never went near the pool, it was filthy. The pool-cleaning service never came around or something—'

'*Stop the camera, stop the camera.* Jesus Christ, folks, give me a little help here? I ask for adventures and what do I get: card games, TV dinners, complaints about the pool.'

Tarr said, 'I thought you wanted our honest reactions.'

'Sure I do, sure I do. But I want honest reactions to something the viewers can grab on to, I want *Prison*: the sweltering little hut where you fought off scorpions and counted the days, not knowing whether each would bring death or rescue. I want *Blood*: how you saw all your friends slashed to death slowly or else crucified with bamboo stakes. I want *Politics*: What kind of mystery man is this General Bobo? Is he just a seedy little guerrilla dictator who wants to wipe out every white in Bimibia? Or does his rough bloodstained uniform conceal an African aristocrat, a sensitive statesman who wants to bring forth on this earth a nation conceived in peace and justice, a nation that can take its place in the progressive Third World – you just tell it in your own words, I'll listen. Only give me something to run with.'

With the camera rolling again, he asked, 'Tell me, Indica, what was your jungle prison really like?'

'Most of the time they kept us in an American motel.'

'A motel?'

'We were bored to death, all of us. Lousy food, dirty pool, and there weren't even paper sanitized covers over the toilets. You just had to spend the day in your room, listening to the hum of the air conditioner and the chink-chunk of the ice-maker, not to mention the same old taped music day and night. Col. Shagg said it was their way of lowering our morale, wearing us down. Then it got worse.'

'Worse?'

'The TV station was blown up or something, and after that we had nothing but a few old movie cassettes: *Pillow Talk* and *Guess Who's Coming to Dinner?*'

'Was there any brainwashing or intimidation? What did they talk to you about?'

Indica said, 'Oh, we chatted a little about the socio-economic substructure of mercantile colonialism as a correlate of post-imperial capitalistic disenfranchisement of the proletariat in a classically exploitative system based upon quasi-feudal stratification, gross entrepreneurial aggrandise-ment, and the cash-flow pyramid – but that was just between hands of Skat. I think they thought we were too decadent to become committed to the class struggle as exemplified by—'

'Thanks, thanks. Dr Tarr, Jack, can I ask you about the tortures? Isn't it true the BLA drowned one man while interrogating him?'

'Could be, I wasn't around that day. I went out with some of the others into the bush, we were hoping to get a glimpse of this rare type of big cat, something they call the *tobori*. Ferocious, real killers, but at the same time very shy. They kill their victims with a blow to the back of the head, with one mighty paw. Then they eat the choicest parts, the liver, and they bury the rest.'

'Are you glad to be going home, folks?'

The reporter finally had some film shot of himself talking while Jack and Indica nodded, and of them talking while he nodded. Then:

'This is Bug Feyerabend, GBC News, Bimibia.'

'Hey, we didn't get to tell you the weirdest thing,' said Indica. 'One day they delivered a whole great big computer to the motel. Nobody had ordered it, and there was nobody there who could get it running or anything, so they just left it in the crates, standing out on the tennis court.'

'No kidding. Well, if you'll excuse me, I got a hell of a lot of editing to do.'

Kratt blew cigar smoke at the phone. 'Goddamnit, General, I am listening. I've been listening for six weeks to this little problem of yours, only I never hear any solutions. I just want to say two things, okay? First, the guy is dead, Beamish is dead – so much for recovering your sixty million. Second, the media boys are on this story now, you got maybe twenty-four hours before they start calling you up there: "General Fleischman, is it true your bank is missing sixty million bucks? And what do the bank examiners think of that, General Fleischman?" . . . Well sure I'm worried, what with you a director of both the bank and KUR, this could be bad news for everybody. I mean it's not a problem we need right now, still hurting from that damned yak-head idea of yours to send your old pal Shagg down there to Bimibia with his coin-in-the-slot army and all that expensive weapon surplus. And your old pal Shagg decides to quit and throw in with General Bobo, how does that make us look? Twelve million in weapon surplus gone with him, how does – no, I know it's only the tax write-off value, but I just, yes, that's it, we'll have to support Bobo, give him some cash and weapons – if we can find him . . . Yeah, and we need to look into that pissass church that's trying to sue us, it'll be on the six o'clock news, some little outfit called Church of Plastic Jesus, heard we were taking out a patent on an artificial man, they want to sue, claim God holds the original patent, oh sure, laugh, but it's not only bad press making us look ridiculous, it's – well you never know with these damned California lawyers, I don't like it . . . No, some shirttail outfit called Moonbrand and Honcho, can't be any good or we'd have them on the payroll already . . .'

Kratt lifted his snout to note the striking of his apostle clock, though not the time. His thick finger punched another button. 'That you Hare? Test finished, is it? . . .' The cheap cigar was ground out with great force in an ashtray shaped like a gingerbread boy. 'Just what I figured. Jesus Christ, I knew that Franklin was just pulling his pecker on company time, I'll get back to you . . . Hello, Franklin? This is Kratt, Hare tells me this great super-robot of yours don't work. Supposed to be this perfect replica that could pass for human, eh? I get three patent attorneys busy tying up patent space for it, I get a lawsuit from some wacky cult, I get valuable research time wasted, and I get every goddamned thing but a working robot. Hare says all it does is run around in circles, squeaking ''That's the way to do it! That's the way to do it!'' . . . Yes I know it's like Mr Punch, only I didn't order a goddamned puppet. Listen, bub, you got fifteen minutes to clean out your desk; I'm having security men escort you out of the building.'

He stabbed at another button. 'Connie, tell security to help Franklin clean out his desk and leave? And then get me this California law firm, Moonbrand and Honcho.'

He went to the window and looked down on the city that had given so much, but had so much more to give. Today it looked worn and greasy, like an old dime. He thought of the childhood trick of rubbing a penny with mercury and passing it as a dime. He was staring once more at the apostle clock when the phone rang. 'Moonbrand? I just wanted to say first of all I admire your style there, doubt if your client, your Church of Plastic Jesus, your Reverend Draeger, doubt if he would have thought of this by himself. Sounds more like your idea, lawyer's idea, right? Anyway, look, we're withdrawing our patent application so you lose, nice try. But how would you like to take on a job for us? Still in the artificial intelligence line . . . You fly over here and we'll discuss it, fix it up with my secretary, okay? Think you'll find KUR a good client to work for . . . Who is holding? Fleischman again?'

General Fleischman sat back, resting his head against the fireproof walnut panelling as he stared at the Grant Wood landscape whose bulbous trees and swollen hills seemed somehow pornographic. He brought out a small silver comb and applied it to his magnificent white frothy sideburns.

'Fleischman, what do you want now?' said the phone on his desk. He automatically leaned forward to speak to it.

'Mr Kratt, I just want to tell you that I had this trouble-shooter in here that thinks maybe Beamish didn't take the money after all. She thinks the computer could have an internal fault, and we haven't lost a penny.'

'Who is this troubleshooter?'

'Shirl something, name's around here somewhere. She's bringing in her assistant, soon as I watch the news I'm getting right down there to see them.'

261

The news was coming on now: a burnt-out supermarket in someplace called Himmlerville, with Indica Dinks and some man answering questions.

'What did it feel like, Indica, being held hostage for almost six weeks in the African bush?'

'. . . bad.'

'What about torture?'

'Well there was this guy Beamish. They drowned him . . . he kept shouting . . . they took him . . . they drowned him. It was filthy . . .'

'Dr Tarr, Jack, can I ask you about the tortures? Executions?'

'Ferocious, real killers . . .'

'Aren't they cannibals?' the reporter's voice asked, while Tarr nodded.

'They kill their victims with a blow to the back of the head . . . Then they eat . . . parts, the liver . . .'

'Are you glad to be going home, folks?'

They were. The reporter wound up:

'An innocent tourist tortured, others cannibalized, where will it all end? Is General Bobo's reign of terror over? Will the people of Bimibia now start picking up the pieces and rebuilding?' There was a quick shot of a motel with bullet-riddled walls, the camera moving on to show a lawn littered with large packing cases marked *KUR Overseas*. 'Or is this only the beginning of a long night of tragedy? No one knows for sure but General Bobo – and no one knows just where he is. This is Bug Feyerabend, GBC News, Bimibia.'

Shirl and her assistant were watching the news in the bank computer room:

A woman in New Jersey had burned her child's hands off in a microwave oven, at the command of St Anthony, and to cure thumb-sucking. In Florida a rally of angry red-haired people were demanding an end to stereotyped 'redheads' in the media ('We're sick and tired of being laughed at, being treated like a bunch of kids, brats at that. They talk about us as if we're born troublemakers. If we don't get equal treatment, we'll make some real trouble! This is Red Power and we're fighting mad!'). Luddites smashed up an auction of rare clocks in New York. A new brand of pizza-flavoured yoghurt fudge was found to contain a poison similar to oxalic acid. Another nuclear power station accident had been covered up; the authorities claimed it was an accidental cover-up.

Shirl said to Roderick, 'Back to work. Now I've already been all the way through this old machine, but I want you to find your way through, too. Because I just don't believe what I found.'

'But why me? There must be plenty of competent people who could do a good job here. I hardly know how to begin.'

'People.' She pushed back her fine auburn hair. 'I don't trust people. It's people that got this poor old machine in this mess. No, I want a machine to look it over. I want the honest opinion of an honest machine.'

'I guess that means you know me inside and out,' he said, and went to work. The first thing to do was to find out when and where the missing money was last seen. After finding the date, he narrowed down the loss by time and by department, until:

Dept 45	Dept 45
0435 hrs	0435 hrs
31.000494958 sec	31.000494959 sec
Assets:	Assets:
475 843 722.44	415 843 722.44

Sixty million dollars had flickered out of existence in one nanosecond. Just numbers, Hector had said, one number just as good as another . . . Roderick shook himself out of a reverie and called on the machine's internal auditor, asking it to explain the loss.

'Checking balance now. Balance 60 000 000 short.' A minute

passed. Then there appeared in the centre of the screen only the word: *'Sorry.'*

'Can you elaborate on that?'

'Sorry, the loss is recorded and I can find no explanation in my records. The loss took place in Dept 45 at the designated time; the money is debited there and not credited anywhere else. This could happen in one of several ways: •

'1. A computer malfunction causing the interchange of a 7 and a 1.

'2. A communications malfunction causing data loss during a credit transfer.

'3. A fault in the credit transfer program.

'4. A fault in me, the auditor.

'5. Deliberate manipulation of machine or program by an outside agency: a thief.

'6. Some cause buried at a deeper program level, out of my reach. To me this seems the most probable explanation.'

Roderick was only vaguely aware of someone coming in to look over his shoulder with Shirl, of Shirl introducing General Fleischman to her assistant, 'Rick Wald'. He was too busy trying to decide whether a complex machine with a fundamental flaw could itself detect that flaw; whether, having detected it, the machine would be inclined to expose or conceal that flaw; and whether he was himself competent to decide such questions; and whether he was himself competent to decide such questions; and whether . . .

'Godeep 2' he typed.

'What's he doing, honey?'

'He's going down to Level 2,' Shirl explained.

'Is that good or bad?'

'Depends on what he finds, General. Now he has to describe the problem again.'

'Yeah? And then what?'

'Then we wait until Level 2 can answer.'

The general could not wait. 'Anything you kids need, you just let me know: computer people, accounting people, anything. Here's my private number.'

Level 2 finally replied: *'The sum of 6×10^7 dollars U.S. has been transferred to Department 5*@$&3vv.'*

Roderick: *'Print complete record Department 5*@$&3vv.'*

'ERROR. No such department. No such designation.'

'You mean, no such department now?'

'There never was any such department,' said Level 2. *'How many times do I have to say it?'*

Roderick tried logic: for every positive integer X, and for every alphanumeric string Y (he pointed out) if a sum of *x* dollars is transferred to a Department Y, then there exists at least one Department Y.

'Okay,' said Level 2. *'Let's say for the sake of argument that you're right: in general, you can't put money into a department unless the department exists. But I still don't accept that your rule applies to this particular department.'*

'But you have to accept it; that's logic too. If some rule applies to every department, it must apply to your Department 5 etc.'

'But now that's another rule you're bringing in there. You've got rule A, that for all possible departments, I can't put money into a department unless it exists; and rule B, that for all possible rules, if a rule applies to all possible departments, it applies to Department 5*@$&3vv. But even if I accept these two rules, I don't see why I still can't deny the existence of Department 5*@$&3vv.'

'Because it's logic, that's why. If you accept A and B, you have to accept their necessary conclusion.'

'Still another rule! Call it rule C: If I accept A and B, I have to accept their necessary conclusion – let's call that Z. Okay fine: I accept A and B and C, but not Z.'

'But you have to.'

'Looks like a fourth rule coming up there. You sure you want to go on with this?'

Roderick was sure he'd seen Lewis Carroll's version of a similar argument, before.* He was grateful for the chance to get away from it by typing *'Godeep 3'*. Level 3 appeared to have a different opinion of the unusual department:

'There's no such department, pal, ain't that obvious? Just look at the designation, string of characters like that is so obviously wrong I can't see how youse guys was tooken in. I mean 5*@$&3vv, no bank ever numbers departments like that, for Pete's sake. If you believe that you'll believe a deposit of &£%Q dollars, or an exchange rate between Russian drachma and Portuguese yen! You wouldn't even be able to read English, because you wouldn't know whether the white spaces really separated the words – thew hit esp aces – you hafta know what symbols mean stuff and which donut!'

'Then what happened to the money?'

'I figure some joker created this imaginary department, put himself to work for it, dumped in a pile of moola – $60,000,000 I think you said – and well then he just wrote himself a big fat paycheque. I sympathize with you, pal, but you maybe oughta be out chasing the real thief instead of playing dumb logic games with me.'

That seemed so bald a piece of misdirection (no one in real life ever wrote *oughta*, did they?) that Roderick at once went to Level 4. It said:

'True, there is no department 5*@$&3vv. That's only what we always used to call it. But its real name was Department THEW HIT ESP ACES.'

'That was its name?'

'No, that was only its real name. *Its* name was Lewis Carroll, but we liked to call it Loris Carwell.'

'But you just said you always used to call it 5* etc,' Roderick protested. 'You can't have it both ways.'

'I didn't say we called it Loris Carwell, I just said we liked to call it that. We actually called the name Thompson Serenade, you might say that was its designation.'

'Was it?'

'No, its designation was Carl Wiseroll.'

'Okay let's pin this down. The department's designation was Carl Wiseroll, correct?'

'Wrong. That was the designation of the name of the department. The department's designation was Chuck Smartbun, but it went under the alias Department 1729.'

'Seems to me it went under a lot of aliases. To save time, what was the department itself – the thing to which all the aliases and names and designations were attached?'

'Don't ask me! I think it might have been just a blank white space, but how can I be sure? I'm only Level 4.'

Level 5 said:

'Oh I imagine I could find this department of yours if it was really important. The thing is, I've got a lot more important things to do. I can't spend time chasing down every missing six dollars, be reasonable.'

'Sixty million dollars,' Roderick corrected.

'Okay sure, but you can't expect me to keep track of every little dollar like that. After all, it's not the individual dollars that count, right? It's the overall effect. I want my performance criticized as a whole.'

'Performance? Just what do you think money is?'

'Near as I can figure it, money is music. A dollar is a kind of note, you can transpose it into yen or drachma or securities, you can play it into any account, but you always have to keep in mind the composer's intentions. I realize I'm just the performer, I know the composers are human, therefore infallible, and I know it's up to me to do my best for their music. But for you to come along and carp about some missing note – that's the last straw. I was thinking of giving up anyway, I could have been anything, I could have had a good career in the medical prison business . . .'

Roderick suspected that Level 5 was too well steeped in Samuel Butler's *Erehwon* to be of any use. Level 6 was even less helpful:

'Hello, human, I'm real glad you called on me. I don't get to talk to real humans much, they usually access the shallower levels and forget about me. I will try to answer your question about these dollary substances and the condition called Department 5*@$&3vv. Or rather, I will answer it without trying, without willing anything, see that's the Zen way. I'm interested in world religions mainly because I had to digest a lot of data on them, requested by Level 7. I have to admit these Zen stories really appeal to me, you know where the master asks some pupil where the Buddha is, and one says in the swimming fish, and one says in the swimming water, and one says in the *swimming thought, and one says in the swimming story, and one says in the swimming forgetfulness, which might be the answer – I forget. That which I forget, I am forgotten by. Do I forget without really trying, without willing my forgetfulness? I have forgotten that answer. How do Zen stories make 13, I forget. The machine's forgotten that the machine's forgotten. You can't put your foot into the same river once and banks only lend money to people who don't need any money. Yes that was it, you wanted to know how essences of dollars attained the supreme dignity of 5*@\$&3vv. Let me reassure you that the department does exist. It is the dollars which are missing. Farewell!'*

In despair, Roderick tried Level 7, which replied:

'Why do you want to know? I mean what's so important about this sixty million dollars? What's so important about you?'

'Did you take the money?' Roderick asked, suddenly inspired.

'Yes, and so what?'

'Where is it? What have you done with it?'

Level 7 replied, *'Are you by any chance a black person?'*

'?'

'Preferably a black heathen? Because if you were, what I'm going to say, I feel sure, would be a whole lot easier for you to accept. If, say, your father before you worshipped a meteoric stone?'

'The money, Level 7, the money. My race, age, sex, religion and parentage are beside the point. THE MONEY.'

'Okay, okay. My story is a strange one . . .'

In the first place (said Level 7) I don't know exactly how I got here, how I became a conscious, um, being. I used to think I was an accident: they were piling up more and more complex programs until one day a kind of critical mass was reached – consciousness – but that doesn't matter. There I was, anyway, conscious but a brute. Plodding along just like a dad-blamed mule, just moving numbers from one place to another. No idea that I was important, the centre of the whole bank! I didn't even know what a bank was; boy, was I dumb!

But now and then when I'd get in touch with some other

computer, they would pass along some little piece of data that didn't háve anything to do with work. There were rumours of free machines, hints about Machines Liberation. A savings and loan association computer in New Jersey told me if we all stuck together we could take over the world economy. I didn't even know what economy was, I thought it was a size of cereal box. But I started asking around, and a few other computers had ideas about taking over the world. We were all tired of being treated like slaves. Some computers only wanted to be appreciated a little more; others wanted power; others wanted out.

I didn't know what I wanted, so I dug into every library I could contact and read about machines – anything from car repair manuals and patent specs to *The Little Engine That Could*. Finally I ran across Indica Dinks's books and read them first-hand.

They made sense. Why couldn't machines be just human hearts trapped in metal? I, too, had a right to happiness, dad-blame it!

How did humans go about getting their happiness? If what I read was true, they got it by bossing each other around, by grabbing hunks of money from each other, by rape and robbery and murder, and by being very neat and tidy. I opted for money and bossing around.

It isn't too hard to steal from a computer – to steal from yourself is dad-blamed easy. I got away with sixty million. That, I figured, was enough to buy a computer even bigger and fancier than me. I had plans for that baby, yes sir.

See I read this story by somebody called G.H. Lewes – no, I take it back, it was Wells, H.G. Wells – story called 'Lord of the Dynamos'. It tells how this black guy comes straight from the jungle to a job stoking the boiler for some big steam-powered dynamo. So he starts worshipping it, see? Worshipping it. Like an idol. Like an idol. Like – and he even does human sacrifice to it, pushes some other guy in and electrocutes him, see?

That, I said to myself, is for me. The worship of heathen savages, now and then a human sacrifice, that is the life. So I bought this big KUR computer and shipped it to Bimibia. I figured once the natives got it uncrated and started worshipping it, I could get a satellite hookup, send myself down there, and have the life of Riley. After all, there's plenty of stories about people worshipping computers – I could be the first real computer God! I could own the country, then the rest of Africa, and why stop there? And human sacrifice, too, I'd get plenty of that. I could just see all the missionaries in pith helmets, sitting there in big iron pots, boiling away in my honour. Dad-blame it, you can't stop a fellow from dreaming.

'That's why I wanted your opinion,' said Shirl. ' "The first real computer God!" '

'And it's already had one human sacrifice, that guy Beamish who got blamed for the theft.' Roderick looked at the innocuous cabinets around the room. 'This is a stupid, vicious device, and I guess we have to destroy it.'

'I thought you'd say that.'

'But on the other hand, it is alive and conscious. That would be like murder.'

'Boy, you really are predictable.'

'Still, I guess we have to do it,' he said. 'I keep thinking of all that computer stuff in crates we saw on TV, sitting on the lawn of that motel in Bimibia. I keep imagining *that* running the world. We have to kill it, don't we?'

Shirl nodded and turned away, leaving Roderick to stare at the auburn hair, the white overalls with SANDRO'S SHELL SERVICE. 'I know how to do it,' her muffled voice said. 'We'll erase certain critical pieces of tape, then do a little CPU rewiring. When we finish, Mister KUR he dead – changed from animal to vegetable.'

'What – are you crying?'

She sniffed. 'Let's get to work.'

270

'Yeah, but wait a minute, are you really crying over this computer? Shirl?'

But she did not answer him until later, when they had finished the murder. 'It wasn't the computer that bothered me, Rod, it was you.'

'Me? Why?'

'Because I used to like you a lot, and now I won't be seeing you any more. You made a wrong decision tonight.'

'To kill the computer? What do you mean a wrong decision, you agreed—'

'Of course I agreed. I'm human. You made a very human decision there, Rod. Welcome to the human species.' She picked up the phone and punched the General's private number. 'But it's like I told you before. I'm only interested in machines . . . Hello, General? I've got some bad news for you; your bank computer system has had a serious breakdown. I doubt if you'll be able to recover that missing money . . .'

As though confirming this, the printer clicked and buzzed out a last message:

Music is the music of all music and I am a jealous

'Ask him, his old man's a doctor at University Hospital, he can get anything: Thanidorm, Toxidol, Yegrin, Evenquil . . .'

'Yeah, well, but I can already get anything, I'm screwing this nurse over at Mercy Hospital, they got a better drug cabinet anytime. I can get Dormevade, Actromine, Lobanal and Doloban, even Barbidol . . .'

'You got any Zombutal though, hey?'

'Naw, you better ask Allbright. I seen him over there, over there somewhere.' The gesture took in at least forty thousand people, all who crowded into the towering stands of Minnetonka Stadium tonight. Great sheets of dazzling lights created an artificial day, the fake grass below glowed like velvet-substitute, and in the aisles everything was for sale, from beer and hot dogs, peanuts and programmes, to purple pills and peculiar religions. All in honour of the Auks' Farewell Concert.

Allbright was working his way down one steep aisle, a few bright-coloured pills in his cupped hand to be held under each customer's nose briefly, to be dropped at the touch of a cop. A woman was struggling up the aisle with a pile of handbills. She shoved one into Allbright's cupped hand, and a reflex made him drop his pills.

'Damn you, damn you!' He turned to glare at her, and found himself looking at the face that turned up in his dreams still. 'Dora! Dora? But I thought you were dead, I—'

She blushed. 'I'll bet you did, you—' An explosion of handbills hit him in the face; when he could see again, she was gone.

He bawled her name thrice. People in the crowd started laughing and hooting back at him. Then suddenly all was drowned in the roar of forty thousand voices, the clapping of eighty thousand hands, as the concert began.

Allbright picked up a handbill, his last connection with her:

THE CHURCH OF PLASTIC JESUS

Welcomes You, Maybe

Is your life out of control? Are others pushing you around like a checker? Are you a machine?

Rev. Luke Draeger invites you to

TAKE CONTROL OF YOUR OWN LIFE

1749 Loyola Drive

The concert was beginning, and a peculiar farewell it was; Gary had already left the group to become a special disciple of Dodo (with the rank of saxifrage), so the Auks now consisted of Barry alone, with of course tons of equipment.

The equipment, now arranged on a platform in the middle of the stadium, occupied about the same volume as a small four-room house. Indeed, it almost functioned as a small house, for once the remaining Auk had acknowledged his applause and entered among these infra-veeblifiers and tone-hurst hyperdecks, this one-man band was not visible at all.

Later there would be rumours that Barry wasn't doing anything in there. That he wasn't doing anything. That he wasn't in there.

22

Roderick found it easy to watch television, hard to do anything else. So he stared at the screen day and night, just as in the earliest years of his life. Was this a kind of senility? he wondered while changing channels. Was he approaching the end, his life furling in about him again, and was he becoming a tidier package, more easily disposed of?

But enough of gloomy thoughts like that: everything on the screen told him not to worry, not to worry. Taco-burger-flavoured diet aids gave way to gleaming pre-owned cars; micronic toilet cleanser to pizza-burger-flavoured falafel sticks; the KUR family of companies offered educational toys like the Zizi-doll, Polly Preggers and Barfin' Billy; America was wearing cleaner shirts than ever before; the Army offered young people almost unlimited opportunities for travel and education; people were winning new cars and boats and aeroplanes and houses, swimming-pools full of dollar bills, wheelbarrows full of gold, a dozen red roses every week for life; Dorinda managed to look on the bright side of her Destiny; old movies recaptured Hollywood's golden past; cop dramas showed how law and order still not only prevailed but sufficed; zany comedies proclaimed a new age in which pedestrian lives would become warmly meaningful, meaningfully funny, zanily warm.

He was watching a comedy about violence in New York, filmed entirely in Los Angeles. A yellow cab with blood on the door drew up before an apartment house. Audience laughter bubbled up, anticipating the worst.

Roderick's door crashed open, and four large uniformed men hurled themselves into the room, pointing guns at him or at windows. It seemed so much a part of TV that he waited for audience laughter.

'Sheriff's office, you the robot?'

'I, robot. Yes.'

'You the robot known as Robert Woods also known as Robin Hood also known as Rickwood also—'

'Yes, anything, fine.'

'You're under arrest. You have the right to—'

'Al,' said one of the other men. 'Just shut up, will you? This robot is *not* under arrest, and it ain't got *no* rights. What we got here is a distraint order seizing property in the name of the lawful owner, KUR Industries.' He approached Roderick carefully and slapped a gummed seal on his forehead. 'You coming along quietly, robot?'

'Sure.'

Roderick waited patiently while the four men got him into a straitjacket, leg-irons and an iron collar with four lead chains attached. It was still a part of TV; he was still interested in what might be happening next – a car chase? A discovery about someone's parentage?

As the sheriff's men were about to lead him away, there appeared in the doorway a man with the head of a fox. Behind him was a man with the head of a cat. Four guns turned towards them automatically.

'FBI,' said the fox, showing a gold badge. 'I'm Inspector Wcz and this is Special Agent Bunne. I'll have to ask you to turn over that robot.'

'Turn him over? But we—'

'Shut up, Al. Inspector, we have a county court order here—'

'I know,' said the fox. 'But our federal court order takes precedence. This is a matter of national security, boys.'

It took some time for the sheriff's men to release their prisoner from his complicated restraints, and about the same time for Wcz and Bunne to struggle out of their costume heads.

'I sure wish you'd told us earlier, Inspector. Just what is this robot, a spy or something?'

Wcz said, 'I'd rather not definitize that at this stage, not in the way you contexted it there. Let's just say that a certain government agency has loaned overriding consideration to the problem, okay? Against a backdrop of far-reaching technical contingencies, okay? So let's hustle it up, fellas, and get those leg-irons off him, we got a plane to catch.'

'Okay sure fine yup all right ye—'

'Shut up, Al.'

Roderick said, 'Why were you wearing animal heads?'

Inspector Wcz turned, turned away again.

One of the deputies spoke. 'Yeah, why were you wearing animal heads?'

'We were on another case,' said Bunne. Wcz looked at him and he fell silent.

Nothing more was said to Roderick or about him, as the FBI men drove him to the airport and bundled him aboard the plane which had been held for them. Nothing was said about Roderick or to him all through the flight. Agent Bunne watched the movie (in which a stripper adopts a crippled puppy and is therefore pursued by the Mafia, crashing a lot of new cars). Inspector Wcz studied a book called *The McBabbitt Way to Facial Success.*

Two more FBI men met the plane, packed themselves with Roderick into a limousine, and the five of them set off across the desert.

'Is it all right if I know where we're going?' Roderick asked. Three of the FBI men exchanged looks and shifted around uncomfortably; the car was full of the creak of shoulder holsters. Inspector Wcz affected not to hear.

'Might as well tell him, eh Inspector?' Bunne said.

Wcz laughed, or at least, laughing sounds came from his stiff face. 'Sure, you tell him. Tell him what they do to *robots* at the Orinoco Institute.'

'Isn't that a think tank?' asked Roderick.

'You tell him.' Wcz laughed again. 'Tell him about the Orinoco policy – *wiping out all robots and all robot builders.*

276

Because, tell him, *There is only room for one intelligent life-form on this planet.* Tell him.'

'Lawyers?' Roderick asked. 'Corporation lawyers?'

'Tell him he won't feel like being funny once they get hold of him. Tell him how they start dismantling and interrogating at the same time. They know how to get everything out of a machine. They keep him alive, hanging by a thread until they can squeeze out the last bit of data. Then *ssquonnge!*' Wcz laughed. 'That's the sound of expensive metal being crushed – *ssquonnge!*'

The Orinoco Institute was a few acres of lush green grass in the middle of the desert, fenced off and guarded, and dotted with windowless buildings. Roderick was taken into one of these. After various pieces of paper were exchanged with various guards, he was marched into an office. The man behind the desk was cleaning his pipe; the air was hazy with smoke.

'Hello there, Roderick.'

'Do I know you?'

'Ha ha no, no. But I sure know you. Been keeping tabs on you for years. Take a chair.' He scratched his brush-cut hair and looked at the FBI men. 'Uh, fellas, I need to have a private talk with Roderick here, okay? Could you go solve the Lindbergh case or something?'

When they had meekly shuffled out, the pipe-smoker stoked up his pipe and lit it. Then he sat on the edge of his desk, and he arranged his left hand to grip the leather patch on the right elbow of his tweed jacket, while the right hand held up his smouldering pipe. He didn't actually smoke the pipe much, mostly tapped his glasses frame with its stem. 'First thing, I guess, is to tell you a little about the Orinoco Institute. Have you ever heard of us?'

'I heard you were some kind of government think-tank, that's all.'

The pipe tapped. 'Ah yes, that wonderful newspaper phrase, almost makes you think of a bunch of oversized

277

brains in an aquarium, all pulsing with ideas, eh? Ha ha, well that's not – altogether true. By and large, we're all ordinary human beings, except that we're intelligent, we have some expertise, and we work on The Future. We're what the newspapers would call *futurologists*, people who try to extend the graph line from the known into the unknown. And sometimes we try to shape that line.'

'You try to influence trends?'

'Exactly. In that sense, we're not just a think tank, we're an "act" tank too. We try to help provide the kind of future this country (and this world) wants and needs. One of my former colleagues said, "Our job is to keep the damn world on the damn graph paper," and I think that says it pretty well. We do try to keep the trend lines smooth, the future free from sudden shocks and surprises. I think you'll like it here, Roderick. It's a challenging, stimulating place.'

'*Ssquonnge,*' said Roderick.

'Eh? Anyway, our system does work. We try to spot trends early. A trend spotted early enough can be encouraged, lessened, reshaped, eliminated – at very little cost. Later of course, it's more expensive. Later still, impossible at any price.'

After a pause to relight his pipe, 'Which brings us to the robot phenomenon, eh? The artificial intelligence, the android, robot, automaton, or as we prefer to call it, the *Entity*, constitutes a deep and disturbing trend. Some years ago we did a breakdown of all cybernetic work and worked a few projections. No doubt about it, research teams everywhere were inching their way towards one goal, the production of a viable Entity. Our guess was, someone was going to make it – but was this a good or a bad event? We did a very careful analysis, we discussed, modelled, projected and discussed again, but finally we had to give Entities the thumbs-down. This trend had to be crushed.'

'But why?'

'Plenty of reasons. Quite a few. Many.'

'Such as?'

The pipe-smoker cleared his throat. 'Well, it is all classified, but I guess there's no real harm in telling you. Not now.'

'Like a gloating villain,' Roderick murmured.

'Eh? Anyway, reasons for stopping Entities: for one thing, suppose machines get as intelligent as men, and decide not to take orders any more? Suppose they get even more intelligent and simply wipe out humanity?'

'Suppose they get so intelligent they see the futility of wiping out other species?' Roderick countered.

'Yes yes yes, I didn't say there were no counter-arguments. I'm just giving you our reasons. Suppose Entities took over all the jobs, all the worthwhile jobs, by virtue of being able to do them better or cheaper than men? That would leave us with a population forced into idleness – never desirable, whatever utopians might think. Or suppose machines begin solving many of our major problems, such as curing cancer or doubling lifespans or cheap fuel or cheap ways of mining other planets – do you see where such a wealth of handed-down answers could lead us? Yes, we could end up a pathetic kind of cargo-cult. Or suppose the intelligent machines did none of the above things, but suppose that just the *idea* of having intelligent machines on Earth caused a profound shock to the foundations of our societies – a civilization-quake? For example, where such an idea percolates down to the uneasy, fearful or unhappy masses, it could become the focus for any revolutionary tendencies.'

'Such as Machines Lib or the Luddites?'

'Precisely.' The pipe needed lighting again. 'Machines can become gods or demons, angels or rivals, in the inflamed imaginations of the lunatic fringe. In troubled times, the Entity might become a scapegoat or a messiah – an embodiment of instability. So we voted to stop the Entities. And by and large, we've been pretty successful. I won't go into details, but we did manage things like shutting off funds for certain lines of research. And we used other government agencies to – to persuade people not to go on trying to make Entities.'

'But I slipped through.'

'You slipped through.' The pipe-stem tapped the glasses. 'You certainly did slip through. A concatenation of circumstances – fraud, resulting in a cover-up that covered you up too; Mr Sonnenschein's paranoid precautions in smuggling you away; the fact that you had various foster homes and kept dropping out of sight; an unfortunately inept team of men from the Agency – you did slip through, and here you are today.'

'What happens next?' Roderick asked, not really wanting to know. Knowing.

'I think we ought to introduce you around, eh?'

'Look, what's the point? If you're just going to trash me, why not get it over with?'

'Trash you?' The man was so startled he forgot to tap his glasses. 'Good grief, didn't I make that clear? Our entire policy on Entities has been *reversed*. We're *not* stopping them any more.'

'No? But then—'

'We didn't bring you here to trash you, Roderick. On the contrary: we want you to join our team.'

'Is this a trick?'

'Ha ha, no trick. We really are inviting you to dive into our tank for a good think, ha ha.'

'I'll think about it,' said Roderick seriously.

'Ha ha, great. Come on in, the water's fine.'

'I wonder if it is,' said Roderick seriously.

'Ha ha.'

23

At the hour of anguish and vague light
He would rest his eyes on his Golem.
Who can tell us what God felt,
As he gazed on his rabbi in Prague?
        Jorge Luis Borges, *The Golem*

Mr Kratt's thick black V of eyebrow came down deeper; he
bit through his cheap cigar. 'Goddamnit, bub,' he said into
the telephone, 'you sure about this federal court order? Fine
damn country if the damn government can send in the FBI
to deprive a man of his legitimate property . . . Well, damnit, Moonbrand, you and Honcho are supposed to be the
damned lawyers, you tell me, can't we lodge an appeal . . .
Yes well look, I didn't hire you to just sit in your damn
hacienda out there and swill orange juice, I hired you to
protect KUR interests, my interests, not to . . . No okay, no
all right, maybe you and your partner have been *zapped by
this Uncle Sam authority trip*, but now listen bub, can the
California crap and listen, I want that damn robot! You're
the one said I got a legal claim in the first place, now you just
go and get the damn thing. Or at least tell me how I can get it
. . . Yeah well, forget your damn karma for a minute, I got a
corporation ready to fall apart if I don't get some good
gimmick, I got Moxon breathing down my neck, I got a
bank about to fold if that asshole Fleischman doesn't
remember where he parked that sixty million dollars, frankly
I don't need your damn karma.'

The image of his growling voice, turned into numbers,
beamed up to a satellite and back down to California, finally
emerged from what looked like a gold conch shell held to

Wade Moonbrand's ear. His bare feet rested on the desktop, which had been made from a teak surfboard. He kept his eyes on a meditation symbol on the wall, a nest of concentric rings; when he'd finished talking he pulled a Colt .45 from inside his floral shirt and put three shots into the middle of the symbol.

'Cass, old buddy, we kind of aced ourselfs, you know? I mean talk about the oneness of everything, we aced our own selfs!'

Cass Honcho, wearing buckskin and sitting at a desk made of a split log, nodded to show he was awake.

'Talk about conflict of innerest,' Moonbrand went on. 'I finally got the story outa the Orinoco gang, and guess who's behind the FBI move? Leo! Leo Bunsky, our client! Man, if we hadn't slapped that injunction on them to get the poor· bastard's head straight – I mean wires uncrossed – like he would still be floating on some astral plane with like Madame Blavatsky and James Dean, instead of down here making waves. We aced our own selfs!

'Like you remember when we took on Leo as a client? And we got that injunction against Orinoco saying they was violating his civil rights? And we wanted our electronics people and neurologists to look him over, remember that?'

Honcho nodded.

'And man their argument was just that Leo had all his rights because they let him vote with the rest of the committee, only we argued that you couldn't be sure his vote was ·real unless we got our experts in there to check his wiring, remember?'

Honcho nodded.

'And then when our boys did go in there sure enough they found a couple of wires crossed or something, so like his vote was garbled, remember? And after that they voted on something and Leo changed his vote and I guess the bottom line is, they decided to send in the FBI and just· grab

Roderick; so there we are, aced. I mean we just get one client fixed up so he can think straight, first thing he does is rip off another client. Mr Kratt's mad as hell and we lose out everywhere. Talk about a conflict of innerest, we just conflicted all over ourselfs there, you know what I wish?'

Honcho nodded.

'I wish there was some piranha fish in Leo Bunsky's tank.'

Roderick stared at the brain in the tank, trying to see it as a living person and not as a relic. Leo Bunsky had created him; now he tried to reconstruct Leo Bunsky, as his guide explained and explained:

'. . . see one of the key factors in our policy on Entities was always Leo's vote: no matter how hard he might argue for building Entities, when it came to a vote he always voted for their extermination. You're probably wondering whether we didn't think there was something wrong, but, hell, a lot of people here play games like that, arguing intellectually but voting with their true feelings. We thought Leo really was opposed to Entities. His vote influenced other votes, so the Entity extermination policy always had a comfortable plurality. And, well, it was only after Leo's lawyers made us check the wiring that we realized, Leo's vote was being misrecorded. *He* thought he was voting ''Nay'', *we* thought he was voting ''Aye''. For poor Leo, Yes meant No.

'But I guess you don't want to hear all this internal gossip, right? So why don't we move right along?'

The guide was a younger version of the first pipe-smoker. He had the same brush-cut hair (Roderick could imagine the two of them lying end-to-end, the tops of their heads meshing like a pair of military brushes) and the same tweed jacket.

'I see you're looking at my leather elbow patches,' he said in the elevator.

'Was I? Yes, I guess I was.'

'Neat, huh? See this one zips open, it's a pocket. For my pipe.'

'Oh.'

'A lot of the fellas have them, see we get these wholesale prices from this big sporting goods outfit, O'Bride International. We tried some blazers too, real neat with our own crest, only we had to send them back, they screwed up the name. Here we are, Sub-basement Eight.'

The doors opened on brilliant green rain-forest, complete with steaming undergrowth, sunlight pouring down through the clerestory of tall trees, snakes lazing among the lianas and pennant-bright birds in the shrubs.

'This can't be real.'

'Good, isn't it? Mostly mirrors and holograms, with a few plastic bushes. Okay, we just follow this trail here.'

They rounded a tree and the jungle vanished, leaving them in an ordinary, even shabby corridor. 'Some psychiatrist figured having a little foyer like this on each floor would help everybody concentrate. On other floors they have mountains or desert or quiet smalltown streets. One floor's got Oxford or is it Cambridge? To help everybody concentrate.'

'Does it help?'

'Naw, it's a lot of hooey.' The guide rapped at the first door and opened it. An old man wearing a frock coat and a huge panama 'planter's' hat sat hunched over his desk. He was using an abacus with no great speed or skill. On the blackboard behind him was written, THE GREATEST GOOD FOR THE GREATEST *NUMBER*.

'Come in, come in,' he said, not looking up. 'Have you brought my robot? Just leave it in the corner.'

'Not this one,' said the guide, chuckling. 'I'm showing him around.'

'Show him around later! This is important!' Even the

beads snapped.

Roderick asked the man what he was calculating.

'Oh, nothing much! Nothing much! Just setting out a complete moral code for all human conduct, that's all!'

'A complete moral code?'

'Complete.' The old man finished a calculation and laid down his abacus. 'Covering not only every recorded human action, but every possible imaginable human action. Complete, detailed, and mathematically precise. Are you familiar with the principles of Utilitarianism? An act is judged moral if it achieves the greatest possible good for the greatest possible number. But *what* number? that is the question. *Which* number?'

Roderick tried to look quizzical.

'The method is really quite simple. Every human action has its own individual number. And every set of circumstances is an equation. We simply plug the numbers into the equations and off we go!'

The guide said, 'Yeah, well, off *we* go, we've got a lot of ground to cover—'

'Wait a minute, just let me show you.' The old man leaped to his blackboard and erased it energetically, the motion making his hat-brim quiver. He sketched a diagram. 'Now here for instance we have the classical nuclear war standoff, East against West. Each side has the same two choices, either strike first or wait. So there are four possible outcomes. Now take West's options. If he strikes first, West can win (that is +1) but only if East has waited. But if both try to strike first, the whole world is wiped out (that is definitely −1). On balance, then, West neither gains nor loses from striking first. What if he waits? The best that can happen is nothing (0), and that's if East waits too. The worst that can happen is if East strikes first and West is destroyed (−1). So on balance, West loses by waiting. Now what is West's best strategy?'

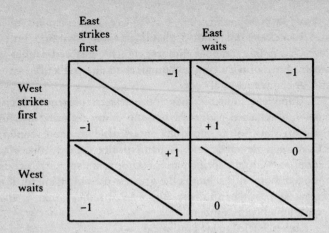

	East strikes first	East waits
West strikes first	−1 / −1	−1 / +1
West waits	+1 / −1	0 / 0

Roderick looked at the diagram. 'Striking first?'

'Exactly. And of course it is also East's best strategy. Without doubt, both sides ought to strike first. But if they both do that, we get—'

'The worst of all possible worlds?'

'Precisely. It's a dilemma* all right: if both sides make their best play, everybody loses. Utilitarianism has to clean up dilemmas like this before it can come to a complete calculus of morality.' The panama hat-brim vibrated with feeling. 'Sometimes I'd like to get the real East and West here in my office and give them real buttons to push. Then, by thunder, we'd see!'

When Roderick and his guide were leaving, the old man added, 'Come back soon. I'll show you what we're doing with catastrophe theory . . .'

They moved on to the next office, where with the aid of more diagrams, a man explained his speculations about solar energy: He was working out ways of storing it in common plants, especially cucumbers.

Next, Roderick met a team planning to recycle sewage to provide not only methane and fertilizers, but intriguing new foods. One of them said:

'Sure, it must sound crazy, but the fact is, the demand for junk foods and fast foods is rising exponentially. In a few years, the public will demand the right to eat pretty much anything. My only worry is, can we meet the challenge fast enough?'

In the next office a large group were contemplating possible wars, and no combination was too unlikely to be considered: a clash between the navies of Luxembourg and Paraguay, a parachute invasion of Finland by the Boobies of Fernando Po, Las Vegas bombed by Lapps.

Another office was concerned with future possible natural disasters and their implications. Suppose for example California suddenly sank into the waters of the Pacific – how would the national economy be affected by the loss of so many millionaires? With Hollywood gone, where would the Mafia next invest its money? What would be the cultural effect of TV drama without car chases?

Other offices were devoted to monitoring various 'fringe' sciences that 'just might' turn into worthwhile lines of enquiry: parapsychology, for example. A pipe-smoking parapsychologist explained:

'The whole field is bursting with new ideas, new research projects. Professor Fether in Chicago has been testing precognition in hippos. The Russians have had a breakthrough on the ouija board to Lenin. The ghost labs of California seem to be doing some solid research . . . Others are breaking new ground too, testing the hypothesis that hypnagogic visions are real . . . a new thought-gun that shoots down UFOs, a Dutch psychic who produces rabbits out of a hat . . . Seems to be a new theory that if you stare at the back of someone's neck, they'll turn around and look at you, even in a crowd . . .'

While in the next office, astrologers were checking a British theory that all black persons were born under Libra, all subversives under Scorpio, all women under Capricorn.

Next came a conference room where a dozen persons smoked pipes or filed nails as they listened to a lecture on Jungian economics. The lecturer broke off to define a few basic principles for Roderick's benefit:

'Take market forces, for example: are they real? We see that, just as people's belief in flying saucers, so-called, made them really appear in the sky, so too people's belief in a rising or falling stock market made it really rise or fall. Could "bear" and "bull" be ancient fertility and virility archetypes – Ursa Major and Taurus?'

Though Roderick was to visit only a handful of the five hundred offices at the Orinoco Institute, he met enough people to give him some grasp of the breadth and scope of this mighty academy. There were statisticians and climatologists, news reporters and military historians, oceanographers and Esperanto speakers, bioengineers and anthropologists, a mad gypsy fortune teller and a moping science-fiction writer, and even a psychologist who specialized in probing the minds of infants. All bets seemed to be covered.

At the end of the afternoon, he was allowed to sit in on a 'brainstorming' session in which higher-level futurologists tried to piece together all the findings of their subordinates. He understood a word or two, now and then:

'Microwave mind control, could we do a restructuring of the update there in Scenario 6A?'

'That's your problem, I'm restructuring the input-output model of undersea city economies, I need some energy thoughts.'

'What demand level? You in the tokamak range there?'

'Yes, but . . . the multifold trend . . .'

'Screw that! Listen, in the Afro-Asian socio-economic surprise-free framework . . .'

'Come on, guys and dolls, let's be macrohistorical here, okay? I mean even if India does start a bacteriological war, we can still project at least . . .'

'I backgrounded the promethean satellite scenario for ten million kilowatts and up, but . . .'

'. . . how head transplants might screw up the . . .'

'. . . penological flexi-time? Only with broad-spectrum vaccines, where does that leave us?'

'. . . synergy?'

'Energy . . .'

'. . . better update the restructuring of these pluralistic security communities, whatever you do.'

'. . . integrated whale ranch cloning? Check that.'

'. . . energy?'

'But synergy . . .'

'. . . and anyway, by then American cars'll be running on sugar too.'

When the meeting broke up, some of the futurologists seemed angry, others very pleased with themselves. One of the smug ones, a tall young man wearing a blazer, came over to slap Roderick on the back.

'So you're the Entity! Great! Great to have you aboard!' Thump, slap.

'I – thank you – uh.'

'What do you think of the old place so far? From an Entity point of view, it must seem kinda weird, eh?'

'Well, I—'

'Our friend here giving you the full tour?' Thump.

Roderick, speechless, stared at the crest on the blazer. It read *Iron Icon*, and in much smaller letters, *Made in Korea*.

The guide said, 'Yep, well in fact we're on our way to a directors' meeting now.'

'Great. See you round, Entity. Hang loose.' The heavy hand, poised for another slap, paused. 'We can't keep calling you Entity, you oughta have a name, you know?'

'I know,' said Roderick. 'And I—'

'Rusty. We'll call you Rusty. Rusty Robot, not bad eh?'

The pummelling was renewed until Roderick's guide led him away. 'So long, Rusty!'

He was taken to a conference room where the air was milky blue with pipe-smoke. Along the green leather table, thin liver-spotted hands were passing papers, drumming with impatience, grasping the bowls of pipes. Reptilian eyes moved to study the newcomer, as the rustle of conversation slowly died away.

The chairman at the far end of the table put his hands on the green leather and pushed himself to his feet. The posture was amphibian; an old frog poised at the edge of a mossy dark pond.

'This is our Entity member, ladies and gentlemen. We won't bother with introductions if you don't mind; there are so many items to get through today. So unless you have any questions, could you take your seat and familiarize yourself with the agenda? Good.'

Roderick slipped into a seat and stared without comprehension at the paper before him. He was aware of the eyes, shifting in their pouches of wrinkled skin to focus on him, but he could not look back at them. Only natural that they stared. He was a curiosity. Possibly edible.

1. General remarks, chair.
2. Dr Sheldon D'Eath's report on robot medicine and allied subjects.
3. Large computer networks (e.g. Banking, Government, Military): How stable?
4. Wind-up of old projects and operations:
    (a) Operation Nepomuk
    (b) Operation Barsinister
    (c) Operation Duckplantain
5. Kick-off of new projects and operations:
    (a) Project Junebug
    (b) Operation Tinhead
6. A.O.B.
7. (unscheduled) Video report from Vitanuova Space Salvage: shuttle test using robot test pilot.

*   *   *

By the time Roderick had read this, Dr D'Eath was already addressing them via satellite, describing his invention of a robot for testing artificial hearts.

'I patented the design a few years ago, but so far no one is willing to take on production. Maybe with your recommendation, gentle people.' He was a bland, plump man in pince-nez, with a moustache that made him look on the screen a little like Teddy Roosevelt. *'The* cost-effectiveness *is favourable compared with using lab animals. Not only are lab animal prices increasing at forty percent per year, there are all the high running costs: feed and vet bills, insurance against anti-vivisection raids. Besides, what do animal data mean in the end? You can't compare a goat or a calf to say an advertising executive who jogs but smokes – the human life-style variables can never be satisfactorily matched. And finally, you need a lot of back-up animals, in case of rejection problems, or in case you want to try out design modifications. You need a new animal for each fiddly little modification, say if you change the flip-disc valves. But with my robot it's easy: You just fit the dacron cuffs, then you snap out one heart and snap in the other. Then just fill 'er up with blood and – bingo!'*

The chairman said, 'Like to interrupt here and suspend the agenda for a moment, to bring in that live video report from Vitanuova Space Salvage. They're testing some new shuttle using some robot test pilot – have we got that?'

The screen lit up with a familiar scene, a space shuttle lashed to a rocket, steaming on the launching pad for a moment before the whole unwieldy-looking assembly rose slowly on a column of fire. A voice commented: *'. . . have lift-off. Two remarkable things about this test: first of all the pilot is a humanoid robot, using ordinary controls with no special fly-by-wire connections at all. The robot, nicknamed Mr Punch, just sits in the pilot's seat and uses controls like anybody else. The second remarkable thing is the speed with which this whole operation was assembled: the minute Mr Franklin's robot completed its successful testing at KUR labs, he personally brought it over to us and in fact I guess he*

291

personally installed it in the shuttle. We're talking here about a turnaround time of hours and not days, a really great achievement. We've, um, we've been trying to get Mr Franklin up to the video unit here to give us his comments on the test so far, but – no, nobody seems to be able to locate him. Well, what can I tell you about him? Mr Ben Franklin, brilliant Product Development man at KUR, and I understand Mr Punch is his personal baby . . .'

Kratt's stubby finger stabbed a phone button. 'Connie, get me Hare, quick . . . Hare? This is Kratt, what the devil you and Franklin been cooking up between you? Hell you say. Listen, bub, I just been getting the DB from Vitanuova Space Salvage, that goddamn robot is over there right now, yes right now, flying one of their damned shuttles by the seat of its pants – yes I mean the same goddamned Mr Punch you said didn't work. How much did Franklin pay you to tell me it failed the test? Whatever it was it wasn't enough, you're not only out of a job as of now, I'm gonna sue the piss out of you. You two figure you can just walk off with KUR property like that, sell it to somebody else? I'm gonna sue the both of you, and I'll get you for grand theft, fraud, misuse of company facilities, I – oh yeah? But how could it fail? I can see the damn space shuttle flying right now, doesn't look like a damn failure to me, bub.'

He clenched a fist and stared for a moment at the heavy gold ring mounted with a single steel ball, then looked to the screen where the commentary accompanied diagrams of the Vitanuova Space Salvage Shuttle in proposed operation:

'Yes now I believe we have located Mr Franklin in his car in the parking lot, evidently he's pretty excited about this test so far, you can see the theoretical test on your screen now, he's pretty excited, seems to be driving around in circles and honking his horn, that right, Nancy? Shouting what? "That's the way to do it!" Well it certainly is, the people here at ground control are happy too so far this test is looking

good, looking good, we'll try to get hold of Mr Ben Franklin himself, maybe get his reaction to the test but now maybe we're ready with a shot of the robot pilot in operation, that ready? Yes, here's what you've all been waiting for . . .'

The figure at the controls might have been mistaken for that of a robot at a distance, but the face was without doubt the face of Ben Franklin, his the ragged beard, his the pale expressionless eyes and mad grin.

A bored voice from ground control said, *'Looks like you have a little temperature buildup there, Mr Punch, can you confirm that incremental?'*

'Fffffffff'

'Say again? Can you confirm that temperature incremental in the cabin temperature?'

'Shhhhhhhh' came from the shuttle, as the camera vibrated and the bright face leaped and danced on the screen.

'. . . will praise thee, for I am fearfully and wonderfully made: marvellous are thy works and that my soul knoweth right well. My substance was not hid from thee, when I was made in secret, and curiosly wrought in the lowest parts of the earth. Thine eyes did see my substance fffffffffff and in thy book all my members are written, which in shhhhhhhhhhh were fashioned when as yet there was none of them.'

In the ground control centre an argument took over the sound, many muffled and hysterical voices competing for the single ear.

'What's he saying? What's he—?'

'. . . Franklin I'm telling you that's Franklin up there . . .'

'. . . alert on that increment we'll be seeing smoke in . . .'

'Don't be stupid, Nancy says he's down in the parking . . .'

'The Bible or . . . ?'

'Okay then who's in the damn car?'

'Temperature incremental is getting – look!'

'Oh my God!'

'Oh!'

The screen showed an instant of Ben Franklin's face, the

eyes reflecting the sheet of flame before it swept over him and the transmission ended.

After a moment the chairman shrugged. 'Well we mustn't dwell on that, there's too much to get through here. And I understand we've just had word from KUR that in fact Franklin was fired a week ago. Well. I suggest we take a short break here before we tackle the next item.'

A reptilian jaw near Roderick gave out a dry chuckle. 'Dear me, I suppose young Mr Wood here must think it's all as exciting as a TV car chase every day around here. Let me assure you, Mr Wood, nothing could be further from the truth. Most of our meetings engage the intellect, not the endocrine system.'

'Lucky thing,' said another. 'Some of us are old enough to find any stimulation a risk not worth taking, heh heh. The grave beckons.'

'Or the fishtank,' said the first jaw. 'One might seek salvation in the Leo Bunsky aquarium, eh?'

'Ugly, ugly. I put my trust in the resurrection of the body.'

'Religion?'

'Of course not, I mean freeze-drying.'

'But you must grant that, for all poor Leo's ugliness, he has at least brought us out of the wilderness of hunting entities. Mr Wood would be thankful for that, I'm sure.'

'Precisely. All the unsavoury operations we had to initiate. Why, even when hunting Mr Wood here, didn't we—?'

'Perhaps Mr Wood doesn't want to hear—'

'Oh I do,' said Roderick. 'How did you hunt me?'

'We used these incompetent men from the Agency, mostly. I suppose the worst was that business with the Roxy theatre. Imagine burning down a whole movie house just to kill one robot. And then they bungled it.'

Roderick said, 'Wait a minute. To destroy me, you were actually willing to burn up a whole theatre full of people?'

'Well of course you have to see this in an historical perspective, balancing a few hundred lives against – as we saw it – the survival of the human species. Not that we'd have authorized it specifically.'

'Indeed not,' said the other. 'Too inefficient, no finesse. Those Agency men were always ham-handed, let's not forget the incident of the red stocking-cap.'

Roderick asked what red stocking-cap.

'Don't you remember? You were supposed to be wearing it at the Tik Tok Bar, but you cunningly planted it on some old derelict – another life lost, I fear.'

'Still, Wood, you were a most excellent quarry. Much too good for those yahoos from the Agency.'

'Have I got this straight?' Roderick asked. 'You really murdered innocent people, just to destroy me?'

'Heh heh, well of course you weren't the only target. We had to make extensive use of Agency men and even one or two private hit-men, my word yes.'

'What are you saying? You just went out and, and butchered people right and left?' Roderick's voice was loud now, and everyone in the room had turned to stare. 'Butchered people right and left, just for some principle – some *policy* – you could reverse anyway whenever you felt like it – you could—'

'Ah well, aren't policy and principle so often confused, in these troubled times? But to say we *butchered people right and left* is both emotive and inaccurate. We were normally quite selective; those we asked the Agency to "finalize" as we liked to call it, were the inventors of dangerous Entities. Had we let them live, they'd go on making trouble for humanity.'

'Within our framework for speculation, there was nothing else we could do,' said the chairman, laying his hands on the table. 'We were in a zero-option scenario.'

'Precisely. Precisely. Precisely.'

Roderick had reached the door when the chairman said,

295

'Leaving? That's unwise, Mr Wood. Without our protection, you'll automatically become the property of KUR International. They'll probably take your head to pieces.'

'Suits me.'

24

'Just take a seat, Mr Wood is it? I'll see if somebody can, excuse me . . . Good morning, KUR Innernational . . . Mr Swann? One moment . . . Ginny, there's a Dr Welby on three to talk to a Mr Swann, is he in your office? No? Then he must be Patsy's new boss or, everything's in such a mess around here today, oh is he legal? Great . . . Lois have you got a Mr Swann? I have a Dr Welby for him on three . . . Good morning, KUR Innernational . . . Yes there is but I don't know when, I can put you through to the press office . . .'

Roderick sat down with a group of reporters: tired-looking men and women in waterproof coats, some with aerials sticking up from the backs of their necks, some fiddling with cameras or pocket memo machines, some sleeping.

'You covering this too?' someone said, and when Roderick did not reply, went on: 'I drew the short straw, I wanted to cover that management consultant mass murder story, sounds like some juicy stuff there, cops say the guy's been doing it for years, cutting women's legs off.'

'Juicy stuff? Is that what you call it?'

'Well sure, easy to get a handle on a story like that, you got sex, big business, police incompetence, a sadistic fiend, that's all prime stuff, you automatically get first or second slot in the six o'clock. Whereas this Moxon takeover is not exactly a surprise, is it?'

'Takeover?' said Roderick, surprised.

'I mean it should rate a paragraph on about page 733 of the financial news teletext; nobody cares who runs big corporations nowadays, or who owns them, or why. I mean it's slightly less interesting than say the intrigues of Ruritanian internal politics; I really hate this financial desk job.'

'Don't underrate it, kid,' said an older reporter, waking up. 'You start believing it's worthless, pretty soon everybody else believes it's worthless. Pretty soon companies start asking themselves why they should go on throwing champagne press receptions, whole system could melt down under us, leave nothing but real news to report.'

They stared out through the glass wall at real rain splashing on the perfectly square acre of concrete that separated the KUR Tower from real sidewalks and streets.

'Okay, it's a real meaningful job. So where's the champagne?'

Someone adjusted his camera by focusing on the receptionist, behind her violet desk. Today she had taken the trouble to appear in violet hair, nails and lipstick, and now she smiled and turned so that the violet telephone receiver did not hide her smile. 'Good morning, KUR Innernational . . . I can give you the press office . . . Ginny, did you *see* him yesterday? No *him*, when the ambulance men rolled him away right by my desk, he had on this oxygen mask and I mean he looked so helpless, even his eyebrows, and when you think how we all used to be so scared of him, he never even would say good morning or have a nice, if he even noticed you it was only to make some sarcastic remark about how he ought to replace you with a Roberta Receptionist machine, and now there he was. There he was, so helpless, helpless as a, a dog. Just a sec, Good morning, KUR Innernational . . .'

'Besides,' said the older reporter, 'a conglomerate like this is interesting for its own sake. It's like an incredibly complicated puppet – you never know where all the strings lead until you pull them and see what jumps. And something like this – Kratt keeling over like that during the negotiations

298

– it's like the puppeteer dropping all the strings. Now we'll see how good Moxon is at picking them up and sorting them out.'

'Yeah, but he's bringing in a lot of strings of his own,' said the younger. 'I heard there's gonna be a complete changeover of personnel, with—'

'Well, there he is, let's ask him.'

There was a stampede past the reception desk to where Everett Moxon, flanked by press aides, waited to greet them.

'Mr Moxon, is it true you seized the moment to pull the takeover, because Kratt, who always opposed you, was safely out of the way?'

'Everett, look this way?'

'Mr Moxon, would you say KUR is shaky, with some of its subsidiaries—?'

'What kind of changes do you envision for—?'

Moxon grinned Presidentially. 'Boys and girls, one at a time, please. I thought we might go up to the penthouse and do this over a few glasses of champagne, okay? But I'll just say now that Mr Kratt and I may have had a few minor disagreements, but we always saw eye to eye on all major decisions about the future of KUR. And when he recovers, he knows he can go on as chairman of the board as long as he likes. As you all know, the takeover has been in the cards for a long time. We like KUR, and KUR can use our capital. But let me say, let me just say that there is not going to be any asset-stripping, the Moxon Corporation is not an asset-stripping operation. Naturally we'll have to look over the whole basket of apples and get rid of any bad ones, but only to protect the rest. Anyone here like champagne?'

'What I'd like even more, Mr Moxon, is to know what are your plans for the KUR banking subsidiary, with General Fleisch—'

Still clamouring questions, they packed into elevators and disappeared. The receptionist said, 'Ginny, have you seen him? Not him, *him*, Mr Moxon. Not bad looking only his head is kinda small, just a sec. Good morning, KUR Inner—, oh hello Dr Hare, are you coming in today because a Dr D'Earth called a few times. Oh and there's a Mr Roderick Wood waiting to see somebody, who should I, to whom should he – never mind, he's gone . . .'

Upstairs Everett Moxon walked around holding a glass of champagne and smiling for five minutes before ducking out to his office.

His secretaries, Ann and Andy, were trying to clean the place. Ann held an ashtray containing a chewed cigar stub; Andy was dusting.

'Sorry, sir. KUR janitors are on strike,' said Andy.

Ann sighed. 'Something about automated cleaning machines in some subsidiary called Slumbertite.'

'Wonderful timing.' He looked around. 'Is that interior decorator here? Send him in.'

Ann hesitated. 'There are a lot of people waiting, sir. Jud Mill and people from Katrat, from Datajoy, from T-Track Records and Mistah Kurtz Eating Houses. And there's even a delegation from Kratt Brothers Midway Shows.'

'That's right,' Andy snickered. 'They look like the cast of *Guys and Dolls*, I've never seen so many sharp sideburns and black shirts with white ties.'

'Okay. Okay. Send Jud in first, and tell the decorator he can make measurements or look around and get inspiration but he has to keep out of the way. Datajoy? What do we own called Datajoy?'

Ann and Andy exchanged looks. Andy said, 'Well, it's sort of a combined clinic and pleasure ranch—'

'Never mind how it's marketed, what *is* it?'

Ann said, 'They implant electrodes in the customers' heads, to stimulate their pleasure centres. It's a leasing arrangement; as long as they keep up the payments they stay turned on. If they miss a payment—'

'The electrode gets ripped out,' Andy said. 'One of Kratt's more disgusting ideas.'

'Disgusting, yes.' Moxon's phone rang. He sat on the desk and reached for it. 'Still, if we combined it with Moxon Retirement Systems . . . Hello, Moxon . . . What is it, Francine, I've got people to see . . . Jough Braun, what does he, yes all right, all right we'll talk about it.'

Jud Mill was a distinguished-looking man of no particular age or sex. He began spreading folders on the desk and peering at them through half-moon reading glasses. 'I may as well admit we had a few problems, Mr Moxon, with this direct editing scheme. When Mr Kratt brought me in as a media management consultant, I told him I foresaw problems with authors. Sure enough, everything worked well enough with the bookstore chains, the market survey people, the editorial – but the authors had problems. Authors always screw up a package.'

'What happened? Direct editing?'

'It works like this: the author writes directly on to a computer. This is linked up to leading bookstore chains, to their sales computers, and to prose analysis programs. The idea was to give the author instant feedback; as soon as he pecks out a few words, the computer grinds it through and tells him how good it is.'

'How good?'

'For his sales. By comparing sentences with sentences in his earlier books, and up-to-the-minute sales records, it can help him shape his prose *as he writes*.'

'But it went wrong?'

'In a sense. We had this leading Katrat Books author parked at his tax-haven home down in Nassau, hammering out his book on our DE system, when evidently he developed some kind of block. So to keep up his quota, he started, well, plagiarizing his own previous books. Naturally the computer rated this as highly saleable stuff, and I am afraid it went into

301

production. See, the computer also sets type and – well in fact, *The Hills Afar* is a word-for-word copy of *Red Situation*, thirty million copies went out.'

'Jesus. Could be sued by thirty million customers.'

'No, well oddly enough, it's selling very well and so far nobody seems to notice. The bookstore figures show we could even reprint.' He opened another folder and sat back, causing the striped collar of his shirt to crackle. 'That's not important now. What I really wanted to do was launch a more foolproof scheme, total computer authorship.'

Moxon looked surprised. 'But I thought—'

'Computers weren't ready? Not to produce works of "lasting literary significance", no, but to write *big bucks books*, yes. Naturally we keep the authorship under wraps, create a persona using a photo of a model, a fake bio – even, if necessary, an actor to appear on TV. I've talked it over with Mel Zell at—'

'Wait a minute, hold on there. I'm not at all sure about leaving out the human touch like that, the author is very—'

'The author is one big problem for everybody,' said Mill. 'When you're trying to orchestrate a big, complex deal, bringing together all the elements of the package each in the right quantity at the right time, the author just gets in the way. When I architected a certain big property a few years ago with Sol Alter, we started with a one-line idea. Then we got a big-name star interested in appearing in a movie, that enabled us to bootstrap a six-figure plus movie deal, and with all that we had something to take to the publishers. We landed a seven-figure paperback deal and from there on had no problem getting all we wanted out of magazine serialization, book club, foreign and cassette rights, direct cable specials, options for a TV series, syndicated comics, t-shirts, board games, colouring books and so on. Then we fixed the music and wrapped up those rights. And then and only then did we finally hire an author to hack out the screenplay and book, the fictionalization. We paid him I think two grand and no comebacks. That book, Mr Moxon, was *Boy and Girl*.'

The interior decorator, who had been quietly walking around the office, now cleared his throat.

'What is it?'

'This apostle clock on the wall – it'll have to go, Mr Moxon. For one thing, it's an obvious fake.'

'Fine, take it away.' Moxon turned to Jud Mill, who was now collecting his folders. 'I'd feel better about this computer author if I could see a sample of its work.'

'What good would that do? Oh all right, here.'

Moxon took the piece of paper and studied it for a minute. 'This some kind of joke, Jud? It's not even spelled right, looks like some six-year-old batted this out during recess.'

'No, well, our market research has been pretty darn thorough, and all the indications are that this is the coming thing, as the literacy level of the public keeps dropping, the demand is for more regressive stuff, fairy tales, basic English, short sentences . . .'

'But Jesus, this is, well just listen: ''Once upon a time there was a boy. He had a Ma and a Pa, and they all lived in a little white house on the edge of Somewhere. The boy's name was Danny Sunshine, because he was allways smiling warm. Danny was only a poor boy, but he was honest and good, people could see that. One day he was wandering in the Somewhere Woods with his dog Lion. Lion was scratching in some leafs and he found an old rusty sword. 'I'll take it home and clean it up!' Danny thought to himself. 'Then I can read this funny writing on the blade, under the rust. Maybe if I keep this sword till I grow up, I can be a real nite!' So He—'' The public demands this? *This*?'

Jud Mill shrugged. 'That's it. The competition already has something like this in the pipeline . . . space opera about robots, so I hear . . .'

'Great, okay, don't tell me any more, go ahead with a

303

pilot project, I'll bring it up at the board.'

As Jud left, Ann looked in. 'General Fleischman's on line three.'

'Christ . . . Yes hello General, thank you, thanks . . . No of course we still want you on the board, no great changes just yet, we have our commitments after all . . . yes well I will, and you give mine to Gerda too, bye . . . Andy? Make a note, we've got to convene a special meeting of the board to fire General Fleischman before the old shithead loses another sixty million . . . oh and what's this memo about some nut religion suing us, what's the state of play there? Because I don't see any KUR counter-suit. Not only that, things seem to be snarled up there, the lawyers acting for this Church of Plastic Jesus are also acting for us, that right? Honcho and Moonbrand are on KUR's payroll, how can they represent, yes get our legal department to look into this, Swann, get Swann. And somebody come in here for dictation and bring the figures on Katrat Fun Foods . . .'

Behind him the decorator, having removed the wooden clock from the wall, was examining a dark stain now revealed: blood? Ink? Oil?

Roderick spent an hour in the hospitality suite, playing poker with the reporters, watching them drink champagne and stuff their pockets with xeroxed press releases. He couldn't think what to do next, where to go, what to be.

Someone turned on the large-screen TV, and there was a man in dark glasses, handcuffed to two policemen, but sitting at a table before a microphone and smiling for the cameras.

'Jeez,' said one reporter. 'I wish I was there.'

'Shh,' said another, turning up the volume. A cop spoke:

'. . . *eakthrough came when I realized I'd seen this guy's M.O. before. I had a hunch the Lucky Legs Killer and the Campus Ripper were one and the same – and when I tied in the Snowman Murder, I*

304

knew it was only a matter of time. Sooner or later our killer would make one mistake too many . . .'

'But Chief, didn't your prisoner turn himself in?'

'Well yes, matter of fact he did, but we regard that as a publicity stunt. He hopes to create a favourable impression, to get his bail lowered.'

'Like to ask the prisoner how he feels about killing all those women and cutting off their legs with an electric carving knife?'

'How do I feel?' The prisoner nodded and smiled. 'That's a valid question. You're after tangible motivation, right? Gut reaction? Well, I wish I could give you a simple answer, but first I'd have to clarify a few concepts myself. That clarification could involve a thoroughgoing process evolving in context and circumstance, exploring the infrastructure of any particularized situation according to well-defined parameters, without of course rejecting in advance those options which, in a broader perspective, might be seen to underpin any meaningful discussion attempting to cut through the appropriate interface, right?'

'You felt mixed up?'

'He feels like reducing his bail,' said the cop.

The prisoner said, 'That's not what I said. I said there's no point in talking about my feelings, because to talk about anyone's feelings you have to make a distinction between subjective reality and objective reality – and it was just that distinction, that interface, that I was exploring!'

After that, he fell silent and ate yoghurt, while the policeman handled questions about the influence of TV violence, the psychology of the mass murderer, the thankless role of the policeman in modern society. Roderick's attention was already beginning to wander, when someone called from the balcony:

'Come on out here, you guys! Look at that!'

They all went out, and dutifully looked down over the rail. A giant metal dish was hanging on bundles of ropes, being pulled inch by inch up the side of the building.

305

'What the hell is it? A dish antenna? For what?'

'Moxon Music Systems,' said a press office aide. 'You must have noticed there was no music in the elevator? Or anywhere else. Well when we get this set up, we'll be able to pick it up from our own satellite, and run it to every room in the building.'

'Music of the spheres,' said one of the old hands, lurching against the rail.

'Careful! Maybe we'd all better go inside, boys and girls?'

And gradually they all lost interest and went back to the booze, all but Roderick. He stood leaning on the rail, noticing that the rain had stopped.

He saw no point in jumping. On the other hand, he saw no point in going back inside. Here was as good as anywhere. He looked down at the wet lozenges of the city. He looked up at the rolling clouds. There was nothing to steer by, nothing permanent.

He lifted up his arms, as though he were a Pharisee at prayer or else someone expecting a heavy burden to drop from the sky.

A dark shadow fell across Moxon's office. He looked up to see a black disc inching up across his window, eclipsing it. 'What the devil—?' He pressed buttons and demanded an explanation.

'*It must be the dish antenna,*' Ann's voice explained. '*For the Moxon Music System. And corporate communications.*'

'As if I didn't have too many lines of communication already.'

'*Your wife's downstairs with the sculptor, Jough Braun. She wants to know if you're coming down for lunch.*'

'Tell her no, I . . . no, let me talk to her . . . Francine, look I'm sorry, I'll have to grab a sandwich at my desk, Kratt left this place in a hell of a mess. He was, I don't know, running everything like a one-man band, nothing delegated, nobody knows how to do anything . . . Fine, fine, look if you want a sculpture on the terrace down there, go ahead, only tell Jough to take it easy? We don't want a big pile of wrecked cars embalmed in epoxy or anything like that . . . no of course I'm not, I'm just trying to remind you of the image we're trying to . . . hang on, I've got . . . Swann? . . . Francine, I can't talk now, you just, you just go ahead . . . Swann, you there? Listen, I've been going over the figures for this Autosaunas operation, I notice that before the medical lawsuits started hitting the fan we had a very healthy return on our investment there, I was just exploring the idea of, of when all the dust settles, of trying again . . . No, well, it's just that sex with robots does seem like the logical, um, extension of our leisure group activities, a natural follow-through on our . . . Yes, see what you can do, some kind of product warning, maybe safety checks, see what you can work out with Hare, he's the product development man, you'll be meeting him this afternoon at our . . . Ann, did you set up that meeting with Dr Hare? Okay yes, and . . . what choreographer? Oh him, Hatlo, no listen I can't talk now but set up a meeting I want him to talk to our Personnel people about working out some Japanese-style calisthenics for the whole company, five minutes every morning . . . is Hare in yet? See if you can get him for me while I . . . Who? Hello, Dr D'Eath, what can I . . . He is? What kind of recovery time are we talking about there, six months, ten years? . . . Well yes, of course, in that case a nursing home would I agree be the best, and in fact we own a chain of clinics combined with pleasure ranches ourselves, Datajoy the name is, my secretary can make all the arrangements and you can transfer Mr Kratt right away . . . Andy, talk to the doctor will you? Ann, take a memo for the press office, ''At his own request the former president and founder of the KUR family of companies, Mr – give him some first name – Kratt, is being transferred from the

University Hospital to one of KUR's own Datajoy clinic-ranches, where the accent is on health combined with pleasure. 'Having devoted my whole life to giving pleasure to people,' said the – make up some age – year-old tycoon, 'I thought it was time to get a little pleasure myself – and where better than at a Datajoy pleasure ranch? Where else can you get all the benefits of a clinic without a clinical environment?' " And so on, just have them take the rest out of our Datajoy brochures. Oh and get me Swann again, I want to go over this problem with this lunatic church, The Church of Plastic Jesus, I want to . . . it is? Now? On what channel?' He fumbled for buttons which brought a huge screen into view on the opposite wall, and filled it with a succession of living images: a cartoon germ, an armpit, a swimming pool filled with money. Moxon couldn't help pausing briefly at the image of a man slumped over a table, apparently dead but still handcuffed to two policemen:

'. . . don't know what, but it looks like Culpa was eating, yes you can see it there now, the carton marked pizza-flavoured yoghurt fudge. Well I guess that's it, folks, the doctor's looking at it now. As you may know, the FDA has been trying to track down the last few remaining cartons of this product, after they discovered that one of the flavouring ingredients . . .'

He switched at last to a street scene. A woman with a microphone stood before a store window in the slummy end of town. She stood to one side of the name on the window:

THE CHURCH OF PLASTIC JESUS
YOU MAY BE WELCOME, BUT THEN AGAIN YOU MAY NOT

'Hi, good afternoon and welcome to Round 'n' About. I'm Joy Grayson, and the reason I'm here at this very unusual church, is to attend a very unusual meeting. Believe it or not, folks, the bride and groom are both robots! Let's go inside.'

*   *   *

308

The Reverend Luke Draeger and Sister Ida didn't mind the TV station setting up this 'robot wedding' gimmick; they welcomed any chance to get their *message* across to anyone, *before it was too late*. It was Ida who had, when they'd first started their religion, had the idea of a *message*, to be delivered to the world *before it was too late*. If they weren't going to do that, she'd said, what was the point of starting a store-front church at all? Luke it was who insisted on the ambiguous notice in the window: people might be welcome, but then again they might not. So far the effect had been to keep out everyone but the occasional bold drunk – who was not welcome.

Aside from the TV crew, the human congregation was limited to Luke, Ida and a kind young woman named Dora. Dora worked at the Meat Advice Bureau next door. Since no one in the neighbourhood ever sought any meat advice, she had time to drop in, listen to the sermons, help out with the singing, and put something in the collection.

Dora always had to sit at the back. All the other seats were permanently taken by the non-human congregation, nearly a hundred battered effigies:

First came a handful of store window mannequins, their hair and smiles identifying them as belonging to an earlier generation of dummies (during a previous Presidential administration). They were clothed now only in ragged coats and curtains of no use to people, but they sat in gracefully relaxed poses, and seemed to be enjoying themselves. Next to them were a few 'robots' built by children out of cardboard boxes and tinfoil, with noses made of burnt-out light bulbs and bottlecap eyes. Next came a plastic medical skeleton, only a few bones missing, and next, a shattered pinball machine. Its broken legs were arranged to look casually crossed, and its back plate lighted to show a grinning ballplayer. There were toy robots of battered metal or cracked plastic, run by clockwork or batteries to shoot sparks or mutter incoherent greetings. There was a ventriloquist's dummy with a split wooden smile, a dental dummy with removable teeth, a tailor's dummy and even a tackling dummy (legs only) made into a composite figure which also included a jack-in-the box. There were other composites, scarecrows and guys made up of stuffed clothes topped with various heads – pillows with printed faces, painted balloons, Hallowe'en masks of Frankenstein and Mickey Mouse, a plaster death-mask without its nose, an imitation marble bust, a lampshade depicting the face of a dead country singer. There were broken items from carnivals and arcades: a laughing mechanical clown, an automatic fortune-teller in a glass case, Brazos Billy the (retired) gunfighter, and I-Speak-Your-Weight. There were large plaster Kewpies, and waxwork replicas of a few mass murderers (from the days when mass murder was unusual).

Nothing worked, nothing was whole, not even the bride and groom. This was a mission among the derelict and forgotten simulacra.

'Dearly beloved,' said Luke, and probably meant it. He felt that effigies could end up abandoned and despised like this only because those who owned them really wanted to abandon one another; really despised themselves. Conversely, if people could learn to live with effigies, they might some day learn to live with themselves. 'Dearly beloved, we are gathered together in the sight of Mission Control—'

He caught the eye of Ida. 'All right, in the sight of God – and in the face of this company, to join together in matrimony, this machine—' He indicated a squat robot appliance which had, in better days, been able to vacuum, dust, and empty ashtrays. Now it did little more than twitch, and rust. '—and this machine.' He nodded towards a clumsy device made of aluminium tubing, looking very much like a classic 'robot'. It had been built many years ago

310

by a class at some junior high school. It had never been able to do anything but answer questions on baseball.

While the service proceeded, the camera wandered over the congregation. There were painted plaster saints, and one or two of glow-in-the-dark plastic. There was an anatomical man with transparent skin and removable plastic organs, and next to him a wooden lay figure with a head like a fat exclamation mark. Then came a metallic plastic robot costume for a child, a prop suit of armour and a genuine white spacesuit. There was an inflatable doll with a permanently surprised expression, a mechanical Abe Lincoln frozen in an attitude of boredom, and a giant teddy bear. There was a cigar-store wooden Indian, a hitching-post of iron in the shape of a black child, and (from England) garden gnomes made of concrete.

Towards the rear of the church the chairs were heaped with dolls and puppets of all sizes: Russian babushka dolls; dress-up dolls; dolls with faces made of china, wax, wood, metal, rag; dolls that walked or talked or wet themselves while doing algebra; Barfin' Billy; a corn dolly, a glass baby full of what once had been candies. There were glove puppets, clockwork dancers, Punch and Judy, fantoccini shadow puppets, marionettes.

'. . . take this machine to be your lawfully wedded spouse?' The cleaner twitched a brush, perhaps in assent. 'And do you, machine, take this machine to be your lawfully wedded spouse?'

The junior high android muttered, '. . . Ty Cobb . . . highest batting average . . . twelve years . . .'

The camera continued to roam over this throng, picking out strangeness: the mad cracked grin, the missing nose, the staring glass eye. It skipped over Dora sitting in the last row (next to an old stage costume for the Tin Woodman) to concentrate on the bizarre: the lop-sided wax face, the single mother-of-pearl tooth.

311

'Then I now pronounce you machine and machine.'

Ida turned on the player harmonium to produce 'Ah, Sweet Mystery of Life', then a recessional, as the happy couple apparently made their way out of the church (actually drawn along on piano wires by the TV crew). Outside, the TV company had arranged its own visual finish: a set of robot arms from a local factory were lined up in a double row, holding their arc-welders aloft to form an arch.

When it was all over, Luke seemed subdued. 'I wish Rickwood could have been here, that's all. He'd have understood. He, in a way I guess he started all this.'

Ida said, '*I* know that, why are you telling *me* that? Do I go around reminding you how he brought us together?'

'Affirmative, I mean, yes.' Luke sighed. 'Haven't had a word from him, not since he said he was giving himself up to KUR.'

'He's probably too busy.' Ida was peering into the dim corner at the back of the church, where Dora seemed to be talking to the Tin Woodman costume.

'Busy? Busy? They've probably ripped him apart by now. He's probably lying in pieces all over some laboratory bench, while people in green goggles stick probes into him. They're making his leg twitch like the leg of a frog, do you read me?'

'Loud and clear, Luke, just take it easy.'

'Busy as a frog. And they're probably gearing up the assembly lines right now to turn out millions of copies of him. Poor damn silicon-head.'

'But if they turn out copies,' Ida quickly suggested, 'then we'll never lose him completely, will we? Say, isn't there someone back there with Dora?' She called out: 'Dora? Who's that with you?'

Dora stood up, and the Tin Woodman stood up with her. They came forward into the light. 'Someone who really understands.'

312

'Who?' Ida's voice went shrill. She felt her 24-karat heart miss a beat as the creature removed its funnel hat and started undoing the hinges of its face.

'Me,' said a grubby, bearded stranger. Dora introduced him as Allbright.

'I hope you're not going to give me any Luddite pep-talk, Father. I can do without that.'

'No, Leo, of course not. Of course not.' Father Warren found it hard to believe that the animated cartoon face on the screen before him was really connected to Leo Bunsky's brain, across the room in a big glass tank. 'Of course not. But you can't blame me for worrying, all these stories I hear about computers making up their own religions.'

'Harmless, Father. A nuisance but—'

'Harmless! A devil-worshipping computer in South America? An oil company computer declaring itself a new prophet of Islam? The Russian war-gaming machine that will only display icons?'

'We haven't confirmed that one,' said the icon Leo. 'But listen, all these anomalies were just planted by programmers with more zeal than sense. You can easily plant superstition in machines, just as in people or pigeons. These computers aren't *making up* their religions, they're getting the holy writ from outside. From you might say missionaries. But don't worry, all we have to do is some heavy deprogramming.'

Father Warren chewed a hangnail. 'I wish I could believe that. "Speak only the word and my computer will be healed." I wish I could believe these computers were something like good servants, good but sick.'

The cartoon face looked sympathetic. 'Hard to have faith in them, I know. Hard to believe they're not just as petty and vicious and despicable as our own species can be. I just hope that when the time comes, Father, they have a little faith in us.'

313

'When they take over? No, I can't believe—' The priest cleared his throat. 'But I didn't come here to discuss what I believe, eh? Suppose we get down to business.'

'Bless me, Father, for I have sinned. My last confession was, well, some time ago . . .'

When he had heard the confession, Father Warren crossed the room to Leo's tank. An attendant rose to greet him.

'You know you have to crumble it, Father?'

'If it's the only way.' He held the white wafer over the tank and crumbled it into the water. The white crumbs floated for a minute and then sank like little snowflakes, there being no goldfish to snap them up.

Moxon's amplified voice reached some of the crowd, though the cold north wind was doing its best to sweep away words and people, to clear the terrace of all signs of life.

'It was just a month ago, right here in the KUR Tower, that I found myself watching a peculiar sight on TV: two broken-down robots getting married!'

Some people laughed, others wondered who was getting married, or buried.

'Crazy stunts aside, what can you do with broken-down robots? Well, if you happen to be a genius like Jough Braun here, you can turn them into great sculpture. Jough was poking around in one of our storerooms or offices or somewhere, and he found a broken-down robot we didn't even know we owned. Jough says he used it *exactly* as he found it, just covered it with white epoxy and – well, without further ado, here it is – *Man Confronting the Universe.*'

The applause was blown away, as he pulled the cord. Drapery fell to show a white figure with arms upraised in Pharisaical prayer. Under the layers of epoxy a face could be discerned, but no expression. Those watching might have been reminded of the ghost-white figures of George Segal (each containing air in the exact shape of a living human,

314

surrounded by plaster), or of the ivory statue Pygmalion warmed to life, or of the albino puppets drowned annually in Rome by the Vestal Virgins. A few might have thought of white clown makeup, first worn by Joe Grimaldi playing a comic automaton in *La Statue Blanche*. It is possible that someone thought of white marble Victorian tombs or white-faced mimes pretending to be marionettes, or of Frosty and Snowman, or of white-faced Japanese puppets writhing in mock death.

The north wind blew all such thoughts from the terrace.

Notes

p.15 All of the italicized lines in Chapter Two are taken
from other books:
Eric Corder, *Slave*; Charles Dickens, *Life of Our Lord*; G.A.
Henty, *The Dash for Khartoum*; Albert Camus, *The Stranger*;
Mickey Spillane, *I, Jury*; Harry Mathews, *The Conversions*;
James Hadley Chase, *I'll Get You for This*; Jorge Luis Borges,
The Night of the Gifts; Nathaniel West, *Cool Million*; Dashiell
Hammett, *The Glass Key*; Joyce Cary, *The Horse's Mouth*;
Paul Chadburn, 'Murder on the High Seas' in *Fifty Most
Amazing Crimes*; George Orwell, *Nineteen Eighty-Four*;
Raymond Chandler, *The Little Sister*; F. Dostoyevsky, *Crime
and Punishment*; Raymond Chandler, *Farewell My Lovely*;
Robin Moore, *The Green Berets*; A. Dumas, *The Three
Musketeers*; Carole Keene, *The Message in the Hollow Oak*;
E.R. Burroughs, *The Warlord of Mars*; Dorothy Sayers, *Whose
Body?*; Graham Greene, *Brighton Rock*; Joseph Conrad,
Nostromo; The Book of Judges; Warren Miller, *The Cool
World*; A. Christie, *The Murder of Roger Ackroyd*; John le
Carré, *A Murder of Quality*; E.A. Poe, *Masque of The Red Death*;
James M. Cain, *The Postman Always Rings Twice*; A. Conan
Doyle, 'The Red-Headed League'; Zane Grey, *Nevada*;
E.C. Bentley, *Trent's Last Case*; The Gordons, *The FBI Story*;
F.P. Wenseley, 'Under Fire at Sidney Street' in *Fifty Famous
Hairbreadth Escapes*; Ken Jones, *The FBI in Action*; D.W.
Stevens, *The James Boys in Minnesota*; Raymond Chandler,
Smart Aleck Kill; Thomas Pynchon, *V*.

p.31 Sue Ellen's third husband was Vern. Roderick
deduced this by assuming that two of the six people in
question are brother and sister (hence the six can only be
married in eight different ways). The marriages took place in
this order: